Ramage's Challenge

Also by Dudley Pope

NAVAL HISTORY

Flag 4
The Battle of the River Plate
73 North
England Expects
At 12 Mr Byng Was Shot
The Black Ship
Guns
The Great Gamble
Harry Morgan's Way
Life in Nelson's Navy

NOVELS

The Ramage Series:
Ramage
Ramage and the Drum Beat
Ramage and the Freebooters
Governor Ramage R.N.
Ramage's Prize
Ramage and the Guillotine
Ramage's Diamond
Ramage's Mutiny
Ramage and the Rebels
The Ramage Touch
Ramage's Signal
Ramage and the Renegades
Ramage's Devil
Ramage's Trial

The Yorke Series:
Convoy
Buccaneer
Admiral
Decoy

Ramage's Challenge

a novel by
DUDLEY POPE

An Alison Press Book
Secker & Warburg · London

First published in England 1985 by
The Alison Press/Martin Secker & Warburg Ltd
54 Poland Street, London W1V 3DF

Copyright © 1985 by Dudley Pope

British Library Cataloguing in Publication Data

Pope, Dudley
    Ramage's challenge: a novel.
    I. Title
    823′.914[F]   PR6066.05

ISBN 0–436–37746–2

Made and printed in Great Britain by
Richard Clay (The Chaucer Press) Ltd
Bungay, Suffolk

For Kay
who crossed a rubicon
with me and sailed
past Cabo Trafalgar
in the moonlight.

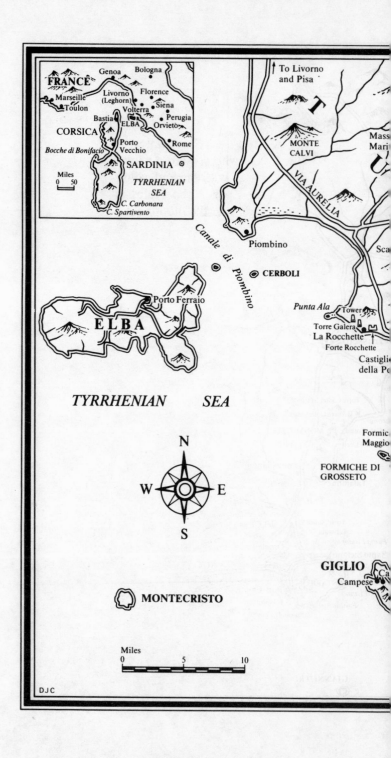

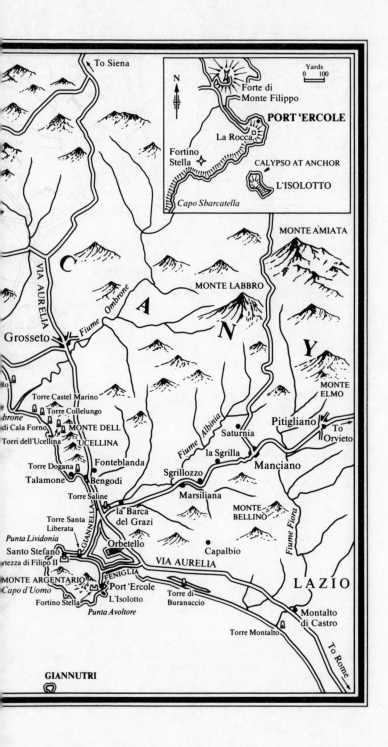

Yards
0   100

N

Forte di
Monte Filippo

PORT 'ERCOLE

La Rocca

Fortino
Stella

CALYPSO AT ANCHOR

L'ISOLOTTO

Capo Sbarcatella

To Siena

MONTE AMIATA

C

Fiume Ombrone

A

MONTE LABBRO

N

Grosseto

Y

MONTE ELMO

Torre Castel Marino

Torre Collelungo

brone
di Cala Forno

Fiume Albinia

MONTE DELL'

Torri dell'Ucellina

UCELLINA

Pitigliano

To Orvieto

Saturnia

la Sgrilla

Fonteblanda

Torre Dogana

Sgrillozzo

Manciano

Talamone

Bengodi

Torre Saline

Marsiliana

MONTE BELLINO

Fiume Fiora

la Barca
del Grazi

Torre Santa
Liberata

Punta Lividonia

Santo Stefano

rtezza di Filipo II

Orbetello

Capalbio

VIA AURELIA

MONTE ARGENTARIO

Capo d'Uomo

Fortino Stella

FENIGLIA

Port 'Ercole

L'Isolotto

Punta Avoltore

Torre di
Buranaccio

LAZIO

Montalto
di Castro

Torre Montalto

To Rome

GIANNUTRI

VIA AURELIA

GIANNELLA

Author's Note

The Porto Santo Stefano of today was originally just "Santo Stefano" and there were only two causeways between Argentario and the mainland until the third was built to carry modern traffic. Forte della Stella was also known as Fortino Stella: Torri and Monte dell' Uccellina were also spelt Ucellina; Filippo Secundo was often Filipo Secundo at the time.

Dudley Pope
Yacht *Ramage*
French Antilles

Chapter One

The Atlantic entrance to the Strait of Gibraltar always reminded Ramage of a gigantic funnel lying on its side, its spout pointing towards the Mediterranean and forever replenishing the warm inland sea from the cold ocean. The lower side of the funnel was shaped by the North African coast between Casablanca and Tangier, the upper by the Spanish shore from Cadiz to Tarifa.

However, this present stretch of Spain reaching from off Cadiz down to the actual Strait (which was known to generations of British seamen as "The Gut") brewed the most unpredictable weather in Europe. No, that was not quite fair: perhaps the Texel, off the north-west corner of the Netherlands, was as bad: sudden and vicious thunderstorms spawned there too out of a clear sky.

Anyway, for once the wind taking the *Calypso* frigate diagonally across the Gulf of Cadiz, from off Faro down to the Strait, was remarkable only for its lightness: light enough to decide him to go in close to Cadiz and then stretch down towards The Gut, giving all his officers (and young Paolo in particular) a chance to have a good look at this part of the Spanish coast, which must be guarded by more forts and towers (one every half a dozen miles, it seemed) than anywhere he had ever seen except the Tuscan coast of Italy, which had coincidentally belonged to Spain for many years. Obviously the Dons favoured towers.

The light breezes (admittedly from the north, giving the *Calypso* a soldier's wind and calm sea and ensuring she was not off a lee shore) and a packet of sealed orders (to be opened once past Gibraltar) made him want to attack Cadiz just to placate his impatience.

He glared at Paolo. "Where did Columbus sail from on his third voyage?"

"Sanlúcar de Barrameda at the southern end of those marshes, Las Marismas," the midshipman answered promptly. He pointed to the eastwards and added: "Just over there, sir."

"And Magellan?"

"Same place, sir."

"And where did the Spanish plate fleets arrive when they bought back the gold and silver from the Main?"

"Same place, sir, but they had to cross the bar and then sail or warp their way more than thirty miles up the River Guadalquivir to Seville, so that the bullion could be inspected by government men and officially weighed and stamped . . ."

Ramage nodded and pointed first at the chart spread on the top of the binnacle box and then at the shore running south-east five miles away over on the larboard side. "And where are we now?"

"Those low reddish cliffs have the Cortadura Fort at the northern end and the Torre Bermeja at the southern – you can just see the tower."

Ramage nodded and let his thoughts wander. He was looking at the coast of Andalusia. For more than a hundred years (beginning not so long after the Moors were driven out of Spain in 1492) an enormous quantity of gold and silver had poured into Spain from Mexico and Peru, yet a couple of centuries later Spain had nothing to show for it: no splendid palaces or new universities or even towns had been built with the money. No fleet, no army that mattered. The reason was simple enough: Philip II, who had sent the Armada against England (paying for it with the riches from the Spain Main), and the kings succeeding him, had spent money on armies intended to turn the Protestants of Europe into Catholics, particularly the Netherlanders.

When the navies of France and Britain, the buccaneers, pirates and the Dutch had managed to prevent the plate fleets reaching Sanlúcar, the Spanish kings had borrowed heavily from the great bankers of Italy and Austria; the Fuggers and the Welsers, the Bardi and the Strozzi had been more than willing to lend – against the security of all the gold and silver of the Indies waiting on the Main to be shipped to Spain.

Then the king (he could not remember which one, but it was soon after Charles II was restored to the English throne) was trapped. His enemies' ships waited to catch the plate fleets at sea, so no bullion arrived in Spain, and with no bullion the king had no money to fit out the plate ships anyway.

Nor did he have the money to pay the bankers' interest on principal, so he defaulted on his debts. And that was how the Habsburgs broke the Fuggers, the enormously powerful family of merchant bankers which had (until it overextended itself with loans to Spain) financed wars, emperors and nations.

The *Calypso*'s white-haired master, Edward Southwick, stood patiently to one side, recognizing the look on Ramage's face and waiting for him to come back from wherever his thoughts had led him.

He offered Ramage a telescope. "That round tower is the Torre del Puerco, sir, and you can just see the waves breaking on the off-lying reef, Banco de los Marrajos, which is a couple of miles to seaward."

Ramage swept the coast with the glass. "Then there are cliffs and a headland, a small one."

"That's right sir," Southwick said. "That's Cabo Roche, a good marker for the next reef, which is Lajas de Cabo Roche, three miles offshore."

Ramage walked to the ship's side and looked down at the water, and then aft at the *Calypso*'s wake. "We're making about three knots and there doesn't seem to be much current."

"About a knot, southgoing," Southwick said, "but we can expect a couple of knots once we get a few miles past Cabo Trafalgar."

"Not often the current favours us," Ramage commented. He walked over and smoothed down the chart. "Hmm, I could just see the low reddish cliff beyond Cabo Roche. This is a good chart – where did you get it?"

"Bit o' luck," Southwick admitted. "My old one didn't have many details, but once I heard we'd be bound through The Gut, I saw an old friend o' mine who was the master of the flagship.

I remembered he'd been along this coast several times, and he gave me a sight of the chart he'd drawn from three captured Spanish ones so I could copy it."

Ramage ran his finger along the coastline drawn in on the chart and beckoned to Paolo. "Medina Sidonia. What does that name mean to you?"

The young midshipman's brow wrinkled. "*Accidente!*" he exclaimed, lapsing into Italian. "An old Spanish family. That's all that comes to mind, sir."

Ramage pointed over the larboard bow. "That headland there, Cabo Roche . . ."

Paolo nodded.

"North of it you see a few hills, with the mountains behind. Then you come to that sugarloaf (which must be a thousand feet high) and if you had a glass you'd see a tower on top. That sugarloaf is called Medina Sidonia."

"Indeed, sir," Paolo said politely.

"But that sugarloaf is not the Medina Sidonia I'm referring to. Tell him, Southwick!"

The master grinned sympathetically. The captain often shot questions like this at Midshipman Orsini as part of his self-appointed task of educating the Marchesa di Volterra's nephew and heir.

"Philip II put the Duke of Medina Sidonia in command of the vast Armada he sent against England in 1588, but Drake and gales did for the poor old duke, who knew nothing of the sea and was a coward anyway," Southwick explained.

"This was probably all the duke's land, then," Paolo commented.

"Exactly," Ramage said. "This small section of the Spanish coast, from Sanlúcar southwards, is really Spain's history squeezed into a few miles. The duke led the Armada and was beaten, the plate fleets arriving with the gold and silver later stopped, Spain went broke and has never recovered . . . It's all here. And Medina Sidonia's estates are just inland.

"So now study the chart," Ramage continued. "Get a glass and watch for the towers. If you know which is which you'll know exactly where we are: they're like beacons all the way along this coast."

4

For the next couple of hours Paolo alternately bent over the chart and then scowled at the coastline through the telescope, occasionally scribbling a name and time on the slate kept in the drawer of the binnacle box, and careful to add a brief description of each one – the captain was sure to read the daily journal which all midshipmen were required to keep and which was supposed to form a diary of the voyage, noting particularly anything of navigational interest and importance.

Well, Paolo thought, we passed Cabo Roche a couple of miles back, so that castle must be the Castillo de Sancti Petri. The Medina Sidonia sugarloaf came next, and then the village of Conil, built on a hill sloping back from the coast and easily seen in the glare of the afternoon sun because most of the buildings were white. A cluster of spinning windmills on top of a nearby hill looked in the distance like a bunch of flowers. Inland the bulky Monte de Patria was spotted by a series of towers – Torre La Atalaya, followed by the square-shaped Castilobo, which was hard to see because its grey stone blended with the land behind. Then on a small headland was Nueva, a round tower standing out among the rocks.

As the *Calypso* sailed south-east along a flat stretch of the coast which ran for five or six miles, blurred by the haze thrown up as the Atlantic slapped the beaches but backed by the line of mountains, blue-grey in the distance, Paolo studied what seemed to be a small island lying just off the coast.

Yet the chart did not show an island and, puzzled, he was just examining it with the glass for what seemed to be the tenth time when Ramage walked over. "You look worried."

"That island, sir," he said, gesturing over the larboard bow. "It isn't on the chart!"

"Perhaps it isn't an island . . ."

"But . . ." Paolo guessed the comment was a hint.

"If you went aloft with the bring-'em-near, the extra height would show that your 'island' is a headland, the end of a long and low sandy spit. Look inland – that flat-topped high ridge running back to the mountains is the Altos de Meca, so . . ."

"So that's Cabo Trafalgar, sir!" Paolo exclaimed, the relief very apparent in his voice.

"Exactly, and remember if you pass this way again close

5

inshore, that from the north (and the south, of course) it does look like an island." Ramage bent over the chart. "Yes, there's a very prominent round tower at the seaward end of the Altos de Meca. Not surprisingly it's called the Torre de Meca."

"Trafalgar doesn't seem a very Spanish name," Paolo commented, "especially compared with the towers."

"It's not, and although the English call it Traf*AL*gar with the emphasis on the second syllable, it should be on the third, Trafal*GAR*, because it's taken from the Moorish name."

"What was its original name, then, sir?"

"*Original* name? Well, the Romans were probably the first to name it – from memory something like *Promontorium Junonis*. Then the Moors called it *Taraf el gar*, which means (so Mr Southwick tells me) 'the promontory of caves'."

"Are there caves there, sir?"

"Presumably – I've never visited the place. By the way, the chart shows a reef just south of it, the *Arrecife de Canaveral*, quite apart from these reefs further offshore. Remember that, if you're ever leading a shore party from the south!"

"With all these towers and forts, I'd sooner stay at sea," Paolo said with a grin. "The next tower is only three miles south-east of the cape, Torre del Tajo."

"No, I don't think we shall be visiting Spain on this voyage," Ramage said, and then remembered that until they were off Gibraltar and he could open the sealed orders, he did not know.

At that moment the sails began to flap, and as Ramage swung round to glare at the quartermaster, he saw that the telltales were hanging down: the thin lines on which were threaded corks into which feathers had been stuck, showed that the wind was dying. Damnation, this wasn't the pleasantest of places to be becalmed.

By dawn the fitful wind was just beginning to freshen and the *Calypso*, like every one of the King's ships at sea in wartime, greeted the first light of the new day with her ship's company at general quarters: guns loaded and run out, Marines, with their muskets, ready for any enemy emerging from the night.

Ramage stood alone in the darkness at the forward end of the quarterdeck beside the rail, almost overwhelmed with memories.

6

Entering the Strait (particularly at daybreak) was an exciting experience: it beat the first sighting of the flat eastern coast of Barbados after crossing the Atlantic: it even beat seeing the Lizard again after a couple of years away from England. It was hard to know why the Strait of Gibraltar was different except that there was always the air of mystery. Yes, even now he could hear the distant bray of a donkey away over on the larboard bow – probably its protest at being whacked into activity by its peasant owner. And the smell of pines and woodsmoke and spices borne out to sea by the whiffles of chilly wind tumbling down the mountains and cliffs.

As the sun rose slowly ready to peer over the mountainous eastern horizon, he could just make out the dark bulk of Spain. There were many more towers along this coast, black fingers jutting up from rocky hilltops. Were the Spanish sentries asleep? Would they soon be passing the word that a British frigate was passing southwards into The Gut? Did they care?

He seemed to have spent all his life in the Mediterranean or the West Indies. He recalled those years ago when he had been the junior lieutenant in a frigate and had ended up, after a disastrous brush with a French ship of the line, as senior surviving officer. He had gone on to rescue Gianna – then known to him as just a name on a list, the Marchesa di Volterra – from (quite literally) under the hooves of Bonaparte's cavalry.

He shook his head, as if trying to rid himself of the idea that in the end it had all proved a waste of time and the wheel had turned a circle: Gianna was even now either dead, a victim of Bonaparte's secret police, or a prisoner. Young Paolo, her nephew, who was now standing down there beside his division of guns, was the only sign that Gianna had ever been part of Ramage's life, and there were even times when his memory refused to summon up her face.

The junior lieutenant had rescued her; the junior post-captain commanding a frigate had lost her. Was she dead? If so, then Paolo inherited Volterra, the tiny kingdom in Tuscany which she had ruled and which had been invaded by Bonaparte's Army of Italy.

The Marchesa di Volterra had been (is, he corrected himself hurriedly) tiny, beautiful, imperious, tender, hot-tempered,

7

autocratic and a dozen other contradictory things. He had loved her (and, he knew, she had loved him), and the years she had lived as a refugee with his mother and father, either down in Cornwall on the St Kew estate or in London, had been happy, except for the powerful sense of duty and obligation she had always felt for her people in Volterra.

No, the two of them could never have married, since she was a Catholic, and always, *noblesse oblige*, there was the pull of Volterra. So he had failed her in the end: as soon as the Treaty of Amiens had brought peace between Britain and France, she had decided to return to Volterra and her people, even though Ramage and his father had tried to persuade her that the peace would be brief; that it was another of Bonaparte's tricks, and as the ruler of Volterra returning from exile she would be seized or assassinated by the Corsican's men the moment war started again.

Nevertheless, in the company of the British government of the day, she decided that Bonaparte genuinely wanted peace (it was as though she dare not think otherwise) and set out for Volterra while the Admiralty sent Ramage and the *Calypso* thousands of miles away across the Equator on a voyage of exploration.

Yet, as if to compound misery with happiness, Ramage had then met, fallen in love with and married Sarah, the daughter of the Marquis of Rockley, and the two of them had been on their honeymoon in France when the war began again. After a narrow escape they had reached the Channel Fleet as it arrived to resume the blockade off Brest. Was it so fortunate, though? The admiral had sent Ramage across the Atlantic and Sarah back to England in a small brig which had vanished: no one knew to this day whether Sarah and the brig's men had perished in a gale, been killed in a French attack, or captured so that now they were prisoners.

As for Gianna – she had reached Paris. Beyond that, there was no news. Had she reached Volterra and been assassinated? Or imprisoned in France by Bonaparte's hirelings? He sensed that she was no longer alive.

Two women, and both dead or prisoners. But for knowing him, both might still be alive. Gianna would probably be a prisoner in Tuscany, but Sarah would be living with her father and mother, or perhaps married to some young sprig who rode well to hounds, dressed elegantly, drank and gambled in moderation, and never put anyone's life at risk – least of all, Ramage added bitterly, his own.

And there, showing as dawn crept up from the east, was the low black line on the southern horizon which would very soon reveal itself as the Atlas mountains: the northern shoulder of Africa and the southern shore of the Strait. Over there to the west, thrusting itself westward into the Atlantic, was Cape Espartel, still hidden in the darkness.

Southwick broke the night-induced gloom. "Looks as if this wind'll veer to the north-west as we turn east into The Gut, sir."

"Yes, it'll probably follow the mountains round and funnel past Gibraltar. Anything so long as we don't have to fight a levanter!"

The strong easterly wind that often blew out of the Mediterranean and into the Atlantic kicked up vicious seas in the Strait with violent squalls, so that beating against it with a strong current (usually flowing eastward) could make the last few miles through The Gut very unpleasant.

It was soon light enough "to see a grey goose at a mile" and then the men stood down from general quarters with the lookouts going aloft. A few men then waited on deck, looking across at the mountains of Spain, less than three miles off, and speculating about the Admiralty orders for the *Calypso*.

"Blackstrapped again – who'd have guessed that a couple o' weeks ago?" one of them commented. "Still, a drop o' red wine, as long as it ain't Spanish, 'll make a nice change from rum and small beer."

"Ah Stafford, you start to learn about the wine, eh?" said a plump, black-haired man whose accent revealed he was Italian. Alberto Rossi was (as he proudly told anyone who cared to listen) from Genova: the birthplace of Cristoforo Colombo, the man the English obstinately persisted in calling Christopher Columbus and the Spanish unforgivably Cristóbal Colón – "As though," Rossi protested, "he was a Spaniard! *Accidente!* He never went to Spain until he had thirty years."

"Still, the Spanish paid his fare to America," Jackson said.

The only American on board, he was the captain's coxswain, having served with Ramage for several years. He owned a properly executed Protection, recognized by the American government and issued and attested by an American Customs collector, which certified that Jackson was an American citizen and born in Charleston, South Carolina. This meant he could not be impressed into the Royal Navy (or, if he was, an appeal to an American consul would get his release).

However, Jackson was happy enough serving – was it George III or Captain Lord Ramage? People like Southwick often wondered; men like Stafford were certain: Jackson served the captain even if the King paid his wages. Not that Jackson needed the money. Stafford knew only too well that like all the men who had been serving with Mr Ramage for a few years, he had done well from prize money. They could all look forward to a comfortable old age – if they lived long enough! Death or prize money – they were the choice if you served under Mr Ramage, Stafford knew, and if you lived long enough you would end up a rich man . . .

"Whatcher reckon, Jacko?" Stafford asked.

"Well, we won't be joining a fleet, that's for certain, because there ain't one out here. I reckon Mr Ramage doesn't know himself, yet. Probably got sealed orders. Something special, anyway."

"Why special?" Rossi asked.

"Obvious, ain't it. There are only a few (if any) of our frigates in the Mediterranean, and the Admiralty's very short of them at home. Why not send a cutter with orders for anyone out here? Why send a frigate specially?"

"Is sense," Rossi said grudgingly. "The Admiralty knows Mr Ramage understands Italian and Spanish, and knows the Mediterranean well. Hasn't brought him the happiness, though."

Stafford glanced up at Rossi. "How so?"

"The Marchesa. He rescue her, he love her, she go back to Volterra – though by now this Bonaparte probably has her locked up in a jail. Or in a grave."

"But Mr Ramage is now married to Lady Sarah," Jackson reminded him. "Happily too, and she's a fine lady."

"I know, I know," Rossi said impatiently waving a dismissive hand. "But you know for a long time it was always the Marchesa, and we all thought he would marry her . . ."

"You did, but I always said no: she's a Catholic, and that matters in a Protestant country. Anyway, Lady Sarah is much more suitable as a wife, even if – " he hesitated, unwilling to say it aloud. "Even if the ship she was in is missing."

"*Accidente!* Don't say anything against the Marchesa!"

"Don't be so damned Italian," Jackson said. "You forget Mr Ramage and I rescued her. Who carried her wounded down the beach and got her into the boat, eh? That was Mr Ramage and me, and you were still skulking in Genoa at the time, slitting a throat here and there if anyone paid you the right price."

Rossi grinned contentedly: he liked the reputation of having been a dangerous man in Genova, although glad enough to exchange it all for service in the Royal Navy after escaping from the Genovesi authorities, who had a narrow-minded outlook about life, sudden death and the ownership of property.

"Yer know," Stafford said sadly, "seems a shame, dunnit, that a man like Mr Ramage, him been wounded a dozen times and the best frigate captain in the Navy, can't marry the first woman he falls in love with 'cos of a lot o' religious nonsense, and *then* loses the second one at the end of 'is 'oneymoon.

"I wonder what *did* 'appen to Lady Sarah. A real lady, she was. I'm not saying nothing against the Marcheezer, Rosey, but you must admit she was a bit of an 'andful at times. Very Italian, when she got angry." He looked round warily at Rossi. "Nothing wrong with that, o' course – after all, she was used to being the ruler of Volterra, with a palace an' all. 'Ad to laugh when she used to come the empress with the captain!"

"He had the measure of her," Jackson nodded understandingly. "He could handle her. She never did realize that however much she stamped her foot and rolled her eyes and demanded this and that, she usually ended up doing just what the captain intended all the time. But he always left her thinking she'd won the day – that was the secret of his success."

"Ho yes, the captain was smart enough," Stafford agreed. "But Lady Sarah was always calm. A proper *English* lady. They're different from foreigners, you know." He nodded con-

11

fidently, as if remembering the lessons learned during a long string of amorous and cosmopolitan conquests. "They don't yell and wave their arms about an' put on airs and graces."

"Is very dull, though, married to the calm sort. Like having sunshine every day: you need a gale occasionally for comparing," Rossi said emphatically.

"Don't you believe it," Jackson said firmly. "That's why I like the Tropics. Always warm and most of the time sunny. I don't want to be for ever wondering if tomorrow we're going to have snow or rain or a minute's glimpse of pale sun. An English summer is like getting a sample of the year's weather all in one week!"

Stafford patted his stomach. "Breakfast . . . and it's Louis's week as messcook."

Louis was one of the Frenchmen who had escaped with Ramage and Sarah to join the fleet off Brest, and because the tiny group were royalists, they had accepted the bounty and now served in the Royal Navy. They had joined the trio of Jackson, Stafford and Rossi, and as a result they now spoke with the sharp vowels of a Genoese accent mingling with its English equivalent, the slang of the Cockney.

Chapter Two

Ramage stood at the taffrail looking astern. The sun had lifted clear of the eastern horizon and as the *Calypso* stretched into the Mediterranean, keeping to the middle of the Strait to avoid being becalmed under the Spanish cliffs, he stared at the African coast. With Gibraltar and Spain on one side and the mountains of Africa on the other, the Strait was known to the ancients as the Pillars of Hercules – and the pillars were perpetuated in the Spanish dollar sign: the Spaniards drew two vertical lines for the two pillars, and then entwined them with an "S" shaped garland.

In the distance Ramage could now see the Ras el Xakkar of the Arabs, the north-western tip of Africa and known to British seamen as Cape Espartel, the southern gateway to the Strait and unmistakable because of a long ridge of rounded mountains which ended just behind it in a great black hummock, Jebel Quebir. Two or three miles beyond as the coast trended south, out of sight just now, was Yibila, only 450 feet high but a perfectly shaped breast with a dark-coloured cairn on top – the reason for its Arab name, The Nipple.

The African coast lining the Strait was harsh: indented cliffs seemed to have been chewed by some great prehistoric monster, and were littered by many rocks, white-collared where the sea broke round them. The first port was Tangier, known to the Romans as Tingis and later called Tanjah by the Arabs. What a mixture of Spanish and Arab names there was along this coast: in fact both the Spanish and the Moorish sides of the Strait showed just how much the two peoples had been bound together

13

in years past. Until, in fact, Ferdinand and Isabella drove the Moors out of Granada, their last stronghold in Spain, only a few months before Columbus sailed to discover the New World.

The Moors had occupied Spain for seven hundred years. How much of their character, habits and morals had spread to the Spaniards, Ramage wondered. More than the Dons cared to admit, he suspected.

Looking down at the *Calypso*'s curling wake, Ramage was thankful that she had a fair wind and even more thankful that his preliminary orders from the Admiralty were to "proceed with all despatch" to the Mediterranean, opening his sealed orders only when Europa Point bore northwards.

Their Lordships were not being overprecise: Europa Point is to Gibraltar what the white cliffs of the South Foreland are to Dover. Much more to the point, he was instructed not to call at Gibraltar. Why? Did the Admiralty know that port admirals delighted in sending off visiting frigates on wild goose chases of their own?

Or were Their Lordships afraid that the contents of their secret orders might be revealed? Yet what in the Mediterranean could be so secret that the port admiral in Gibraltar (or a commander-in-chief if there happened to be a fleet at anchor there) did not know about it?

He turned to look forward over the *Calypso*'s bow. The ship was making good time despite a slack current. Sticking out from the Spanish shore (as though a pedlar was offering him an onion by its stalk) was Tarifa, a small island linked to the Spanish mainland by a causeway. Tarifa had for centuries been a sally port for pirates and privateers who lurked behind its steep cliffs, waiting to pounce on passing merchant ships. It was the southernmost point of Europe, beating Europa Point by five or six miles.

Well, Ramage admitted, the Pillars of Hercules held many memories for him; it had been the gateway through which, as a young midshipman, he had first passed to see and smell the black smoke of guns in battle and hear the calico-ripping noise of passing roundshot. Promotion, fear, opportunity, boredom, excitement . . . the smell of pines on a hot summer day along the Tuscan coast . . . Gianna . . . the excited chatter of Italians . . . a

14

jumble of experiences . . . and what were those secret orders going to add to the pile?

He saw the new officer of the deck come on watch. William Martin, lieutenant and son of the master shipwright at the Chatham yard, must be about twenty-four by now. What were *his* thoughts on returning to the Mediterranean? His last visit brought him plenty of excitement – and had given the ship's company a good deal of pleasure, because Lieutenant Martin played a flute as though the instrument was part of his body, and its music as the sun went down at the end of a clear Mediterranean day brought cheers from the seamen who, expressing their pleasure rather than mocking, had nicknamed him "Blower".

Martin listened carefully as the small, red-haired and freckled lieutenant he was relieving passed on such details as the course to steer, the currents to be expected, and any of the captain's orders which had not yet been executed. Lieutenant Kenton, who must be the same age as Martin, was the son of a half-pay captain in the Navy and, like Martin, was a competent and well liked officer who had also been in the *Calypso* when she was last in the Mediterranean. In fact as the sun lit up the Strait he and Ramage had been reminiscing about the time they had attacked Port' Ercole with bomb ketches and, in another operation, captured several of Bonaparte's signal towers dotted along the French coast.

Now, as Kenton turned away to go below, Martin walked to the larboard side and stared at Gibraltar just coming into sight, and Ramage watched him pick up a telescope to examine the fortifications of Tarifa – a high wall with several towers.

This was an impressive stretch of coast: the mountains rolled inland like giant petrified waves and were given the resounding name of Sierra Nuestra Señora de la Luz (and, as if to carry on the Arab tradition of Yibila, one of the peaks just east of Tarifa was named Tetas de la Luz). The next peak, Ramage noticed from the chart, had an earthier name, Gitano.

Southwick came on deck and glanced round. Seeing Ramage walking to the quarterdeck rail he came over to join him. "We're far enough out not to have to worry about the off-lying dangers, sir," he commented.

Ramage said teasingly: "Yes, one of the fastest ways of being put on half-pay must be to run aground on La Perla!"

"Easy enough to do as you go into Gibraltar if you lose the wind with a strong eastgoing current, or a white squall hits you."

"A court of inquiry will have heard it all before!"

"True," Southwick admitted. "I wonder how many of our own ships over the years have ended up on those rocks, let alone Spanish and Moorish. But who named them? 'The Teeth' would be fitter!"

La Perla was in fact a group of rocks usually covered and lying half a mile offshore, just where an unwary ship from the Atlantic and bound for Gibraltar might be tempted to take a short cut. Or, as Southwick had noted, where a ship losing the wind and caught in the currents and eddies (which often ran at three knots) would end up.

The Rock: one of the most impressive places in the world, Ramage thought: perhaps *the* most. One can compare it with an enormous block of wood attacked by a madman with an axe. The north and east sides are almost vertical, like the end of a box; the western side, now on the larboard bow, is a steep slope, while the side facing the Strait is a series of steps, or terraces, which end at the aptly named Europa Point.

Ramage felt hungry and thirsty, and irritated by the slack current which was slowing the *Calypso*: Nature was determined to make him wait and wait before opening those damned orders. "Come down and report when Europa Point bears due north," Ramage said, "and bring Aitken with you."

Captains hated sealed orders which were to be opened at a certain position, or on a certain date. There was always the chance that one might subsequently be accused of opening them earlier. The best method was the one just adopted by Ramage: telling the first lieutenant and master to report to his cabin at the time appointed for opening the orders. Then there were witnesses and (if it could be allowed) they could read the orders and discuss the ways and means of carrying them out.

He went down to his cabin, unlocked a drawer in his desk, and took out a canvas bag. It had brass grommets round the opening and a sturdy drawstring passed through the rings. The bag

16

was heavy because inside there was a small pig of lead to make it sink quickly if thrown over the side in an emergency to avoid capture.

Ramage took out the packet, secured the bag again and returned it to the drawer. Sealed orders. Well, they looked just like any other letter from the Admiralty – an outer cover of thick paper folded once from each side and the overlapping flaps joined by a large seal, the red wax covered with thin white paper before the Admiralty seal was impressed. Ramage wondered for the thousandth time how the Admiralty acquired that seal. Presumably it belonged originally to their predecessor, the Lord High Admiral, who would have used it until his office was "put into commission" – handed over to several individuals who became the Lords Commissioners of the Admiralty. But a fouled anchor – one with the cable twisted round the shank – was hardly suitable; in fact it would be hard to think of a more lubberly symbol.

The Mediterranean – well, it was a change from the West Indies (and that brief foray south of the Equator). "Being blackstrapped" the sailors called it, a catch-all phrase that meant not only serving in the Mediterranean but being issued with red wine instead of rum. The word probably came from Blackstrap Bay (locally known as Mala Bahia), and referred to the fact that a ship bound for Gibraltar and losing the wind would be carried eastward past Europa Point and might then spend several days waiting for a fair wind, anchored off the bay and below an ancient watch tower, nearly one thousand feet up on a long ridge known as the Queen of Spain's Chair.

Names – one thing about cruising in the Mediterranean was that you quickly become aware of the sweep of history: the successive sweep of civilizations, rather. Gibraltar, for instance. Its first name (first to be recorded, anyway) was Calpe, given by the Phoenicians, and when the Romans arrived in their galleys they kept the name. Then, as the Roman Empire crumbled (after holding all the land that mattered round the Mediterranean), the Moors came and gave The Rock the name of Jebel Tarik. "Jebel" meant a hill or mountain. What about Tarik? Ramage remembered he was a Moorish leader – perhaps the man who first captured The Rock and had the

17

mountain named after him. Then the Spaniards drove out the Moors seven hundred years later and named it Monte de Gibraltar. Presumably this was a Spanish corruption of Jebel Tarik, particularly as the Dons rendered "Jebel" as "Hebel". He rolled the words round with his tongue. Yes, "Hebel Tarik" could eventually emerge as "Hebeltara".

He heard the clatter of shoes coming down the companion ladder and then the Marine sentry at the door announced the first lieutenant and the master.

As soon as they came in he gestured to them to sit down. Southwick sat in a creaky armchair to one side of the desk while the first lieutenant, Aitken, sat on the sofa. This was an arrangement which respected Southwick's spasms of rheumatism rather than his seniority, since as master he was only a warrant officer (holding his rank by virtue of an Admiralty warrant), while Aitken held the King's commission.

"Europa Point bears due north, sir," Aitken reported formally.

Both men looked expectantly at Ramage, who held up the packet so that they could both see that the seal was unbroken. "My new orders from the Admiralty, to be opened as we pass Gibraltar."

Southwick sniffed. He had a repertoire of a dozen or more different sniffs, and anyone knowing him well could translate each into a word or a phrase, even an attitude. This particular sniff, Ramage recognized, had two meanings: first, it's time Their Lordships stopped play-acting with sealed orders, and second, a return to the Mediterranean at this time can only mean trouble.

In this Ramage had to admit that Southwick was probably right: for a long time now the Mediterranean had been Bonaparte's private sea: he had captured bases used by the Royal Navy, and defeated Britain's allies.

Ramage slid a paperknife under the seal, then opened and flattened the sheets of paper. Only two sheets. The thickness of paper had led him to think the orders were bulky, but he saw at a glance that in fact they were commendably brief – although brief orders tended to be the toughest . . .

There was all the usual preamble used by Evan Nepean, the

18

Board Secretary, wording which had probably been in use long before the Board was first created. Then came the second paragraph . . .

Since the resumption of war following France's abrogation of the Treaty of Amiens, His Majesty's Government has been attempting to discover the whereabouts of many British subjects, and subjects of countries which are our allies, who were visiting and found themselves trapped by hostilities in France or its occupied territories. Among them, of course, is the Marchesa di Volterra.

Among the British subjects particularly concerned are five admirals, seven generals and eleven peers of the realm, who were in France or Italy.

Our agents have traced certain of these persons to prison camps in France, although the French Government has not included their names among those usually submitted through their Agent resident in London in order that exchanges may be arranged, nor have they answered specific enquiries made by His Majesty's Government through their Agent. The situation is exacerbated at the present time because in any case we have no French prisoners of suitable rank to make any exchange. My Lords have instructed me to give you the foregoing information by way of introduction to the following.

It has now been reported to His Majesty's Secretary of State for the Foreign Department that a few of these naval and army officers, along with certain peers of the realm, are imprisoned in conditions of great secrecy by the French Government at a town in the Kingdom of Tuscany called Pitigliano and it is further believed that it is the First Consul's intention to use these persons as hostages in an attempt to strike some bargain with His Majesty's Government, the details of which cannot at present be determined.

The Secretary of State has instructed my Lords that these prisoners must be rescued at any cost because of the dangers ensuing should they be used as hostages, or bargaining pawns.

My Lords, having duly considered their instructions, and

having in mind that it was from this area that you rescued the Marchesa di Volterra several years ago, and that you are fluent in the Italian language, hereby request and require you to make the best of your way in His Majesty's frigate under your command and rescue the aforementioned officers and civilians.

Although it is understood from the Secretary of State's sources that none of the hostages has been offered nor given his parole, Their Lordships are particularly concerned that any person who might in fact have given it should be left behind.

On the successful completion of these orders you will carry these hostages to Gibraltar and acquaint the port admiral of these orders so that he can arrange suitable transport to bring them safely to the United Kingdom.

My Lords impress upon you particularly the need for absolute secrecy to ensure the safety of the hostages and of the source of the intelligence which has resulted in you receiving these orders, and it is considered imperative that in the event of you or any of your ship's company being captured by the enemy, none of you shall reveal any of the foregoing, lest you fall under the terms of the third Article of War.

Hmmm . . . to threaten a post-captain with one of the Articles of War showed the importance that the government (in the person of the Secretary of State) attached to the rescue. Article Three – "If any officer, mariner, soldier or other person of the Fleet shall give, hold or entertain Intelligence to or with any Enemy or rebel, without leave from the King's Majesty, or the Lord High Admiral, or the Commissioners for executing the Office of Lord High Admiral . . . shall be punished with death."

Strong stuff, and Pitigliano was many miles inland. Many miles.

"That's what comes of speaking Italian," Ramage said as he handed the sheets of paper to Aitken. "But now I understand why we weren't to know about it until we had passed Gibraltar. Calling in there and accidentally revealing any of that . . ."

20

Aitken read swiftly. "I wonder how the government discover these things? About Bonaparte holding hostages in secret camps?"

Southwick sniffed. "By the time they finished Captain Ramage's report on rescuing the Count of Rennes from Devil's Island, along with all those other French royalists, I should think the count's friendship with the Prince of Wales led Prinny to ask a lot of questions.

"That probably led to the Foreign Department – or whoever handles our agents abroad – suddenly waking up. Why, just comparing the names of naval officers we know have been captured with those offered by this French agent in London arranging the exchange of prisoners must show a number missing. And Army, too, of course. And civilians," he added quietly, knowing that both the Marchesa and Lady Sarah came under that heading.

Ramage nodded, as much to show Southwick it was all right to discuss the two women as to agree. Yes, it was strange that neither Sarah nor a captain being sent home in the *Murex* had been mentioned so far by the French, and although Bonaparte was not fussy about involving civilians (against all the rules of war used up to now) it was surprising that the *Moniteur* had not crowed about capturing the daughter of the Marquis of Rockley, and the Marchesa di Volterra.

All of which left question marks. The *Moniteur*'s silence about Sarah might be simply because the *Murex* had never been captured: perhaps she had sunk in bad weather or because she had sprung the butt of a plank. And Gianna – if Bonaparte's secret police had seized and murdered her, obviously the *Moniteur* would stay silent. Plenty of question marks, but no answers . . .

"Do you know where Pitigliano is?" Aitken asked. "Is it far inland? It'd be just our luck if it was surrounded by mountains!"

"No," Ramage said, shaking his head. "Pitigliano is likely to be the only piece of luck we have. It's about thirty miles or so inland, a small hill town. I've been there once, and from what I can remember, it's built on a wedge of land in the middle of a valley. Obviously a river ran through the valley once and

21

Pitigliano (or the hill on which it now stands) was an island in the middle.

"Yes, now I remember . . . the town is actually built so it forms the flat top of the hill, and there's only one gate – which is at the top of a steep track."

He thought of a better way of describing it. "Think of a dunce's cap. The point at the top cut off and that's where the town is built, with a high wall all round it, so that from down in the valley you would see only the walls and the roofs of a few buildings.

"At the bottom there are several caves cut into the tufa, and there many of the peasants keep their donkeys. The town hall is in the piazza with a sort of pulpit built outside, so the mayor can harangue the people.

"Dust, donkeys braying and laden with firewood, their owners hanging on to their tails for a lift to windward up the hill to the town gate, the caves, tracks covered with white dust . . . that's all I can remember."

Aitken crossed his legs and then scratched his head. "I wonder why Bonaparte picked Pitigliano? There must be dozens of other hill towns he could have chosen."

"Hundreds," Ramage said. "The length of Italy, although more in Tuscany than anywhere else because there are so many sugarloaf hills. Bonaparte knows the area well, of course, from the time he marched through with his Army of Italy, but one of his underlings probably chose the town."

"Can't place it," Southwick admitted.

"You remember Santo Stefano and Port' Ercole well enough," Ramage said. "And Talamone. Thirty miles inshore from there."

"That's most convenient: I still have all my charts and the notes I made. Not far from where we – you, rather – rescued the Marchesa," Southwick said. "Might be an omen, sir."

"A bad one," Ramage said gloomily. "All this to rescue some admirals and generals who'll stamp round the deck and get in the way of the sailors."

"Yes, sir, but with Rossi and Mr Orsini speaking Italian . . . they'll be able to help you."

"Rossi yes, I don't know that I dare risk using Orsini. He's the Marchesa's heir, so if anything has happened to her, he's now the ruler of Volterra. If Bonaparte has murdered the Marchesa, then he'll quickly do away with Orsini."

"You'd have trouble leaving Orsini behind, sir," Aitken said. "And if he was captured, what Frenchman could guess he'd just caught the ruler of Volterra? He speaks like an Englishman."

"You sound as though you're both selling Orsini," Ramage said. "I recall hearing you frequently criticizing his mathematics, Mr Southwick . . ."

"Indeed you have, sir, and not for the last time. He takes a good sight; it's just the calculations that do him in. Two and two often make five, although he's not the first midshipman to have that trouble. But I doubt if we have a better seaman on board. Turn in a splice, have the men send down a yard, lay a gun . . . An' the men would follow him anywhere."

"In Tuscany, since they don't speak the language, that mightn't be a help," Ramage said sourly. "Anyway, now we know where we're going, are we all right for water to get us there and back to Gibraltar?"

"We've thirty-six tons remaining sir; plenty, even allowing for having the hostages on board," Southwick said.

As the first lieutenant and master stood up to leave the cabin, Ramage said: "Don't discuss this with anyone else for the time being: until I decide how we'll do it. I don't want people pestering me to be allowed to join in. It may end up with Rossi and me going alone . . ."

Chapter Three

When you were beating down Channel against a strong westerly gale, spray slashing like buckets of icy water slung violently at anywhere you are unprotected (neck, third button down on the oilskins), and the dreadful chill while the cold and wet gather before their slow creep down the spine, the sky just a swirling grey mass merging with the rain squalls, two reefs in the top-sails and deck seams dripping water on to hammock, kitbag and last items of dry clothing, you thought wistfully of the Mediterranean.

Blue skies, purple seas, a warm wind always from the right direction; the smell of pines when close in with the shore; the air clear and bracing when out of sight of land . . .

Yet the reality of the Mediterranean was nearly always different, Ramage reflected: heavy rain, gale-force winds (usually heading you) and the clouds the same swirling grey mass. *Perhaps* a degree warmer than the Chops of the Channel, but the wind just as violent with the seas shorter, but that made them much more uncomfortable.

Oh yes, and the winds had fancy names – take the French, for example. A nor-wester was the *mistral*, but getting caught by a *mistral* meant three or four days of fighting a gale. Then the *tramontane*, "across the mountains", and because of that it was a bitterly cold north to north-east brute that blew hard and chilled your very marrow. Then the *levant*, blowing at gale force for days from the east, hell if you are trying to get through the Strait into the Mediterranean (though usually you could shelter in Gibraltar), but murderous on ship, men and sails when you

24

are trying to reach the Tyrrhenian Sea along the west coast of Italy, whether by rounding the southern tip of Sardinia at Cape Spartivento or sneaking through the Strait of Bonifacio between Corsica and Sardinia.

You left that decision until the last possible moment in the hope that the levanter veered a little and became the *céruse*, blowing from the south-east so that, with luck, sheets could be eased. (It was beyond even thinking about a *ponant* to put in an appearance, from between south and south-west, or the *labé* from the west-south-west.)

Yet, Ramage thought sourly, if you have sailed enough you think of the West Indies with the constant trade winds blowing briskly from the north-east – if there was not a calm lasting days, or a hurricane, or a week of south-east winds bringing torrential rain which reduced visibility to a ship's length.

Usually, however, whatever the wind direction, it had some east in it, and *usually* your course had some east in it too, so you were still beating to windward, but the difference was that the buckets of spray hitting you in the face were *warm* – at least for the first few minutes, until they soaked your clothing.

So why did a sane man go to sea (unless encouraged by the pressgangs, which were very persuasive)? Few men beating to windward in heavy weather would admit they ever had a choice: poverty, pressgang, dodging debtors, sent to sea as a midshipman because of a family tradition . . . dozens of reasons. Of course, given a decent wind, a clear sky (or one speckled with Trade wind clouds), and the attitude immediately changed: hurrah for the life of a sailor . . .

Ramage noted that the only man in sight who seemed to be enjoying this *levant* at the moment, blowing at what the French would term at least *grand frais* with a sea *très grosse*, was George Hill, the new third lieutenant. He was the thin and nonchalant lieutenant (debonair, one might say, when his sou'wester and oilskin coat were not streaming spray and rain and his face not white and tinged with blue) who had been appointed provost marshal "upon the occasion", guarding Ramage while he was under an arrest during the recent court-martial brought by the madman, Captain William Shirley.

After starting off as a very officious young lieutenant, Hill had by the end of the trial, been asking Ramage to be considered when the next vacancy occurred in the *Calypso*. And that had come almost at once when Wagstaffe was made first lieutenant of a seventy-four, which allowed Kenton to step up to take Wagstaffe's place, leaving the third lieutenant's berth vacant for Hill.

"Blower" Martin stayed as fourth lieutenant, but he was content: indeed, he had confided to Ramage that he needed another year's experience before being promoted.

Hill, despite his (when dry) debonair, almost flippant manner, was proving a good seaman. His manner for the first week or so had put off Southwick and Aitken: they were not used to a man who could make light of the most important things in their world. Hill used the expression "putting a fold in the laundry" to describe reefing; "that hook thing" was an anchor; rope of any size became "string" (including the ten-inch cables); and splicing was "that embroidery stuff". Taking a sight was "having a wink at the red eye", and all caused long faces until they discovered that Hill could splice with the best of them and liked nothing better than racing the topmen aloft and laying out along a yard "to get a bit o' exercise".

Southwick had to admit that Hill worked out a sight as though he had been navigating since childhood. In fact, the master had grumbled: "Whatever Hill has mathematically, I wish young Orsini would catch it." From there it was a short step to putting Hill in charge of drumming mathematics into Orsini, and Hill was apparently having some success (according to Southwick), although his teaching methods were unorthodox. Ramage often heard Orsini hooting with laughter while working out a noon sight under Hill's watchful eye, but Southwick reported that nine times out of ten the calculations were now correct: Orsini's habit of adding when he should subtract, or being just one out in all additions and subtractions, now seemed to be a thing of the past.

Both Kenton and Martin liked Hill and soon dropped into his habit of treating life with levity, and even Aitken confided to Ramage that the gunroom was a good deal more cheerful now Hill was on board.

Ramage saw the master, looking like a wet bear in his oilskins, lumber up the ladder and work his way across the quarter-deck, walking cautiously from one gun to another so that he had handholds against the violent rolling.

"Cape Spartivento's about fifteen miles on our larboard bow, sir, unless the current is stronger than usual."

"I'll be glad to bear away a bit when we round it," Ramage admitted.

"Fighting a levanter the length of the Western Mediterranean doesn't make for accurate dead reckoning," Southwick muttered, "so Hill had better keep a sharp lookout."

"Come now, you had a sight of the sun a couple of times yesterday," Ramage said teasingly. "I saw you scurrying around with your quadrant, and chasing Orsini, too."

"Sometimes I'm overwhelmed by Nature's benevolence," Southwick growled, and Ramage detected the influence of Hill in the remark.

"You should be. I assume you are ready for the sun to break through?"

Southwick glanced up at the thick, shapeless clouds streaming overhead. "Oh yes, sir; I have my quadrant tucked in my sou'wester, and I left my books of tables open in my cabin – along with sharpened pencils."

Ramage nodded: if Southwick could still joke, things were not too bad, although as far as Ramage was concerned he seemed to have been beating to windward for most of his life.

The grey skies, the endless waves racing past to the westward, the *Calypso*'s labouring progress (she seemed to plunge her bow down in the same place every time, throwing up welters of spray), gave him too much time to think. To reflect. To feel guilty. The First Lord of the Admiralty, Lord St Vincent, admittedly a crusty old fellow, said that when an officer married he was "lost to the Service", and Ramage began to suspect he was right. Hardly a minute passed without him thinking and worrying about Sarah, and he was damned sure he could not be blamed because he worried whether his wife was dead or a prisoner. Killed or captured, he told himself bitterly for what must be the millionth time, before their honeymoon was properly over. If only he knew for certain, one way or the other. Yet if he knew that Sarah was dead, there would not be much

27

purpose left to life: it was only the thought that she was a prisoner that gave his life any direction.

And Gianna. He still loved her, but (he now realized) as though she was a sister. And just as if she was a sister who had done something rash against the family's advice, he was haunted by the question of whether she too was dead or a prisoner. The two women to whom he had been closest . . . and both could be dead. Dead because of him. If he had not rescued Gianna and brought her back to England as a refugee to live with his family, she would not have rushed back towards Volterra in that brief period of peace. And if he had not been sent south on that voyage of exploration, he would not have met Sarah and married her, thus ensuring that she would be on board that damned *Murex* when it sank or was captured.

"Don't keep on blaming yourself, sir," Southwick said, realizing the mood: when the captain's deep-set brown eyes became unfocused, the normally hard line of the jaw was slack, the skin was taut over that slightly hooked nose, the hands were clasped behind the back, knuckles white – then Captain Ramage's thoughts were hundreds of miles away, reliving some episode concerning her Ladyship or the Marchesa. It was understandable, but all the worry in the world would not restore either of them. And at this moment it was better for the captain to worry about those extraordinary orders from the Admiralty.

Southwick considered they *were* extraordinary orders. Parole was a touchy business. British officers held as prisoners of war in France (and French officer prisoners in England) were usually offered parole, which meant giving your word of honour that you would not escape. In return, you were allowed either to lodge (at your own expense!) close by, or be allowed out from the actual prison each day.

The Admiralty viewed parole very seriously – as far as *British* officers were concerned. If a British officer gave the French his parole and in return received a degree of liberty, then woe betide him if he used the opportunity to escape and reach England.

Almost the first question asked an escaped British naval officer on reaching England was whether he had given his parole. If he had, then he was sent back to France, where he would have to wait his turn to be exchanged in the normal way for a French officer held prisoner in England.

It occurred to Southwick that Bonaparte must laugh at the quaint and punctilious British, because no one had ever heard of the French sending back a French officer who had broken his parole and escaped.

By the same token, he thought contemptuously, as far as he knew no British consul ever considered that a Briton abroad could be right in an argument with foreign authority (unless, of course, the person involved could influence the consul's career). By and large – according to Mr Ramage – all Britons should avoid British consulates or embassies if they ever needed help: the hirelings of His Majesty's Secretary of State for the Foreign Department were chosen for their vapidity and their dancing and conversational skills, not their brains (which, if discovered Mr Ramage maintained, could wreck a diplomat's career).

So what happens, Southwick wondered, if we get to Pitigliano and find that two admirals, three generals, four colonels and five peers of the realm *have* given their parole? It is all very well for the Admiralty to say they must be left behind, but what happens when these people's friends hear about it in England? Once again the government would be looking for a scapegoat, since no government could be wrong, and no politician would ever risk losing a vote . . .

"Who else is to blame if not me?" Ramage asked quietly, seeming to have come back from a long journey.

Southwick's sniff implied that the answer was so obvious he was having difficulty in remaining patient. "Sir, have you ever considered the answer you'd get if you asked either lady if given the opportunity she'd change anything?"

"That's absurd," Ramage snapped. "No one chooses death."

Southwick gave a shrug sufficiently violent to be obvious in spite of the newly tarred oilskins encasing him. "Supposing you'd been killed rescuing Lady Sarah in the *Murex*, or the Marchesa in that affair with the Post Office packet – would you have changed anything that went earlier?"

"That's not at all the same thing," Ramage said angrily. "I was doing my duty. If I am killed in the process, that's too bad."

29

"And that's just what both ladies would say. The Marchesa felt it her duty to go back to her people in the Kingdom of Volterra, even though you and your father warned her of the risks from Bonaparte's police. Lady Sarah was, I'm absolutely sure, proud of having helped you capture the *Murex* and escape from Brest: that was her duty – to her husband and to her country. *Noblesse oblige*, they call it, sir."

"You talk up a gale of wind," Ramage said bitterly, "but it doesn't bring 'em back."

Southwick looked at him squarely, the grandfather talking to his grandson. "Nor does moping."

Finally Ramage nodded. He glanced across at the feathers on one of the windvanes. "If those men are steering the right course, the wind is starting to veer."

Chapter Four

A steady *céruse* gave the *Calypso* a brisk beat up to Cape Carbonara, the south-eastern tip of Sardinia, and then once round it the frigate was able to ease sheets and steer northward along its east coast, ignoring the watch towers perched on the cliffs.

Because she was French built, the *Calypso* would almost certainly be identified as a French national ship by the thick-headed lookouts, and in any case to most of them ships with more than one mast were the same. A single frigate was therefore unlikely to cause an alarm: her very course and obvious destination – Leghorn or Genoa on the mainland, Porto Vecchio or Bastia in Corsica – made it obvious that her voyage was routine.

With the sky clearing and the *Calypso*'s bow not shouldering up spray, the frigate now looked more like a laundry than a ship o' war. Ramage had given permission for lines to be rigged so the men could hang up their wet clothes. The sailmaker had carefully unrolled a bolt of canvas, one end of which had been soaked by a random deck leak, and draped it across three guns because, left in its rack, the cloth would breed mildew on a hot day.

Ramage had read the Admiralty's secret orders once again, reflected on parole, which had concerned Southwick (and realized that if all the prisoners had given their parole none could be rescued and the Calypsos would have risked their lives for nothing), and then settled down with pen and paper for some mapmaking.

31

Pitigliano. Yes, it was easy to sketch a map from memory showing the section of the Italian mainland between the coast and Pitigliano, and the towns (most of them really large villages) between: Manciano, with the turning north to Saturnia and its sulphur baths (much favoured by the Romans, and the Etruscans before them), and which might have given its name to Saturnalia; and Osteria and Farnese and Valentano to the south. And then, he remembered, Marsiliana, Sgrillozzo and la Sgrilla, hamlets on the road before one reached Manciano.

Scale, that was the problem: he was trying to remember how many miles it had been from Orbetello on the coast to Manciano, and then on to Pitigliano, while on a boyhood journey to Orvieto. His strongest memories were white dust and thirst . . . Still, Pitigliano was about thirty miles south of Monte Amiata, which was by far the highest mountain around, and perhaps a dozen miles from the foothills of Mount Elmo, so in daylight there were some unmistakable reference points.

No problem, *signore* – except that Pitigliano must also be about thirty miles from the coast . . . miles covered presumably by French mounted patrols as well as gendarmes and Italian farmers and villagers who might consider it wiser to help the French (who, after all, had been in occupation for several years) rather than a crowd of passing Englishmen who had done nothing to help them . . .

But in what disguise would the Calypsos be? A troupe of buskers, tumbling to the tunes of "Blower" Martin's flute? The problem comprised two halves – going and coming back. Going, they would be a group of the *Calypso*'s officers and ship's company, in some sort of disguise. Coming back (assuming parole had caused no problems) the Calypsos would be escorting freed hostages of unknown rank, age and physical condition. How could *they* be disguised? A crowd of widows going to early mass, rigged out in black?

The captain of the *Calypso* frigate might grumble that the Admiralty was picking on him, but in fairness to Their Lordships (how one hated being fair to the Board) he was an obvious choice. He spoke fluent Italian, thanks to a childhood spent in Italy. And he knew much of Tuscany quite well – not that Their Lordships would consider that: as far as they were concerned

Pitigliano could be anywhere between Genoa and Venice, Milan and Naples or Bergamo and Bari. Ramage spoke Italian and knew the coast: that was all that mattered. Oh yes, and he had on board as a midshipman the nephew of that Marchesa who was the ruler of Volterra – the one who is missing . . . Ramage could picture the conversation round the long table in the boardroom: St Vincent nodding to save words, Captain Markham (who had intervened on the Board's behalf at that travesty of a court-martial), another one or two members of the Board to make up a quorum, and Evan Nepean, the Board secretary, busy taking the minutes.

Two Italian speakers: that would settle it. But, Ramage realized, he was in a better position than the Board knew because, thanks to them helping to get the *Murex* out of Brest, he had on board four French seamen: four royalists who, until a few months ago, had lived in France and knew a good deal about the way the new regime conducted its affairs. And of course there was Rossi, the Genovese seaman. Rossi's life as a youngster in Genoa had taught him the same skill with a dagger that the Cockney Stafford had learned with a set of pick-locks.

And there was Hill. A couple of days ago the new lieutenant had made a pun in French to Orsini. Ramage, happening to overhear it, discovered that Hill's mother was French, a royalist who had married a London banker many years ago but who had absolutely no ability to learn English. This resulted in the house being staffed with French servants (refugees once the war had started) and Hill being bilingual from the time he started to talk.

What a happy little party they would make, Ramage thought sourly: Gilbert and his Frenchmen led by Hill and singing *Ça Ira*; Paolo (who in fact was developing a healthy baritone) and Rossi singing a rousing duet from an Italian opera; and he and Jackson humming some old English sea chanty, and all of them coughing from the white dust covering the flat rock forming the roads, slapping mosquitoes and cursing their sore and swollen feet.

Life on board one of the King's ships was no training for marching over rough tracks – or, come to that, well-made roads. Running barefoot on wooden decks was one thing; marching to

Pitigliano was another, especially since most of the men owned only light shoes. The Marines had boots, but they spoke neither French nor Spanish. Some of them had such local accents, Ramage remembered, that only their proud parents would claim they spoke English . . .

Tongues and feet: they were the first considerations. Who could speak what language, and who could be fitted with boots from the purser's store on board, even if it eventually meant borrowing from the Marines. Borrowing from the Marines would, of course, mean that the Marine lieutenant, Rennick, would want to join in. He was a brave and competent officer, but his life had necessarily been governed by the drill book, so that now he lacked the flexibility of the sea officers who had to handle the ship amid sudden squalls, sails blowing out, or the thousand and one emergencies which gave no warning, no time to look up any answers in a notebook.

None of which answered the question of how to get to Pitigliano – and how, once there, to get in touch with the British hostages. Nor how (if they had not given their parole) to rescue the hostages and get them on board the *Calypso*. That, my friend, is why orders can be written in a paragraph, but the subsequent report of proceedings, describing how the orders were carried out, usually takes several pages.

Pitigliano . . . Manciano . . . Saturnia . . . All small but interesting places he had once dreamed of visiting again with Sarah when Bonaparte had been defeated and a lasting peace signed. And, assuming that Gianna had survived, they would visit her in Volterra, the old city with its scores of towers lying just to the north.

Yes, in his daydreaming (while they were still honeymooning in France, before the war started again) he had taken Sarah on his own Grand Tour of Italy. Not the usual one, when most of the time was spent looking at painting and sculpture in Milan, Florence, Siena and Venice, and in Rome visiting all the Romans one could not avoid but whose conversation would be limited to social gossip and the same vapid comments that Romans had been making for centuries about paintings, and the activities of cicisbeos.

No, he wanted (*had* wanted, he corrected himself) to show

34

Sarah the Italy that ranged from the glorious palace at Caserta (splendid to look at from the outside but bare and cavernous inside) to the so-called beehive houses of Friuli. To so many English people Italy, after the Grand Tour, was simply the jumbled memories of social visits and picture frames.

He unrolled a map of southern Tuscany. It covered from Cecina on the coast, eastwards across to Siena and ended with Arezzo forming the top right-hand corner. Then it ran south to include Perugia, passing just east of Orvieto and then down to the border with Lazio. It followed the border westward, skirting Lake Bolsena, arriving back at the coast between Montalto di Castro and Capalbio. There was a lookout tower at Montalto and, he remembered vividly, the next one north: the Torre di Buranaccio. Several lifetimes ago (or so it seemed) he had landed there with Jackson to rescue a group of Italian aristocrats escaping just ahead of Bonaparte's advancing troops. One of them was supposed to be the aged Marchesa di Volterra, by chance an old friend of his parents. Damnation, what mis-understandings had arisen when it transpired that the Marchesa was in fact young and beautiful (and wilful, too!), the daughter of the one they had expected.

Somehow the Torre di Buranaccio (where at one point in the misunderstanding she had presented a pistol at him and was quite prepared to fire it) was a beginning. It had brought him to the notice of Nelson, then of course only a commodore, and Lord St Vincent (then only Sir John Jervis, since the battle for which he received his earldom and title – and in which Com-modore Nelson and Lieutenant Ramage had played an exciting part – had not yet taken place).

Maps, he reminded himself firmly and stared down at the one spread on the desk, weighted down to stop it rolling up again. So there it was, a slightly skewed square of land with the small lump of Argentario hanging off the left-hand corner. Argentario was a diamond-shaped, mountainous island joined to the mainland by two causeways. Between them on the main-land was the small fortified town of Orbetello but, more im-portant, the northern causeway joined the mainland just oppo-site where the track to Pitigliano turned inland from the Via Aurelia, which ran along the coast only a few yards inland and along which so many Roman armies had marched to and from Rome.

So follow that track from the Via Aurelia. After a couple of miles it went through the first village, which was not as big as its name, la Barca del Grazi, and whose sole importance seemed to be that it was a fork where another track branched left to many more hill towns forming a chain round the foot of Monte Amiata.

Damnation, it was hard to follow the track without traipsing off along the side roads of boyhood memories, when he and his mother and a couple of coachmen (there were plenty of bandits across the Maremma, and highwaymen lurked near inns favoured by wealthy travellers) explored Tuscany. They had stayed at most of the hill towns where the inns were so small that often mother and son occupied the only available rooms and the two coachmen had to lodge with friends of the inn-keeper. And a church built after 1300 was regarded as recent.

So on the road to Pitigliano . . . That was the shortest and easiest approach by road and without going down to Montalto di Castro and taking the road – little more than a track – that ran along the edge of Lake Bolsena, twisting to come into Pitigliano from the east, the opposite direction, it was the only way. One could start off from Montalto di Castro and scramble across country through the corner of Lazio, but that meant risking running into marshes at the northern end of the Maremma. More important, apart from the swampiness of the marshes forming the Maremma (which extended all the way down to Rome) they were notorious for malaria: there was something in the damp air which meant that people living in the hamlets on the road to Tarquinia and then on to Rome were plagued with ague. He did not want to risk any of his men falling victims – not after years in the Tropics when he and the surgeon, Bowen, kept the *Calypso* free of all the diseases which so far had killed thousands more men out there than fighting the French.

Very well, he told himself, you have refreshed your memory about the track to Pitigliano; now decide how you get to the track to start off and how you then *proceed* along it. How the Admiralty people loved that word "proceed": along with "whereas" it must be their favourite. No captain was ever ordered to "go", and no captain in his report ever "went":

36

always "proceed" or "proceeded". Along with "prior" and a few other words which fools and lawyers used like pointing fingers because they were almost illiterate or too lazy to think, "proceeded" had a high place on the list of words Ramage would like to remove from the language.

So, picking up where you interrupted yourself at the thought of "proceeding", consider first just how you will "proceed" along the dusty track to Pitigliano with your merry men. And, of course, when you get there, what you do about finding and rescuing the British hostages. Let us (for the moment) not bother with getting back to the coast with them: there will be time enough to consider that when you find (to your astonishment) that the plan so far has worked. Ah, yes, he thought, I must remember to start that section of my report to the Admiralty with the Board's favourite word, "whereas". Indeed, after the traditional "I have the honour to report", he would slip in a "whereas" to introduce his reference to the orders he had received.

Ahem. He coughed in a little mime for his own benefit. We are getting ahead of ourselves; at the moment the Italian mainland is a good hundred miles away from the *Calypso*, and Pitigliano is another thirty miles inland . . .

Did the French carry the important prisoners in carts or coaches, or did they have to march? And if march (which was most likely), was it all the way from France? Or were these the Britons caught when the war began again while visiting southern France, and the Grand Tour cities of Italy? That was more probable. Marching along those dusty roads . . . still, it might have been winter, when they would be ankle-deep in mud. They probably spent the night in barns, sleeping on straw. Just as unpleasant for the French guards, of course, if that was any comfort. He pictured a column of men, possibly in chains, trudging along a muddy road, with French guards, unshaven and just as muddy, trying to count them from time to time, and cursing them and telling them to hurry . . . And he also pictured men like Stafford and Southwick and Hill and Kenton and Martin, up to all sorts of tricks to make the life of the guards more miserable. With that picture in his mind he bent over the map once again. It was now obvious how to do it – wasn't it?

Chapter
Five

For once Ramage was thankful that his clerk was an unimaginative man: when Ramage hastily transferred from the *Murex* to the *Calypso* after the escape from Brest, he had stuffed all his documents into a canvas bag and forgotten them.

Now, when he wanted to examine some of those documents again (they included excellent original French passes with only the names faked), he assumed they had been thrown away – until he casually mentioned them to the clerk, who disappeared without comment to return a few minutes later from his tiny cabin–cum–office with the greyish-blue sheets, several of them headed by the French National government seal. Six sets of documents, used for the escape of the four Frenchmen (who were now members of the *Calypso*'s crew), for himself, and for Sarah . . .

Like rescuing Gianna, that wild rush in Brest seemed a lifetime ago; the only proof that it had ever happened was the sight of the four Frenchmen carrying out their duties on board the *Calypso* – and yes, these documents he now held in his hand. No Sarah, no *Murex*. But do not start thinking about all that now, he warned himself. Examine the documents and think how you can get hold of some more sheets of this crudely made paper so favoured by French authority.

There were three types of documents. He was not so interested in the wording as in the seals of the various ministries at the top of each page. The first paper was a *passeport*, issued by the local Committee of Public Safety. He remembered Gilbert (who had obtained them so that they could go into Brest from the Count of Rennes' château, where they were trapped) explaining that there were in fact two kinds of *passeport* – one for foreigners, and another for French citizens visiting another town. A *passeport* for a Frenchman allowed the holder to travel back and forth from his own town or village to a named town: visiting a third town required yet another *passeport*. Anyway, at the top of the first page were the arms of the French Republic and underneath was a printed form, the various blank spaces filled in with a pen.

The next document (intended for Sarah) bore the coat of arms of the province of Brittany and certified that she had been born in Falaise, in Normandy, but on marriage had removed to Brittany. More important, it was signed by the *préfet* of Brittany.

The third document was headed with the printed words *"Liberté Egalité"*, and centred between the two words was an oval with an anchor symbol in the centre and "Rep.Fran.Marin" round the inside. Yes, he had remembered correctly the stationery of the Ministry of Marine and Colonies. Although the document itself and the signatures were genuine, the rest of the details were false – it was a discharge from the Navy of France.

Unfortunately, he had no document issued by the French War Ministry; but he decided that of the Ministry of Marine (with a sufficiently bullying manner when presenting it) would be enough.

He held up a page to the light. Very poor-quality paper: it had a sad greyness that with a black border would serve for sending a letter of condolence to a defrocked cleric. Yet would a guard or the commandant of a prison expect documents always to be written or printed on the same quality paper? Surely a few ministries must have decent notepaper. This stuff was the best that the papermakers could produce (or all that the Republic would pay for) after years of blockade by the Royal Navy. Now, during that eighteen months of peace, surely some ministries had managed to get better paper. Anyway, that would be a good enough explanation, particularly if given in the sort of hectoring voice which implied that anyone doubting it was not *au courant* with the present situation in Paris.

Now he must talk to Gilbert, who had obtained these documents in France. Presumably the French system, with *barrières* every few miles along most roads and at the approaches to all towns, would not be used in Italy, if only because it would need thousands of men. Nevertheless the French Army of Italy was one of occupation . . . sentries, paid spies, cavalry patrols, all would be needed.

Ramage called the Marine sentry to pass the word for Gilbert. A couple of minutes later he told the Marine to send for Midshipman Orsini as well: it was now two or three years since Paolo had escaped from Volterra and made his way to England by way of Naples, but he might remember some French regulations which could help prevent mistakes.

How much to tell them? It would be asking a lot of Gilbert not to relate to the rest of his mess (Jackson, Stafford, Rossi and the other three Frenchmen) why the captain had sent for him. Orsini would keep his mouth shut because, apart from anything else, it concerned his own country, and he would not want to risk any slips. Which led to the decision whether or not to take him.

Paolo might by now be the new ruler of Volterra: that was the first consideration. If Gianna was dead, he would certainly be by right of succession, even though Volterra was at the moment occupied by the Army of France.

If Paolo was captured and identified by the French, his throat would be cut – having murdered Gianna, the French would be delighted to dispose of the Marchesa's nephew and successor. Yet one must consider that Paolo knew all this countryside like the back of his hand. Italian was, of course, his native tongue but, being an educated young man, his French was fluent and his English marred by only a very slight accent.

So, Ramage thought, by not taking him I lose a guide, a young man speaking French and Italian, and perhaps more important, one who *looks* French or Italian: a sallow skin, jet-black hair, a narrow face which anyone who had travelled would at once identify as Italian or Spanish. A *Mediterranean* face, in fact.

What would Gianna have expected? Suddenly he could see her face and hear her voice: for a moment she seemed to be in the cabin with him: a memory, or a ghost, but most certainly Gianna, and at her most decisive. "Paolo has been in action with you a dozen times. More, in fact. A French roundshot could have knocked his head off at any time. One is, my dear Nicholas, just as dead from a roundshot as a dagger thrust – or the musket balls of a French firing squad. And, dear Nicholas, can you bear the reproachful look in the boy's eyes when you tell him you are not taking him?"

Gianna's voice was so firm, so determined, so *real* in his imagination that the sentry's knock bringing him back to reality made him blink, still expecting her to be there.

"Send them in!" he called, and waved Paolo and Gilbert to sit down. Paolo sat in what had become known as "Southwick's chair" and Gilbert perched on the edge of the settee, combining the discomfort of a servant sitting in his master's presence (a hangover from the château) with the nervousness of a seaman unexpectedly summoned to the captain's presence.

Ramage then realized that with the *Calypso* just off the Italian coast, even if both Paolo and Gilbert bellowed the Admiralty's secret orders through speaking trumpets, there was no enemy close enough to hear them.

He spoke first to Paolo. "You remember Pitigliano?"

Paolo looked startled, and then said: "Near Orvieto – a hill town?"

Ramage nodded and turned to Gilbert. "The road running along the coast here and down to Rome is the Via Aurelia – you've heard of it?"

"Only because it's one of the great roads down which Julius Caesar marched. One of them crosses the Rubicon, doesn't it, sir?"

"That's it – I hardly expected you to know about the Rubicon, though."

"I don't, sir," Gilbert admitted. "Just the phrase."

Ramage glanced at Paolo. "Go on, you explain it!"

Paolo grinned broadly because, second only to the sea and naval tactics, his interest was (as Ramage knew) the complex history of the Roman Empire. "Crossing the Rubicon – well, in English it means reaching a line where you have to make an important decision one way or the other. If you stay your side,

41

you're safe: if you cross, you're committing yourself to something drastic."

"Go on," Ramage urged, "let's have the details. Why is it
called the Rubicon, this line of yours?"

"It's a small river running into the Adriatic between Ravenna
and Rimini, where the Via Emilia and Via Flaminia meet. Not
deep or fast. But we have to go back to 59 BC, when Julius
Caesar was neither famous nor feared: he was simply a famous
man's nephew with little experience as a soldier. He was governor of an area of what is now northern Italy and southern
France. The Helvetii, in what is now Switzerland, were causing
trouble so he went up to Geneva to deal with them.

"But he knew fame and fortune in the Roman Empire came
only to victorious generals, so Caesar carried on north to
defeat the Gauls (the French of today), the Germans and the
Belgae – three hundred thousand barbarians living in northern
Gaul (the Netherlands of today). He beat them and went on to
cross the Channel and conquer Britain.

"By the time he was ready to return to Italy – after fighting
many more battles – he was famous and his nine legions were
devoted to him. (They were not paid by the government: their
leader, in this case Caesar, let them plunder, so a successful
general always had loyal troops!)

"Left in Rome all this time," Paolo continued – and Ramage
saw that the youth had slipped back more than eighteen
centuries, so that he was a centurion marching at the head of
his hundred men, part of the six hundred who made up a
cohort, ten of which, six thousand men, made up a legion –
"was Pompey, a great general who had conquered Spain but
had done no fighting for a dozen years.

"Obviously the two of them had to be rivals: rivals in a
competition with the Roman Empire the prize. Well, Caesar
was coming back from Gaul with nine legions of men who had
been victorious everywhere. Pompey had ten legions – but unfortunately for him, seven were away in Spain.

"By January 49 BC, Caesar and his legions had reached the
northern bank of the Rubicon in the march back to Italy. The
southern side of the river was Pompey's territory. The question
facing Caesar was, should he cross the Rubicon and attack, or

should he stay where he was. Obviously the stakes were enormous. Well, he did cross – and Pompey retreated right down the coast to Brindisium – Brindisi – and fled across the Adriatic. Within ten weeks of crossing the Rubicon, Caesar ruled the Roman Empire. So, *mon cher* Gilbert, when you have to make a great decision you've reached the banks of the Rubicon: when you make it and carry it out, you've crossed . . . such a muddy river it is, too."

Gilbert nodded and, turning to Ramage, asked quietly: "Have we reached a Rubicon, sir?"

"We're approaching it," Ramage said, "but for the moment we're concerned with the Via Aurelia, and in particular a small stretch where it passes Monte Argentario, which looks from the sea like a small and mountainous island but which is linked to the mainland by a couple of causeways."

Paolo had looked up sharply. "Monte Argentario, sir?"

"You remember it, then, even though it's not now part of the Roman Empire! Yes, Port' Ercole at the southern end is where we had our little affair with the bomb ketches, but now we use Argentario only as a landmark – the northern end, this time. More precisely, where that northern causeway meets the Via Aurelia."

"Surely that's where the road to Pitigliano branches off, sir?"

"Exactly. And about thirty miles along that road is Pitigliano."

"It's a rotten road, from memory. Not much more than a track, sir. Marsiliana is about a third of the way, Manciano about two thirds and then you reach Pitigliano, with Monte Labbro and Monte Amiata over on your left. Why – may I ask why – are we interested in Pitigliano, sir? It's so far inland – for a cutting out expedition, anyway!"

"Their Lordships don't think so," Ramage said drily. "I have their orders here." He tapped a drawer. "We march, not row," he said grimly. "Thirty miles there and thirty miles back, only we'll have company when we return."

"French prisoners, sir?" Paolo asked.

"No, they'll all be British."

*

43

At dawn, Argentario was lying fine on the starboard bow, standing four-square like a rocky island close to the shore, the causeways hidden by its bulk. Ramage held the telescope steady and examined it, finding that almost every headland and mountain nudged a memory. There was Monte Argentario itself, towering over the rest of the island and, for the moment, Punta Avoltore at the southern tip was in line with it. Just round to the east there was Port' Ercole, which he had attacked with the bomb ketches not so long ago, and for the moment Orbetello was out of sight, hidden like the causeways by Argentario itself. On the mainland to the south was Torre Montalto, the next one down the coast from the Torre di Buranaccio. In a moment he had a picture of Gianna, hidden in the shadow of the doorway inside the candlelit tower, heavily cloaked and suddenly aiming a pistol at him until she was satisfied he was not an enemy, not one of Bonaparte's officers.

Argentario . . . yes, that almost-an-island, with Port' Ercole at one end and Santo Stefano at the other, always seemed more of a home to him than St Kew. Would his father ever understand that a small piece of Tuscany could in many ways mean more to him than the estate in Cornwall that the family had owned for generations?

It was not because here he had fallen in love with Gianna: that was all over long ago, and he was married to Sarah, if she was alive. If Gianna was alive, if Sarah was alive . . . So many question marks, all of which finally asked: were the women he loved and had loved now dead?

The early light now showed up the whole of the mainland, from the mountains inland from Argentario, with Monte Amiata the distant queen and not yet crowned with snow, to where it dropped away as the land trended south to the tedious flats of the Maremma marshes where a paddled duck punt or, on the occasional track, a galloping horse stirred up clouds of mosquitoes that would linger like smoke and sting like demons.

But on the Tuscan edge of the marsh there were always bluish-white plumes of smoke, or, if it was windy, the faint hint of it. The busiest man in Tuscany was always the *carbonaio*, the charcoal burner. Anything wood was a living for the *carbonaio*.

Trees, bushes, twigs – put into his ovens made of turf, which sat on the ground like gigantic anthills with twists of smoke escaping here and there, and turned the wood into the charcoal that everyone used for cooking. The *carbonaio* stripped the *macchia* more effectively than the goats which, wrenching up roots instead of grazing, destroyed the shrubs and bushes completely. At least the *carbonaio* only lopped off the growth.

Here he was standing at the quarterdeck rail of the *Calypso* with dawn now broken over the Italian mainland, the tiny whitehorses tinged red, and the few streaks of cloud a light pink, a maiden's blush if ever he had seen one, and he was thinking of charcoal burners (who usually looked like rural chimney sweeps) and of blushing maidens. In the meantime the *Calypso*'s ship's company was still at general quarters, standing by the guns, even though the lookouts had already given the familiar hail, "See a grey goose at a mile", and the men sent to the mastheads had reported no ships or vessels in sight. Not even, Ramage noted, fishing boats from Port' Ercole or Santo Stefano returning with their catches after a night out. Or did Bonaparte forbid that now?

All the watch towers scattered round Argentario, perched on top of cliffs and headlands, had been built by the Aragonese or later by Philip II when he ruled this part of Italy and was planning to send the great Armada against England. The position of the towers, each in sight of the next on either side or in view of a central tower, meant that signals, presumably warning fires, could be passed either round the coast, as though round the rim of a wheel, or directly like one of its spokes when a valley gave a sight of a central tower. Did Bonaparte now use some of the towers to give his troops warning of enemy ships approaching? Most probably not, because the Royal Navy was so stretched that there were very few British warships in the Mediterranean today: in fact, the Barbary pirates, forever lurking in their fast galleys, and rowed by Christian slaves, must be more of a threat to the local people.

However, if anyone of consequence did see the frigate passing northwards under easy sail he would almost certainly report her as French, and no one could blame him, although anyone with an eye for a ship would be puzzled by the cut of

45

her sails. An experienced sailor would wonder, because they were British cut. But the wind was so light that now they flapped and thumped and jerked the yards, occasionally hanging like heavy curtains until a random gust bellied them.

Ramage called to Aitken: the ship's company could stand down now. Once the guns were run in, cutlasses, pikes and tomahawks replaced in their racks, cartridges returned to the magazine and decks swabbed, then they would all go to breakfast.

Then, Ramage decided, His Majesty's frigate *Calypso* will become a vast tailor's shop. Instead of the rumble of the trucks of the guns being run out for exercise and the thump of round-shot being rammed home, there will be the snick of scissors and a silence punctuated by curses as needles slip and prick fingers. Men will be cutting, stitching and fitting: hands more accustomed to thrusting thick sail needles through stiff canvas, using a rawhide palm for leverage, will be sewing with the comparatively dainty needles, making clothes.

They would be stitching five French uniforms (for an officer and four men), plus those for an officer and two men from the Grand Duke of Tuscany's forces. The rest of the men would not need any special clothing. It was fortunate that it was summer; even more fortunate that the purser had a few rolls of cloth very similar to the colour favoured by the French Army – when its soldiers were not still dressed in the old clothes they were wearing when they were swept into the Republic's armies.

As soon as the men finished their breakfast, Ramage told Aitken to furl the courses and topgallants: the *Calypso* would make her way along the coast under topsails alone, cutting her speed to a couple of knots if the present wind held, and this would not put them too far north of Argentario by nightfall. As Aitken picked up the speaking trumpet, Ramage gave him a list on which were written several names. "I want these men sent aft in an hour's time."

He had finally included Rennick. It was simply cowardice, in a way, but it would be unfair to leave the Marine officer behind. There was not much that Rennick could do, but on the other hand it could easily be misinterpreted in a despatch to the Admiralty if anyone wondered why the Marine officer was left behind. And Rennick, with his red face and jovial manner, was one of the bravest men in the ship. The Marines remaining would be under the command of Sergeant Ferris – who would also be indignant at being left behind, but the safety of the ship was the prime consideration, whatever the Admiralty's orders about hostages.

Southwick was already grumbling, refusing to admit that a sixty-mile march would be too much for him – and Ramage could guess the reason: the old master was hoping there would be a good fight somewhere along the way, not realizing that the moment a shot was fired or a sword drawn in anger the whole expedition would be doomed.

He went down to his cabin, sat at his desk, and pulled out of the overhead rack the chart which Southwick had made some years ago of the coast between the little fishing village of Talamone and the deep bay sweeping south round to the causeway which curved in a half moon out to Santa Liberata, on Argentario itself.

The Via Aurelia passed two or three miles inland of Talamone itself but because of the sudden curve of the land it soon met the sea at the hamlet of Fonteblanda. The road then hugged the coast just behind the sandy beach although the sea was often obscured by small woods of pines. Near the northernmost causeway the Fiume Albinia ran into the sea close by a big square tower, Torre Saline. Just a wide-mouthed stream, in fact, which spent the summer dried up and in the winter prevented nearby fields flooding. More important now, however, was the fact that it met the coast (and, with Torre Saline, would be as good as a signpost in the dark) only a hundred yards or so from the turning on the Via Aurelia for Marsiliana and Pitigliano.

Ah, the nostalgia that a map created. Up to the north was Punta Ala; then Scarlino, Massa Marittima, Castelnuovo – all places on the road to Volterra. That was the wonderful thing about Italy – many of the place names sounded like musical notes. And many of the derivations of the names were now hidden in the shadows cast by time. Did the silver in the name "Argentario" come from a Roman banker who once owned a villa there (*argentum* being Latin for silver) or from the thousands of olive trees growing on its slopes? The underside of an olive leaf was silvery; a breeze sweeping the olive groves turned the leaves so that from a distance all the grove – indeed the whole island – seemed coated in silver.

Talamone, too, was an odd name unless you knew it was named after Telamon, the King of Salamis who landed there after returning from the Argonaut expedition. The Calypsos, some of them anyway, would be landing tonight very close to where Telamon went on shore . . . Now Telamon's monument here was a small walled fishing port with a square tower rising up from the middle of it. And Santo Stefano had been a small but powerful place in medieval days: important enough for Philip II to build the Fortezza which was named after him, and had not the Santo Stefanesi sent a dozen ships to fight the Saracens in the Battle of Lepanto?

Port' Ercole, at the other end of Argentario, was the Port of Hercules of Roman times, and important enough for the Spaniards to build Forte della Stella (star-shaped and strongly built) and the Forte di Monte Filippo . . . both reminded him once again of sailing into Port' Ercole with the bomb ketches . . .

Tuscany, what an area! One's own memories (yesterday's history) spilled over into ancient history: here Philip II had built forts even before sailing the Armada against England, and Captain Ramage had attacked some of the forts two and a half centuries later. Tonight he would be landing where Telamon landed (in legend, anyway) after sailing with Jason and the other heroes to fetch the Golden Fleece, and once you went back to the Argonauts, Spain's activities only two and a half centuries ago became stale news.

Two and a half centuries hence (around 2050) would some young Royal Navy officer land there in the darkness? What would the map of the world (Europe, anyway) look like then?

At this moment, Ramage mused, with Bonaparte holding everything from the Baltic to the Levant, it is hard to think of the Mediterranean as anything *but* a French lake – until you remember that it has at various times been a Phoenician, Greek, Roman, Carthaginian and Saracen lake, not to mention the periods much later when the Spaniards and Austrians claimed it.

For the moment, though, he reminded himself, it was enough to know that the turning to the left along the Via Aurelia which went to Pitigliano was just past the mouth of the Fiume Albinia. Within a few hundred yards was the massive square tower, Torre Saline. And a mile further along the coast was Orbetello, whose history started *before* the Etruscans . . . So the Calypsos needed to find the Torre Saline.

The sentry's knock warned of Aitken coming down to report that the men on the list were waiting at the after end of the quarterdeck. "So you are taking Rennick, sir?"

"Yes, it'd look bad in the despatch if I left him behind."

"But you're not taking me, sir." The first lieutenant's voice was neutral: a comment rather than a protest.

"No I'm not!" Ramage exclaimed crossly. "I'm leaving you in sole command of His Majesty's frigate *Calypso*. If I don't come back you'll have the responsibility of sailing her back to England."

Aitken decided to brave the asperity in Ramage's voice. "Kenton and Southwick could sail her back, sir."

"Damnation, Aitken! You don't speak Italian, your French is rudimentary – what good will you be on the road to Pitigliano, compared to being on board, able to deal with any emergency that arises?"

"You need prisoners, sir. Only the guards have to speak French."

"You don't possess –" Ramage was going to say "an admiral's uniform" but realized in time that no admiral or general would be wearing uniform while on a peacetime visit to France or Italy. "Look Aitken, I seem to be commanding a ship full of fighting cocks. I want just a handful of men who can march, and a few that can speak French."

"Aye, sir, I know that; but Hill will be with your disguised Frenchmen, you'll be with the Italians, so who'll be in charge o' the prisoners?"

"You will," growled an exasperated Ramage taking the easiest way. "If anyone asks you, you're the Earl of Dunkeld and when the Treaty of Amiens was signed you came to Italy hoping to shoot boar in the Abruzzi. Or bores in Florence."

"The *third* earl, I'm thinking, sir," Aitken said grinning.

49

"You make just one mistake on this jaunt and you'll be the last and the title becomes extinct . . . Mine, too."

"I'll mind m' step, sir," Aitken said, picturing the expression on Southwick's face. So command of the *Calypso* would be left in the hands of young Kenton, the second lieutenant. Quite a responsibility, and for a few moments Aitken had misgivings about his request. Then he remembered what Mr Ramage had done before he was anywhere near as old as Kenton. Responsibility matures and advances the competent and ages and breaks fools. That was one of his father's favourite pronouncements and in Aitken's experience it was true.

Ramage followed Aitken up the steps of the companionway. Muffled oars, he told himself; I must remember to have Jackson supervise the work. The landing had to be silent – the barking of a *carbonaio*'s dog could raise the alarm before they had even started.

On the quarterdeck he looked at the group of men in front of him. "I have a job for volunteers," he said. "You won't be risking broadsides, musket balls, boarding pikes or tomahawks. No, if things go wrong you'll end up with your back to a wall and facing a French firing squad aiming muskets at your gizzards. I've picked your names more or less at random –" (would that I had, he told himself) "– so any man who reckons serving in the Navy should not make him risk being shot as a spy is free to go about his duties on board and no one will think any the worse of him."

Not a man moved, and Ramage heard Jackson mutter: "You're stuck with us, sir." Agreement came in a variety of English regional accents and Ramage also heard Rossi's Italian and Gilbert's French.

Ramage looked round at the men. "Thank you. Belay that last pipe about me choosing your names at random, and now I'm going to tell you what we have to do.

"Then Jackson will tell you how he and I and some other men once landed at night on the coast just south of here. This is Tuscany, not England or France. Different bird calls, different smells, different dam' nearly everything. The point is I don't want you firing at friendly owls or thinking that a charcoal's burner's banked fire is a volcano about to erupt.

50

"Then you'll go down to the waist of the ship where your shipmates will be waiting with cloth and thread to fit your new clothes. I want you to think of yourselves as a strolling band of actors, because if you don't put on a good performance the audience won't jeer at you, they'll shoot."

Chapter
Six

It was still too damned light: although the new moon had already set the clouds were small and slow-moving, obscuring only a few stars, and pushed along the coast by a light north wind which might at any moment turn west into a land breeze.

Argentario was a bulky dark mass on the starboard beam; ahead was the northern causeway, a long thin crescent like the new moon, narrow and little more than a sandy beach backed by a scattering of pine trees and with the lake formed by the two causeways a silver sheet of water beyond. Over on the larboard bow was Capo d'Uomo (with a tower on top), then Monte dell' Uccellina (little bird: a splendid name!) which sloped down gradually to the sea at Talamone and formed the corner of the cliffs on which Talamone was built. Yes, with the nightglass, even allowing for the irritation that it showed everything upside-down, Ramage could see the walled village with the square tower in the middle. At that moment a break in the clouds let the starlight display the tower clearly with its battlements – at a guess four guns a side. He turned to Southwick. "We're about right?"

The master waved his quadrant: he had been using it to measure the horizontal angles made by the peak of Monte Argentario to starboard, Torre Saline and the tower at Talamone to larboard, so that he could work out the *Calypso*'s exact position inside the great bay.

"Time for me to go to the fo'c'sle, sir," he said. "As soon as we get nine fathoms on the lead, we can anchor."

The *Calypso* was gliding: the sea was smooth and the north

wind meant that the land beyond Talamone gave the bay a lee.

He listened to the singsong reports of the leadsman and pictured the man standing in the chains, the thick board jutting out from the ship's side and down to which the shrouds were led. The man would be wearing a thick leather apron to keep off the streaming water as he hauled in and coiled the leadline after each cast, feeling with his fingers for the twists of leather and cloth which let him distinguish the depth of water in which they were sailing.

Ten fathoms. He swung the nightglass forward so that he could search along the coast midway between Talamone and where the causeway met the mainland. Starting from the tower at Talamone, he looked to the right. A few houses – that will be the hamlet of Bengodi and those dark objects like spearheads planted point upwards in the ground are a cluster of cypress, probably planted a century ago as a windbreak. Then the occasional sparkle when the starlight catches a wavelet as it breaks on the beach. Pine trees behind but between them and the sand a low grey line of what must be flat clumps of *fico dei Ottentotti*, growing long fingers across and under the sand above sea level and always ready to trip the unwary. Then a few more small houses – and a faint red glow, a *carbonaio*'s banked fire. More cypress – they sound better in Italian, *cipressi*. The beach, a few more pines – ah, there is the Torre Saline, squat, the largest tower for miles and its square shape throwing shadows round it like a cloak. And there the Fiume Albinia and – yes, he could just distinguish the bridge for the Via Aurelia, so the turning to Pitigliano would be easy to find.

There was the leadsman again. Ten fathoms. Bottom soft mud. "Arming the lead" – that was a curious use of the word "arming". A landman would think it warlike, even though it must be the most peaceful activity in the ship. It meant putting a handful of tallow in the cavity at the bottom of the lead (itself looking like a weight from a grandfather clock) so that when the lead hit the sea bed a sample of whatever composed it – sand, mud, coral, fine shell, and so on – stuck to the tallow. A good chart gave not only the depths of water but the nature of the bottom, and often experienced fishermen navigated without charts merely by knowing the pattern of the sea bed. Many claimed they knew where they were by the smell of the mud . . .

Once again he looked round. The *Calypso* was making under a knot now: the headland at Talamone and the mountains behind were stealing the wind, but there was no hurry. The frigate's cutter and gig had long since been hoisted out and were towing astern; the Pitigliano party of men waited in the waist of the ship with Aitken and Hill; now Southwick stood on the fo'c'sle and Kenton was at the quarterdeck rail.

Ramage handed Kenton the nightglass, noting that the clouds were becoming more scattered. "That's Talamone – you can see the tower. Start there and work your way south, telling me what you see, and I'll identify it for you."

Carefully Kenton described what he saw, and finally reached the Torre Saline. "Carry on to the south. You see where this causeway from Argentario joins the mainland? Now follow the causeway round – it's called Giannella – and you'll see where it joins Argentario itself."

At that moment the leadsman reported nine fathoms. "Carry on," Ramage told Kenton, "you're officer of the deck – and you'll be in command of the ship very soon."

Kenton told the quartermaster to bring the ship head to wind while ordering the topmen aloft to furl sails. Only the foretopsail would be left drawing, so that as the *Calypso* turned north the wind would press against the forward side of the sail and, like a hand pushing against a man's chest, bring the ship first to a stop and then slowly move her astern, giving her sternway which would help dig the anchor in once it had been let go.

Kenton went to the ship's side to watch the water. He reported as soon as the ship stopped, and then as she gathered sternway Ramage picked up the speaking trumpet and gave the order "Let go!" to Southwick, heard the answering hail, and a moment later the heavy splash of the anchor hitting the water, followed by the rumble of the thick cable running through the hawse.

With the foretopsail aback and the anchor dug home, Southwick came up to the quarterdeck to report how much cable had been let out and that the anchor was holding well. Then he corrected himself by saying to Kenton: "I should be reporting to you."

"Thank you, Mr Southwick," the youth said gravely, and

gave the order to furl the foretopsail. Then, turning to Ramage, he said: "I'd be glad if you'd repeat my instructions in front of Mr Southwick, sir, because if I have to carry them out I know they might not sit well with him."

Southwick gave one of his sniffs, one which Ramage interpreted to mean: the orders of my superiors always sit well with me. However, Ramage could well see why Kenton was taking the precaution.

"As the senior lieutenant left on board you will of course have command of the ship," Ramage said. "You know we have sailed in here without any show of secrecy, so that French lookouts will assume we're a French national ship just anchoring in a quiet bay for a couple of days."

"But if a French boat comes off and questions us sir?" Kenton prompted.

"I can't spare you a Frenchman to answer any hails, so do your best to fool them, but if it seems the boat will raise an alarm, sink it, sail with the *Calypso*, wait out of sight and then return here in four days, anchoring in the same position. At the same time you'll send three boats to pick us up at the mouth of the river Albinia.

"If we're not there, you'll return two nights later, same time, and send boats to the same place. If we're still not there you'll go to Gibraltar, report to the port admiral, and give him my secret orders. You'll also report that I and my men have probably been captured."

"That gives you only six days to get to Pitigliano and back, sir," Southwick protested. "Supposing some of the hostages are crippled, or so ill they have to be carried on litters? Let's come back a third time. That'd give you eight days."

"No," Ramage said patiently. "If there's any delay I'll send someone – it'll probably be Midshipman Orsini – to bring you fresh instructions. So, after six days no Orsini means no anyone else."

"Very well, sir," said Kenton. "But –"

"But they're not the sort of orders you like getting," Ramage said sympathetically. "Well, young man, they're not the orders I like giving, because if you have to carry them out it probably means I've gone over the standing part of the foresheet, and

55

taken all my party – and probably the hostages – with me. But that's what promotion and responsibility entail."

"We'll see you on the fourth night, sir," Southwick said, "and, if you've room in your knapsack, a bottle of that Orvieto wouldn't come amiss."

Ramage chuckled. "Marching thirty miles carrying a bottle of Chianti just to satisfy a whim of a mutinous master . . ."

"I wouldn't mutiny if you brought the wine," Southwick said. The two men shook hands and, after he had shaken hands with Kenton and was walking down the quarterdeck ladder to join the men waiting in the waist, Ramage could not remember ever having shaken hands with Southwick before starting off on an expedition. He shrugged: Southwick heartily distrusted anything "foreign", and this expedition involved more things "foreign" than Southwick had ever dreamed. The master was still puzzled by Ramage's wish to spend his honeymoon in France and, Ramage was quite sure, still reckoned that dabbling with foreigners was the reason why Lady Sarah might well be dead . . .

He reached the maindeck and paused for a moment. Just over there, on the mainland, more than twenty centuries of recorded history had unfolded. Invasions by men speaking many languages, from the Phoenicians and Carthaginians to the Romans, from the Goths to the Vandals – and, the latest, the French. Battles, political plots, religious quarrels – and all had ended up with men (and women, for that matter) being buried in the rich Tuscan soil. Devil take it, he told himself sharply, you cannot lead men with that attitude. Yet he was neither scared nor sad. One never set foot on Italian soil – or, indeed, arrived in Italian waters – without thinking of the past centuries. The galleys of Santo Stefano sent to help fight the Saracens in the Battle of Lepanto (nearly five centuries ago) must have been rowed out of this bay, turning southward to round the foot of Italy to join the Spanish and Austrian fleets whose admirals' orders were simple: to prevent the Saracens from conquering Europe – which would be easy enough if they defeated the combined fleets of Spain, Italy and Austria.

You think of great fleets of galleys when you are giving orders to your men on board the cutter, gig and jolly-boat . . .

Ramage followed the last man down the ladder and found himself in the gig with Jackson at the tiller and Orsini and Rossi crouched in the sternsheets, ready to help him on board.

He gave the order to cast off and then looked round. From down here the *Calypso* seemed enormous, but curiously enough the dark shapes of Argentario, the mountains behind Talamone and the Torre Saline seemed to have shrunk. Ramage pointed to the tower. "Very well, Jackson, we lead the way and that's where the mouth of the river lies . . ." Oars slid into the water; Jackson's commands came crisp, pitched so that the men in the other boats could hear.

Even in the darkness Ramage could see that both Orsini and Rossi looked impressive in their new uniforms, sewn up earlier that day. So that was how an officer in the Grand Duke of Tuscany's army looked!

"I trust you'll lose that Genovese accent," Ramage told Rossi. "The accent of Siena – that's what we need for a good Tuscan."

"*Si, siamo paesani, signore*," Rossi said and the accent in which he had said "Yes, we are countrymen" was almost perfect.

"Careful, you'll find yourself giving big tips," Orsini said, teasing Rossi over the Genoese reputation for meanness.

"Tuscany has no great reputation for generosity, *signore*," Rossi said respectfully. "In fact under the Grand Duke . . ."

"Don't confuse politics with people," Ramage said firmly. "And don't spoil legends. Legend has it that the Scots and the Genovesi are mean, and nothing you can do will change it. The Cockneys are like the Neapolitans."

"What are the other comparisons, sir?" Orsini asked.

"Blessed if I know," Ramage confessed. "Veneto – that'd be Norfolk, Suffolk and Lincolnshire, I suppose. Flat land and wary people. Mestre, Padua and Ravenna . . . well, that land round the Po Valley always puts me in mind of Romney Marsh, though the Italians aren't so secretive as the Marsh folk. Not so much smuggling! Rome – well, Romans compare directly with Londoners. Welsh? They vary so much it's hard to say . . . I'm certain of one thing, though: there's no such thing as a typical Englishman, and since Italy is such a collection of different states there isn't a typical Italian.

"I'm talking of the *nature* of the people, of course. Most certainly there's a recognizable English type of man and woman. But Italian men – you could confuse them with Spaniards, maybe Frenchmen. The women, too. Not now, of course, after the Revolution. The Spanish women would be heavily chaperoned, while the Frenchwomen would be dressed more freely. The Italian women –"

"Would be chattering away to their *cicisbei*," Paolo said.

"I can't see *cicisbei* prospering under the present regime," Ramage commented.

"Sir," Jackson said. From the warning tone of his voice Ramage turned just enough to be able to see him holding the iron tiller under one arm.

And Ramage could smell it. Such a mixture of smells, in fact, that even if you were blindfolded and carried halfway round the world, you would still know you were in Italy, or approaching very closely. The faint scorching wood from the *carbonaio*'s turf oven; the sharper yet sweet scent of pine trees, and was that rosemary or thyme? And the all too familiar odour of seaweed washed up on the water's edge and drying in the sun and at night, when the temperature dropped, absorbing the night damp. And the whine of insects and the distant hoot of a nightjar. It was like coming home, only this time he was unlocking the door knowing there might be a burglar in the house.

"Seems a long time ago – and yet yesterday," Ramage murmured.

"Leaves me flummoxed, sir," Jackson said. "To me it seems only last week we were landing at the Torre di Buranaccio to find the Marchesa. Yet another part of me hasn't been to Italy for years."

Ramage turned to Orsini. This was Paolo's homeland: this would be the nearest he would get to Volterra until the war ended. "How about you?" Ramage asked quietly.

"The pines. Not because we have so many in Volterra but when I escaped I worked my way down the coast through the pine forests. To me now they mean safety. But Volterra – the smells of a town. Donkey droppings, spilled wine and casks being cleaned, boiling pasta, sweaty woollen clothes . . ."

"Yes, the woollens. No Italian peasant on the hottest day will go without his woollen shirt . . ."

"That's because Italian peasants know the danger of catching a chill by losing the perspiration and letting in the poisonous night vapours."

"They may be right, sir," Jackson said to Orsini. "I don't see any Italians overheating themselves rowing round here at night!"

"We Italians are cleverer than we look," Rossi said unexpectedly.

"Certainly you're not rowing," Ramage said dryly.

He looked round and saw the other two boats following closely astern, and in the distance he could just make out the dark bulk of the *Calypso*. Good – the men rowing the three boats back here to meet them after the Pitigliano expedition would have no difficulty in finding their way.

As he surveyed the plan up to date, he was sure that the safest place for the *Calypso* to wait was out there in the middle of the bay, right in front of and between Talamone on the mainland and the Fortezza di Filippo Secundo at Santo Stefano, easily seen by every general, admiral, sailor, soldier, tinker, *avvocato* or pimp taking the Via Aurelia to or from Rome. Who would think that an *English* frigate would be anchored there! *Accidente*, the *commandante* would have to be a *buffone*!

There was the mouth of the river, reduced in summer to little more than a ditch, sluicing a path for itself through the mud and sand.

"Keep this side of it," Ramage said quietly. "That'll save us crossing the bridge."

"Aye, bridges could mean sentries," Jackson commented, as though talking to himself. "Not that Boney would think much of this bridge."

In the darkness Ramage could see the faint white crests of the wavelets curling over on the sand, leaving a narrow line of white froth. Jackson gave an order to the oarsmen, and the boat slowed.

Ramage called to Martin, who was sitting in the bow, and the youth began scrambling aft over the thwarts. He would be in charge of the three boats once the Pitigliano party was safe on the beach and they could return to the frigate. It was all right for the *Calypso* to be openly anchored in the bay, but her boats must be hoisted on board: the French must not have any idea that she had landed men.

"Hold tight," Jackson warned as the gig's stem scraped on the sand. "Grapplers over the side!"

"Grapplers" was Jackson's word for the four men who leapt into the water and, standing waist-deep, stopped the boat slewing and then helped pull it further up the beach so that the men who were landing would not get so wet.

"She's all yours, Martin," Ramage said and, gripping the bulwark, lowered himself into the water. It was warmer than he expected, and he teased himself that once again he was caught: frequently on what seemed a cold night in the Tropics it would feel warmer in the water than out – and frequently it was: the sea would be 80° while the air was 76°. Of course even a slight breeze made it seem chillier, in the same way that putting milk or butter in a pottery dish covered with muslin soaking up water kept everything cool by evaporation.

Now the men of the landing party were leaving the boat, first scrambling barefooted over the side into the water and running a few paces up the beach to put their boots in a dry place, then returning to the boat for pistols, muskets and swords.

A few yards to larboard the cutter grounded, and a couple of moments later the jolly-boat nosed up to starboard. Ramage, having put his boots under a bush, went back to the boat to collect his sword and brace of pistols.

He counted the men in his party: they were all waiting on the sandy beach. He gestured to the "grapplers" and called to Martin: "Right, now you can be on your way. Make sure the other two boats follow." With that he helped the "grapplers" push the boat out, giving it a final thrust as they swung up over the bulwarks and wriggled back on to the thwarts. "Good luck, sir," the nearest man whispered, "wish I was coming with you."

Finally the beach was clear of boats and the three groups of men were among the pine trees, except for two who, under Jackson's guidance, had cut branches from the bushes and, using them as brooms, were sweeping the sand to hide the many footprints. The rise and fall of the tide was only a few inches (leading poets and others to assume the Mediterranean was in fact tideless) but it was still rising and would soon smooth out the three grooves made by the stems of the boats. Half a day's sun and some wind whiffling along the beach would have the sand completely smooth again, except for the lace-like foot prints left by the wading birds that strutted along the shoreline pecking up their food.

Ramage found a small and stubby bush without thorns to squat down on as he pulled on his boots, leaving his sword and pistols on the next bush: bitter experience had taught him that a mere hint of sand was enough to cover a uniform, make a sword grate as it was pulled from its scabbard, and block the touchhole of a pistol.

Hill came up in the darkness to report. "My party's ready, sir. The prisoners are ready with Mr Aitken and Rennick . . ."

Ramage grunted as he gave the last boot a tug and then stood up. "No packs of barking dogs or squadrons of French cavalry patrols yet, eh?"

"You can't trust these foreigners to be punctual, sir," Hill said mildly. "Shall I get my party up to the road?"

"Yes, cross to the other side, and tell Mr Aitken to follow you."

He stood for a couple of minutes, staring seaward and breathing in all the scents that made Italy. Over there, the black shape blotting out the stars behind it was Argentario, and to his left he could make out the curving causeway, the Tombolo della Giannella. What was the southern one called? Yes, of course: the Tombolo di Feniglia, which swept round to Port' Ercole. The pine trees of Giannella at the back of the halfmoon of beach (scimitar shaped, really, considering its length) were black, almost menacing. He could pick out the peak of Monte Argentario, but the shadows were too distorting to be able to sight Santo Stefano. No lights visible at this distance – no lights anyway, in all probability: men who rose with the sun to farm their strips of land and tend the grapevines on the terraces went to bed with the sun.

The occasional quark of the nightjar . . . the insects . . . a splash a few yards out to sea as a small fish leapt in a frantic attempt to escape a predator. When did a fish rest? Dare it ever?

How could it stop motionless, knowing that at any moment it might be gobbled up by its next largest neighbour? It must be like that if you belonged to a country close to France . . . Genoa, Switzerland, Lombardy, Piedmont, Venice, Tuscany, the Papal States, the Netherlands . . . the minnows of Europe had been gobbled up, one by one, in the last dozen years.

"Mr Aitken's compliments, sir," Jackson muttered apologetically, knowing the captain's memory was slipping back over the years, and unwilling to break in on his thoughts, "but his and Mr Hill's party are waiting on the other side of the road now, alongside a row of cypress. He wants to know if the prisoners with Mr Rennick should put on their irons."

Ramage glanced up at the sky. From the position of the stars it must be about midnight. Strange, seeing the Pole Star so high after the years in the Tropics, where it was usually less than a dozen degrees above the horizon. If you know the altitude of the Pole Star you know your latitude – that must be about the first thing a midshipman learned when he began navigation. Well, he was standing at about forty-two degrees thirty minutes North, and since that was his latitude it was also the altitude of the Pole Star.

"My compliments to Mr Aitken: I'll be with him in a moment. Lead our party over to join him."

An hour later Ramage and his men were resting a mile along the road to Pitigliano. Most were asleep beside another cypress grove which had been planted more than a century earlier as a windbreak for a farmhouse long ago deserted. The roof was falling in, the last of the whitewash flaking off the walls, the doors either hung by the remains of a single hinge or were lying flat on the ground, a shelter for scorpions hiding underneath among pebbles and in grass growing white. Ramage had warned the men against the small, black scorpion which was ready in an instant to bring up its tail in an arc over its body to jab with the sting at the end.

One of the "prisoners" sat against a tree-trunk, acting as sentry, and at his feet was the canvas bag containing all the arm irons that could be found on board the *Calypso*. Fortunately, there were just enough to shackle the "prisoners" together when the time came to march.

Ramage sat against another cypress, alone with his thoughts and vaguely conscious that a surprising number of the men snored very loudly. Even more surprising, he thought, was the fact that most of them seemed to find the hard ground as comfortable as a down-filled mattress.

Yes, he could just see Gold Belt, low on the horizon. Strange after all the months in the Tropics when those stars passed high to the south, often overhead.

Now he had reached the track to Pitigliano he was becoming more confident about this bizarre expedition. On board the *Calypso*, with the men snipping and stitching at the make-believe French and Tuscan Army uniforms, it was like play-acting: there seemed no chance that a French cavalry patrol or guards at the gate of Pitigliano itself would be fooled. But now, having made the men parade in their three sections before being dismissed to sleep by the cypress, the whole affair began to develop a strange reality of its own.

First there was Gilbert and his three fellow Frenchmen. They looked genuine in their uniforms. Much too smart, perhaps, but sleeping in them for a few hours (as they were now doing) would make them seem more authentic, plus another day's growth of whiskers. On this kind of escort duty, French soldiers would look more like bandits in stolen uniforms. When the four Frenchmen and Hill spoke French and pretended to quarrel among themselves, they sounded just like the French soldiers he had seen a few months ago in Brest; in fact Ramage was hard put to restrain a shiver.

It was many years since he had seen any of the Grand Duke of Tuscany's troops, but he was willing to accept that Paolo had made no mistakes in the patterns he had drawn for the uniforms. Anyway, Paolo, Rossi and Ramage himself had looked impressive (in the darkness, at least), although for the moment the uniforms were also a little too smart: they needed creasing and a light coat of the white dust that they would soon be kicking up along the road.

The prisoners – yes, they looked just like admirals, generals, colonels and civilians who had been on holiday when caught up in an unexpected resumption of war. Jackson, wearing Ramage's oldest pair of breeches, woollen stockings, an old frock-coat and a torn stock, with the buttons replaced and the epaulettes removed, could pass for a stranded admiral. He had agreed when Ramage said his queue looked out of place, and his sandy hair was cut short and combed back. Jackson looked like a man who, although a prisoner for many months, had tried to keep up appearances. Stafford – well, Stafford was dressed in some of Kenton's civilian clothes, and the fact was (as Jackson had announced) that he looked more like a prosperous pimp who had been caught by a highwayman on his way back from the races.

The remaining eight prisoners seemed, Ramage thought, reasonably authentic: he had quite deliberately chosen men who by their faces or way of walking would not be mistaken for labourers and who, by nature, carried themselves with something of a swagger. All of them had spent several hours on board the *Calypso* practising under Rennick's sharp eye – Ramage recalled with a smile the instructions Rennick had shouted. "No, no – walk as though you had a smell under your nose . . . Damme, man, treat him as though he's a card sharper flirting with your wife . . . No, no, he's a poacher that your gamekeeper has just caught . . .! Think of him as the husband who knows you've cuckolded him but daren't do anything about it . . ."

Finally Rennick had turned the delighted seamen into a semblance of Britons of considerable importance who were being treated by the French as hostages and now being transferred from one prison to another led by Rennick.

It *could* work: even Southwick was agreed on that. But if the French discovered the deception, then the French "guards" and the Tuscan "soldiers" could be shot out of hand as spies masquerading in uniform. The "prisoners", not being in uniform, might stand a chance of being made real prisoners but Ramage doubted it: the plains and hills and mountains of Tuscany somehow lent themselves to backs-to-the-wall, firing-party-atten-shun! answers.

Finally, Ramage slid sideways, cradling his head against a hump of earth covering a root, and fell asleep.

Chapter
Seven

Soon after dawn the three groups of men were walking (Rennick would call it shambling) along the flat road running beside the river. They would reach the hills, which looked like sleeping turtles, just as the sun reached its zenith. Scorching sun, no breeze, more than a couple of dozen pairs of feet stirring up clouds of white dust lying on the rock and which formed the track . . . Thirst might become a problem. Each man carried a Marine's water flask, and Gilbert's men and Ramage's had haversacks with ship's biscuits. But the farms along the way were going to suffer just as if this was a real French army unit: they would have to provide food and water. There would be no payment because Ramage had no local money – and anyway the French never paid.

The "prisoners" each carried arm irons. It only took a couple of moments to slip their wrists through and hold their arms as though marching in irons.

"Nice to 'ave a walk in the country just as the birds is waking up," Stafford remarked to Jackson.

"Yes, but when was the last time you did it?"

"Don't fancy it too often," Stafford said airily. "Not that fond of the country. Mosquitoes buzzing most o' the night, scorpiongs waiting –"

"Scorpions," Jackson corrected.

"S'what I said, scorpiongs lurking under the rocks to prod you – hey Jacko, wasn't it a scorpiong that did for that Egyptian doxy, her that danced for Caesar?"

"I think someone else danced, but Cleopatra did herself in by holding an asp to her bosom."

65

"An asp? That the same as a scorpiong?"

"I reckon so," Jackson said carefully.

"Then it must be big if she could 'old it. Like a small lobster."

"Maybe them Egyptian ones are, but those here don't run to more'n a couple of inches."

"'Ere, 'old 'ard. Mr Ramage said they just give you a nasty sting, but one did poor Cleopatra in."

"Don't worry," Jackson said reassuringly.

"S'trewth, I don't remember these scorpiongs when we were last here: and, so help me, the mosquitoes are so much bigger." He slapped the side of his face, and then held out the palm of his hand. "See? Look at the blood in that one. 'Ere, you don't arf look a sight: your face is all swolled up."

Jackson looked at Stafford and laughed. "My oath! You ought to see yourself: you look as though you've got gumboils all over the place!"

Stafford pointed to a small turning leading away to the left and crossing the river. "Where's that go?"

Jackson shrugged. "From what I saw of Mr Ramage's map, it goes across that valley and then twists and turns through those hills. See how the hills get higher and higher? Well, it goes on to the foot o' that mountain. Amiata. We have to keep the same distance and we'll come up on Pitigliano."

"You've never been there, this Pitigliano, 'ave you?"

"No. Mr Ramage says it's a hill town and very old."

"Roaming, you mean?"

"No, older than Roman. Etruscan, I think he said."

"Who? I thought the Roamings came first!"

"No, and the Etruscans gave this area its name, Tuscany. Very clever people, according to Mr Ramage. They built big stone-lined cellars to store the grain and dug caves and painted the walls with things like leopards and people: they painted the women one colour and the men another."

Stafford looked at Jackson startled. "Why the hell did they do that? Couldn't they tell the difference? Must 'ave been uncomfortable, covered in paint."

As soon as Jackson realized Stafford's mistake he roared with laughter. "Different colours in the cave paintings! What did you think, the women were gilded and the men striped green?"

"Well, no," Stafford said, embarrassed, "but don't forget the Druids in England – they used to paint themselves, didn't they?"

"Yes, at times," Jackson said carefully, knowing he was out of his depth. "But most o' the villages round here were originally Etruscan, so Mr Ramage says. Most of 'em have still got ruins to show for it. Huge rocks, specially carved so one fits perfectly into another. Puzzle how they did it."

"My feet ache already," Stafford announced. "They're swelling up. How much farther?"

"Only about twenty miles," Jackson said. "By the time we get there your legs will be worn down to the knees."

"All this marching is for the Marines," Stafford declared and with the dust drying up his mouth lapsed into silence.

At the head of the column, in the uniforms, now rumpled, of officers in the Archduke of Tuscany's army, Ramage and Orsini talked. Ramage was surprised to find that the Grand Duke's army of about three thousand men were very poorly paid because the soldiers were allowed (indeed, expected) to carry on their own trade.

"That's why foreigners find it hard to tell private soldiers from the officers," Paolo said. "The privates like to cut a good figure too, and if they have successful businesses they can afford good tailors."

"I can see that. This uniform –" Ramage tapped his chest, "– makes me look like a general, and Rossi could be a colonel."

"Perhaps the archduke is wiser than we think, sir. A man who can strut before the ladies in a smart uniform will be content with less pay."

Ramage nodded. Pander to a man's vanity *or* put a guinea in his pocket. Ramage chuckled at the phrase, then realized he had missed a comment by Paolo. "What did you say?"

"I was saying, sir, that the archduke has done away with the death penalty. I'm not sure if it was the present one or his father. Anyway Tuscany is one of the few states where you can murder someone without fear of execution. Mind you, that might be preferable to a lifetime in a Florentine jail!"

That reminded Ramage of another remark which Paolo had made but which at the time Ramage had not pursued. "You said we could have cut across the top end of the Maremma if we wanted to get at Pitigliano from the south-west. But what about the marshes?"

"The archduke is draining them, or he's made a start, anyway. You'll find grain growing where there was marsh. Rice, too. Mind you, it's a vast marshy area to drain!"

"And the mosquitoes?"

"The *zanzari* are flourishing – at least they were when I passed through when I was escaping. They seemed as big as eagles . . ."

At the other end of the column, Gilbert led his Frenchmen, marching with Hill. He was thoroughly enjoying his role as the officer in charge of the escort, although Hill and the other three frequently teased him. Their uniforms were already baggy and creased: none of the five men had shaved for several days.

"Citizen," said Hill, who was accustomed to shave every day, "my whole face itches with this damned beard. It's making my neck sore."

Gilbert shook his head, as though exasperated. "A *sensible* soldier carries a razor, not a field marshal's baton, in his valise."

"Oh, but I have both," Hill exclaimed, much to the amusement of the others. "All I lack is water and some soap."

"I'll speak to the citizen general about it," Gilbert said. "Meanwhile don't drag the butt of your musket on the ground."

"I'm not!" exclaimed a startled Hill.

"I know; I was just warning you in advance. What a dust those Tuscans and English *aristos* are stirring up with their feet. We'll be dried out long before we reach Manciano."

Louis coughed before saying solemnly: "Have I the citizen captain's permission to speak?"

"As long as you pay proper respect to my rank and age."

"*Sacré bleu!*" Louis exclaimed. "Service in the English King's Navy is preferable to being in this Republican army. Every officer and non-commissioned officer makes his own revolution! *Alors, mon général*, this citizen would like to point out with respect that there are several farms along this road. Look, two on the right, and one across the river on the left. I would not care to drink the river water here, because the river is in reality

68

a stream and a dozen cattle upstream can turn it into a veritable *pissoir*, but –"

"Hurry, citizen," Gilbert said, "we shall be in Manciano before you've finished."

"But, as I was saying before the citizen interrupted me," Louis said with dignity, "where there is a farm there must be water. Water for the farmer, his oxen –"

"– his wife, his children, his aged mother, his thirsty aunt who won't take wine, the priest when he visits on feast days, the farmer's donkey –" Auguste interrupted.

"I understand," Gilbert said. "A well, a rope, a bucket and –"

"A shave, perhaps?" Hill said with mock plaintiveness.

"Citizen Hill," Gilbert said gravely, "everyone must make some sacrifice for the Republic, One and Indivisible."

"Oh indeed," Hill said promptly. "I'll sacrifice my beard! And my indivisible back will ache and my hands blister from the promptness with which I haul up that bucket!"

"I'll remind you of that, citizen," Gilbert said, "and the other citizens are witnesses."

"To be serious, do we spend the night in Manciano or do we sleep in the fields again?" Louis asked.

Gilbert looked at Hill, who said: "Mr Ramage will decide when we get to Manciano. There'll be no inn in such a small town, so it'll probably be a choice of fleas in houses and sleeping on straw, or lying on the grass in a meadow giving the mosquitoes a feast."

"I prefer the mosquitoes," Louis announced. "With mosquitoes you can put a jacket over your face and hands, and they go away in the day. Fleas bite worse, creep in anywhere and travel with you."

"He's right," Auguste said, his voice sonorous. "We expect you to register our preference this evening when the citizen general from Tuscany calls you to his council of war."

"There might be some pretty girls in Manciano," Hill speculated. "You never know, in these remote towns."

Louis gave a cynical laugh. "Citizen, a hill town in Tuscany, a market town in Brittany, a large village famous for its apples in Cornwall . . . they are all the same. All the eligible unmarried young women are guarded more carefully than emperors guard their treasuries. You forget a reputation for virginity is more highly prized (among the possessors' parents, anyway) than bullion."

"Well, it'd have to be for love anyway, because none of us have local money," Hill said sadly.

"Don't worry, it's a long way to Manciano, and by the time we get there you may be more interested in sleeping than flirting with a young lady's grandmother, who will in any case be dressed from head to toe in black and trying to sell you wine about to turn into vinegar."

"Wait, citizen!" Auguste said. "The revolutionary committee did not make you a captain to commandeer vinegar in the name of the Republic, One and Indivisible. No, you are expected to commandeer only good wine, and decent bread that has been ground properly and is not so full of husks it tastes like chewing a brush. The meat, too. Fresh, even if they have to slaughter a beast and the meat is still warm when they begin to cook it."

"I'll do my best," Gilbert said wryly, "but I think you have an exaggerated idea of the Republic's influence among these Tuscan hills. I should think of rice, or perhaps polenta, soft and soggy, washed down with the wine they were keeping to make vinegar."

Auguste, hitching his musket on to the other shoulder, said sourly: "To think that every man we left behind on board the *Calypso* envied us, thinking we'd eat like kings and drink like seamen should. I never expected that one day I'd be glad to get back on board one of His Britannic Majesty's ships so that I could have a decent meal . . ."

"My heart *bleeds* for you!" Gilbert said dramatically, slapping his chest. "Here you are seeing new sights, visiting yet another new country, collecting dozens more improbable stories to tell your grandchildren, and all you do is complain. Yes," Gilbert said sadly, in the voice of a man discovering an unpleasant truth. "I have to admit it: you grumble with the skill and perseverance of an English sailor."

"And we march with the perseverance of a charcoal burner's donkey bound for home," Auguste added, then qualified it with: "Once you've got him started."

At that moment Rossi, walking beside Orsini at the head of

the column, pointed up the track. "Something is coming. You see the dust?"

Ramage, having to look into the glare of the rising sun, pulled down the peak of his cap. "Yes – one person, I think, on a horse or donkey. Yes, a donkey, because a horse would make more dust."

"A farmer going to Orbetello?" Rossi suggested.

"No threat to us, anyway. He can tell us what there is in Manciano – always assuming there *is* something in Manciano!"

As it came nearer, the donkey seemed to be walking along by itself, head down, its large ears flapping and carrying a shapeless sack on its back. Then Ramage thought he could distinguish a barrel at the bottom of the pile, balancing on the wooden frame, shaped rather like a sawing horse, which served as a saddle or repository for whatever load it was carrying. The shapeless mass was in fact a man draped over the flanks of the donkey and partly over the barrel, a man who was either asleep or drunk.

Ramage held up his hand to halt the column and with Orsini and Rossi walked over to stand in front of the donkey, which seemed grateful for the opportunity to stop.

This woke the man, who rubbed his eyes but did not seem startled to find himself facing soldiers. "What have I done now?" His tone was surly but deferential; these were the enemy, he seemed to imply, and they made so many rules and regulations that it was impossible for a simple *contadino* to understand or remember.

"I do not know yet," Ramage said evenly. "Where have you come from and where are you going?"

"From just this side of Manciano, and I'm going to Orbetello to sell wine." He slapped the barrel with his hand.

"Have you seen any strangers in the fields, or along the road: people who are obviously enemies of the Republic?" That, Ramage hoped, would reveal the attitude of at least one *contadino* towards the French and anyone who might be their enemy.

"No one. Just Giuseppe, who is my neighbour: he was out at dawn. A wise man gets as much hoeing done as possible before the sun gets hot."

Ramage nodded affably. "Can't you sell your wine in Manciano? It's a long ride to Orbetello."

"Manciano?" The man sounded disgusted by the name. "In Manciano half the men press their own grapes and the other half are too mean to pay a decent price."

"They're thirstier in Orbetello, eh?"

The man shrugged his shoulders and finally slid off the donkey. He stretched one leg and then the other and, after apparently reassuring himself he could still walk, said: "Different people. In Orbetello, many men fish in the lagoon, others make charcoal. Several shops there. Not many people grow grapes. Most of the land is used for olive trees, so they need to buy wine and sell oil."

Again Ramage nodded. "And the French troops there – they buy your wine?"

The man looked him up and down and said nothing.

"What about the French in Manciano – where do they buy wine, eh?"

"French troops do not *buy* wine from anyone," the man said finally, as though explaining something to a child. "They just commandeer what they need. Anyway, there are no French troops in Manciano." He stopped and thought for a moment. "Are you going to Manciano? A garrison, perhaps?"

"We are just passing through – on our way to Orvieto."

"Yes, you would be," the man said. "Many French there."

"And Pitigliano, too?"

The man looked at him warily, and then agreed. "And Pitigliano, too. Now, Colonel, can I go on?"

Ramage nodded: there was little more that the man could tell him. Then suddenly he remembered a question. "Why don't you sell your wine in Pitigliano?"

"The same reason that I can't sell it in Manciano. Too many men grow their own grapes. Anyway, I don't like Pitigliano. My wife's family live there and they've never liked me: think she married beneath her – and her father only a tailor! You'll see his house just inside the town gate. You can't miss his sign, a pair of wooden scissors hanging over the door. Between two *falegnami*, although I wouldn't recommend either of them if you wanted a table made with four legs the same length. Can I go now?"

Ramage nodded and watched the man step back a couple of paces and then run at the donkey, jumping on to its back like a boy playing leapfrog. The donkey did not move and the man reached down beside the barrel and found a stick half as thick as his wrist.

He whacked the donkey with it, but the animal took a deep breath, stretched its neck and brayed, the noise as always reminding Ramage of a cow being strangled. The man whacked again, and reluctantly the donkey began to move. Ramage waved to his column and they continued their march.

"He didn't seem to know much, sir," Orsini commented.

"Obviously not a lot happens on the outskirts of Manciano," Ramage said dryly. "But he knows there's something unusual at Pitigliano."

"Yes, yes," Rossi said excitedly, his Genoese accent strong, "you noticed it too, sir! That was a strange expression on his face after you mentioned French troops in Pitigliano – as though he thought you were trying to trap him."

"Yes, but I decided more questions would only make him more suspicious. Those hills ahead of us are just the sort where partisan bands live. He saw we were escorting prisoners so he might get word to them . . ."

"You think there are still partisans, sir?" Orsini asked. "There were when I escaped from Volterra, but that was a long time ago."

"I'm sure the French have done nothing to make the partisans change their minds about the French Republic, One and Indivisible."

"But how can partisans survive?"

"I doubt if they live like a group of bandits on the Maremma; they're probably like the man we've just seen: tilling fields most of the time, and then one night joining up for a raid on a French garrison, or to ambush a convoy of carts carrying supplies for garrisons."

Rossi nodded his agreement. "That's what happened round Genoa when the French first came," he said. "*Accidente*, I wish we had some *somaro* to ride on. That man did not look comfortable, but his feet weren't sore."

"Not his feet," Paolo said.

Rossi thought for several moments. "I see what you mean. He could harm himself, too."

They reached Manciano shortly after noon, and as soon as Ramage had commandeered bread, all the cheese he could find (some extremely strong *pecorino fresco*, made of goat's milk and, according to Stafford, likely to make your hair fall out) along with several salami sausages and *fiaschi* of red wine, the column continued along the road to Pitigliano. Ramage soon halted them where they could sit in the narrow shade made by a row of cypress trees. The sun was high – but Ramage remembered the Tropics where, at certain times in the year, the sun was directly overhead and a man made no shadow.

"Take your boots off, and as soon as you've eaten, rest with your feet up. You have two hours to sleep."

Hearing Stafford's startled but delighted exclamation, Ramage explained to the men: "No Italians or French would be marching at this time. Any movement during siesta time would make people suspicious."

The bread was fresh, obviously baked early that morning: the salami was good, the slightly smoky taste almost overpowered by garlic, and the *pecorino fresco* was as strong as Stafford anticipated but cleaned the mouth of the greasiness left by the salami. Ramage had a sip of wine, curious about the taste of the product of Manciano's vineyards.

He pulled off his boots, rolled up his coat as a pillow, and lay back on the parched ground, his sword and two pistols beside him. The dark green cypress were like jutting spearheads, he thought sleepily. Cicadas buzzed monotonously – and Ramage realized how much the countryside was part of him because he had not paid them any attention until now, although they were loud enough. A single lark, in line with the sun, sang as if to welcome them. Five minutes later a sparrowhawk (or was it a kestrel – difficult to tell in this bright sun) poised over a small sugarloaf hill; then it dropped like a stone on its prey.

That is how we should arrive in Pitigliano, he decided: swift and unexpected. They must leave the French guards content and unsuspecting, because no one should raise the alarm for the couple of days it was going to take to shepherd the freed hostages back to the beach and on board the *Calypso*. They would need more than two days if an alarm was raised.

An alarm would mean they could not risk using the roads (even at night they might walk into ambushes), and leading the hostages across this rough country would be difficult. For a start, few would be wearing suitable footwear. And, he realized wearily, there was bound to be some damned admiral or general who would try to take command of the party. Well, Ramage had made up his mind about that right from the start: the Admiralty orders put him in command, and anyone, of whatever rank, who disagreed would be given the time and position of a rendezvous near Orbetello and told to make his own way. Orbetello would be near enough – Ramage had to take into account that such hostages, not speaking Italian, would almost certainly be captured, and the French would not take long to extract the rendezvous from them. Men who had faced broadsides and barrages without flinching would quickly discover it took a different type of courage to withstand torture, although, come to think of it . . . yes, give two rendezvous, the second a false one which would sound plausible when "revealed" to the French.

When he woke, a glance at his watch showed he had slept for nearly two hours, and already Hill was sitting up, pulling on his boots.

Before the three groups of men fell in on the road – which was no more than a layer of white dust settled on the rock, distinguishable as a road only because no trees or bushes grew on it, and mule and donkey droppings marked the way like pencilled dots on a map – Ramage looked round carefully. The *contadini* still dozed; there was no sign of a French cavalry patrol.

As soon as they were formed up, Ramage inspected his men: not with the eye of a Rennick, but with the eyes of Frenchmen and Italians. Starting at the rear, he looked at Hill. His chin and cheeks were covered in black stubble; his hair was tousled beneath the cap. His coat was creased and dusty with a grease mark round the collar where the hair touched. The trousers needed a hitch, but there was no dust on his musket. Ramage nodded. "Napoleon the First, Emperor of the French, is proud

75

of you: beneath your feet –" Ramage glanced down at the dusty boots, "– Italian states have crumbled into white dust. Austria cringes. The English tremble with fear."

"Yes, sir," Hill agreed. "It's because these feet throb so much they must sound like five armies marching . . ."

He spoke in French and the other men laughed. "Auguste," Ramage said, "wearing that uniform, do you feel any nostalgia?"

"For Brittany, yes, *mon capitaine*. But –" he waved a hand towards the fields, "– when I think of what my people are doing to these poor people I am ashamed."

Ramage nodded but said: "Don't feel too guilty: not 'your people', just a few men who seized power. Meanwhile try to think of yourself as one of the Emperor's soldiers – just in case we are challenged!"

He looked at Louis. He would put him among a thousand French soldiers and defy anyone to be suspicious. His chin was greasy from the salami: crumbs lodged among the bristles; his musket was slung over his shoulder with all the nonchalance of an old soldier who had marched across many hills and plains and fought many campaigns.

Ramage grinned at him. "Marengo with Bonaparte," he said, naming the famous victory. "Then he reorganized Italy, and made the Grand Duke of Tuscany the King of Etruria, and you've been here ever since . . ."

"Indeed, citizen captain. Pay months in arrears, eating only what we can forage, welcome nowhere, hated everywhere – but nevertheless a soldier of the Republic, One and Indivisible!"

Ramage laughed drily. "Well spoken; the Emperor is proud of you.

"And as for you," he said turning to Gilbert, "you have the harried look of a veteran of Osterach, Cassano and Jovi." In all three battles the French had been beaten by the Austrians.

"That's true, sir," Gilbert said sorrowfully. "I intend to learn German: none of these Austrians speak French."

"Very wise of you," Ramage commented and walked on to inspect the prisoners. He looked them over and said: "You hostages are supposed to be aristocrats and naval officers of flag rank and army officers of field rank, but to me you look like pimps and panders and unlucky gamblers on the run from creditors, cuckolded husbands and cast-off mistresses!"

"If I'd known it was goin' ter be like this," Stafford said contritely, "I'd never 'ave cast 'er orf . . ."

"It's those French guards," Aitken said haughtily, "they bully us. They don't treat us with the respect due to our station in society. They all seem infected with a most noxious revolutionary fervour. Most disturbing. I'd complain to our ambassador, but I can't find him."

"One can *never* find an ambassador or a consul when he's needed," Ramage said sympathetically. "It's their training. They must avoid responsibility, never take sides, never give an opinion, always smile and employ a good chef."

Ramage inspected the rest of the "prisoners" and then had a hard look at Paolo and Rossi. They were Italian all right, combining raffishness with an easy-going stance and a realistic approach to war. To a casual onlooker, the sound of a distant pistol shot would seem enough to send them scurrying into the hills for cover. Which, Ramage thought, just shows how clothes and a few days' growth of whiskers can be deceptive.

The march continued and the road twisted and turned but generally trended to the south-east along a valley. Finally, at nightfall, they reached a river, the Fiora, which started life somewhere up near Santa Fiora, among the mountains near Amiata, and snaked its way across Tuscany, crossing the road a few miles short of Pitigliano and going on to meet the sea near the Torre Montalto. But as spring had turned into scorching summer, so the Fiora had now shrunk to little more than a stream. But at least there was some water, and Ramage gave permission for the men to bathe. As soon as they were dry again and dressed, the remaining rations were issued and all the men, with the exception of a sentry, hid hands and faces under their jackets and, still able to hear the whine of hungry mosquitoes, went to sleep.

Just before the sentry was posted, Ramage spoke to Orsini, Hill, Aitken and, to make sure the Frenchman understood that he would be in command of his section if anything happened to Hill, Gilbert.

"We start tomorrow as soon after dawn as we can. Apart

77

from what's left in our haversacks from the *Calypso*, we've no more food. But it's only five or six miles to Pitigliano, and you all know what to do when we get there. Don't forget, Gilbert – your men answer any friendly shouts from other French troops. We've got to march through the Porta della Cittadella as though we own the place. It is a big gateway, but leave Hill and me to argue if we are challenged: the rest of you keep marching (as smartly as you can) towards the Palazzo degli Orsini, which is large and obvious. What we do after that depends on whether we've been recognized or not. You know the plan if we are accepted as genuine; you know the plan if we are discovered. I hope we shan't need to make up a new plan . . ."

Chapter
Eight

Both Rossi and Ramage sniffed at the same moment, like hunting dogs, as they marched up the hill and Ramage held up his arm to halt the column. In fact there was an odd, almost contradictory mixture of smells – bread baking, thyme, rotting cabbage, rosemary, donkey stables (caves more likely) that should have been cleaned out months ago.

"Pitigliano must be just round this next corner," Ramage said, pointing to windward.

On the left of the road as it climbed a small hill there was a valley of scoured rock on which a few bushes clung, out of reach of goats. Orsini commented that it was obviously the bed of an old river – a river which many centuries ago had run deep and fast.

"I remember now," Orsini said. "Pitigliano is in the middle of the valley, built on an old rocky, mountainous island, which looks like a back tooth. The river must once have divided, swept on round each side of the island like a moat, and then joined up again. That was probably why the Etruscans came here originally: they paddled across to the island and dug caves in which they could live safely. It's all soft tufa. Easy to cut, and then it hardens when the air gets to it and becomes like rock."

"Come with me," Ramage said, telling the rest of the column to stand fast and the "prisoners" to be ready with their arm irons. The two of them walked to the top of the hill, rounded a corner and saw Pitigliano across the valley like a huge painting on a distant wall. "You were right," Ramage muttered to

Paolo. "An enormous tooth. Yes, and a river used to sluice along both sides . . . it would have joined just there, below where we left the men . . . There's the town gate . . . yes, and the Orsini Palace with the battlements."

The road in front of them turned sharply and went down steeply to the bottom of the valley – the old river bed – before turning at a sharp cliff and running beside several caves, now used to stable donkeys (Ramage could see two of them, both grey with a black stripe running along their backs from head to tail), and then climbing up the side of the great rock on which the town stood. And at the top, commanding the road and forcing it to take another sharp turn to the left to reach the town centre, was the town gate.

"Well, sir, no chance of surprising 'em: pity we haven't a band!"

"I'd settle for a bring-'em-near. I wonder how many sentries there are?"

"The whole place seems to be asleep. Ah, there's a man coming through the gate on a donkey. And yes, his wife walking behind."

"That's a familiar sight," Ramage commented. "But no sign of a sentry checking them."

"No, sir, everyone else is still asleep!"

"They're guarding the Emperor's hostages, don't forget," Ramage said sharply. "It's a great mistake to underestimate the enemy. That's how you get a pistol ball between the eyes."

"I understand, sir," said a chastened Paolo. "Actually I'm not underestimating them. I'm not looking forward to going in. The walls round the town, that huge gate, the long drop from the walls into the valley . . ."

"We're lucky. We'll be marching in through the gate in broad daylight. But how would you like to cross that valley and then have to climb the walls in the dark . . .?"

"*Mamma mia*," muttered Paolo. "Even climbing in daylight with no French to greet us would be bad enough. Far too steep even for goats!"

"Go back and bring up the column: the longer we wait here the more impossible it all seems."

A few minutes later, as the column swung round the corner,

Ramage resumed his place and, with Rossi and Orsini, led the way down the hill. A donkey, looking sleepily over the half-door closing off its cave, brayed at them and was answered by another up in the town. Half a dozen dogs came rushing out of the town gates, the first one yelping in terror and the rest barking as they chased it, and the old woman lashed at them with a long staff as they raced past. Neither her husband nor his donkey took any notice. The donkey had a small sack balanced on its wooden frame: the man, sitting astride the animal and, it seemed to Ramage, in grave danger of falling off, tugged at the brim of his big black hat. The wide brim flopped with the donkey's jerking, helping to keep off the flies. Then, adjusting the angle of the hat so that the brim kept the sun out of his eyes, the man whacked the donkey with a stick. The donkey took no notice; Ramage guessed that the man did it out of habit, and would repeat it every hundred yards until they reached their destination.

Ramage half turned as he marched and called back: "Come on, now smarten yourselves up. Only the hostages may speak English. Gilbert – be ready to come up forward with those papers of yours. Remember, Aitken – you and the rest of the prisoners are foreigners and can talk and stare and point. Your men, Gilbert, just take it all in your stride: you've seen it all before so act as though you're hot, bored and tired."

By then they were at the bottom of the hill and rounding the bend. At the top of the hill in front of them the town gate, *la Porta della Cittadella*, seemed to be growing bigger, but the shadow the archway cast and the dark line under the battlements made it seem as menacing as the gateway to an enemy city.

They met the old couple with the donkey almost halfway up the hill and the man looked directly at the donkey's flopping ears. The woman, her face seamed like old leather left too long in the sun, dressed in black that had a rusty hue from too many summers and winters out in the open fields, looked up for a moment, spotted Ramage as the officer most likely in charge, and nodded her head nervously: to Ramage she seemed to be asking him to ignore her husband's snub – and, at the same time, fearful of what these extra soldiers might mean to their lives.

Looking across the valley at the base of the great tooth of

rock Ramage could now see dozens of caves cut into the tufa like a vast rabbit warren, and there were tracks in the valley floor where the *contadini* walked daily to and fro between the caves and their fields. They must keep their implements in them, and their donkeys – and perhaps for the unluckier people some of the higher caves were homes. Certainly a peasant coming home weary from working his land (because land was divided among all his children on the owner's death, a *contadino* might own a dozen small strips, each a mile from another) would be thankful to rest in a cool cave with a jug of wine and postpone the weary trudge up to the town.

And, of course, the caves provided fine cool storage for the big casks in which the year's wine was kept until sold at the next pressing: huge casks lying on their sides with the bung higher than its owner was tall. Every day (if he was a careful man and the weather hot) the *contadino* would come to the casks, pour some wine into a jug from a small barrel, and then climb the short ladder and remove the bung from the cask to see if the level of wine had dropped because of seepage between the staves. He would then top up the wine from the jug and then replace the bung. Air getting at wine could turn it all to vinegar . . .

Topping up was usually done in the evening and the wine left in the jug disappeared down the owner's throat. The heavy drinkers, besotted men who every day stumbled through their work in a drunken daze, cursing their wives and cuffing their children, kicking their donkeys, topped up their casks first thing in the morning. The leavings in the jug (which was often topped up in its turn) was their breakfast.

The door of the last cave on the right of the road swung back and a protesting donkey lurched out, its wooden saddle empty, and turned up the hill towards the gates. The owner, with black hat awry and wearing a faded blue woollen shirt with black trousers tied just below the knee, staggered after it, not seeing the marching column, and seized its tail, whacking it with a stick in his left hand and screaming a stream of blasphemy. The donkey plodded up the hill, apparently oblivious to the stick and ignoring the curses, dragging its master behind.

"That's what you call getting a lift to windward," Ramage

muttered. "I hope that tail is firmly attached."

Man and donkey proceeded up the hill thirty yards ahead of the column, and judging from the man's wavering course he was very drunk. "That's a bit of luck: we'll be able to see what the sentries at the gate do about him."

"Do about the donkey," Rossi murmured. "The man's too *spronzato* to answer questions!"

The donkey reached the gate but no uniformed man stepped from the shadows. The man was pulled through the gate and he neither looked round nor appeared likely to notice even if all the stonework suddenly fell on his head.

"Twenty-five ... twenty ... fifteen ..." Ramage counted the remaining yards to himself as they marched towards the gate. They seemed to be moving faster, although their pace did not change. In fact, time was playing its usual tricks. Ten ... five ... and then he was under the archway and in its shadow and, apart from the column, no one else moved, except that he just caught sight of the donkey as it hauled its owner round the corner into the piazza. He saw only an old man dozing in the shade on the steps of a house, a sleeping dog which had ignored the pack, two goats tied to a stone hitching post on the right ...

Through the archway ... no lounging soldiers ... and there, towering over the town, was the Orsini Palace. The family, once powerful in Tuscany, had long since gone; this palace, one of many they must have built for themselves through the centuries (or did they inherit it from the Aldobrandeschi? He recalled a mention of it), had buttressed walls. And there were the wide stone steps leading up to the entrance. The heavy wooden door was shut; no soldiers lounged. There were no sentries, no carts that the army would use, no horses. One might have expected a carriage or two; the officers of such an egalitarian army were not expected to march.

Then Ramage realized what must have happened: the hostages were not being held in the Orsini Palace. There would be enough rooms, surely, but perhaps hostages need not be so carefully guarded. A lieutenant or young post-captain might be expected to try to escape but rheumatic admirals, quirkish generals and bucolic landed gentry were unlikely to steal off across the Tuscan landscape, seeking their freedom. They were, in all fairness, equally unlikely to give their parole. There was a vast difference between not escaping and actually promising the enemy not to try.

He held up his arm and the column halted outside the palace. Yes, he had seen the scissors sign hanging over the door of the Manciano peasant's father-in-law, but the man could not have been here for some time because only one of the two *falegnami* who were his father-in-law's neighbours was still in business: the door of the other one was boarded up.

Now what? That was the splendid thing about Tuscany and the Tuscans – always expect a surprise to arrive at siesta time. Pitigliano slept just at the moment he expected to be using his wits (and those of Gilbert) to bamboozle French guards, or all of them would be fighting their way out, with the hostages. He expected to be outnumbered three or four to one. Instead, he could tell Orsini and Rossi to capture Pitigliano using only belaying pins as weapons.

Unless . . . there were several unlesses. Why should French soldiers expect there would (or could) be an attempt to rescue the hostages? It sounded too unlikely to disturb the siesta of the most nervous of Frenchmen, be he a private soldier or one of the Emperor's best generals. After all, *mon ami*, Tuscany sleeps through the siesta, and the nearest Englishman is probably having his afternoon nap in Gibraltar.

So, Ramage admitted, there was nothing very surprising about the lack of French soldiers. The great doorway of the Orsini Palace with its enormous lock was shut, but that could just be for the siesta: after all, a locked door kept someone inside just as securely as it kept a stranger out. Lock the door and sleep off a heavy meal. A sergeant's guard inside a palace with walls this high and this thick and such a door would be enough to keep the hostages under control. A summer's day in Pitigliano was the most peaceful thing he could think of, so either the French had shut the palace door or they were in another part of the town. Or perhaps they had moved to a house outside the town. Somewhere cooler?

There was only one way to find out. He beckoned to Gilbert and together they mounted the steps. Ramage drew his sword and used the hilt to bang on the door. The thuds echoed, but no one gave an answering shout. Ramage banged again. A woman came to an upper window of a house opposite, ostensibly to take in some bedding which was airing. Ramage waved to her and pointed at the door.

"It's empty," she shouted back, her voice shrill and nervous. "The French left several weeks ago."

And who the devil would know where they had gone? The mayor? If the French really had left Pitigliano for good, the senior person left would be the mayor.

"Where is the mayor?"

"At home having his siesta."

"Which is his house?" Ramage asked, trying to keep a grip on his patience.

"This one. I am his wife."

"Please ask him to come down here."

"He is asleep."

"Three minutes," Ramage snarled. "Then I send some of my men to fetch him!"

The woman vanished and Ramage and Gilbert walked over to the house. In less than three minutes the front door suddenly burst open and a dishevelled and still sleepy man hurried out, saw Ramage and stopped suddenly, obviously expecting to find him at the door of the Orsini Palace.

The man bowed and introduced himself, his voice and manner polite but neutral. "Can I help you, sir?" he said in Italian.

"The French troops over there," Ramage gestured towards the palace, "do you know where they have gone?"

"They left – well, almost a month ago."

"Where have they gone?" Ramage repeated.

"I am not authorized to say, sir," the mayor said. "You must understand that such information is secret, and if I . . ."

"I quite understand," Ramage said. "But look over there – you see those scoundrels with irons on their arms? They are more *Inglesi* to join the others. If I can't find the rest of them – the ones who were held in the Palace – I'll have to billet them here. Some in your house."

"*Accidente*," the mayor sighed. He was stocky, bald and his face was sun-tanned. His hands were large and calloused. His face was open, his eyes met Ramage's squarely. An honest mayor doing the best he could for his little town, but like grain in a mill, caught between the upper grindstone of the French with their new laws and demands and the lower of his loyalty and duty to his own people.

"Do you have orders which I could see, to assure myself?"

"Of course, but they're in French." He spoke in fast French to Gilbert, who pulled folded papers from a pocket and, opening them, offered them to the mayor, who examined the crest and the name of the ministry. "I don't speak French," the mayor said helplessly. "You must understand, Major, that I am afraid I shall be shot if I reveal anything to you."

The man's wife suddenly came through the door and stood beside him, arms akimbo and brown eyes glaring at Ramage. "It's all right for you," she said sharply, "You make a mistake and your colonel shouts at you. My husband makes a mistake, and the colonel shoots him. Down there –" she gestured to where the road from the town made its sharp turn, "– on the day of *Ognissanti*, they shot three of our men. On All Saints' Day: three *paesani*. Why? I'll tell you why. They accused them of helping an *Inglese* to escape. How did the French know? Because they knew the three local men left the town after midnight, and soon after they could not find the *Inglese*.

"The men must have helped the *Inglese*, the French said, so the three men – two of them my husband's cousins – were shot at once when they came back at dawn. You might ask how the French knew the *Inglese* had escaped? Because he did not attend the evening roll call.

"Later they discovered why. They found him dead in his bed. He was a sick old man who had a separate room and who had died alone. That was why he did not attend the roll call. And us? You might well ask. We were left to bury our dead. I tell you, Major, and I say it without fear: the *commandante* responsible for those *Inglesi* prisoners was a wicked man. An assassin!"

"Be quiet, Anna you've said more than enough!" her husband said, pushing her back towards the front door. He had not attempted to stop the woman, Ramage noticed until she had completed her account. Yes, people of Pitigliano obviously had little reason to trust or help the French.

"Be sensible," Ramage snapped. "The moment I know where

86

the rest of the *Inglesi* prisoners are being kept, I shall march my company out of Pitigliano and you'll never see us again."

The mayor thought for a moment and his wife, who was listening just inside the door, called: "Tell him, Alfredo. Anything to make them leave us alone!"

"Orbetello," the mayor blurted, as though he could not withstand the agonizing pressure of thumbscrews any longer. "Orbetello first, but I think only to stay there for a day or two. Then I think – but this is just a guess – they were going to take them on a long journey."

"Thank you," Ramage said, and held out his hand, which the startled mayor shook.

"You understand my position?" the mayor muttered.

"Perfectly. You've told me all I need to know. I bid you farewell. My respects to your wife."

Within five minutes Ramage was leading his column down the steep hill out of Pitigliano, explaining to Hill on one side and Aitken on the other, what the mayor had told him. Paolo, marching just behind, said: "That explains that strange look the *contadino* on the road to Manciano gave us. You remember, sir, you asked him if there were French troops in Manciano, and then – implying we were going to Orvieto – if there were any in Pitigliano. He must have seen the Pitigliano garrison marching the prisoners to Orbetello . . ."

"Do we go there and look?" Aitken asked.

"The mayor said he thought they would only stay there a few days before starting on a long journey," Ramage said. "I suppose we have to follow – if we can."

"*Mamma mia*," Rossi muttered, "more marching. I worry about the Marine whose boots I'm wearing. How do I explain I wore them out?"

As Ramage marched he thought first of the Admiralty orders, then of the hostages. Why were the French moving them? Taking them to more comfortable quarters, or to a place where they would be more secure? He had only guessed that the French were satisfied with the security of Pitigliano. Yes . . . there might even be yet another prison where important prisoners were being kept as hostages, and the French were now collecting them all together. But where? And why?

Chapter Nine

As the column passed through Manciano on the last leg of its journey back to the coast, it seemed to Ramage that he had spent his life marching, and coughing as white dust swirled up from the track like fog and made his throat raw.

Orbetello was a walled town, and the Via Aurelia on its way to Rome passed just to the east. A town with a big jail – he, Jackson, Stafford and Paolo had become familiar with the piazza at the time they attacked Port' Ercole with the bomb ketches. Yes, Orbetello could provide temporary lodging for hostages and their guards if they were on their way to Rome. Or perhaps not so far – Tarquinia, maybe, which was just short of halfway to Rome. And the port of Civitavecchia was less than halfway between there and Rome. But why go all that way to find a port when within ten miles of Orbetello there was Santo Stefano at one end of Argentario and Port' Ercole at the other? It made no sense, and Ramage realized that he was not thinking clearly, as though the thudding of his heels on the hard track was numbing his brain.

As if understanding his problem, Paolo said: "Why Orbetello, do you suppose, sir? I can understand the French using the town jail to punish people, but it's a bad place to keep important hostages. They're likely to die of prison fever. I should have thought that Pitigliano and the Orsini Palace were just right."

As they marched along the track the setting sun was ahead of them, glaring in their eyes. Now Paolo had rounded it all off. Why Orbetello? It was convenient for Santo Stefano or Port' Ercole, and that was that. Ports meant ships.

Except . . . yes, except that Santo Stefano had the large Fortezza di Filippo Secundo. That would be a good place to lodge hostages. And Port' Ercole had at least two suitable fortresses. But . . . the more Ramage considered the merits of either place the more the "but" intruded. Two of them, in fact. The first was, "But why move them from Pitigliano?" and the other, "But why Orbetello?"

Paolo said: "Perhaps they wait in Orbetello until a ship arrives at Port' Ercole or Santo Stefano."

"I've thought of that," said Ramage, "but to take them where? If the French wanted them up in the north they'd make them march – they probably haven't enough ships to spare to carry them to Genoa by sea. Or down to Civitavecchia, come to that. There'd be no point in taking them to Corsica or Sardinia: the bandits and guerrillas make enough trouble already."

"The islands off the coast?" Paolo ventured.

Ramage shrugged his shoulders. "If it was Elba, the French would have marched them north to Piombino, not Orbetello, and put 'em on board the ferry. Giglio? That's possible and only a few hours' sail from Santo Stefano. A small, mountainous island, small harbour, at least one fort . . . but enough room to house the hostages and their guards? Vulnerable, too: don't forget the Barbary pirates still raid such places, and I don't think the Emperor would be very pleased if his valuable hostages became galley slaves.

"That leaves Montecristo – yes, possible: sticks up out of the sea like a back tooth, just like Pitigliano in the valley. Then Pianosa and Capraia to the north. All vulnerable to pirates."

He shrugged his shoulders again as he marched. "Who the devil knows: we're looking for logical moves, but generals and admirals and emperors are usually more quirkish than logical. Damn and blast this sun; the glare makes my head ache."

"We're not due back at the beach to meet the *Calypso*'s boats until tomorrow night, sir," Paolo reminded him.

Which meant, of course, that now they were clear of Manciano they could stop and, after a meal from the provisions he had commandeered in the town, rest, starting again tomorrow when they had the whole day for the march. It would be wiser to halt well this side of the Via Aurelia, crossing it and getting to the river mouth only an hour or so before the *Calypso*'s boats arrived. Providing the *Calypso* had not been trapped and sunk or captured by a couple of French frigates which happened to be passing . . . I'm very tired, he told himself; as soon as it is dark the ghost of Hamlet's father will appear from among the dark green cypress to tell me ever sadder stories of death and duplicity.

He took a few quick paces to get ahead of the column, turned to face it, and held up his hand. As soon as the men halted he pointed to the row of cypress just back from the road and told the men to fall out for the night.

While Jackson and Stafford and Rossi issued the rations, Ramage sat with his back to a tree, Aitken, Hill Rennick and Orsini sitting in a half-circle round him.

"Before we start, sir, I'd like to ask Orsini a question."

Ramage nodded to Aitken, and Paolo looked startled.

"That Orsini Palace in Pitigliano – is that your family?"

"A distant branch of it," Paolo said just as Ramage realized that he had not connected Paolo with the palace.

"So you won't inherit it," Aitken commented.

Paolo looked embarrassed. "Well, it's not quite the same as England – or Scotland," he added tactfully. "The big English and Scottish families usually own single castles, and estates, which pass from eldest son to eldest son. Here in Italy we do not have primogeniture; the eldest son has no more (and no fewer) rights than his brothers. If – I take an imaginary example – the Count of Orbetello has three sons, then all three are counts, and so are each of their three sons. When the father dies his estate is divided into three, and so on when each of the sons die. In two generations it will have been divided twelve times – three times, and then three times for each of their sons.

"So the Palazzo degli Orsini in Pitigliano has not been passed from eldest son to eldest son. Quite apart from primogeniture, the Orsini family is large and owns many palaces (what in England would be called large country houses), and when the head of a particular branch of the family dies, his property is divided among many people."

Aitken asked bluntly: "How does this affect you not having a claim on that place in Pitigliano?"

Ramage realized that the real explanation was embarrassing Paolo, who was afraid that Aitken and Hill would think he was boasting. "What Orsini hasn't told you is that he's the present head of the Orsini family. He might well be the ruler of Volterra, if his aunt – the Marchesa, whom you know, Aitken – is dead. The Palazzo degli Orsini in Pitigliano probably belongs to a distant cousin who fled when the French came."

Aitken's curiosity was aroused and both Ramage and Orsini realized that the *Calypso*'s first lieutenant was genuinely interested, not prying.

"So if – if anything has happened to the Marchesa and you are now the ruler of Volterra, where – what, rather – is your home?"

"The palace in Volterra. Or would be if the French had not occupied Volterra, along with the Kingdom of Tuscany."

"So you own a lot of land," Aitken commented.

"My aunt does – or did. If she is dead I inherit a kingdom. But to no purpose: at the moment everything I own is stowed in my trunk in the midshipman's berth on board the *Calypso*."

Aitken nodded and said quietly: "I'd never thought about this very much. We're really marching across your land."

"Not quite that," Paolo said hastily. "All this area belongs to the Grand Duke of Tuscany. Or did. Who knows what Bonaparte has done now he calls it the Kingdom of Etruria."

"But it's as though we were marching across the hills of Perthshire," Aitken said. "I come from near Perth," he added. "Aye, laddie, you carry a heavier weight on your shoulders than I realized."

The youth shrugged. "If I'd stayed, the French would probably have shot me – or at least let me rot in some prison. By escaping I can at least –" he gave a dry laugh, "– pay occasional visits."

"Aye, this'll be your second that I've been on. Port' Ercole's not that far away."

"But out of range of a bomb ketch," Orsini said, and moved over as Jackson came up with food and the flasks that were full of water when the Marines used them, but now contained wine.

That night Ramage slept fitfully: mosquitoes seemed to

whine past him in line ahead, and from nearby a nightjar kept up its drearily monotonous "quark . . . quark . . . ." Occasionally a nightingale began singing and Ramage found himself wakening fully so that he could listen to its song. One of the few drawbacks of life at sea was that apart from the mewing of gulls when they were close to land, the sea was barren of birdsong.

For too many nights now waking meant only lying and thinking about Sarah. He recognized that the worst part was the uncertainty. If he knew for sure that the *Murex* had been sunk in a gale or by the French, he could mourn her. She would be dead and (the thought seemed harsh but was not) that would be that, because she could not still be suffering in any way. But because she might have been captured (perhaps by privateers) anything could have happened. He forced himself to think about it, even though it made him shudder. If by privateers, they could have raped her and now be waiting for a chance to ransom her. If captured by a French national ship, she would be a prisoner and, given that Bonaparte appeared to be collecting the important and the famous as hostages, she might be a closely guarded prisoner in Paris.

Yet . . . yet . . . there was no point in having hostages unless your enemy knew about them. Their value was that the enemy knew you had them and that something unpleasant would happen to them unless he did whatever was demanded as the price of their lives or liberty.

Dead or a prisoner? And the same went for Gianna: assassinated or a prisoner? Yes, he thought bitterly, fear is not knowing, and he thought he would never sleep, but eventually he did, wakened as dawn broke by Jackson's insistent, "Sir . . . sir."

Another day . . . another march . . . more decisions . . . hell fire and damnation, he was more tired than he realized. He wanted to sleep, free of those nightmares which were not nightmares because he was still awake.

Jackson passed him his boots and then waited to see if there were any orders. Ramage shook his head. His mind had never been so empty of ideas or, for that matter, so hostile to them. Ideas meant action, and every bone in his body seemed bruised from marching and sleeping on the hard ground, every muscle stretched beyond its limits.

92

There was a smell of burning and he glanced round to see that the men had lit a small bonfire and over it swung a pot suspended from a tripod of three tree branches.

Sailors always wanted something hot to drink for breakfast, and the fact that they were in the lee of a row of cypress on the road from Manciano to the sea apparently made no difference. Well, to the onlooker it was natural enough: soldiers were always lighting fires to cook their food . . .

An hour later the column was marching westwards: for once the sun was cool and at their backs, and by noon they expected to be resting in the shade of the cypress only a mile short of the Via Aurelia, free to swim in the Albinia river. Wash in it, any-way, as long as oxen had not been sloshing about upstream. Ramage rubbed his chin, the bristles rasping. Within the first hour he was back on board the *Calypso*, he vowed, he would shave . . .

They had just come in sight of the cypress grove when Rossi laughed and pointed ahead. Coming towards them in the distance was a donkey, and on its back the same hunched figure they had first seen going the other way.

"He's sold his own wine," Orsini said, "and from the look of it he spent some of the money sampling the wine of Orbetello."

"Let's hope he's sober enough to talk sense," Ramage growled, "otherwise you can dip him in the river a few times. Though come to think of it, that won't put him in the right frame of mind to help us!"

The man turned out to be tired, not drunk, but he was extremely nervous, though there seemed to be no obvious reason. Ramage gestured to his men to fall out and rest along the side of the track, and then, with Orsini and Rossi, squatted down on the ground, offering the man some wine from a flask. He shook his head.

"You sold your wine for a good price?"

"Yes," he said abruptly, as though he did not want to discuss it.

"Is Orbetello crowded?" Ramage asked casually.

"No more than usual."

"You stayed longer than you expected?"

"Yes," the man said and rubbed his head as though trying to

erase an unpleasant memory. "*Mamma mia*, when my wife hears . . ."

"What happened?" Rossi asked sympathetically, responding at once to Ramage's wink.

"Gambling," the man muttered. "I can't resist it. I used the wine money."

"But you won!" Rossi said jovially.

"Yes – to begin with. The first night I doubled it."

"Why are you so miserable, then?"

"You know *scopa*. I lost nearly all of it the next night. *Scopa* . . . *Mamma mia*, they swept me up." The man still had a sense of humour. *Scopa*, the name of a card game, also meant broom.

"Anyway, you still have some *soldi* left, so cheer up!"

Again the man shook his head. "I felt so badly – I knew my wife would be angry. Miserable, I was, and so I started drinking . . ."

"And that's where the rest of the money went," Rossi commented.

"No, only some of it. But I drank so much I went to sleep in the road outside the *taverna*, and when I woke up . . ."

"Your pockets were empty."

"Yes, some thieving *stronzo* . . ."

Rossi looked at the man and rubbed the side of his nose with a forefinger. "Perhaps your wife would not be so angry if she thought that *ladrone* stole *all* the wine money."

The man thought for a few moments and then shook his head. "No, I've been away too long for that. If I had come back the next day with that story it would have been all right, but I stayed longer . . . she knows."

"Not the first time, eh?" Ramage said understandingly. "Is this why your father-in-law speaks so badly of you?"

"You know about that, then?"

"At Pitigliano, at the sign of the scissors? Yes, of course. By the way, one of those *falegnami* has closed."

"I'm not surprised," the man said, shaking his head. "The one on the gate side? Yes, well, he drinks, you know."

And now, Ramage thought, we are all friends together. Time to ask some more questions without arousing the man's sus-

94

picions. "You didn't play *scopa* with any of the French soldiers, then?"

The man looked up at him, his eyes bloodshot and squinting as though the light was too bright. "The French soldiers went two weeks ago. The ones that came from Pitigliano, that is. The usual garrison is still there, but they don't play *scopa*. Some French game they have, with different cards from ours."

"So the taverns are quieter now," Ramage commented. "Where have the French taken their money to now, I wonder?"

The man looked directly at Ramage. "*Signore*, I don't know what you are doing, but if you are on the side of the French, surely you would know the answers to all these questions?"

"The Army of Italy is a big one," Ramage said vaguely. "Orders go astray, mistakes are made . . ."

"*Permesso*?" Rossi asked.

Ramage nodded, giving the Genovese permission to say what he wanted. Rossi understood people instinctively; he had a knack probably learned in the stews of Genoa, and it was a knack which would still work in the open fields of Tuscany.

"*Amico mio*," he said, "I think you have guessed."

"I never make guesses, I'm always wrong. And just now –" he looked at the pistols tucked in Ramage's belt, "– making guesses could be dangerous."

"All right, don't guess," Rossi said. "All we ask is that you answer our questions if you wish, but if you want to remain silent, then please don't betray us the minute you get to Manciano."

"You mean I *could* betray you? That you are not with the French? What about those men?" He gestured to where Gilbert was sitting.

"Yes, you could betray us, and they are not French. They are simply dressed in French uniforms."

The man turned from Rossi and looked directly at Ramage, paused a moment as though reassessing him, and then said: "You are the leader, eh?"

Ramage nodded.

"You are Italian?"

Ramage shook his head. "I was not born an Italian, but these two were."

"*That* I can tell. Once a Genovese always a Genovese. And the youngster, he is Tuscan. *Allora*, I help you. You have my word. Not," he added, "that that means much to you, but I am known as an honest man."

"Yes," Ramage said, "I see that. We are looking for the French soldiers who were in Pitigliano."

"The French soldiers or the *Inglesi* prisoners?"

"If they are still together, does it matter?"

The man grinned and shook his head. "Two weeks ago – I know the date because I had to go to Orbetello to do some shopping – the French took their hostages to Santo Stefano. As I rode back along the road (along the Via Aurelia, before taking this turning) I saw a French ship sailing into the port. I think it took them all away."

"You don't know the destination?"

The man shrugged his shoulders. "No. It was not a big ship, but there are many places. Giglio, Elba, Montecristo . . . Even Corsica or Sardinia."

"Thank you," Ramage said. "I know you have told us this because we are *paesani*, but I wish we could help you with *soldi*, so that your wife is not so angry, but unfortunately we have neither French nor local money in our pockets."

"I guessed that," the man said, "and I would not have accepted it anyway. I am not a soldier or –" he winked at Ramage, "– a sailor, but I am a *proprio Toscano*, even if my father-in-law says bad things about me. Tell me, did all go well in Pitigliano?"

"Quiet. The few people we saw helped us. We were there only a few minutes."

The peasant nodded. "When I first met you, I wondered but dare not risk saying anything. Even now, you could shoot me, saying I am a traitor."

Ramage pulled one of the pistols from his belt, flicked open the pan so the man could see the powder, and shut it again. Then he cocked the gun and gave it butt-first to the man. "If you think you are going to be shot, you can take me with you."

The man handed back the gun. "*Grazie, signore*, but let us both try to stay alive – me to face my wife, you to find the prisoners . . ."

Chapter
Ten

Back on board the *Calypso*, once more dressed in breeches and stockings, shirt, stock and uniform coat, Ramage again reflected wryly that as far as he was concerned the one benefit brought about by the French Revolution was substituting trousers for kneebreeches.

The *sans culotte*, the "without breeches", could kneel or sit in comfort. Breeches were one of the most uncomfortable, confining garments yet devised for men, and the revolutionaries were sensible to dispose of them, thus ensuring a liberty not envisaged in their windy rhetoric. And, from what he and Sarah had seen during their honeymoon, French women had achieved a similar freedom in refusing to wear corsets. However, this often gave men an unfair advantage: a fellow with skinny shanks or bow legs looked much better in trousers: the tubes of cloth hid the defects. Women in abandoning corsets all too often looked – well, abandoned! Those lucky enough to have slim figures looked very beautiful in the new Grecian style now popular, but the plump women looked like barrels draped in sheets of muslin.

Looking around his cabin at Aitken, Southwick and Hill, all of whom were watching him attentively, waiting to hear his plan for their next move in finding the missing hostages, he wondered what their reaction would be if they knew he had been thinking of *sans culottes*, and how he hated having to wear breeches, and how plump Frenchwomen fared badly in the Revolution.

"They might be kept prisoner in Santo Stefano despite what

our gambling friend said," he commented, "but I doubt it. The Fortezza is the only place big enough to hold them and the guards – and the obvious question to ask ourselves is: 'Why there?' The Orsini Palace in Pitigliano is large, much more comfortable and in every way more suitable. This makes me certain that Santo Stefano was being used simply as a port and that by now a ship has called and taken them somewhere else."

"Dare we risk sailing off to look for them somewhere else when they might still be at the Fortezza, sir?" Southwick asked, adding one of his you-might-be-mistaken sniffs.

Ramage recognized the sniff and smiled. "No, we daren't: I was just coming to that. Because I know Santo Stefano quite well, the cutter will land me tonight on a stretch of beach about a mile east of the port and I'll go in and find out."

"Sir!" Aitken exclaimed. "Surely that's too big a risk compared with what we could possibly gain. Rossi could easily find out. Or young Orsini – it's just the sort of job he'd be good at."

"You'd sooner risk the probable ruler of Volterra than me?"

"Most certainly, sir," Aitken said flatly. "We've Admiralty orders to carry out, and losing you means risking that we can't complete them. It's unfortunate that Orsini might have inherited Volterra at this particular time, but he's simply a midshipman in the King's service. And," he added as an afterthought, "we've never worried before about risking his life."

That was true enough and Ramage imagined Orsini's reaction if he thought he was deliberately being kept out of danger. "Very well, we'll send him in tonight with Rossi."

"May I command the cutter, sir?" Hill asked quickly. "I've a lot to learn about this sort of work. I'm afraid being a lieutenant on board the *Salvador del Mundo* didn't help much."

"Made you a very good escort for accused officers," Ramage said teasingly.

Hill sighed and then grinned: "With respect, sir, your court-martial changed my life. If I hadn't been your escort and asked if I could serve with you, I'd still be in Plymouth Sound chasing after the admiral and worrying that my stock wasn't properly ironed."

"You're more likely to reach a ripe old age serving in a

guardship, waiting on an admiral, than serving as the second lieutenant in a frigate," Ramage said ironically.

Hill shook his head. "No sir, guardships are *much* more dangerous than frigates."

Ramage raised a questioning eyebrow.

"Yes, sir: every day in a guardship you risk dying of boredom!"

"At least that's painless," Ramage said. "Now, tell the sentry to pass the word for Orsini and Rossi. In the meantime, Hill, let's look at our rough chart of Santo Stefano: I'll show you where the beach is. You have to land there because there are rocks and cliffs everywhere else."

"Jackson, sir," Southwick said.

Ramage stared blankly, then realized what the old master meant. "He'd never have forgiven me!"

When Aitken looked puzzled, Ramage explained. "Some years ago, when we were rescuing Orsini's aunt, Jackson and I had to walk round Santo Stefano without anyone realizing who we were. You'd better take Jackson in the cutter – he'll be able to point out various landmarks to Orsini and Rossi, though there's no need for him to land." He looked round at Hill. "Pass the word for Jackson as well."

When Orsini and the two seamen arrived, Ramage explained what they were to do. When he had finished, Orsini asked: "What arms do we carry?"

Ramage shook his head. "None. As I've just explained, the pair of you are supposed to be from Lucca: you spend half the year traipsing round Tuscany, just pruning olive trees. That story will be convincing to the French provided your clothes are ragged enough, your hands grimy enough, and your pruning knife sharp enough. And you have a sharpening stone tucked in your belt, too."

"We're out of pruning knives, sir," Southwick said ironically. "A few handstones, yes; pruning knives no. You didn't tell me about the olive trees when were were commissioning . . ."

"Do you know what a pruning knife for olive trees looks like?"

"Well, no, sir. I suppose it's a short knife with a curved end."

"That's for pruning grape vines, and disembowelling rabbits;

99

it'd take you a month to prune an olive tree with a small blade like that. No, you need something like a short cutlass, or the machete they use in the West Indies for cutting sugarcane."

"We're out of them, too," Southwick said lugubriously. "You didn't mention sugarcane, either."

Ramage sighed, as though despairing. "I need a new master for this ship. A young man with imagination."

"Maybe," grunted Southwick, "but all that's the gunner's job." With that Southwick knew he had played a trump card, because the *Calypso*'s gunner was a useless man who fled to his cabin rather than accept responsibility for anything. Because he was appointed by the Board of Ordnance (which was controlled by the Army), it was almost impossible to replace him, so Ramage simply ignored him.

Ramage, remembering it was early in the season for pruning but guessing that French soldiers would not know that, looked up at the deckhead, as though thinking. "Ah yes. That two-handed sword of yours. We could put that on the grindstone and grind it down to half its length, and then shape it up."

In a moment Southwick was on his feet, remembering just in time to duck so that he did not bang his head. "Sir! You can't be . . ." His voice tapered off as he realized the other officers were laughing. He had made the rare mistake of taking Ramage seriously when he made a straight-faced joke. To recover himself he said: "But of course, for the King's service I'd be willing to sacrifice it."

"Good, thanks: that settles it," Ramage said. "Rossi can have that. Now Orsini, your midshipman's dirk is about the right length."

"It will be fine, sir," Orsini assured him. "Wrapped in a greasy cloth, it'll look just right."

By now Southwick had sat down again and was scratching his head. "I'm sure we could find something like Mr Orsini's dirk . . . the cook must have a big knife. The butcher, too."

"But they need them so that we can eat," Ramage said. "No, don't bother your head: your sword will do, and you might get the men to hoist the grindstone up on deck: I expect most of the cutlasses need sharpening as well."

"If you say so, sir," Southwick said, knowing he was beaten.

He had owned the sword for many years; it was the only one he had ever found that had just the right balance. "If you'll excuse me, I'll see to the grindstone now."

Ramage nodded, and Southwick made for the door. Just as he was going through, Ramage said: "Oh, Southwick. It'll take hours of grinding to shorten your sword. Have some men grind down a cutlass to a couple of feet, and round up the point."

The master grinned: it was not often the captain caught him twice . . .

"We'll go up on deck and survey Argentario's beaches with the glass, and it'd be a good idea," Ramage said to Hill, Orsini, Rossi and Jackson, "if you get those little headlands fixed in your memory."

For the next half an hour the five men passed the telescope between them. Ramage found the names came back easily. From where the northern causeway joined Argentario, as the telescope swung to the right towards Santo Stefano, there was the Torre Santa Liberata at the end of a small headland; then still going westward the land cut back into a small bay next to a larger one, Cala del Pozzarello, with Torre Calvello guarding it. Then came three small headlands, the last of which was Punta Nera, and then the land sloped sharply down into Santo Stefano itself.

The little port was scooped out of the hills, with several fishing boats hauled up on the only stretch of beach, and looking down on it was the bulky, four-square and curiously dignified Fortezza di Filippo Secundo. And then, at the western end of Argentario (or as far west as they could see from the *Calypso*), was Punta Lividonia.

Ramage let his memory take over. Just round that headland, the third or fourth bay to the south, was Cala Grande. Some years ago he and Jackson and a few men in an open boat had rowed into there from the Torre di Buranaccio on the mainland with Gianna, badly wounded, a pistol or musket ball still lodged in her. They had put into Cala Grande in the darkness and he and Jackson had climbed up the cliffs and over the hills to Santo Stefano, looking for a doctor to kidnap and take down to the beach . . . Was that doctor, who had in fact proved

101

to be a loyal Italian, still alive and living in his house just by the Fortezza? What was it called – ah yes, the *Casa di Leone*. Yes, that plump little doctor had a lion's heart; his house was aptly named.

Ramage caught Jackson's eye. The American seaman had guessed where his thoughts were. "That doctor, sir. *Casa di Leone*, wasn't it?"

Ramage nodded. But it was all years ago. Gianna had recovered, spent years in England, and then left for Volterra at the signing of that wretched peace treaty. Now her nephew was going back to Argentario – like Ramage and Jackson he would be disguised. It was curious how Argentario played such a frequent part in all their lives.

The cutter's stem grated as it nosed up on the sand and Rossi jumped over the bow, boots and cutlass in hand. He turned to make sure that Paolo Orsini did not slip as he too jumped. The two of them, after putting their gear higher up the beach out of reach of the wavelets, returned and helped shove off the cutter. The arrangement was simple: the cutter would stay a hundred yards off the beach, out of sight in the darkness, until Hill heard a nightjar call four times, pause and then call again. Paolo was very proud of his imitation of a nightjar, a trick he had learned as a boy in Volterra, where a nightjar regularly hooted from a tree below his bedroom window.

After the boat, oars muffled, disappeared into the night, the two men sat down on long strands of *fico dei ottentotti*, which grew flat, spreading like a thick net over the sand and in places as deep as a mattress.

"You've got your cutlass?" Orsini asked.

Rossi held up a canvas roll. "All ready, sir."

Rossi was a proud man. He knew he had been singled out by Captain Ramage from some two hundred men on board the *Calypso* and that his orders were to go into Santo Stefano and find out, *at whatever cost*, if the hostages were in the Fortezza or had been taken away by sea. *At whatever cost*: Rossi liked the phrase and rolled it over in his mind again. English was a good language for being exact. Not like French, for instance. No wonder (judging from what Gilbert and his mates said) that

French was the language of diplomacy. It seemed to Rossi that in French you could make a violent speech lasting an hour and, even though it was full of bold words and fine phrases, at the end of it you could have promised nothing nor announced anything that mattered, yet leave your audience impressed and inspired. Perhaps that was how the seeds of revolution were sown.

Italian was different. Yes, you could also make long-winded speeches full of fine words, but your listeners would soon spot that although you were throwing up a lot of spray, you were not making a yard to windward. With English you could distinguish the "blow-hard" (another splendid English phrase!) even quicker. That was why elections in England were often violent: the candidate might blow hard for five minutes, but the moment the crowd became bored, the eggs and rocks and jeers flew thick and fast.

Half an hour before the pair of them left the ship Mr Ramage had spoken to them alone in his cabin. A wise man, he was, and a tactful one too. There was Mr Orsini, a midshipman and the head of one of the great families in Italy, and there was ordinary seaman Rossi, late of Genova, about whom no one on board the *Calypso* knew much, except for Mr Ramage.

Rossi had told him something of his past and Mr Ramage must have guessed the rest. Anyway, Mr Ramage made it clear that Rossi was going because he would not hesitate to slit a throat, and Mr Orsini was going to help Rossi if he needed a lookout, or something like that. Well, Rossi thought, if they succeeded, ordinary seaman Rossi got all the credit; if they failed – well, Midshipman Orsini was in charge and took the blame. This seemed a very fair arrangement to Rossi because, apart from being killed, he could not lose.

Rossi felt a moment's guilt as they reached the track at the back of the beach and turned right towards Santo Stefano, almost immediately finding it became steep as it wended over the small headland marking the western end of the bay. Yes, he did feel rather guilty about the chance of Mr Orsini getting holystoned if they failed because he was one of the nicest people on board the *Calypso*, officer, warrant officer, petty officer or seaman. He loved going into action (with that damned silly

103

dirk of his, which had too short a blade to keep trouble at a respectable distance); he was curious about everything connected with seamanship. Thoughtful about the men, too: as soon as he saw a rain squall in the distance when he was on watch, for example, he sent the men below for their oilskins. He was the only officer who regularly said "please" except for Mr Ramage, and if you were the captain you could afford to say please.

"This catches the muscles in your shins, doesn't it?" Orsini commented, beginning to puff.

"We need a *somaro*, so we could hold its tail," Rossi said. "My feet have never worked so hard as this last week. Sixty English miles to Pitigliano and back, I heard Mr Aitken say."

"Yes, sixty. The last time I walked so far – that was a long time ago . . ."

"When you escaped from Volterra, sir?"

"Yes. Most of it at night, like now. I fell into so many ditches that I must have swum a quarter of the way."

"What Mr Ramage said about cutting throats," Rossi said conversationally, "he meant it, and you leave it to me."

"I know. He thinks I couldn't cut a throat in cold blood, but he knows you could."

"Something like that," Rossi said tactfully.

"He's wrong though. I could cut a Frenchman's throat in cold blood just as easily as in action when we board a French ship. You see, I hate them. Mr Ramage and the other officers don't really *hate* the French: their job is to fight the enemy, and the enemy today is the French, so they fight them. In ten years time it might be the Spanish, or the Austrians. I see it differently. The French have stolen Volterra from my family. They have corrupted many of the leading families, using fear or bribes. Bonaparte rules Europe from the Baltic to the Ionian Sea. His soldiers and sailors glory in it. So people who steal my land and kill my family and corrupt or imprison my people – well, just line up the throats."

Rossi stopped and turned to Orsini in the darkness. "Listen sir, I could have told Mr Ramage that. Being Italian as well, I can guess how you feel. But it's very hard for the English to understand because their country has never been occupied by an enemy. At least, not for hundreds of years. But believe me, even though I'm sure you can cut a throat in cold blood, don't be in a hurry to do it. The first time – well, afterwards you have nightmares. The second and third times aren't much better. So leave it to me. I can sleep soundly when it's over."

"Thank you," Orsini said. "I *could* do it, but that isn't to say I want to."

The two men walked along the track as it twisted over two more headlands which formed small, rock-strewn bays, and as they began climbing another steeper hill Orsini said: "I think this is Punta Nera: from the top we should see Santo Stefano."

Five minutes later, breathless, they looked down on Santo Stefano: a large bay and a smaller beyond it and the Fortezza above in the hills, keeping guard over both of them. Houses lined the big bay and Orsini could see fishing boats hauled up on the beach, and what must be nets drying on frames. Yes, just as it looked from seaward in daylight: a small fishing port surrounded by hills and guarded by (unless one knew the part Aragon and Spain itself had played in Tuscan history) a fortress which seemed larger than necessary.

"*Andiamo*," Rossi said, but Orsini held his arm for a moment.

"Can you see the *Calypso*?"

The two men stared into the darkness. They knew where she was anchored, and finally Rossi said: "I think there's a darker patch. Look, can you make out Talamone in the distance? Well, in line with Monte dell' Uccellina behind it and halfway to Talamone – the dark –"

"I see it," Orsini said. "A long way to swim."

Rossi shivered. "Don't even joke about it, sir."

The hill running steeply down into Santo Stefano was long and deeply rutted where sudden rainstorms had washed away the thin layer of red earth to lay bare the rock beneath. At times the track twisted like a snake to show where donkeys and their owners scrambled from one side to the other, as though each rock was a stepping stone, but even in the darkness both men could see that some of the exposed stone was vertical, miniature precipices only a few inches high but enough to cause a fall, to break a limb of donkey or man.

105

"No need for us to be quiet," Orsini said, "so we can curse as much as we like. Do you know any choice Lucchesi curses?"

"I don't care how they curse in Lucca," Rossi said, tripping as he spoke, "but I know what they say in Genova and Volterra and it means the same as I'm saying now!"

Slowly they worked their way down the hill and in the darkness it seemed to Orsini that the little town of Santo Stefano was slowly rising to meet them: already the Fortezza, though still distant, was higher. In daylight a sentry on the battlements would see them clearly.

The Fortezza was their target. Mr Ramage reckoned that if there were no signs of a French garrison there, then the hostages had gone, because there was nowhere else to keep them. So it was down into the valley (which ran into the bay, and gave its name to one of the town's quarters) and up the other side, a careful look round, question someone and then back again to the cutter. Then Orsini began to have doubts: he had been at sea long enough to worry when everything appeared to be going well.

The track turned now to cross the nearer side of the town and first one and then several dogs began to bark as they passed the first few houses. A man came to a door and swore at them, his voice sleepy.

Rossi and Orsini spoke to each other in Italian, the gossiping conversation to be expected of two men arriving at night in a strange town. The track forked but a glance upwards showed which was the more likely to lead to the Fortezza.

It took them fifteen minutes to reach the open square in front of it, and Rossi muttered to Orsini: "You stay here while I have a look. The gateway is on this side."

With that the seaman disappeared silently into the blackness before Orsini had a chance to argue. Suddenly, squatting down on a large rock which, from the foot and hoof prints surrounding it and dried in the earth, was used by the peasants for mounting mules, Orsini felt tired: for most of the walk from the boat he had been excited, but now he was almost sure the town was empty of the French: if there were hostages in the Fortezza, surely there would be French soldiers on patrol, or a sentry on the track, which was the only way to Santo Stefano by land.

The shout was followed immediately by the crack of a pistol shot. For a moment he heard the noise echo and re-echo across the valley below. He had not seen a flash, but it was close and must be at the Fortezza. Should he go there – and risk missing Rossi, who would expect to find him here (assuming Rossi had not been killed)? A second pistol shot was followed by scurrying feet: one man was coming towards him. The footfalls were not regular; they were more like those of a drunken husband trying to stagger home without his wife hearing. Then Orsini heard cursing at regular intervals: not loud – but now the Genovese accent was unmistakable.

"Rossi! Over here, Rossi!"

"*Andiamo!*" Rossi said as Orsini ran towards him and led the way down the track.

"What's happened? Are the French after us?"

"Yes, but don't worry; *sono ubriachi.* The whole lot of them."

"All drunk? You're sure? How many?"

Rossi lurched and Orsini grabbed his arm to prevent him falling. "I'll explain when we get up to Punta Nera."

"Are the hostages there?"

"No . . . just a small garrison . . ."

At that moment Orsini felt a curious dampness soaking through Rossi's sleeve.

"You're wounded! Here, let me look!"

"It's nothing and it's too dark to see," Rossi said hurriedly. "Come on, we've got to get back to the cutter. The hostages aren't there: that's what matters. We'll find out where they went before we leave the town. Have you got your dirk?"

"Yes, why?"

"I'll need it. Lost my cutlass when they caught me, before that *stronzo* shot me."

Rossi was swaying on his feet. Orsini did not know whether to force the man to have a rest or hurry him back to the cutter quickly: it was a toss up either way if he was bleeding badly.

Together they stumbled down the hill and at the first house showing a light Rossi said gruffly: "Your dirk."

Orsini handed it over. "What are you going to do?"

"Wait here!" Rossi said and walked up to the doorway, ripping aside the sacking which covered it. Orsini saw him

107

point to something inside the room and hurried up to stand at the doorway.

Rossi now stood, white-faced, just inside the tiny room. A plump and bleary-eyed man sat at the table, a mug in one hand and a jug of wine in front of him. A raddled old woman sat at one end of what passed for a bed, watching Rossi with sharp but frightened eyes. A young woman was at the other end of the bed holding a baby in her arms and breast-feeding it.

With a tremendous effort the man raised his head and focused his eyes on Rossi. "Wha' did you say?"

"The French: did they have any prisoners here?"

"Don' know. Shoot me, because they would if I told you."

"I'll cut your throat if you don't," Rossi said waving the dirk, "so it looks as though your mug of wine is turning to vinegar."

"His arm is bleeding badly," the young woman said, and as if she thought the man was too drunk to notice, added: "He's a Genovese, like my cousin Umberto. He's not French."

"You seem to know everything," the man said, his voice slurred. He reached for the jug and knocked it over, the wine spreading across the table and dripping to the floor. He muttered a curse, folded his arms on the table in front of him, and pillowed his head. To Orsini it seemed he was snoring in a moment.

Rossi spoke to the young woman. "You have nothing to fear. We are Italians. All we need to know is what happened to all the English prisoners the French brought to the Fortezza."

"They were English?" The old woman asked, lisping because she was toothless. "The French are supposed to fight them but –" she cackled mirthlessly, "– but not here. All they do here, the French, is steal our wine and get drunk and chase the young women. No one is safe. My daughter here, and her nursing the baby, well, I could tell you a story –"

"Quiet mother," the young woman said, tucking one breast back into her shift and bringing out the other, and holding the baby to it. "*Segnore*, sit down here –" she touched the bed beside her. "You look as though you will faint. Get him some wine, mother. Quickly now!"

Rossi lurched forward and Orsini helped him to sit down, taking the dirk at the same time. The old woman produced another jug, picked up the mug in front of the sleeping man, wiped it with the hem of her skirt and filled it. "Drink this," she told Rossi, "although you're in no state to appreciate how good it is. We have no food until my son-in-law goes fishing tomorrow. Just some bread and goat milk cheese."

Rossi shook his head. "No, the wine is enough. It is good wine. I must apologize, ladies, for my rough appearance, but we have little time."

The young woman nodded. "Yes, we heard two shots. Were you hit twice?"

"No, the first hit me with a ricochet. The second missed."

"Shall I bandage it for you – washing in wine cleans a wound."

Rossi turned to the young woman. "It is kind of you *signora*, but the wound is of no significance. But if you could tell us . . ."

"The French arrived with their prisoners about three weeks ago – from Orbetello, I understand. Then a week later a French ship came into the port, and the prisoners and the new French soldiers went on board. The old French soldiers – the ones always at the Fortezza – stayed there. Then the ship sailed."

"Was it a big ship?"

"You can see for yourself when it gets light: she has come back. She is anchored out in the bay, halfway to Talamone."

Rossi nodded. So it had been a French frigate, and the good people of Santo Stefano thought the *Calypso* was the same ship. "Yes, I saw her out there. You are sure all the prisoners – the English, I mean – were taken away in this ship?"

"Yes. My husband was selling the French some fish to feed them. The French actually paid. My husband was sorry to see the prisoners go. We need the money," she added, as if justifying selling to the French.

"But you do not know where the French ship was taking the prisoners?"

"No. Once a ship goes round Punta Madonella, one cannot see the direction she takes."

Rossi sat for a few minutes with his head between his knees as another wave of faintness made him feel he was being drawn into a black pit.

Orsini thought of the long climb back to the beach where the cutter was to collect them. He helped Rossi to his feet. "Thank you, *signora*," he said to the old woman, and then turned to her daughter. "*Signora*, have no fear; the French will never know we have been here. Your baby –"

"My son," the woman said quickly, knowing how stupid men were in recognizing the sex of young babies.

"Ah, a son eh? Has he been named yet?"

The woman shook her head. "The priest has been very ill."

"Include 'Paolo' among his names, *signora*, for luck. And one day in the future, several years perhaps, try to find out who rules Volterra."

"You are from Volterra," the woman said quickly, "I recognize the accent. 'Paolo'," she said softly. "It is a nice name. Yours, I think."

Paolo nodded. "In better times, perhaps, I can come back and see how the boy has grown up."

The woman nodded. "Goodbye, *signore*. Look after your friend."

Paolo helped Rossi down to the port, sat him on a pile of nets and then inspected the fishing boats. By chance the smallest one was nearest the water's edge and had oars and thole pins in it. He lifted the bow and pulled, finally getting it into the water. He was just looking round for the painter when Rossi lurched up and half collapsed across the gunwale. Orsini helped him in and then scrambled after him. "More comfortable to row round to meet Mr Hill," he said. "And not a throat cut."

Rossi's arm throbbed. Mr Bowen had cleaned the wound with spirits (giving him a tot of rum first, saying with a reassuring grin that it would take the sting away) and then put in five stitches. Rossi had often heard of people "being stitched up" but had never thought much about it. Watching Mr Bowen at work with needle and thread he realized that it was just that: stitching, like mending a shot hole in a sail; holding together two flaps of skin that would otherwise gape open and slipping the needle in. Rossi had done the same sort of thing hundreds of times, only he was joining torn canvas.

Mr Bowen was thorough. As soon as Rossi had described

110

how the bullet had ricocheted off the wall before hitting him, the surgeon had wanted to know about the wall. Was it brick, stone, stucco? It was a startling question, and Rossi had been able to answer only by elimination. No, it had not been stone. Nor brick. Then he remembered noticing soot from the lamps and round the big fireplace. Yes, it was stucco, and as he thought more he remembered the cracks in it looking like veins in an old man's legs.

He had wondered why Mr Bowen was so interested, and the surgeon explained as he washed the cut with spirits: a bullet hitting stucco and then bouncing off would pick up some of the sand and *gesso* used to make the stucco and leave perhaps some of it in the wound, so it was best to clean it.

Now, with his arm held diagonally across his chest by a sling, Rossi waited outside Mr Ramage's cabin door while the Marine sentry called his name and, receiving an answer, opened the door.

Rossi found the captain seated at his desk with Mr Hill in the armchair beside it and Mr Orsini on the settee.

"Ah, Rossi, how are you?"

"*Bene, grazie, commandante.*"

"Not too '*bene*', I trust, or Mr Aitken will have you holy-stoning the deck tomorrow morning. Sit down there, beside Mr Orsini. Is that arm of yours going to be all right?"

"Just a flesh wound, Mr Bowen says. He's put in a few stitches. He'd be a good sailmaker in an emergency, sir."

"I'll remember that. And I hope you watched carefully when he fixed up your arm: we might need a surgeon's mate."

"I faint at the sight of blood, *commandante,*" Rossi said quickly. "Since I was a child . . ."

Ramage nodded. "I'll remember that, too. No blood for Rossi. Now, tell me what happened at the Fortezza. Mr Hill has got me as far as the beach, and Mr Orsini as far as the square in front of the Fortezza."

"*Allora,*" Rossi said. "I thought it would be easier for one person to get in, so I asked Mr Orsini to wait outside." Then, realizing that this might be interpreted as a criticism he added: "Mr Orsini is more used to storming such a building: he hasn't had my experience as a burglar."

111

"You too, eh?" Ramage raised his eyebrows. "I thought that Stafford was our only night worker."

Rossi shrugged his shoulders and looked modest. "When times were hard and there was no other work . . ."

Ramage gave a dry laugh, guessing what the "other work" was.

"Well, there was no sentry at the entrance to the Fortezza. You remember the little bridge over that dry moat, sir? Those boards creaked, but the gates were open and I could hear voices – from a guardroom, I supposed.

"The men inside were obviously drinking and playing cards, so I had a good look round the rest of the Fortezza. There was no one. Then, I'm afraid, I was too confident. Going out I thought I'd just walk past the guardroom, but two men came out with a lantern, saw me and made me go inside. None of them spoke Italian and several of them started shouting and waving pistols. But –"

"Did you get any idea who they thought you were?" Ramage interrupted.

"Yes, sir: they suspected I was a local Italian looking for something to steal. Two of them went out to inspect their quarters to see if anything was missing, taking one of the two lanterns with them. One of the men left behind started searching me while another held up the remaining lantern, waving a pistol at me. He was very drunk."

"Then what happened?" Ramage prompted.

"I kicked the man with the lantern. He dropped it but fired his pistol at the same time – accidentally, I think. That was the bullet that ricocheted round the room and hit me. I bolted for the door in the darkness and someone else fired another shot – I don't know where that went. As I ran out of the gateway I heard Mr Orsini call my name, to show where he was, and I was very grateful because my arm was useless and I was beginning to feel dizzy. After that Mr Orsini did everything."

"That's not what Mr Orsini says," Ramage remarked.

"Well, sir, he helped me down the hill and there was a *contadino*'s hut with a lantern. We went in and the women told us that a French ship had taken away the hostages: confirming the unlucky gambler's story completely."

112

"Did you threaten these women?"

Rossi glanced quickly at Orsini, obviously puzzled. "No, sir. There was no need. The man was completely drunk and he fell asleep while we talked to him."

Ramage laughed and reassured the seaman. "I asked only because Mr Orsini said that although you were swaying and he thought you'd faint any moment, you charmed the old woman and the mother with her baby."

Rossi's face went red. He was not a man to blush, but he was pleased at the midshipman's compliment. "Well, sir, the women were *proprie Toscane*. They wanted to help once they discovered we were Italian. I know I *was* nearly fainting," he said with a grin, "but I remember Mr Orsini suggesting a name for the little baby, who hadn't been christened yet."

Ramage looked round at Orsini with eyebrows raised.

"Just polite talk, sir; I wanted to make sure she would not gossip. That reminds me, they thought we – the *Calypso*, that is – were the ship that took the hostages away, and that we had returned to anchor out here."

"Both of you are sure there was no hint of where the hostages were being taken?"

Rossi and Orsini shook their heads, Rossi wincing as the quick movement jarred his arm.

"Very well, my thanks to the pair of you. I gather that Mr Hill was about to shoot you both when you rowed round to Cala Pozzarello in that fisherman's boat. That wasn't the time to forget the nightjar call and start shouting, Mr Orsini."

Orsini looked embarrassed. "I've always dreaded something like that, sir, and finally it happened . . ."

"You were lucky Mr Hill recognized your voice."

Ramage stood up. "Pass the word for Mr Aitken and Mr Southwick as you go out, please," he told Hill, "and hoist in the boats."

When Southwick and Aitken arrived, he pulled the Tyrrhenian Sea chart from the rack above, opened it and held it down with paperweights.

"Very well, Mr Southwick, so Bonaparte's villains have decamped with our birds. Where do you think we should start looking?"

"The islands, sir: that's about all I have to offer. I can't see the French using a ship to move them up or down the mainland coast: they marched them to Pitigliano from somewhere up north."

"From Florence, sir?" Aitken asked. "Isn't that the most likely place to find a crowd of wealthy English enjoying themselves when the war started again?"

Ramage nodded. "I'd *expect* to find them in Rome or Florence. A few in Naples, perhaps. But most of them visiting the artistic treasures of Florence."

He thought for a minute or two, his imagination spreading a map of northern Italy in front of him. Yes, Florence was most likely. All the English visitors (and Scots, Welsh and Irish) might have been rounded up there, like so many cattle, and then the French would have sorted out the important ones and selected their hostages . . . Hmmm . . . *hostages* meant people both special and different, and the French would separate them from the others. And intended to keep them separate? Yes, but where? Well, the obvious needs were reasonable accommodation and good security. The Palazzo degli Orsini at Pitigliano had been perfect in every respect.

He opened a pair of dividers and measured the distance between Florence and Pitigliano. About one hundred miles, more by the twisting roads. So . . . that told him the French did not hesitate to march the hostages one hundred miles. That in turn probably meant they would not hesitate to march them two or three hundred miles: there was no hurry, and there was precious little else to occupy the Army of Italy at the moment.

The conclusion to be drawn from all that? Well, the fact that the hostages had been put on board a ship (on board a frigate that by chance looked like the *Calypso*: a sister ship, probably, because it was a very successful design) must mean that they were being moved to somewhere not accessible by land.

An island, in other words. Sardinia, Corsica? No, he had ruled them out earlier because of bandits and guerrillas. The French were not popular in either island and the hostages might be killed or freed: there was no certainty either way.

Which left the tiny islands just off the north coast of Sicily (which did not seem likely) or those in the Tyrrhenian Sea.

Which was what Southwick had just said, although, Ramage noted ruefully, that was Southwick's instinct; Ramage had reached the same conclusion by a more devious route.

"It won't take long to check them all, sir," Aitken said.

"Providing we don't meet a French squadron – or even the French frigate that took them away from here."

"Heh," snorted Southwick, "it's been a long time since we had a decent action: the ship's company are getting soft."

"Don't tell Rossi that," Ramage said as he measured off a distance on the chart with the dividers. "We'll weigh at dusk – then no one keeping a watch from Argentario or Talamone will be sure where we are bound. Not," he added, remembering Orsini's words earlier, "that anyone thinks we are anything but a French national ship."

Chapter
Eleven

Daylight showed they had anchored in the darkness at just the right position with the island of Giglio half a mile away on the starboard hand as the *Calypso*'s bow swung slightly to a southerly breeze.

Ramage stood with Aitken and Southwick while they examined the island with telescopes. "You see, it's just a mountain put down haphazardly in the sea, like so many islands round here. Just look at that village on the top – you could mistake it for a castle. Castellated walls with a hundred or so houses inside, judging by the roofs we can see. I'll bet none of the people up there are fishermen! Imagine the long walk downhill to the port, and then the climb back up the hill again with the day's catch. Castello, that's the name of it. Strong enough as a refuge if the Saracens are sighted."

Aitken nodded. "Yes, everyone would bolt up there from the port and from that village on the other side of the island – Campese, isn't it? – and slam the gates shut. Load the rusty muskets, boil up some olive oil – water, too, I expect – and be ready to pour it down on the heads of the Saracens as they try to batter the gate down and climb the walls. If I was inside the Castello with those heathens shouting and screaming for my blood and my wife's body, I think I'd sooner rely on boiling oil than damp gunpowder in rusty muskets."

"The Saracens – the people here always call them *i Saraceni*, incidentally, not Barbary pirates – have been raiding this coast for hundreds of years: to these people a Saracen raid is about like a severe storm to the Isle of Wight," Ramage said. "When the Aragonese owned this part of the coast they did these people a service by building the lookout towers, forts and places like Castello, though I doubt they received much thanks at the time because the local people had to quarry the stone and do the work

"Just look at that terracing on those slopes: they must press a good deal of wine. Come to think of it, they produce a very good white, and it travels. The trouble with that Argentario wine is that it hardly reaches Orbetello before the shaking of the cart (or donkey if they use small barrels) has turned it to vinegar."

Ramage resumed examining the island. "That's a tiny harbour, just big enough for fishing boats. No one seems interested in us. But – that's odd. Very odd . . ."

Aitken and Southwick waited for an explanation and when none came the master gave a sniff that Ramage recognized as "You don't have to tell us *but* . . ."

"Castello," Ramage said. "They have a flagpole. Seems to be the only thing up there that's been erected in the last hundred years – and it's been painted. Once the sun is up it'll stand out like a pencil."

"And if they hoist a Tricolour . . ." Southwick said.

"If they hoist a Tricolour it'll save you walking up the hill to see if the French are there," Ramage said.

Aitken looked again with his telescope and then said: "But that doesn't actually prove the hostages are there, does it sir?"

"No, only that there's a French garrison, which one would expect. A small garrison, anyway: probably less than fifty men."

"Well," Southwick observed, "no one over there in the port seems very excited that we've arrived. If the commander of the garrison thought we had anything for him, I'm sure he'd have sent out a boat by now."

"Perhaps they don't get up early," Aitken said. "If I spent much time here I'd probably slip into these Frenchified habits – eating and drinking too much and sleeping late."

"Hard life for the Italians, though," Ramage said. "Ask the first hundred people you meet when they last tasted meat, and the answer will probably be months ago – and that was a tough old goat which had dried up and gave no more milk. Fish, artichokes, bread made from the flour they grind from the bit of wheat they manage to grow (as long as a *colpo di vento* didn't knock it flat just before harvesting time). But no flour means no *pasta* and no bread. Ask them about *dentice, polpo, mormora, triglia* and *seppia* – they're the fish they catch and live on – but don't look for meat."

"I fancy some fresh fish," Southwick said.

"We'll get you some *polpo*," Ramage promised.

"What's that?" Southwick asked suspiciously.

"Octopus. A great favourite. Good if you're hungry – you can chew it for hours, like tanned leather."

"Do we hoist a Tricolour, sir?" Aitken asked.

Ramage thought a moment and then shook his head. "If they look down at us from Castello they won't even notice we're not flying any colours. They'll assume we're that other frigate, since we look alike. That is, if the first frigate ever came here." He eyed Southwick. "You haven't convinced our first lieutenant yet that the French Navy aren't quite as fussy as the Royal Navy about day-to-day routine."

"I don't want them setting him a bad example," Southwick explained. "Anyway, now we're at Giglio what do you propose doing, sir?"

Thinking he wished he knew, Ramage closed his telescope with a snap and turned to look back eastward, where the sun was beginning to lift over the mainland, a golden orb in a clear sky. It was almost in line with the peak of Argentario which, being less than a dozen miles away, stood out dark and almost menacing, its western sides streaked black and grey with shadow. To the right in the distance the land was flat, the Maremma marshes. To the left of Argentario was Talamone, distinguishable only because of the mountains behind it and, fading northward into the distance, Punta Ala, with more mountains. But the peaks near the coast were small compared with those inland, the distant ones merging blue grey into the horizon – the Apennines, which reached across into western Tuscany. Monte Amiata, Monte Labbro and Monte Elmo, near Pitigliano, were high, but mere anthills compared with those around Arezzo. And that, he told himself, is a useless survey of Tuscany's geography, and neither Aitken nor Southwick will have failed to notice that you do not have a plan waiting on the tip of your tongue.

"Giglio is like Pitigliano except it's surrounded by water," Ramage said casually, speaking in a deeper tone than usual, as though making a wise comment.

"Indeed it is, sir," Southwick said, his politeness just skating round the edge of sarcasm. "Yes, indeed. To get to one you march along dusty tracks; to get to the other you walk on the water."

"Yes," Ramage said, ignoring the sarcasm. "We won't have to walk on the water because we have boats, but the routine will be the same. We'll march our 'prisoners' up to the top of the hill (to Castello) to help our bluff and with luck we'll march 'em down again, with the hostages."

Both Aitken and Southwick looked up at Ramage and the first lieutenant said: "But sir, if they have the hostages up there, surely they'll have a bigger garrison?"

Ramage walked to the taffrail and the other two men followed. "It doesn't really matter how many French there are if they have the hostages."

When he saw the puzzled look on the faces of both Aitken and Southwick he explained evenly: "Just consider the word 'hostage'. Supposing we had a squadron and could land five hundred seamen and Marines and storm Castello. If you commanded the French garrison and guessed Bonaparte wouldn't listen to excuses if you let his hostages be rescued, what would *you* do?"

Aitken nodded slowly. "Yes, sir. *Hostages.* I'd tell the commander of the British force that if he didn't go back on board his ships and sail away again, I'd hang the hostages one at a time from the battlements."

"Exactly," Ramage said. "Which leaves us back with our only weapons, guile, cunning and deception. We're in the same position as a married woman's lover: it's all right to cuckold the husband but he must never find out – or at least not until long after the affair is over. I'm talking from the lover's point of view, of course."

"And because I don't speak French or Italian, and because I'm a bit broad in the beam these days, sir, I suppose –"

119

"You suppose correctly, my dear Southwick: you and Kenton and Martin are going to be left behind to look after the *Calypso*."

"And if you don't come marching back again," Southwick grumbled, "I suppose those of us left behind will have to come storming up the hill to rescue you all."

Ramage nodded. "Yes, we'd appreciate that. But if you see bodies hanging by their necks from the battlements don't bother: just sail away again. I'm sure any survivors would prefer to remain prisoners in Castello than corpses hanging outside it."

"When do you intend starting off, sir?" Aitken asked.

How one's choice of words changed with promotion. A lieutenant making a suggestion to a senior officer (his captain, for example) would "propose" doing something, leaving the captain free to say no. But when the captain was telling the lieutenant, or the lieutenant was asking for the captain's orders, "intend" was the word.

Captains intend, lieutenants propose. That was a good rule of thumb, and of course captains "proposed" to admirals, while admirals "intended" (unless they in turn were writing to the Board of Admiralty). And the Board of Admiralty, of course, neither intended nor proposed; they disposed.

"We might as well start early and make a day of it," Ramage said lightly. "Tell the French and Tuscan armies to get dressed in their appropriate rigs as soon as they've finished breakfast, and have the prisoners ready, looking suitably chastened. You expecially," he said to Aitken, "you don't look as though you've been a hostage for very long!"

"I thought I was the laird of thousands of acres, sir, and just visiting Florence so that I could listen to the boring conversation of the English visitors who prefer Rubens to Raeburn."

"Surely talk of Leonardo or Michelangelo – or even where you tasted the best Chianti – must come as a welcome change from all that mist covering the glens, or chasing a reluctant stag only to have your musket flash in the pan."

Aitken shook his head sadly. "All those foreign painters – why, any self-respecting Scot would have his portrait done by Raeburn. I remember that Captain Duff – he commands the *Mars* now, I think – used him. Fine Scottish family, the Duffs."

120

"Raeburn's a painter? Damn me, I thought a raeburn was like a brae or a loch or a glen: somewhere a stream trickled or a stag lurked."

Aitken grinned. "I also remember Captain Duff saying he reckoned one of Raeburn's finest works was a portrait of Admiral the Earl of Blazey."

"Ah yes, I remember, it's hung where we hang the game . . ."

"That," Aitken said solemnly, "might be more of a reflection on your father than on the artist, surely sir?"

As soon as he heard that the selected men were dressing up in their uniforms, Rossi requested to see the captain. Aitken had told him he would not be going on this expedition and then listened patiently to the Italian's protests. Normally he would have said that the first lieutenant's word was final, but because the Italian was so distressed at being left behind, he mentioned it to Ramage.

"But what good could he do if he came?" Ramage asked. "His arm is in a sling, and a mile or so's marching up a steep hill over a rocky track will just about finish him off. We'd end up carrying him."

Aitken, however, was having second thoughts. "Perhaps it depends on what he's supposed to do, sir. Did you take him to Pitigliano because he's Italian and speaks the language, or because he's quick with a pistol and sword?"

"Obviously because he speaks Italian: we have scores of men quick with guns and cutlasses."

"In that case, sir, I suggest we take him. We only need his tongue. If the marching shakes him up too much, he can always wait beside the track until we come back, but if he endures to Castello, we can use him."

"You're afraid that if you leave him on board he's going to put the Evil Eye on you," Ramage said amiably. "All right, he can come. But I've been thinking about Orsini, Rossi and myself leading the column. When we went to Pitigliano, the chances were that we'd have to bluff our way past Italians first. Here we're more likely to bump first into the French. No Italian is likely to challenge us down here at the harbour or on the road up to Castello."

121

Aitken agreed, knowing that in any case he was one of the "hostages" in the middle. "I suggest two men, sir: Gilbert and Louis. Better to have two men answering questions – preferably at once – to create confusion?"

"Very well," Ramage said. "Tell Rossi to dress himself up. I see the boats are ready." He pulled on the strange jacket, that of a captain in the Duke of Tuscany's army (the King of Etruria's, he corrected himself), and tugged at his sword belt. "Let the men start boarding. The boats' crews know they are to return to the ship the moment we have landed?"

"Yes, sir," Aitken said patiently, "everyone has had his instructions – I'm just going to tell Gilbert and Louis of the change."

As the first lieutenant went down to the maindeck, Ramage sighed. There were a dozen possible islands to the north and south which *could* be used as a prison for the hostages, but really none seemed very likely. Giglio – well, it was a possibility, even if a remote one. He had pointed out the new flagpole to Southwick and Atiken because it was necessary to keep their spirits up. Now was not the time for them to realize the hopelessness of the search. That damned frigate could have taken the hostages anywhere; she could have gone round the foot of Italy and across to the Morea: there were hundreds of islands in the Ionian Sea that were suitable (if rather parched: many of them had little or no rain in the summer).

In fact (the most chilling thought of all) the frigate might have taken them up to Toulon. Even Bonaparte would not expect his hostages to march hundreds of miles back into France, but if a French frigate was also due to go to Toulon for, say, a refit, she could take the hostages with her. So at this moment, while the *Calypso*'s motley force climbed down into the boats to assault Giglio – a tiny island which was less than a fly-speck on a chart of the Mediterranean – the hostages could be prisoners in the great citadel at Toulon. By now they could, for that matter, be sitting in carts (or even carriages, if Bonaparte acted on some whim) on their way from Toulon to Paris.

Paris? Yes, there Bonaparte could use them in some charade or other. Perhaps he might want to parade some of the English nobility as prisoners through the streets to show the sturdy

French republicans how right they had been to strap down their own aristocracy on Dr Guillotine's infernal machines.

That was almost ten years ago. The guillotine blades had not been used much in the past few years: indeed, most of the recent victims had been French revolutionaries disagreeing with Bonaparte. He shook his head to clear away the pictures flashing across his imagination like those of the new magic lanterns being advertised in the *Morning Post* and *The Times*. Giglio, he told himself: we march up to the top of the hill, and we'll probably march down again, tired and no better informed about the hostages, but we've no choice.

"I'm sorry, gentlemen, I looked everywhere in the Mediterranean but couldn't find them . . ." His report to Their Lordships would be written in more formal phrases, but that would be the sense of it. Sitting in the Board Room in Whitehall, even looking at the chart of the Mediterranean pulled open from one of the rollers over the fireplace, the inland sea would not seem so big. But it was nearly as far from the Levant to Gibraltar as it was from Plymouth in England to Plymouth Rock in America . . . Giglio (pronounced Jeelyo) would hardly show, and it was a name he was beginning to hate, along with Montecristo, Pianosa and Capraia.

"I'm coming," he called as he saw Southwick waving to him. Tradition – the senior officer was the last man to board a boat, and the first to disembark. The King of Etruria's uniform, he thought as he walked over to the break in the bulwark, hitching his sword round, is quite unsuitable for sea service.

There was the circular watch tower (almost obligatory along this coast) at the far end of the village and a score of houses lining a narrow stretch of sandy beach with a dozen or more small fishing boats hauled up on it, and a surprisingly large church a hundred yards inland. At the back of the beach a few posts, each as high as a man, were joined by fishing nets hanging in bulky loops. Drying – or waiting to be repaired. Yes, he saw two men and a woman (dressed in black except for a once white scarf over her grey hair) who, from the darting movements of their hands, were busy mending.

A third man stood at the doorway of the nearest house. Was he particularly interested in the two approaching boats?

123

Ramage guessed not: had he thought they might want to buy fish, he would have made the effort to walk the thirty yards to the water's edge. Nor did the net menders look round. They would have seen the boats leave the *Calypso*, so those swiftly moving hands made one thing quite clear: the French were not popular among Giglio's sturdy islanders. Perhaps the French pressed Italians into the Navy. Did they hate the French or, like many other islanders, just hate (and fear) everyone not born within their shores?

It does not matter why, Ramage told himself; it only matters that they do not like the French. If there is shooting, then these people will not help them. Nor will they spy for them. Perhaps there will be one man in a hundred, the usual informer and opportunist who curries favour with the French, but he will be the village outcast, safe enough while the French remain but who knows his life will not be worth a *fiasco* of vinegar the day the French leave.

The seaman at the cutter's tiller ran the bow up on the beach within thirty yards of the net menders and unshipped the rudder, but even when they heard the stem scraping the sand and the oars splash as the men gave a last thrust to wedge the boat firmly to let the landing party jump on shore without getting wet (and in lightening the boat make it easy for the oarsmen to get it afloat again), neither the two men nor the woman turned.

The jolly-boat arrived a few feet away and within five minutes the motley column was drawn up on the sand with the two boats pulling back to the *Calypso*. Four yelping dogs, one chasing the other, came racing round the last house in the row, saw the column of men, turned and ran away again. A donkey tied outside a front door of the last house brayed impatiently and was answered by another in the hills above the village. Impatiently? Was a *somaro* ever impatient? Bored, perhaps, or hungry.

Orsini muttered to Ramage in Italian: "It's hard to believe the French are up there, isn't it, sir?"

"Don't judge by these people," Ramage said grimly. "These poor beggars, and their father and grandfathers and the rest of them going back five centuries have seen many an enemy of one sort or another land on this beach. *Saraceni, Aragonesi,*

124

Francesi, Inglesi . . . and none of them came to buy fish. Rape, rob, pillage or just destroy . . . no wonder they hate the sight of a stranger."

"Would it be worth it if I . . .?" Orsini ventured.

Ramage stared at him. "From Castello (which Southwick tells me is fifteen hundred feet high) you can almost see Volterra, or the mountains round it, anyway. But just think: to these people you're just as much a *straniero* as any of the rest. You may speak Italian but to them you have a strange accent: strange enough, probably, to make them more suspicious of you than if you were a Frenchman . . ."

Orsini gave an involuntary shiver. "There's not much advantage in being an Italian these days."

Ramage shrugged his shoulders and said with deliberate harshness: "It is no advantage – in the Mediterranean, anyway – being anything but French. We'll change that eventually, but it'll take time. Until then, people like these fishermen are going to snub you. Be thankful it's only a snub: it could be a pistol ball in the back."

Ramage walked a few paces to one side and looked at the column, led by Gilbert and Louis in the sober uniform of the army of Revolutionary France, who were followed by Orsini and Rossi in their garish outfits. Then the hostages, with Aitken, Jackson and Stafford in the front row. All the hostages were by now apparently chained to each other: a suspicious French guard would have to tug a chain to discover that the "prisoners" were holding their manacles.

And there, at the rear, muskets over their shoulders, pistols in their belts, and swords hanging from belts over their shoulders, were the other two Frenchmen, Auguste and Albert.

Ramage nodded: yes, it all looked realistic enough, a few more hostages being delivered, to be added to those already (he hoped) in Castello: sign this receipt please . . .

Except it was all a waste of time; there were no hostages in Castello; Castello had a garrison of a few French soldiers, probably the scoundrels that various company commanders had been wanting to be rid of since they first crossed the Alps . . .

The winding track began beside the last house, and Ramage could see how it twisted and turned as it snaked the fifteen hundred feet to the top of the mountain, where the gate of Castello, a town gate in fact, waited like a dark mouth to swallow them.

Over a hill, down into a small valley and up again . . . the men whose feet had worn the track in the rock over the centuries had been concerned with finding the easiest route for themselves and their donkeys, tired from an exhausting day's labour under a scorching sun.

A scorching sun . . . yes, the sun was already getting some heat in it. He raised his arm, saw that he had everyone's attention (so that he did not have to shout an order), and with an overhand motion started the column marching.

Three dark-eyed, black-haired children watched from a doorway; a woman appeared at a window, moving aside the sacking that covered it. She was holding a baby, and she spat before pulling the sacking back. A black and white cat streaked across the road, chased by the same four dogs. The cat made for the nets and the old woman turned and picked up a stone, but the dogs had obviously played this game before and suffered from the woman's markmanship because they bolted back behind the houses.

"They are poor, these people," Rossi said, as if to himself. "I've never seen a thin cat in a fishing village before . . ."

The track led out of the little port and then passed half a dozen more small stone houses and an equal number of tiny little buildings with half-doors.

"*Mamma mia*, even the donkeys live as well as the *cristiani*," Rossi said. "The donkey huts are as well built and roofed as the houses."

"You've lived in a city too long," Ramage said. "If you had been a *contadino* instead of a *ladrone* in Genova, you'd know that in the country a man values his donkey as much as his wife."

"In Volterra, *more* than his wife," Orsini said.

Rossi, although not disputing Ramage's taunt, thought for a few moments. "It makes sense," he said matter-of-factly. "A wife can't carry a couple of barrels of wine, or a load of firewood."

"No," Orsini said. "Just one barrel, or half a load of wood.

126

And the baby slung over her shoulder, and two more clutching her skirt."

The track started to lead up over the first hill. Castello, Ramage thought, seemed to be floating above them on great petrified waves, the rock lightly dusted with red soil. Grapevines and olive trees planted in well kept terraces grew in even lines, the olive leaves already silvery in the early sunlight. Suddenly (although the noise must have been there since daylight) he became conscious of the fast, highpitched buzzing rattle of the cicadas, and perhaps because he always associated them with the sun, he began to feel the heat through his coat.

Who would be a soldier, with all this marching? One could join a cavalry regiment (given the choice) but horses meant aching thighs, tight breeches, and fellow officers with hearty, back-slapping manners, and anyway a horse tended to break wind at awkward moments, such as when the colonel's lady was patting it. That sort of thing, he was sure, could blight a young subaltern's career.

So, heigh-ho for the life of a sailor. Flogging to windward through heavy seas, sheets of spray and curtains of rain, clothes never dry for a month, always eating salt tack, and the knowledge that foreign climes, so often written about ecstatically by poets, could mean the black vomit, ague, typhoid and the plague; that the thunder of broadsides, also written about by poets, could take your head off, or part you from a beloved and trusty leg. Or you could drown. There was, he reflected, a lot to be said for living the life of a landowner, riding to the hounds once a week – and having a horse refuse a hedge, so that you made the jump alone, head-first, and broke your neck. I must write about it in my Journal, Ramage thought; the happy thoughts of a post-captain marching up to Castello . . .

"It's quiet here, sir," Gilbert said unexpectedly, his French voice jerking at Ramage like a leash. "If there was a large garrison up there –" he nodded towards Castello, now going out of sight behind yet another hill, "– I'd expect to see a soldier coming down to buy fresh fish for the commandant, or one of the bad girls of the village returning home after a night . . . well, after visiting a friend up there."

"A bit early for the trollops," Ramage commented, "and

there wasn't much sign of a fish for sale back there: the fishermen did not go out last night."

"Just as well, sir," Orsini commented. "We'd probably have run down some of those boats in the darkness!"

"I think I preferred marching to Pitigliano," Rossi muttered to himself. "This is like climbing up the side of a mountain."

"This *is* climbing up the side of a mountain," Orsini said, "but have you forgotten all those hills in Genova?"

"I thought I had, but this is bringing back the memory."

"Your arm – is it hurting?" Orsini asked.

"No, it's the muscles in my legs," Rossi grumbled. "It's never like this in the *Calypso* . . ."

Castello came into sight once again, but after they had marched another hundred yards along the track, winding over a ridge, it vanished as they dipped into a small valley. Now they could see the rocks and cliffs on the west side of the island, and the sea seemed a long way below them. Not as far down as Castello was up, Rossi pointed out in a complicated joke which relied more on a Genovese accent than a sense of humour.

When they reached the top of the next ridge, from which they could see the track entering Castello in the distance as though it was a fuse leading to a powder keg, Ramage called a halt because, to a casual onlooker, it was a logical place for a rest. For the column, as Ramage walked back to tell them, it was their chance to have a good look at what they faced at Castello, whether the hostages were on the island or not.

Aitken, after making sure that no French soldiers or *contadini* were watching, joined Ramage and sat down beside him.

"Supposing the hostages aren't up there, sir?" he asked. "What do we do?"

The eternal question. Ramage laughed and with his finger pushed a small twig in front of the black beetle which also seemed intent on going up to Castello. "I could hand you over to the garrison and make Kenton the first lieutenant! However, if the hostages aren't there, then we get angry with the garrison, blame the commandant of the fort at Santo Stefano for giving us wrong information, and hope the commandant here at Castello actually knows where they are. That way we'll save ourselves having to search any more. I don't particularly want to march up to every fort in the Tyrrhenian Sea. With the exception of Pianosa, which is very flat, the rest are very mountainous. Gorgona, Montecristo . . . more climbing."

"Do you think we'll get away with it, sir? Just going up to the commandant and asking?"

"We're not 'just asking'," Ramage said impatiently. "As far as we *and* the commandant are concerned, we have more hostages we were ordered to deliver to Giglio. Very well, the others are not here, and there's been the sort of mix-up made in anyone's army." Ramage held his arms out, palms uppermost, and looked despairing. "So we march back to the port. If the hostages *are* there, we keep quiet about our 'prisoners', and relieve the commandant . . ."

Aitken added two more twigs to the barrier in front of the beetle. "I haven't seen a scorpion yet. What size are they, sir?"

"About twice as long as that beetle, but not nearly as fat. You won't mistake one – long thin tail, which it arches up over its back like a dog's tail and points forward if it meets an enemy, and jaws like this –" he held up his hand, the thumb and forefinger making a half-circle. "The jaws don't hurt you – they just get a firm grip so that he can give you a jab with his tail, which looks like a bent fishing rod and has the sting in the end. Probably a couple of them under that rock – just the sort of place they like."

"I'll leave them in peace. The gate of Castello seems to be open. And look, just a few wisps of smoke: cooking."

"Cooking and baking," Ramage said. "Don't forget, that's more of a small walled town than a fortress. Many more local people live up there than down at the port, where we landed."

"They have a quiet life!"

Ramage shook his head and gestured down into the valley separating them from the high peak on which Castello was built. "Look down there carefully. Wherever it slopes it's terraced with vines – see? And the groves of olive trees to the right of those big rocks. The *contadini* are already working. Weeding, pruning – and see, those two men at the foot of the terraces are sorting out the right size rocks: they're making another terrace."

"Plenty of rocks, not much soil. Reminds me of parts of the Highlands in summer."

Ramage nodded and stood up. "We must be on the move. The next time we speak English we'll know – I hope – where the hostages are."

"Better still," Aitken said, "we'll have them with us. But –" he stopped as the thought struck him, "how are you going . . .?"

"I've no idea," Ramage said with a grin. "You draw me a plan of Castello and where the garrison is, and where the hostages are held, and I'll tell you. Until then, let's keep an open mind. Or, to be honest, let's see what opportunities present themselves."

In the last valley a surly *contadino* jogged past on his donkey, whacking it with a monotony which indicated it was a habit rather than a spur to the animal, which ignored everything with a raffish unconcern. "I wish I could talk with that donkey," Paolo said. "I think he could tell me much about life."

"I'm sure he could," Ramage commented, and Rossi laughed.

The muscles along the front of Ramage's shins ached: he had a stitch like a knife in his side. Ramage had thought the march to and from Pitigliano would have put him in trim but now he realized the difference between marching horizontally and (it seemed) almost vertically. Admittedly the track twisted and that took out the worst of the steepness, but the fact was, as Southwick had announced with something like glee, Castello was fifteen hundred feet high . . .

Chapter
Twelve

There it was! A sudden turn in the track brought them to the gateway and Ramage saw at once that the most fearsome thing about Castello was its name: the thick, turreted walls built round the village were crumbling. Obviously only a garrison from an occupying army was likely to do repairs – and then an enemy would have to be threatening.

Certainly the present garrison saw no threat, and the villagers clearly left it to the Church and the French to defend them against *i Saraceni*, so shrubs and cacti grew between the carved stones and the roots slowly but quite relentlessly levered many of them apart so that, helped by decades of winds, hot sun and torrential rains, one stone after another tumbled down the slopes, making the steep hill look as though Castello had been through a siege.

Luckily for the future of Castello, the blocks of stone which had been cut by masons long since dead were too big for the villagers to carry off to build houses for newly wed sons. Obviously, since the French had arrived, *i Saraceni* had been forgotten; it was not in the people's character, Ramage reflected, to remember that they were still there, lurking along the distant coast of Africa with their galleys ready to raid as soon as the French had gone.

The Saracens, Moors or Barbary pirates (the names changed, the people remained the same) had plagued the Mediterranean for a thousand years, and their strength was that they raided small towns and their victims had short memories. Short memories and too preoccupied with their own quarrels to unite and crush the raiders.

131

Half a dozen children stood shyly at the gateway, not afraid because they recognized Gilbert's and Louis's uniforms. A pack of dogs led by a mongrel as big as a wolf, scarred along its back and one ear almost torn off, came rushing out, a mass of hysterical yelping until a couple of the children set about them with sticks and cries of abuse.

The noise brought a French soldier to the gateway, bleary-eyed and unshaven for a week. He stared at the column of men outside, and Gilbert stepped forward, pointing at him and snapping: "Report at once to your commandant that the special party has arrived."

The soldier stood there obviously befuddled with sleep and a numbing headache from last night's wine. "He won't like that. He's never called before roll call at noon."

"Noon!" Gilbert exclaimed and pointed dramatically down at the harbour. "By noon we shall have sailed again!"

"I'll tell the corporal," the soldier muttered. "Let him have the responsibility."

As the man lurched away Gilbert muttered to Ramage: "Soldiers are the same, whatever uniform they wear –"

"Snarl at the corporal," Ramage advised, "otherwise we'll be standing here all day!"

When he arrived the corporal could have been the other man's older brother, except that he squinted at the column as though he had a bright light shining in his eyes.

"You!" snapped Gilbert. "Fetch the commandant at once. I have orders from the general. Are we to be left standing here all day with the dogs pissing all over us and the children throwing stones?"

"At once, Major, at once," the corporal stammered and disappeared, leaving only the wide-eyed children, who had not understood a word. A breeze started blowing through the gateway and Ramage cursed: it brought them the smell of the village – rotting cabbage, stinking fish, donkey dung, the sewage of centuries ripened and refreshed by hot sun and warm showers.

"I'll have the first tilt at the commandant when he arrives," Ramage said. "Anger and outrage sounds better in Italian than French. He probably won't understand a word but he'll

132

guess the meaning. Then you can take over for the *coup de grâce!*"

Gilbert chuckled: his original dislike of wearing this version of the uniform of Bonaparte's Army of Italy was disappearing rapidly at the prospect of abusing the commandant of Castello.

A good five minutes passed before the commandant appeared, still buttoning up his coat, the corporal carrying his sword and hat. He was a plump little man, swarthy, with perfect teeth beneath sagging black moustaches which had not been combed after a night's sleep.

"Good morning Major," the commandant said, obviously having taken the corporal's word for Gilbert's assumed rank. "No one told me you were coming . . ."

Ramage stepped forward and released a torrent of abusive Italian, but the man stood helpless, his hands held down, palms outwards as though submitting. With feigned ill-grace Ramage gestured to Gilbert, who snapped out crisply: "You've had no orders? No orders – I can't believe it! What about your hostages?"

Ramage could hardly breathe as he waited for the reply.

"But Major, they are well enough. I feed them properly and let them exercise. Why, I've even given them playing cards, and they gamble and drink wine like – well, like my soldiers."

Gilbert turned to Ramage. In a few moments the whole position had changed. Was the commandant still half asleep? It was worth a chance. Ramage stepped forward and began speaking to the commandant in Italian, mixing in enough halting French that Gilbert would be able to repeat once he had grasped the idea.

"The orders . . . they said a frigate with other hostages would – how do you say – collect your hostages to take them all away, to Toulon. Look!" He turned and, with as much drama as he could summon without laughing, gestured towards Aitken and his men. "There you have some of the cream of the English aristocracy who were in Italy when the Emperor went to war again, and whom I'm exercising. You have some here. At Toulon are many more caught in France. I do not know what the Emperor intends, but he wants them all assembled in Toulon.

"Which is why we arrived in the frigate. Clearly you have not even noticed that a frigate waits just off the harbour. Where are your sentries – asleep in the clouds?"

The commandant had understood perhaps a quarter of what Ramage had said and looked appealingly at Gilbert, who repeated everything in rapid French.

The commandant finally took his hat from the corporal and put it on. "Major, I have not received any orders, but we are a long way from Florence and it is not unknown for messengers to be delayed. But I understand what the Emperor intends, and I will prepare my hostages at once for the voyage. You won't want provisions for them, will you?"

Gilbert, seeing the man's greedy eyes already calculating for how much he could sell the food to the villagers, shook his head. "No, we have provisions enough on board."

"It is hot out here," Ramage grumbled in Italian. "Let us get into the shade. A drink would be welcome."

Gilbert translated, and the commandant led the way into the square. The streets were narrow with the houses crowding each other. It was, Ramage saw, still a medieval town: nothing had changed in the last four or five centuries, except the stucco peeled and was never repaired, paint flaked off. Tiles were replaced after a storm – though judging from a few houses some people did not bother. On one side of the square there was a shallow stone bath used as the laundry place; close by, a well had a cranked handle for winding up the bucket, which looked worn enough to be the original. Beside many doorways were eyebolts for tethering donkeys and, he guessed, where there were no piles of manure, the owners of the houses owned strips of land on the slopes.

There was the butcher's shop, an open-fronted house with two strings of dead wild birds hanging up for sale. Birds whose feathers were red and black, green and yellow, their beaks revealing they were finches and caught in traps. Two doors further down was the *verdura*, but not much produce was on display – half a dozen cabbages, the outer leaves yellowing, and strings of garlic (regarded by Italians as the best protection against the Evil Eye). At the far side of the square, draped over a brick wall but facing the sun, were what looked like hundreds of short lengths of white string: the *pasta* made early that morning and now hung out to dry in the sun. Spaghetti has the same importance to Italians as potatoes to the poor in northern France and Britain. The difference being, Ramage reflected, that the Italians had the good sense to disguise the taste with various sauces.

A raucous screaming suddenly froze everyone except the commandant who, after finding himself walking on alone, turned back and explained. "It's Monday so the garrison's butcher is slaughtering a pig."

"Of course," Gilbert said, "I was thinking it was Thursday."

They followed the little commandant to the far end of the town, where a sentry sat on a chair inside a crudely made sentry box.

"The hostages live in the last five houses in this row. I commandeered them because there was nowhere else suitable. My soldiers live in billets, of course."

"The owners of the houses will be thankful we are taking the hostages away," Ramage said in atrocious French.

"So shall I," the commandant said fervently. "It is a grave responsibility. English generals and admirals, nobility – supposing they escaped! I would be a private soldier again – if I was not shot!"

Ramage nodded his head judiciously. "So now you will have the opportunity of being a field marshal . . ."

"Just leave me alone, I am quite content," the commandant confided. "Giglio has good wine and is far enough from Florence . . ."

"But your wife . . .?"

"It's far enough from Paris, too," he said with a wink. He banged the side of the sentry box and woke the soldier, who without being asked and showing no curiosity about the strangers behind the commandant, handed over a large bunch of keys.

"None of the houses had locks on the doors, so we had to fit them," he explained. "At least, those were my orders. But no one can escape from this island. Still, I made the owners of the houses pay me, and Florence sent me locks for ten houses." He winked again.

"Tell him to parade his hostages here," Ramage said to Gilbert. "Keep talking to him: I don't want him to wonder why we marched *our* hostages up the hill for exercise when we could have had them running around on deck."

"He's so thankful to be rid of them I don't think he'd do anything," Gilbert said. "As long as we sign his receipt, he'll be quite happy."

By now the commandant was unlocking the door of the first house and shouting orders to the people inside. Then he went on to the other houses, and by the time he reached the last the hostages were emerging from the first.

They all gathered at the sentry box, obviously conforming to a drill established when they first arrived. Ramage looked at them carefully. Yes, they were well dressed, though here and there breeches and coats were patched, clearly sewn by the owners, because the stitching was more workmanlike than neat. Boots and shoes – clean, though not polished, but it had not rained for three or four weeks so all they needed was a flick of a cloth to remove dust.

And all the hostages looked fit. Three or four men, although portly and red-faced, had obviously benefited from a year's frugal wine ration in place of unlimited brandy and port, and a more frugal diet than they had previously enjoyed. Only one man walked with a stick though, Ramage guessed, from habit rather than disability because the stick was a Malacca cane with a gold top: anyone with a walking problem used a stick with a handle.

It was devilish difficult to distinguish between the admirals and generals, since they were not in uniform. Certainly the one man who stood so erect he might be tied to a post must be a general, and those two might be admirals, while that foppish fellow would come under the commandant's description of an aristocrat.

Only one of the hostages, coming from the last house, showed the slightest interest in Ramage's men. Or, Ramage corrected himself, only one man *revealed* any interest. The admirals and the generals had long ago learned the art of apparent disinterest: it was not easy to watch the world tumbling about one's ears and merely comment: "By Jove!"

Finally the commandant came back, returned the bunch of keys to the sentry, and with a stentorian "*Messieurs!*" gestured towards Gilbert. Obviously, with the hostages about to be taken off his hands, he was not going to strain himself trying to explain things in English – or even in French, which a good half of the hostages probably spoke.

Ramage beckoned to them, muttering to Gilbert to wait until they were gathered round. Then, with the commandant talking to the sentry, who was still seated in his box, Ramage began speaking to the hostages in Italian. With every fifth or sixth word English and together making complete sentences, he explained that they were being rescued but must act as though they were about to be transferred to France. Above all, they must show no excitement. "Fall in behind those men, who are also acting as hostages," Ramage said, the English words interspersed with what was another long burst of Italian.

The real hostages walked, slouched or ambled: Ramage guessed this was how they formed up for roll call and was an expression of defiance. Two of them winked as they passed close. There was no doubt that they all understood what was going on, and Ramage was thankful that they could adapt themselves so quickly.

Suddenly the commandant came scurrying over, a hand uplifted to halt everything. "You must sign for them!" he exclaimed to Gilbert. "I must have a receipt. My adjutant will write it out but we must list all the names."

"And those of their wives, children, mistresses and grandparents!" Gilbert exclaimed disgustedly. "No wonder the Emperor fears for France's future. The Republic, One and Indivisible, will sink under the weight of the paper and we shall all drown in a sea of ink. That's what the Emperor told my general, who told my colonel, and now I tell you."

"And I'll tell the goats," the commandant sneered, "but you don't leave Castello until the receipt is signed."

"Well, go away and write it out," Gilbert snapped impatiently. "We will be waiting in the piazza. But bring pen and ink: I left my desk on board the frigate."

Chapter
Thirteen

Ramage's cabin on board the *Calypso* had never been so crowded and, he thought, never would the occupants look so strange. At the moment they were all standing and each had his head bent – some to the left, some to the right, some forward so that they seemed to be glowering from under lowered eyebrows, and all looking like bodies cut down from gibbets. Occasionally one of them would forget and, straightening his neck, would bang his head against the low deck beams.

Ramage had purposely left introductions until all the eleven hostages were safely on board. They had marched down the hill from Castello behind Aitken's group; at the beach which comprised Giglio's harbour they were still (as far as an onlooker was concerned) carefully guarded by a few French soldiers and the three men of the King of Etruria's army. And the frigate's two boats had to make two trips to ferry everyone on board.

Ramage had come out with the first boat and gone straight down to his cabin to strip off his gaudy uniform and dress himself once again as a post-captain with less than three years' seniority (revealed by the single epaulet he wore on his right shoulder). It felt strange (and constricting) to be wearing knee-breeches and silk stockings again, and the stock seemed like a hangman's noose about his neck. But the eleven hostages would, he surmised, provide enough problems with precedence and authority for the captain of the *Calypso* to need all the symbols of authority he could muster.

He had left the hostages waiting on the quarterdeck under the awning, where they seemed happy enough chatting and exclaiming on the sudden change in their fortune. Finally he passed the word for Aitken to invite them all to join him.

The sentry, already given his instructions, formally announced each arrival, and the time he took getting the names and the titles right allowed Ramage to greet them one by one and note who they were.

"Sir Henry Faversham, Admiral of the White, sir," the sentry bellowed.

The admiral came through the door, bent almost double: he was tall and thin, and clearly had not been in a ship as small as frigate for a long time. Carefully, almost warily, he stood more upright until he was sure he had enough clearance above him.

"Ramage? Ramage, eh, must be Blazey's son? Well, thank you m'boy; very well executed, that operation. Fooled the French, eh? And damn nearly fooled me!"

By that time the next person was being announced, and Ramage excused himself.

"Vice-Admiral the Earl Smarden, sir."

Ramage found that the old Marquis of Folkestone's son looked more like a cheerful and successful farmer than heir to one of the country's oldest marquisates.

"Splendid, Ramage, splendid! I should have recognized you – like your father when he was younger!"

The next person was Vice-Admiral Sir William Keeler, who was one of the most colourless men Ramage could remember meeting. He squeaked his word of thanks and then had to move aside as the sentry announced the first of the two soldiers. "Lieutenant-General the Earl of Innes," the Marine said carefully, as though not fully convinced that a lieutenant could also be a general.

Ramage could not remember any campaigns with which the earl was associated, and when he came into the cabin he guessed why: the earl must be at least seventy-five years old, although when the hostages had marched he had not given the impression of being an old man. His voice was brisk, although his eyes were watery.

"Thank you, young man," he said, shaking Ramage's hand with unexpected vigour. "I don't know where you collected that gang of gipsies but they fooled the commandant!"

139

The next man who came into the cabin a minute or two after the sentry announced Major-General Alfred Cargill looked as though he had spent the time in front of a looking glass, combing his hair, trimming his moustaches and wetting his eyebrows to make them bristle more fiercely.

Apart from that, General Cargill had the carefully tended look of a haberdasher and the ingratiating smile of a man trying to conceal from his creditors that he was on the verge of bankruptcy. But his voice (surprisingly soft but unsurprisingly querulous once one studied the narrow face and beaky nose) was unfriendly. "Suppose I should thank you but God knows you took long enough getting here. More than a year," he said.

Ramage bowed. "I received my orders only six weeks ago," he said politely, "and the Admiralty understood you to be at Pitigliano. We went there first and lost about seven days, for which I apologize . . ."

Cargill was not the man to give credit to anyone finding him at Giglio. "The Admiralty must be asleep," he said loudly and querulously.

"They had no frigates patrolling so far inland," Ramage said coolly, "and presumably received the information from other sources." He turned to greet the next person, who had been announced as the Marquis of Stratton.

"Most grateful, most grateful, sir. I'm a neighbour of your father's y'know. Couple of miles from St Kew. Never met you, though: you must've been away at sea, I suppose. I spend a lot of time in Town, too. Very quiet, the country. Too quiet."

The marquis spoke in disconnected spurts, like water from a hand pump, but he had a friendly face. Ramage guessed that he and his father were about the same age, and although the marquis had confessed to preferring London to the Stratton estate in Cornwall, he had none of the dissipated look of the older bucks haunting the gaming tables of the fashionable clubs.

The next man was Viscount Ball, who was plump, cheerful and grateful. There was nothing he could do to hide the fact that he was *nouveau riche*, nor did he try. Ramage remembered that Ball was a very wealthy Navy Board contractor. Had there not been a scandal a few years ago about overcharging? Giving him a viscountcy in place of further contracts was the normal procedure.

The Earls of Oxney and Beccles clearly lived on their estates, and Ramage speculated on what had induced them to make the Grand Tour. The last two men were the youngest: neither looked more than twenty. The Honourable John Keene was, from memory, the heir of the Earl of Ruckinge, who was a friend of Ramage's uncle in Kent, and the Honourable Thomas Lewis was the son of the Earl of Granton, one of the old King's newer creations. Both young men seemed in awe of Ramage, and both thanked him profusely.

Noting that General Cargill was already slumped in the only armchair, Ramage turned back to Admiral Faversham, the most senior of the officers unless the Earl of Innes wanted to quote dates of commissions.

"I hope *you* don't think we wasted time, sir," Ramage said.

The admiral shook his head. "Don't take any notice of Cargill," he said quietly. "Makes trouble all the time. Once –" the admiral chuckled at the memory, "– the French commandant in Pitigliano locked him in a room by himself for a week as punishment. Bread and water. We all had a little laugh, I can tell you, and we were thankful for the rest."

At that moment Cargill shouted: "Is this the Royal Navy's hospitality? What about a tot o' rum? I'm dried out, walking down that damned hill. Come on, Ramage, where are your manners?"

Ramage looked down at the general. "I am sorry, sir, we are in the Mediterranean, so we have only wine, not rum, which is issued in the West Indies. Apart from the issue to the seamen at noon and in the evening, it's customary for officers to wait until the sun is over the yardarm before having a drink."

Ramage saw both admirals turn away to hide smiles: they guessed that the *Calypso* had not stopped at Gibraltar and probably had no wine on board, except for Ramage's own store, and that there was plenty of rum, but Cargill's abrasive manner to a person so much his junior in rank deserved such a snub.

But Cargill was a man impossible to snub: he was too crude and sure of his own importance. "Well, serve some dam' thing,

Ramage, you've two thirsty officers of field rank, and three flag officers!"

Ramage thought of the thousands of miles back to England in this man's company and he turned deliberately to Admiral Faversham. "May I offer you a glass of wine, sir?" Faversham shook his head, followed by the other two admirals. The Earl of Innes clearly had had enough of Cargill and also politely declined. Ramage turned to the marquis and the other men, all of whom had heard Cargill and all of whom shook their heads.

"You seem to be in the minority, sir," Ramage said, "so perhaps you would be kind enough to wait for dinner which will be served in –" he looked at his watch, "– an hour's time."

"No, I'll be damned if I'll wait. Generals aren't kept waiting on board one of the King's ships by some damned whipper-snapper!"

Admiral Sir Henry Faversham did not move, but in the silence that seemed to echo through the cabin he said quietly: "I should make it clear to everyone present that the captain of one of the King's ships is in complete command of the ship and everyone on board."

"He's not in command of *me*," Cargill growled with ill grace. "By God just wait until the War Office hears about this!"

"Gentlemen," the admiral said, deliberately talking to them all although obviously warning Cargill, "the captain's functions are laid down by various Acts of Parliament, the King's Regulations and Admiralty Instructions, and particularly the Articles of War. Captain Ramage holds the King's commission, so it behoves us all to obey his orders or face the consequences, and help him when possible."

Cargill snorted and muttered something, which sounded to Ramage like: "A year late and full of excuses!"

The marquis and both the earls moved across the cabin to talk to Admiral Faversham: instinctively they tried to help Sir Henry out of what could be a direct confrontation. Cargill remained sitting in the armchair like a sack of potatoes, staring at the desk, quite unembarrassed; oblivious, Ramage noted, to the atmosphere his boorish manner had created.

The two young men, Keene and Lewis, came over to Ramage and started asking questions about the *Calypso*: her size, how many men she carried, how many guns and, given a good wind, how fast she could sail.

After a few minutes Ramage's raised eyebrows brought Aitken to his rescue and he was able to talk to Admiral Faversham, although it was hard to hear over the chatter of so many voices in the confined cabin – everyone, it seemed to Ramage, might well have been in solitary confinement for the past year and suddenly wanted to make up for the long silence.

Sir Henry had obviously been waiting for Ramage to escape from the rest, and asked: "How did you know where to find us?"

"We marched to Pitigliano, sir, and found you had been taken to Santo Stefano. When we heard a frigate had carried you all away from there I didn't have much choice. If the French had taken you somewhere like Toulon, we'd never catch up, but there was just a chance that you'd been imprisoned on one of these islands. Giglio was the first one we – ah, inspected."

"Dressing up as Italians and French, with a gaggle of seamen pretending to be more hostages – whose idea was that?"

Ramage shrugged his shoulders. "It just evolved, sir. I have some French seamen on board who were recently in France, and they sewed the French uniforms and forged French documents. And I have an Italian midshipman and an Italian seaman."

"You spoke Italian to us – seemed to be very good Italian."

"I spent my childhood in Italy, sir."

"What puzzles me is why you came to look for us."

"Admiralty orders, sir."

Sir Henry looked puzzled. "Yes, so you told Cargill, but what did the Board's orders say – you don't have to tell me, of course," he added tactfully.

Ramage paused a moment, thinking of the Admiralty's warning about secrecy. "Well, sir, Their Lordships knew that Bonaparte was keeping a number of people hostage, and they simply ordered me to rescue them."

"Just like that, eh?"

"They had some idea where you would be, sir. Pitigliano, I mean."

Sir Henry nodded. "Well, you made a superb job of it, and I shall make that clear in my report."

Ramage nodded appreciatively in turn. Nods and winks seemed to be the routine for conversation in such a crowd.

"The others," Sir Henry asked, "are they already on their way to Gibraltar?"

Ramage felt suddenly chilled. "What others, sir?"

"The French kept us in two groups. I haven't seen my wife since we were arrested in Florence more than a year ago, when the war started again. Nor has the marquis, who was in Siena, the Earl of Innes, nor the other two earls."

"Where are they being kept, sir?" Ramage asked, hoping Sir Henry did not notice the hollow note in his voice.

Sir Henry had changed visibly in a few seconds from an admiral near the top of the Flag List to being a husband worried sick about the safety of his wife. He shook his head. "We don't know. We were allowed to write a letter to each other once a month, although there's no reason to think they were regularly delivered. Questions asked in one letter were rarely answered in another."

"But you know they're in Italy somewhere?"

"No, I've just assumed it. The commandant at Pitigliano refused to tell us; he just jeered and said they were safe in the hands of Hercules."

"Hercules?"

"Well, pronounced the French way, of course. I suppose he was making some obscure reference to the Strait of Gibraltar since the old name was the Pillars of Hercules. A crude joke telling us that they were still in the Mediterranean area, not sent to France."

"Yes," Ramage said. "Yes, I suppose so."

"Your orders," Sir Henry asked carefully, "how do you interpret them now, in the light of what I've just told you?"

Ramage began to feel a liking and respect for the tall man with pale blue eyes, bristling white eyebrows and hair which was short by usual standards (in fact Ramage had the impression that while a hostage the admiral cropped it himself). The admiral was not asking the question as senior officer present and a man who could blast Ramage's future career with a few strokes of his pen: no, he was being punctilious. He acknowledged that Ramage had orders from the Admiralty which could not be

144

overridden by anyone else, be he at the top of the Flag List or an ambassador. No, Sir Henry was the husband, enquiring because his wife was still in the hands of the enemy.

What a different type of person from General Cargill. Ramage guessed he could easily trace Cargill's career so far – a commission bought for him in a "good" regiment by a wealthy father; then a captaincy and later majority. Then Lieutenant-Colonel Cargill would have his own battalion, and finally – with how much experience of actual battle? – he had become a major-general. But only one of dozens – what made him so important? One of the King's favourites or a friend of the Prince of Wales? Unlikely – the fellow was crude and blatantly *nouveau riche*, and even allowing for the Prince's notorious lack of taste . . . still, it did not matter; Cargill was in the group of hostages and had been rescued, and that was all that mattered.

Sir Henry had seen Ramage looking at Cargill slumped in the armchair.

"The general joined us recently," he said quietly. "I have the impression that in – how shall I put it? – well, in trying to explain to the French how important he was (no doubt to hurry an exchange, which would be natural enough) he gave them the impression that he was very important to the British government, so the French decided to put him in with the hostages instead of exchanging. I don't know the present rate, but I'd expect a couple of dozen captains for one major-general."

"That would explain it," Ramage said, trying to keep his voice neutral, and Sir Henry smiled.

Ramage's cabin slowly began to empty as Aitken and Kenton started showing the former hostages to their cabins. Orsini was the first to have to stow his trunk and then move out of the midshipmen's berth. Because Ramage had only one midshipman on board, instead of the more usual six or eight, Orsini for a long time had the entire midshipmen's berth to himself. Now eight hammocks had been slung and eight of the hostages were about to be shown how to get in and out of them.

Sir Henry refused Ramage's invitation to use the small dining cabin and took Aitken's. Admiral Lord Smarden had Kenton's cabin and Admiral Keeler had taken over Hill's. The

145

marquis had wanted to sling a hammock among the Marines, who were quartered by tradition between the seamen and the officers, but was finally persuaded to take Martin's cabin.

While the purser worried about feeding the *Calypso*'s distinguished guests (a problem which concerned the purser and first lieutenant a good deal more than the guests, who with the exception of Cargill and the admirals, were as excited at their new surroundings as schoolboys starting off on a picnic), Ramage worked at his desk as his steward collected linen from Ramage's stock for Sir Henry and found a tin water jug and handbasin from somewhere.

Hercules. A man making a joke which he thought would go over his listeners' heads might accidentally give away a good deal. Hercules in Latin, and coming from the Greek Heracles. Ramage cursed his inattention while a tutor had tried to drum Greek mythology into his head. Hercules . . . famous for being so strong. While serving a king (whose name Ramage could not recall), he had to perform twelve labours. Ramage opened a drawer, taking out pen, ink and paper.

He wrote down the first task he could remember – killing a monstrous lion. Then he had to kill the Hydra, the many-headed serpent breathing fire. Catch the Arcadian stag – yes, that was the third, and capturing the Erymanthean boar was another. Cleaning the Augean stables. Catching the man-eating mares of Diomedes. And the Cretan bull. And destroying the Stymphalian birds.

Hmm, that made eight. The Queen of the Amazons came into it – yes, she was Hippolyte, and Hercules had to get her girdle. And get the golden apples of the Hesperides. Ramage dipped his pen in the ink. Two more labours to go – for Hercules, anyway. Yes, the oxen of Geryon: he had to capture them. Then the worst one of the dozen – bring Cerberus up from Hades.

He counted up his list. Yes, twelve, and the only one which looked inviting involved Hippolyte's girdle, though come to think of it that led to a battle and Hippolyte was killed. That was the trouble with Greek mythology . . .

Ramage suddenly realized that the sentry had announced Sir Henry, who was now standing beside him. "Writing up your journal?"

146

"No, sir," Ramage turned the page round so that the admiral could read it.

"What the devil – oh, twelve. The labours of our old friend Hercules. I've forgotten them all, except cleaning out the Augean stable." The admiral read down the list, nodding his head. "You have a good memory."

He put the list back in front of Ramage. "So you think his reference to the rest of the hostages being in the hands of Hercules might be more than just a joke? After all, he could have said they were awaiting the judgement of Paris . . . It might have been the first thing that came into his head."

"Yes, sir," Ramage agreed, "but it's all we have to go on – unless you can think of some other clue. Was there anything?"

Sir Henry shook his head. "No. Nothing, and God knows we were all listening and hoping. No, we all heard 'Hercule', and none of us could make head or tail of it. But I assure you, young fellow, that at the time we took it very seriously."

"But now you don't?"

The admiral slumped down on the sofa. "Now – well, we've all talked about it for so long we're muddled. Pillars of Hercules was the only association we could think of, and that didn't make much sense. *Any* sense, really."

"That French commandant, sir – was he an educated man?"

The admiral looked up, startled by the question. "Why, yes, come to think of it, he was! More so than the usual run of French officers, who seem to glory in humble beginnings, even if they had to invent them. They must have been farm labourers or butchers or some such thing before they helped in the 'Glorious Revolution'. Yes, the Pitigliano commandant was different: he could have read the classics. Perhaps he was once a teacher. Why do you ask?"

"Just for that reason, sir: if he'd read the classics – knew something of Roman or Greek mythology, in other words – he's more likely to have chosen the name 'Hercules' for a reason."

"Instead of just thinking of a name at random?"

"Yes, sir; there's more likely to be an association. The connection between where the other hostages are imprisoned and Hercules should not be too difficult to guess."

Sir Henry looked defeated: his face showed that the riddle of

Hercules had never been far from his thoughts from the day the commandant had spoken the word. "My mind is – well, just a whirlpool at the moment. I think and think . . . but to no purpose. I've been thinking of the Pillars, now you come along with the twelve labours . . ."

"Perhaps we should forget it for a few hours," Ramage said. "Then we can tackle it with fresh minds."

"It's hard to forget," Sir Henry said wearily. "But anyway I'm grateful for your efforts so far: I'm sure the Admiralty is more concerned with those you've saved than the others. The wives of flag and field officers are not regarded as very important. Reasonable enough, of course. Tell me," he said, making a determined effort to change the subject, "you know these waters well? I seem to remember *Gazettes* printing some of your despatches."

"Perhaps when we destroyed some of the French signal towers?"

"No – that was along the French coast. I remember it well. No, wasn't there something round here?"

"We captured some bomb ketches and used them to bombard a port on the other side of Argentario – that was some time ago."

"That was it," the Admiral exclaimed. "What was the name of the place?"

Suddenly Ramage felt the skin of his face grow cold and the hair at the back of his neck seemed to stiffen, as though he was a dog hearing an intruder.

"The modern name is Port' Ercole, sir, but the Latin name was the Port of Hercules."

The admiral sighed. "Now we really begin the twelve labours . . ."

Chapter Fourteen

The three admirals, after meeting with Ramage in the great cabin, agreed that Port' Ercole was the likeliest place: likely on several counts. Ramage showed them the original rough chart which Southwick had drawn for the bomb ketches' attack and which had ever since remained rolled up in the chart rack fitted to the deck beams above the desk.

The three of them remembered their brief stay at Orbetello, and they exclaimed when Ramage showed how the northern causeway led to Santo Stefano while the southern curved round to Port' Ercole.

Then Ramage pointed out the forts, built by the Aragonese even earlier than the fortezza at Santo Stefano. "Forte della Stella, along this track, some distance south of the port, is still in good condition and habitable. In fact it almost certainly has a French garrison because it commands the approach to the port. Then up here –" he indicated the larger fort built high on a hill on the causeway side, north of the port, "– there is Forte di Monte Filippo. Tho' which Filippo that is I don't know. Probably not the second, who built the Santo Stefano fortress, because I'm sure these two were built much earlier."

Lord Smarden (who, Sir Henry had told Ramage, had been on his honeymoon when war broke out again: his first wife had died several years ago and his second wife, younger than anyone had expected, was "a delightful woman") jabbed a finger on the chart, indicating Forte della Stella.

"This is quite a way beyond the port. Doesn't that rule it out as a prison for hostages – after all, it means carrying provisions a long way?"

"Of the two, sir, with respect, I'd rather put my money on it. As you can see, there's a rocky islet just offshore there. That's Isolotto, and the Forte della Stella covers the channel between it and Argentario. For that reason alone the French would garrison it. And given the way they commandeer people's donkeys and mules, I don't think carrying more provisions would bother them. The fort obviously has water from a well – they all do."

"Why not Forte di Monte Filippo?"

"Well, in the attack with the bomb ketches which Sir Henry mentioned, we showed the French it wasn't much good for defending the port. I think they'd now rely on Forte della Stella, and also La Rocca, which is a half-hearted sort of fort just here, right above the actual entrance to the port."

Lord Smarden nodded. "Well, this seems to be your country. I'm a fox-hunting man, Ramage, so I'll regard myself as your guest – and riding one of your horses, too!"

Ramage nodded to acknowledge the compliment and then said: "But I don't want to raise any false hopes, gentlemen. Forte della Stella is built above steep cliffs which run all round the coast of Argentario. La Rocca is on cliffs right above the port; Forte di Monte Filippo – well, as its name shows, it is built on a mountain."

"But none of these so-called mountains are very high," Sir William Keeler protested. "It isn't as though we have to storm up sheer cliffs."

"No, sir, *monte* often means just a steep hill. But –" he glanced at Sir Henry, "– we shan't be 'storming' anywhere."

"How the deuce are you going to rescue 'em, then?"

"They are hostages, sir," Ramage said patiently. "The point about hostages is that those who have them can use them as bargaining counters."

"I know that!" Sir William said crossly. "I learned the King's English before you were born."

The sneer was very apparent, but Ramage ignored it. "If we 'storm' anywhere, or if we try anything but a surprise attack, sir, the French will use the hostages as – well, hostages. Either

150

we shall be told to go away or the hostages will be killed, or they will be killed anyway and even if we successfully capture wherever they are held, the only thing we can do –" he paused, so that his words would hit Sir William like a blow, "– is to give them a decent burial."

"You don't have to put it so crudely, Ramage. After all, the French aren't holding your wife as a hostage."

Before he could stop himself Ramage said bitterly: "No, they've probably killed her."

"Tell us," Admiral Faversham said, badly shocked but anxious to discover what had happened. "You must remember we've had no news since the war began. We don't want to distress you unduly but – well, didn't you marry the Marquis of Rockley's daughter?"

Using the fewest words possible, Ramage told how he and Sarah had been on their honeymoon in France when the war unexpectedly broke out again, and how they had escaped from Brest in the *Murex* brig to join the Fleet as coincidentally it arrived to blockade Brest once again. The three admirals were appalled to hear that the *Murex* had been carried into Brest earlier and handed over to the French by her mutinous crew.

"Much as I hate hearing of our men mutinying," said Sir Henry, "at least you stopped the French gaining a brig. And those French seamen of yours dressed up as soldiers who brought us out of Castello, are the same Frenchmen who helped you to take the brig? 'Pon my soul, Ramage, either you have the luck of the devil or you know how to choose people." The admiral paused a moment and realized he had made a tactless blunder. "Your wife, Lady Sarah – you know for sure that the *Murex* was sunk?"

"The brig could have been captured, sir. But we haven't heard a word about prisoners being taken. With my wife was a post-captain who'd been commanding this ship temporarily, and of course the prize crew taking the *Murex* to England. Their names haven't been mentioned in the exchange lists sent from Paris . . ."

Sir William looked at Ramage. "My apologies. Fact is, we're all on edge, hearing nothing for more than a year." He suddenly realized that it was worse for Ramage. "I hope you have news soon. This uncertainty – it's like a tumour, it just grows and grows."

"Yes, sir, I know, and perhaps I was being too emphatic about the need for surprise. But the way we marched you all out of Castello, signing a receipt for the commandant . . ."

"It was the only way, but will it work again?" Admiral Faversham asked. "Of course the decision is up to you. Perhaps you've already decided?"

Ramage looked round at the three admirals. He saw three desperately worried husbands, and knew they represented five more. In rank any of the admirals could be the commander-in-chief of the Fleet on a foreign station where Ramage was serving but now, as they watched him, they were anxious husbands. For now, it was easier to think of them as husbands rather than admirals because none would try to override the Board's orders to him, and in a year or two he could find himself serving under any one of them. Tact did not come naturally to Ramage, and he knew it. Good manners, yes; he had learned them as a child and they came naturally, like saying "please" and "thank you", and standing when a woman came into the room, and eating bread with his left hand and so on. But tact – well, often words were spoken before Ramage realized that they had turned into bricks the moment they left his mouth.

"Gentlemen, we looked for you in Pitigliano and Santo Stefano and finally found you in Giglio without having any clearly defined plans, apart from our group of make-believe hostages. We hoped to get you out by guile, but we couldn't rule out violence.

"One of my men was shot in the arm while discovering you were not in Santo Stefano. I said guile or violence but violence was going to be the last resort. We knew we were after hostages who were men, not women. I had in mind that if there was any shooting, most of you would probably escape in the confusion."

Sir Henry looked at the other two admirals and then at Ramage. "Now you have just found out something the Admiralty didn't know, or didn't mention in your orders: that there are several women to be rescued."

"Exactly, sir. Like you, the women don't expect to be rescued, so they'll be startled, they'll be encumbered by bulky dresses, and," he added ruefully, "no woman can leave a room she's lived in for a long time without running back for some valuable she's forgotten."

"You've obviously been thinking about all this," Sir Henry commented. "And you've just described my wife!" He saw the expressions on the faces of the other two admirals. "All wives," he added, "except Lady Sarah. I've just this moment remembered how you first met her – rescued her and her parents and many other people from renegades and pirates at an island off the Brazilian coast. Don't give up hope, Ramage."

"No sir. That and memories are all I have." He thought for a moment. He was not in the mood for Major-General Cargill's crude manners or the two young men's enthusiasm. In fact, apart from Sir Henry he really wanted nothing to do with the freed hostages: he wanted no personal pleas or objections or suggestions to affect his decisions.

That the hostages might be in Port' Ercole – yes, it was a guess, but a good one. The answer seemed plausible. The second guess (or choice: the word "guess" carried a hint of a gamble) was exactly where the hostages were imprisoned. This time there was no clue from the Pitigliano commandant. The fortresses were the most likely and, of the two, della Stella seemed the obvious one. But he knew there were some big private houses in the hills behind Port' Ercole. Surely the Borghese family owned much of the land round the port, and they would have one or two houses there. Houses big enough to hold a dozen or so hostages and their guards? Italian houses have big rooms and high ceilings, and all too often shutters take the place of glass in the windows – in winter such houses were not used. Large rooms, balconies, houses designed for occasional summer living by wealthy people casual about their possessions – they would hardly make secure prisons for important hostages. Did that rule out the big houses? Not really – the French guards, with muskets and swords, could terrorize women prisoners: they might well have made two or three of the older ones responsible for the conduct of the rest – made them hostages for the good behaviour of the others ...

"Guile," Lord Smarden said, trying to prompt Ramage into

discussing his ideas. "You can hardly dress up your seamen as women!"

"No sir," Ramage said as Sir Henry gave his fellow admiral a withering look, "but I might ask for volunteers from among people with grey hair to dress up as old women – long black dresses, and baskets, shawls over the head – to make reconnaissances." He was looking at Smarden's grey hair and Sir Henry said at once: "I'm sure Lord Smarden would be the first to step forward."

"I appreciate that, sir," Ramage said, keeping a straight face, "and it would take only an hour or so to train him to walk with that shuffle that comes from worn shoes and bunions."

Lord Smarden looked embarrassed but could not avoid nodding and saying without enthusiasm: "Of course, of course."

"However," Ramage said, "Lord Smarden is right; it obviously has to be guile. If they're not at Forte della Stella, we go on to the other fort, without raising an alarm. If we have no luck there we must try a few big houses. It could take a couple of days – nights, rather, with our party hiding during the day."

"What about the ship?" Sir Henry asked.

"So far the French at both Santo Stefano and Giglio seem quite happy to accept her as French – not surprising, since she is French built – and there's no co-operation between the Navy and the Army."

"So now we sail for Port' Ercole?" asked Sir Henry.

"It'll only take a few hours. I want to arrive at night. If we arrive in daylight, the port or garrison commandant probably feels obliged to come out at once to greet us, but if he wakes up in the morning and sees us already at anchor and bustling about our daily business, he's more likely to put off coming out: he usually has to commandeer a local rowing boat which will be covered in fish scales, so he prefers to wait for one of our boats to come on shore . . . And if none comes by noon he'll take his usual siesta, and before he knows it another day has passed, and the ship has been there so long there's no need for a visit."

Sir Henry nodded his agreement. "I must say you seem to know these people, Ramage. I'd never realized just how much

154

the siesta is an important part of their day until they took me as a hostage. I'd always thought it a waste of time. Now – I suppose it's advancing old age and the heat at noon, but I see its advantages."

"Indeed, sir, and it's a splendid time to make a reconnaissance before any night operations, whether serenading a sweetheart or looking for hostages."

"Haven't had much experience of either so far," Sir Henry admitted ruefully, "but now we seem to be combining both!"

By noon the wind had backed to the south and was coming up in fitful gusts, with the air beginning to turn sultry. The day had started off with the sky blue and cloudless, and it had stayed like that until after the landing party were back on board with the freed hostages, but then it had slowly, almost imperceptibly, become hazy. Ramage and Southwick, meeting on the quarter-deck, had looked knowingly at each other.

"It's a *scirocco* all right, sir," Southwick said and Ramage took a telescope from the binnacle box drawer to look across the strait to the top of Monte Argentario.

"There they are," he said, "the balls of cotton streaming to leeward of the peak of Argentario." The clouds, the cotton balls, he remembered, were always the outriders of a *scirocco*, reliable warnings which were useful because the glass usually gave none.

Southwick gave a disapproving sniff. "We don't want a three-day *scirocco* blow now," he grumbled. "The seas will fairly pound the cliffs below Forte della Stella. It's the worst wind for Port' Ercole."

"If it's a regular *scirocco*, either we'll move round to the north of Giglio and find a lee," Ramage said, "or go over to Argentario and anchor where we were before. That's fairly sheltered."

He took a chart – a copy of the one in the rack over his desk – from the binnacle drawer and opened it. "Of course, we could use the *scirocco* to get up to the north and inspect these other islands . . . yet I put my faith in Port' Ercole. But if we *do* go north, we must keep an eye on these." He tapped a finger on three rocks drawn in a line almost midway between Argentario and the headland of Punta Ala. "The Formiche di Grosseto."

155

"Odd name," Southwick commented, "and a damned odd place to find a few odd rocks sticking up in the open sea like . . ." he paused, trying to think of a simile.

"Like ants," Ramage said. "That's what 'formiche' means. And they're damn' hard to spot on a dark night! Still, this bit of headland points at 'em, even if it is low. It's the mouth of –" he examined the chart closely, "– yes, the river Ombrone. Sandy beach with pine forests behind. And a couple of useful towers. The one on the north side of the river is round and reddish. Hmm, a note here says it is called either 'San Carlo' or 'San Rocca'."

"Yes, I remember that one," Southwick said, recalling when he had copied the original chart from another owned by a fellow master. "Apparently it was called 'San Carlo' on a captured Italian chart, but it's 'San Rocca' on English ones."

"Well, it's round and it's red, so it shouldn't be too hard to recognize, and the next one, just as far south of the river as the red one is north, is square and high up, Torre Collelungo. And – your writing, Southwick, is abominable –"

"Hold hard, sir," protested the master. "That chart's had a few showers of spray over it since I copied it!"

"– there's a *third* tower half a mile away, Torre Castel Marino, circular, ruined. Also on a hill – and presumably its guns could once cover the whole beach south of the river."

Southwick looked over Ramage's shoulder. "More towers along the coast to the south," he said. "Those Spaniards certainly did a great deal of building while they owned this part of Tuscany."

Ramage ran his finger along the line showing the coast. "Yes, it's beginning to get rocky as you come south towards the Argentario causeways. This promontory is high, four hundred feet, with a square tower on top of it, Torre di Cala Forno. And look here to the southeast, two more. Torri dell' Uccellina. Curious that the two of them should be named together. The northern one, your note says, is tall and red, and the other short and grey."

Ramage put a finger on the Formiche di Grosseto and then squinted at the towers. "Horizontal sextant angles using San Carlo and Collelungo, or either tower and the mouth of the

Ombrone river if you could distinguish it, or Collelungo and Cala Forno, or – why, it's a navigator's dream," he said teasingly, "you should be able to find the Formiche as easily as your own nose."

"I would, if I could see any of those dam' towers, but you can be sure that if the need ever arises it'll be a pitch-dark night with blinding rain – or *scirocco* haze cutting visibility to less than a mile!"

Ramage grinned at the old master. "If the idea makes you so nervous," he said, "we'll stay away from the ants!"

"I should think so," Southwick grunted. "No one in his right mind approaches dangers unnecessarily."

"Of course not," Ramage agreed, and could not resist adding, "especially with a nervous navigator. Still, the choice doesn't always rest with us."

Southwick did not rise to the bait. "All good navigators are nervous," he declared. "A confident navigator is usually a fool who knows immediately the name of the shoal he's just hit."

Ramage nodded his agreement. The Formiche, he saw, were certainly an odd collection of three rocks – they looked like three large pebbles tossed into the sea by a wilful Nature. Three rocks, almost islets, in a straight line stretching north-west and south-east for less than two miles. There was a note written at the bottom of the chart describing them. The northernmost, Formica Maggiore, was the largest and highest rock: whitish-looking from a distance and thirty-two feet high. Near it was a rocky shoal with only – hmm, only nine feet of water over it. A good spot for small fishing boats, no doubt, but shallow enough to tear the bottom out of a frigate. And south of Formica Maggiore yet another shoal stretched out for three hundred yards or so, an invisible trap for the unwary.

The middle one of the three rocks was nearly a mile to the south of Maggiore. Small, low and black, it was surrounded by shoals. The third, southernmost of the trio, was also the smallest and lowest, with the usual shoals round it. "Warning," the note added, "overfalls extend south half a mile in a gale." Some ants, Ramage thought sourly, and wondered why the Italians had given them such an innocent name, It was surprising that the Romans had not dubbed them – something like Scylla and

157

Charybdis, the legendary monsters living in caves beside the Strait of Messina, between Sicily and the mainland.

In fact, Ramage thought idly, the ancient sailors needed to brave legends more than actual tempests. From memory, Scylla was supposed to have six heads, stand twelve feet tall and bark like a dog. Far worse, she had the distressing habit of snatching a man with each of her heads from any ship coming too close (the Strait's toll keeper, in fact!). Meanwhile Charybdis lived on the opposite side of the Strait in her cave hidden by an enormous fig tree. She swallowed all the water in the Strait and then brought it up again, and as she did this three times a day she created a terrible whirlpool, so the wretched sailors navigating the Strait risked either having their heads bitten off by Scylla or being sucked down by Charybdis.

"Not often that a frigate has so many flag officers on board, sir," Southwick muttered unexpectedly. "Not forgetting the field officers and all the aristocracy. Do the men salute 'em every time they pass on deck, or what?"

Ramage thought a moment. "Ignore them. I'll have a word with Sir Henry, because when the hostages want fresh air and exercise, if they are all on deck the saluting will just about stop any movement by the ship's company."

"Just thought I'd mention it," Southwick said.

"I'm beginning to think you don't like having guests."

"Three admirals and two generals . . . they'll soon start arguing, you'll see: they always do. Lucky they don't have orders to execute – otherwise we'd be having three councils of war a day. By the end of a week the last council of war would decide they did nothing."

Ramage laughed at Southwick's bitterness, and then said soberly: "My father's advice when I was made post was: 'Never have anything to do with a council of war: it's a coward's alibi for doing nothing.'"

"Yes, nervous sailors and soldiers call councils of war while politicians appoint committees. Same thing – spreads round the responsibility (and blame) like a farmer spreading dung. Leaves the same smell, too."

Ramage saw his steward Silkin appear at the companionway. "Damnation, it's time for dinner. I have to play host to these

158

people. They're such a crowd they make my dining place hot. And the food is hardly the proper fare for flag and field officers."

"Serve 'em plenty of wine before the first course, sir," Southwick advised. "It makes a sort of pond for the salt tack to float on."

"That's an old trick," Ramage said. "Start 'em talking and drinking for half an hour and then they don't notice what they're eating."

Ramage paused at his bed place to wash his hands, went through to the coach to measure a distance on a chart, and then on to the dining place. The cabin was small, almost entirely filled by the dining table, chairs and the mahogany, lead-lined wine cooler.

The three admirals, two generals, the marquis, two earls and one viscount were already seated, chatting while drinking wine from glasses that Silkin (long since trained in this particular trick) kept filled.

General Cargill's voice was loudest. "Guile be damned," he was telling Earl Smarden. "Land a hundred well armed men and advance in regular order. Only way against this French rabble. Their officers were butchers and bakers only a few years ago: they can't control their men and don't understand tactics."

"Most of Bonaparte's best marshals were butchers and bakers a few years ago," Sir Henry said mildly. "They exchanged cleavers and baking tins for batons."

"And where's it got them?" Cargill sneered.

"I haven't had a chance of looking at a map of Europe lately, but the last time I saw one it seemed to have got them quite far. All of Europe, for a start."

"Ah, wait until we can get at them," Cargill said, "we'll soon send them packing!"

Admiral Faversham shook his head, pretending to be puzzled. "I thought we *had* been able to get at them – Sir John Jervis and Nelson at Cape St Vincent; Nelson at the Nile and at Copenhagen. For the moment the details of the Army's activities escape me – except of course for Egypt."

"Don't be absurd, Faversham," Cargill exclaimed hotly, "we can only fight where the Navy carries us!"

"Probably that fellow Dundas has stopped overwhelming the

159

Admiralty with any more of his silly ideas," Sir Henry said drily. "Our Secretary of State for War is the strongest argument for peace. Ah, Ramage, there you are. How I wish you commanded a ship of the line – a frigate is rather crowded with so many passengers!"

"Yes, sir," Ramage agreed as he took his seat at the head of the table, "and we'll all wish for a three-decker once we have the ladies on board!"

As though the comment was a signal for which he had been waiting, General Cargill turned to Ramage and said crossly: "I was just telling Admiral Faversham that this idea of using 'guile' is nonsense. A frontal attack in regular order, that's the only way of tackling these Frenchmen."

"Oh goodness me, how I agree with you, sir!" Ramage said emphatically, and three startled admirals looked up sharply.

Cargill took a few moments to recover from his surprise and he then turned to Sir Henry. "You see, Faversham – even he agrees with me."

Sir Henry was learning, and contented himself with a nod.

Admiral Keeler said quickly: "I don't think that Ramage quite understood the point you're making, Cargill."

"Indeed I did, sir," Ramage said politely. "The general said the only way to beat the French – on land, of course – is by a direct frontal attack in regular order because by and large French troops are a rabble. I know nothing of French troops, but I am sure he does: such an opinion must be based on a great deal of experience on the field of battle."

He paused, and noted how Cargill flushed. No, Ramage decided, the gallant general has not yet smelled powder. He then saw that while Sir Henry idly turned his glass by the stem and appeared supremely bored by the conversation, the other two admirals, the marquis, two earls and the viscount looked alarmed at Ramage's words, and even Lieutenant-General the Earl of Innes seemed uncomfortable, as though only loyalty to the Army stopped him from flatly contradicting Cargill.

"No, sir," Ramage told Admiral Keeler, "this French rabble that General Cargill so well describes is always met by direct frontal attacks in regular order – the Austrians have been doing

160

it all the time, and I am sure the War Office in Whitehall has it in mind that the British Army will employ the same tactics, once we can fight the French on land."

"But for God's sake!" Admiral Keeler exclaimed, "the French beat the Austrians every time they meet!"

"Oh yes, indeed they do, sir," Ramage said dreamily, and Sir Henry stopped twiddling his glass and put it down on the table, the better to concentrate. He was slightly deaf on the left side; he turned so that his right ear would miss nothing.

"You see, sir," Ramage said to Sir William Keeler, speaking lightly as if telling him the time of breakfast next morning, "there seems to be some misunderstanding about the nature of the enemy. I am a very junior post-captain, and it would not do for me to argue with a general about military affairs. About naval affairs, naturally I am better informed."

"I should think so!" Sir William snapped. "And you have your orders from the Admiralty."

"Of course, sir," Ramage said respectfully, "and I am given freedom in the way I carry them out."

"What the deuce has all this to do with the point I'm making that French troops are a rabble, and we need to make a frontal attack?" asked Cargill.

"Nothing, sir," Ramage said politely. "I don't think anyone is arguing with your professional views on tactics. Most certainly I wasn't . . ."

"Then who decided on this 'guile' business?"

"Ah, I think that's where a misunderstanding has arisen. The objective – perhaps some people are not clear about our objective?"

Sir Henry held up his glass as Silkin came round with the decanter. This young fellow Ramage, he thought, can tie Cargill in knots if he has a mind to, whether the subject is military tactics or wet-nursing a baby. It is a joy to listen to a young man presenting a well thought out argument; it flows smoothly, like this wine. Fortunate indeed, Sir Henry decided, that he had ended up on board a frigate commanded by a fellow like this.

"I'm in no doubt about the objective," Cargill declared. "Damned obvious what it is. The objective, *and* the means of achieving it."

161

Ramage nodded. "I am glad to hear you saying that, sir," he said, "so we are in agreement."

"Agreement?" Cargill repeated suspiciously. "Agreement over what?"

"You're teasing me, sir," Ramage said, "just because I am a sailor, without your military experience."

Sir Henry recognized his cue. "Well, Ramage, I'm sure the marquis and the other gentlemen would like to hear your views on the objective and the means of achieving it . . ."

Ramage looked round innocently at the marquis, who nodded vigorously.

"Oh, in that case . . . well, we are lucky because of course unlike our former Austrian allies, our objective is not the defeat of a French army but the release of several women hostages held by the French army.

"As long as the helpless role of 'hostage' is borne in mind, obviously there can be no direct frontal attack, otherwise the hostages would be killed out of hand.

"I think that was where General Cargill was being misunderstood: he was saying that French *troops* should be attacked from the front, but of course attacking the French troops is the last thing we want to do; after all, we are a band of rough sailors doing our best to rescue a group of women hostages. The wives of several of you gentlemen."

Neatly done, Sir Henry decided. Ramage was clever enough to see there was no advantage in hacking Cargill down with a cavalry sabre; instead he had slipped in a narrow-bladed stiletto. Now Cargill could not disagree with anything Ramage said without appearing both boorish and foolish.

Cargill took out a large silk handkerchief and mopped his face. "Hot in here, isn't it. Yes, Ramage, nothing you've said contradicts the canons of military tactics. You've no trained troops, anyway."

"No, indeed," Ramage said. "If I had, I would of course, with the Earl of Innes' approval, invite you to lead them."

The earl nodded and turned his face away quickly so that Cargill could not see his relief. He had no wish to assert his authority over Cargill in front of three admirals – he could just imagine the Secretary of State for War's comments when the news reached Dundas's office – but damnation, his own wife was one of the hostages, and no clod like Cargill, who'd never smelled powder, was going to put her life at risk.

This fellow Ramage had already marched three admirals, two generals, a marquis, a brace of earls, a viscount and a couple of heirs out of Castello at Giglio, signing a receipt for the French commandant with everyone smiling at each other, and not a pistol waved, let alone fired. Call that guile, chicanery, deception or whatever this dam' fool Cargill chose, but by any gentleman's measure it was a fine piece of cool bravery, and if the Earl of Blazey's son could do it again to get the women out safely, then Cargill had better keep out of the way.

The earl shook his head. Cargill was running true to form – a *nouveau riche* family had brought him promotion, so Cargill had never bothered to learn soldiering, other than primping in front of a mirror and then stamping and shouting his way round a parade ground. Typical of the man was the way he used a loud and abrasive voice to disguise his ignorance and shout down anyone who tried to argue.

Young Ramage obviously recognized the type and had cut Cargill down to size without ever raising his voice above a quiet conversational level. In fact Lord Ball, at this end of the table, had been sitting the whole time with his head forward, hand cupped behind his ear, just to hear what Ramage was saying.

Ramage held up a hand to attract Silkin. "You can begin serving," he said. To the men sitting round the table he said: "Gentlemen, a frigate's fare is of necessity sparse."

He does not apologize, Sir Henry noted, he just explains. The admiral happened to glance up and accidentally caught the Earl of Innes' eye. The earl's name stood second on the list of lieutenants-general; he would be a field marshal in the next lot of promotions. Cargill's name must be well down a list which included a couple of hundred majors-general. The earl was so much Cargill's superior in rank that the men sitting round the table could be forgiven for thinking Cargill was trying to commit professional suicide. In fact, Sir Henry guessed, the wretched Cargill was sublimely certain that he was making a great impression on Lieutenant-General the Earl of Innes. Come to think of it, he was. He imagined the earl drafting a report to the

Horse Guards describing Cargill's conduct. No, it would not be done that way; the earl would simply make a comment, and that would be that. But that was all in the future: the earl could not visit the Horse Guards until all the present problems were solved; until wives were restored to husbands. For a moment he thought of the members of the Board sitting at the long, highly polished table in the Board Room at the Admiralty. They would not be conscious of the ticking of the Thomas Bradley clock just inside the door – a clock which had recorded the time since just after the Restoration. By now there would be a fire burning – and none of the members would recall (if they knew in the first place) that the back of the fireplace comprised a cast iron plate showing the arms of Charles II. Earl St Vincent would be sitting at the head of the table, with the windows overlooking the stables on his left, the fireplace and wall with the chart rollers on the right.

John Jervis, now first Earl St Vincent, was a very lucky man. Lucky because he had little skill handling a fleet in battle, and his great victory against the combined fleets of France and Spain off Cape St Vincent was due to Nelson, then an obscure commodore, who had the guts to quit the British line to cut off the escaping enemy. But . . . the idea fluttered along the edges of his memory . . . was not young Ramage involved in it? Lieutenant Nicholas Ramage? A cutter – the *Kathleen*, or some such name. Yes! Ramage had seen that Jervis had not realized the French and Spanish were escaping, and he sailed his cutter across the bows of the leading enemy ship, the *San Nicolas*.

The Spanish three-decker sank the *Kathleen* and, by a miracle, Ramage and many of his crew survived, but the unexpected move delayed the enemy long enough for Nelson in the *Captain* to quit the line to take advantage of Ramage's action.

Nelson had been followed by some other captains while Jervis sailed on, unaware of what was going on (or, more likely, unable to gauge its significance). But because the British fleet won the battle, its commander-in-chief received the customary earldom and Sir Jervis took his title from the cape, and Nelson received a baronetcy. Not a knighthood, Sir Henry recalled, which had no outward form, but a baronetcy, which gave him something to sew on the breast of his coat.

Yes, Nelson is an odd little man, quite out of the run of the usual flag officers. And that, he admitted, was an ambiguous remark because Nelson had put an end to the traditional idea that breaking the enemy's line of battle and capturing a couple of ships was enough to claim victory.

Yes, Nelson had recently introduced a new fashion at sea, when the complete destruction of the enemy's fleet is the objective: he started at Cape St Vincent, where he had captured three of the four enemy ships taken (leading the boarding parties against two of them); then at the Nile a few years ago, by then a rear-admiral (a promotion which several jealous admirals resented bitterly), he had burned or captured thirteen of the French fleet of seventeen ships. And then had come Copenhagen.

The man was brilliant, even if his high-pitched voice and high-flown opinions sometimes ruffled feathers. Luckily, Earl St Vincent had been magnanimous enough to accept Nelson's brilliance at St Vincent, and he had been responsible for Nelson being at the Nile and then Copenhagen. So the taciturn St Vincent, while not approving of Nelson's private life with Lady Hamilton (who did!), recognized him as the Navy's foremost fighting man.

What the deuce brought on those thoughts? Sir Henry thought back. Oh yes, wives being restored to husbands, and the Board's view.

Well, the Board's view would be a pale reflection of St Vincent's, since no member of the Board would dare to stand up to the earl, whose pithy, abrupt comments were passed round the Navy like children playing "Pass the parcel". "A naval officer who marries is an officer lost to the Service" – the earl (while still Sir John Jervis) had just about broken Sir Thomas Troubridge's heart with that letter, particularly since St Vincent was wrong and Sir Thomas did not intend to marry.

So how would the Board (which meant the earl) now regard Ramage's activities over the wives? Sir Henry realized that he too could be heavily involved in any recriminations, and so could Smarden and Keeler, although Keeler gave the appearance of being a trimmer. After a year's close observation of the man, Sir Henry had decided that Keeler would always be on the winning side – until the last moment, when he would make a fatal mistake which would bring him down. Glib, hale-fellow-well-met, quick to ingratiate himself with the wives of superior officers as he struggled to get to the top, Keeler was what Sir Henry privately regarded as a two of clubs: outwardly the same shape and colour as the card on which was printed the ace of spades – but worthless.

Wives. So if Ramage was delayed in completing the Admiralty orders to rescue the hostages because he was going back for the wives, or if going back meant a failure of any sort, then young Ramage would be done for: the earl would make sure that he ended his days either on the beach on half-pay (not that that would matter: once he succeeded his father he would be a very rich man) or as captain of a transport – the ultimate punishment for someone of Ramage's temperament and calibre.

As he ate, hardly noticing what it was, the admiral reviewed his thoughts. In the light of what he knew about Ramage's orders, and the views of Earl St Vincent, who had drawn them up, he should persuade Ramage to give up any attempt to rescue the wives: the second party of hostages, in other words. Because Ramage was under Admiralty orders, he could not *order* him, but by telling him (in writing) that in his view he should leave for Gibraltar at once, that would cover Ramage.

Sir Henry mentally shrugged his shoulders. From what he had seen and heard of Ramage, the youngster would do what he considered correct, cover or not. He had stood up to Cargill without knowing (or caring about) the opinions of three admirals and a lieutenant-general, and he did it because he had confidence in himself.

Sir Henry looked across the table at Ramage as Silkin began serving the next course. "A very creditable meal, Ramage. We must be dealing your livestock a crippling blow! So let's regard this feast as something special to celebrate our release, and from now on we take our chance with hard tack!"

The marquis looked startled. "I don't quite understand, Sir Henry: is this not the usual Navy fare?"

"Indeed not! The splendid mutton came from one of Ramage's own animals, killed for the occasion: likewise the fowl. And, of course, all the wine. The Navy lives on salt pork and salt beef; if captains want better, they buy it themselves and carry it on board. You commented to me earlier about

166

hearing a sheep bleating. Well, you've probably just eaten the bleat! And although the seamen get wine twice daily in the Mediterranean, it isn't of the quality Ramage is serving you. The seamen call their tots 'blackstrap'. But Ramage, you seem to have drunk little or nothing."

Ramage looked embarrassed. He rarely drank wine and never spirits, but he had learned to keep the fact to himself because too many people regarded a man who never drank as a reproach to themselves.

Cargill belched contentedly and wiped his face with a napkin. "Wine's for women," he said contemptuously. "No guts to it. As much use as small beer to a drayman."

"I'm sorry sir, I haven't offered you gin."

The Earl of Innes glanced at Cargill, but the remark – an insult if Cargill understood its significance – had gone right over his head. Gin was cheap; it was rated the drink for fallen women, debtors and servants: it brought most relief from life's cares for the fewest pennies. Cargill merely belched again and shook his head.

"My steward will look after you now, gentlemen," Ramage said. "If you'll excuse me, I must see what is happening on deck."

"I'll join you," Sir Henry said. "I'm beginning to feel sleepy after such a fine meal."

As the two men began pacing the quarterdeck, both noted that the wind was whining in the rigging and the wave crests were beginning to tumble and break, while the horizon to the south was now joined by haze to the paler sky. Argentario was no longer a sharp mountainous outline but a blurred hump to the east while the mainland was almost indistinguishable.

Sir Henry waved an arm forward, to the south. "No mistaking that, Ramage: stand by for a *scirocco*! And it's going to last three days, just as it always does."

"Not all of them, sir," Ramage said cautiously.

"This one is going to, though. Just look at that cloud streaming to leeward from the peak of Argentario . . . and it's so damned clammy. The Arabs have the right idea about the *scirocco*."

Ramage raised his eyebrows, and Sir Henry said: "If an Arab murders his wife when there's a *scirocco* blowing, he's not blamed. How about that, eh?"

"I'd heard that, sir, but since an Arab has a harem with several wives, it mightn't be the advantage that Christians think."

"Hmm . . . never thought of it like that," Sir Henry said. "Anyway, it'll be knocking up a sea below Forte della Stella . . ."

"The fishermen don't leave Port' Ercole when there's a bad *scirocco*. Those caught out usually make for Santo Stefano and wait there in the lee for it to blow out. There's a fish market . . ."

Sir Henry guessed that Ramage was talking only to avoid the main problem. "It means we can't do a dam' thing for three days – more, if we have to wait for a heavy swell to ease down."

"Yes, three or four days, sir."

"And you should be making for Gibraltar, not hanging round here to collect wives."

"Hostages, not wives," Ramage said gently.

"Lord St Vincent won't like it if anything goes wrong as a result of your waiting."

"My orders cover it, sir," Ramage said.

"Wives?"

"No, 'hostages' sir. My orders, signed by four members of the Board, are to rescue the British hostages at Pitigliano. However, I found they weren't there. Instead half were at Giglio and the other half are – we hope – at Port' Ercole."

"If anything goes wrong, they'll flay you and use your skin as parchment," Sir Henry said. "You realize that, don't you? I couldn't help you: I'd be an involved party. In fact my skin might be nailed up alongside yours." He thought for a moment. "Were the hostages named?"

"Some of them. But neither of us can leave this coast with the wives still in Forte della Stella, or wherever they are, can we sir."

Sir Henry recognized it as a comment, not a question. "Not that many wives," he said bleakly. "Mine, the Earl of Innes's, the other two admirals' (tho' I think Admiral Keeler doesn't feel the separation as strongly as the rest of us), and the wives of the marquis, our two earls and the viscount."

"But not General Cargill's wife?" Ramage asked carefully.

"He's not married – or, at least, his wife wasn't with him when he was arrested," Sir Henry said. "Odd, I don't know for sure whether he's married or not."

"Eight wives," Ramage said. "Not a large party. I'm surprised the French kept you apart."

"Oh, I think there are more than eight hostages in that party,"
Sir Henry said, "and I don't think they're all women. It's just
a feeling I have, but I've always considered our wives simply to
be part of a second group of hostages."

"You mean, sir, that there could be other naval and army
officers?"

Sir Henry shook his head. "No, I think the hostages referred
to in your orders (however you interpret the wording) are the
ones you have rescued. I know that because I know which flag
officers left the country when peace was signed – as you well
know, no serving naval officer can go abroad in peacetime without the Board's permission. Same goes for the soldiers: they
have to ask the Horse Guards, and the earl knows who applied.
So any men held hostage with our wives must be civilians –
people like the marquis."

"Why were the marquis and the others separated and put
with you then?" Ramage mused.

"The French probably have a scale," Sir Henry speculated
grimly. "After all, there's a scale both countries use when
exchanging prisoners: a post-captain equals six lieutenants; a
lieutenant equals ten midshipmen, and so on."

"And a marquis?"

Sir Henry laughed. "This one is probably the first the French
have ever taken. Obviously they don't value them too highly
because he's been put in with admirals, generals, earls and a
viscount!"

"The marquis is lucky," Ramage said. "In France before the
Revolution, the title was not ranked as highly as in Britain.
There are many more of them, of course, and the French didn't
have earls."

Sir Henry's thoughts returned to Port' Ercole. "You have to
waste three days, perhaps more . . ."

"I intend to wait here," Ramage said. Both men noted the
use of the the word "intend"; this was what Ramage was going
to do, and he was telling the admiral, not suggesting (when he
would have used the word "proposing"). "We can anchor off
the north side if it grows too rough *here*. No one suspects
our identity: to the garrison we are a French frigate . . ."

Chapter
Fifteen

It wanted an hour to sunset when Ramage stood at the fore end
of the quarterdeck with Aitken, Hill and Orsini. By now the
wind was much stronger, with the ship pitching heavily in the
swell which had come up from the south, sliding in under the
wind waves. Each time the *Calypso* snubbed at her anchor cable
she groaned as if in protest. Each jerk was felt through the
whole ship: deck beams moved a fraction of an inch, bending to
absorb the weight of the guns on the maindeck: each gun and
its carriage meant a couple of tons pressing down on the deck
planking at four points, where the four wooden wheels, or
trucks, rested.

The pitching of the hull jerked the masts back and forth a
distance almost imperceptible to the untrained eye but increased by the weight of the yards and the sails furled on them.
However, the thick hemp rope of the standing rigging stretched
naturally, giving the masts a certain amount of play. The movement of the hull and of the masts, as Paolo Orsini had learned
during the first few days after joining the ship (a wide-eyed and
very nervous "Johnny Newcome"), was what gave the *Calypso*
her strength. Southwick had explained it to him quite simply:
you could bend a bundle of thin sticks across your knee without breaking them, but a solid stick of the same diameter would
snap.

As Paolo now watched the rigging slackening and tautening
he remembered Southwick's words, and although he had
sailed thousands of miles since then, he was still grateful for the
old master's quiet explanation: coming when it did, it meant

that a young lad yet to make his first voyage as a midshipman was never again frightened by the creaks and groans of a ship working in a seaway.

"We'll move round to the north side of the island and find a lee," Ramage told Aitken. "There's no point in waiting, and I don't want to start feeling my way round in the dark. Man the capstan, and let's have the fiddler play a few tunes: with this sea the men will need some forebitters when they set their chests to the capstan bars."

Southwick bustled up. His station was on the fo'c'sle when weighing anchor, where he could see how the cable was growing (the indication of where the anchor was lying on the sea bottom, in relation to the ship). Skilful use of topsails and the rudder meant that the ship could sail up until she was almost over the anchor, thus taking much of the weight off the cable and so making it easier for the men at the capstan, who would otherwise be hauling the ship bodily ahead.

Many captains, the master recalled, did not bother to help the men, taking the view that a seaman was a seaman, and straining at a capstan bar was part of the job.

As Southwick made his way forward to the fo'c'sle, the boatswain's mates were busy with their calls, the shrill, twittering notes interspersed with orders sending men running forward while the topmen, the most agile seamen in the ship, went to the shrouds, awaiting the orders which would send them aloft and out along the yards ready to untie the gaskets holding the sails tightly furled so that at the shouted words "Let fall" the canvas would drop like blinds.

Ramage looked up at Castello with his telescope. "Nothing," he commented to Aitken. "No one on the battlements. Still having their siesta, I expect. No hostages to guard ... sleep, eat, play cards and read the *Moniteur*. I wonder how many of them can actually read?"

"About the same percentage as our seamen, I expect," Aitken said. "A few minutes' listening to someone reading from the *Moniteur* can't be much of an incentive to the illiterate dullards to take lessons!"

By now the men on the quarterdeck had removed the small wedge-shaped drawers which fitted into the slots round the circular top of the capstan, and which held bandages if the ship was frequently in action, or cloths for polishing brass if she was in port for any length of time. The men were now sliding the long capstan bars into the slots so that they radiated out like the spokes of the wheel of a haywain, but horizontal and at the height of a man's chest. As the last bar slid into place a boatswain's mate took a line and with it clovehitched each end to the next, as though adding the rim of the wheel to the spokes. This swifter, as it was called, made sure that none of the bars accidentally came out (an accident which could happen easily enough, without the swifter) should the men at one bar lose their footing.

Hellfire, Ramage thought to himself, the wind is coming up quickly: had it been out of a clear sky and brief, it would be called a *colpo di vento*, but as it *is* there is no doubt the captain of the *Calypso* has left weighing anchor so late that he is risking having to cut and run. Cutting and running to escape an enemy was all right, but telling the Board that one had to cut a cable and lose an anchor because of bad weather would bring down their wrath: not so much because of the value of the lost cable and anchor but because it revealed poor judgement and worse seamanship.

Ramage glanced at the distant stone wall partly enclosing the port, and then at the rocks at the bottom of the cliffs. "Use the topsails to get the strain off the cable as soon as you can – but you haven't much room to tack."

Aitken nodded and gave Hill an order. In a way it was amusing, Ramage thought: he was going to walk a few feet away apparently to watch the men at work at the capstan and then join Southwick, but actually he was giving Aitken the chance of handling the ship alone under what were difficult conditions. The only way Aitken would ever be absolutely confident was knowing that he could not make mistakes because the captain was not within earshot, ready to take command again. And now in turn Aitken was trying out Hill because this was the first time that the new third lieutenant had sailed with Aitken.

Ramage found the fiddler hurriedly tuning his fiddle. "Hurry up," he said, "it'll be blowing a hurricane and we'll part the cable before you've hove a strain on that blasted catgut!"

Finally Ramage said: "Come on, better flat forebitters than no forebitters at all: up on the capstan you go!"

The man grinned, revealing three or four yellow teeth and, ducking under the swifter, squeezed past two men standing ready to start pushing on their bar and scrambled up on to the top of the capstan.

The *Calypso*'s bow was now rising and falling a good fifteen feet as the swell waves swept in, lifting high on the crests and plunging so quickly into the troughs that Ramage knew the men there would be feeling almost weightless, hard put to stand still because as the bow dropped they would be almost forced to trot a step or two.

The fiddler stood facing outboard, his knees flexing and tensing to keep his balance. He sawed once at the fiddle and then waved the bow confidently at Ramage, who promptly ordered: "Start heaving, my lads!"

As Ramage recognized the familiar tune of one of the men's favourite forebitters, the foretopsail was let fall, the canvas flogging and almost drowning out the fiddle and the groaning of the capstan, until the yard was hoisted. Then the yard creaked as men hauled on the braces to trim it and the canvas stopped flogging as others heaved on the sheets.

"*On Friday morning as we set sail . . .*" the capstan men roared, pressing against the bars, each of the pawls clunking as it fell back into its slot in the barrel, preventing a sudden jerk overwhelming the men and spinning the capstan in reverse.

Further aft yet another sail began to slat, and now Ramage could hear the fiddle giving the tune, and the men bellowed the second line.

"*It was not far from land . . .*"

Ramage heard rather than saw the maintopsail being braced round almost overhead, the sail sheeted home and beginning to draw. Below decks forward, in the cable locker, men would be dragging the cable – as thick as a man's thigh – and coiling it down in a great circle, each ring smaller than the previous one. The nippers would be running back and forth smartly as the capstan turned the long, endless rope, the messenger, which first went round an identical drum beneath the capstan, then led

173

two-thirds the length of the ship and round the voyol block secured right up in the bow (an enormous pulley) and finally back aft to the capstan extension.

The anchor cable itself never went round the capstan barrel extension on the deck below, midway between the mizen and mainmasts; instead it was briefly seized to the messenger by the boys using short lengths of line to nip it – hence their nickname, nippers – so that the cable was hauled along by the messenger until it reached the hatch over the cable locker, into which it slithered like an enormous serpent returning to its lair, the boys hurriedly unhitching their lines at the last moment and running forward to nip the cable again.

"Oh, there I spy'd a fair pretty maid . . ."

Now the men at the capstan bars were finding it easier as the frigate slowly beat up towards the anchor, one short leg before tacking, and then coming round on the other. The capstan swung fast on each leg but the men were slowed down, grunting with effort, each time the *Calypso* tacked and briefly the weight came back on the cable.

"With a comb and a glass in her hand . . ."

Ramage found himself beginning to hum the chorus.

"The stormy winds did blow,
And the raging seas did roar . . ."

Ramage went forward to the fo'c'sle to join Southwick, who strode to the bow and looked down at the cable. He came back to report to Ramage: "At short stay, sir."

Ramage nodded: the anchor cable was now leading down into the water at the same angle as the forestay. The anchor was still holding, and Southwick signalled to Aitken, who was still standing on the quarterdeck near the capstan, speaking trumpet in his hand.

"While we poor sailors went to the top,
And the landlubbers laid below . . ."

It always surprised Ramage that men straining at the capstan bars with every ounce of strength, veins standing out like cords

174

on their arms and necks, could spare breath for the words, but they could and seemed to gain strength, the capstan's revolutions speeding and slowing in accord with the singing and the tacking.

"Then up spoke a boy of our gallant ship,
And a well speaking boy was he . . ."

Southwick walked forward again and looked down at the cable. The *Calypso* swung once more as Aitken tacked her, and the capstan slowed down while the ship wheeled yet again on the cable, like a dog straining at its leash.

"I've a father and mother in Portsmouth town,
And this night they weep for me . . ."

Southwick came back. "Up and down, sir; we're swinging on it," he reported as he waved to Aitken. The next few minutes – almost moments – were going to be critical: with the cable now vertical, Aitken had to time the *Calypso*'s moves so that she was tacking offshore at the moment the anchor lifted off the bottom.

"Then up spake a man of our gallant ship,
And a well speaking man was he . . ."

If the *Calypso* was tacking inshore, towards the cliffs, as the anchor came off the bottom, releasing the ship, there would not be room enough for her to go about because the anchor would not give that tug to bring the bow round. Even worse for Aitken, the sheer size of the anchor, swinging like an enormous pendulum in the water, would slow her down, dragging at her bow like a brake and preventing it swinging across to complete the tack.

"I've married a wife in fair London town,
And this night she a widow will be . . ."

Damnation, the frigate was pitching! This was when Ramage hated command: at a time like this he had no job to keep his mind occupied. Southwick was watching the cable and would soon be stowing the anchor; Aitken was judging his tacks. Hill, Martin and Kenton, and young Paolo, were down there on deck, busy with their allotted jobs. But Captain Ramage, having

175

once given his orders, just had to keep out of the way, his most important tasks being to ensure his hat did not blow off, and nod when Southwick (out of politeness, not duty, because he had to report to whoever had the conn, Aitken in this case) made a report.

The capstan men roared into the chorus once again.

"The stormy winds did blow, and the raging seas did roar . . ."

As they paused a moment before launching into the third line Ramage thought he heard a wild shout. Yes, it was coming from above. The only man left aloft was the masthead lookout and Ramage held on to the breech of a gun as he craned his head upwards.

Yes, there was the figure of the lookout. He was shouting – that much was obvious because his mouth was opening and closing, but the wind was whipping away the words. Frantically the man pointed to the south just as Southwick reported "Anchor apeak . . . anchor aweigh, sir" and signalled to Aitken.

The frigate began to forge ahead slowly while turning to larboard, away from the land, and the men fairly ran round the capstan, cheerfully bawling out the rest of the chorus:

"While we poor sailors went to the top,
And the landlubbers laid below."

From that, Ramage thought inconsequentially, other land-lubbers would assume that the poor fellows were lying down below, victims of seasickness or terror, but to a seaman "lay" meant something quite different. "Lay aft here!" meant come aft, and in the forebitter the wretched landlubbers had simply gone below.

Now the blasted ship had swung round so that the forward lookout was hidden by the yard, and Ramage walked across the fo'c'sle, braced himself and looked aloft again, trying to balance against the pitching. Now the man was gesticulating over the starboard beam.

Ramage looked to the south. Running down towards them under reefed topsails was a French frigate, identical in shape to the *Calypso*, but signal flags were streaming out from the halyards. "What ship?" she was probably asking – the normal procedure when ships o' war met. And normally not a problem – unless the ship challenged was an enemy which would not know the correct reply. Ramage had half expected to meet the frigate one day: no doubt she was the French national ship that had carried the hostages from Santo Stefano to Giglio. But to meet her at the beginning of a *scirocco* while weighing anchor to move to a more sheltered place . . .

For a few moments he listened to the next verse: nothing could be done until the anchor was out of the water and the men began to cat it: the curious order, catting the anchor, which saw it hoisted on the cat davit, a thick wooden beam projecting from the side of the ship forward, often with a cat's head carved on the end. The purchase, or pulleys, were inset and took the tackle (which had a hook on the end) and hauled the anchor close up against the ship's side.

> *"Then up spoke the captain of our gallant ship,*
> *And a valiant man was he,*
> *'For want of a boat we shall be drown'd'*
> *For she sank to the bottom of the sea."*

Just as Ramage turned to hurry aft, Southwick reported that he had sighted the anchor. Ramage nodded and then pointed towards the approaching French frigate.

"Pity we don't know the answer to that challenge," the master bellowed, "then we could lead 'em a dance!"

Lead them a dance, yes, in normal times, Ramage thought to himself, but these were not normal times: the *Calypso* had on board the handful of Britons that Bonaparte regarded as his most valuable hostages. The fact that they had just been rescued would not help much if they were now killed in battle. Or (which was more likely) recaptured.

Back on the quarterdeck after pointing out the approaching French frigate to Aitken, who had not heard the hail and still looked tense from the concentration needed to get the *Calypso* away on the correct tack instead of heading out of control for the rocks at the foot of the cliffs, Ramage listened as the drummer boy marched up and down the maindeck beating to quarters.

Sir Henry was on the quarterdeck but tactfully walking back and forth at the taffrail, well behind Ramage and obviously intent on leaving the *Calypso*'s captain a free hand to do what was necessary.

Aitken gave the quartermaster a course to steer: north-east, roughly the same as the approaching French frigate but also one which gained time: although Ramage had been able to guess that the signal flags were obviously the challenge for the day, the Frenchman would not in turn be able to read flags hoisted in the *Calypso* as the British frigate began running dead before the wind: it would be like looking at a page on edge and trying to read the printing.

The *scirocco and* the frigate: Ramage cursed his luck. By and large he did not believe in luck: bad luck was usually the alibi used by those nincompoops whose plans went awry, although they never credited good luck when their plans succeeded. Yet now was hardly the time for such thoughts.

The French frigate had been approaching fast, the thickening *scirocco* haze and failing light making her seem a grey phantom surging towards them low in the water, rising and dipping over the ridge-and-furrow of the swell waves. But Ramage saw that the distance was now remaining almost constant as the *Calypso* came clear of the island and began setting more sail.

"Fore and maincourses, if you please Mr Aitken," Ramage said, looking towards the west. Twilight. How long before darkness would help hide the *Calypso* in its mantle?

Running away from a French frigate! Still, it was not often that a French ship saw the *Calypso*'s transom . . . But now she had to be a plover. He looked forward, startled for a moment as the forecourse, the largest and lowest of the sails on the fore-mast, was let fall and Aitken, speaking trumpet to his lips, shouted orders for the afterguard to brace the yard and sheet home the sail. A moment later the maincourse tumbled, and Ramage could imagine the maintopmen cursing that the fore-topmen had beaten them by a few seconds.

The *Calypso* surged forward as the brisk wind bellied out thousands of square feet of extra canvas to bring the ship alive, and Ramage saw men running across the maindeck like ants suddenly disturbed. Yet every apparently aimless movement was carefully controlled, sending each available man to the guns to cast off the lashings which prevented the carriages

178

moving when the ship pitched and rolled, and heaving a strain on the train tackles.

Powder boys (the nippers of ten minutes earlier) would any moment be scurrying up from the magazine, each carrying a cylindrical wooden cartridge box containing a shaped bag of powder. Then the gun captains would arrive to bolt on the flintlocks (which because of their vulnerability to rust were stowed below when not in use) and the rest of their gear: prickers for preparing the cartridges, long lanyards which attached to the triggers of the locks, allowing them to fire the guns beyond the recoil, and horns of priming powder.

All you need do – all you have done, Ramage corrected himself – is give the orders: there is no need to stand here ensuring they are being carried out properly: that is why you have a first lieutenant like Aitken, and other officers like Kenton, and Hill (getting ready for action for the first time in the *Calypso*), and Martin, Paolo and, of course, Southwick.

Down below, Bowen would be laying out surgical instruments and bandages, spreading a tarpaulin over a small section of the deck in case there were a number of wounded; the carpenter would be sounding the well, and he would be doing it regularly if they went into action, his sounding rod sliding down the long tube to the bottom of the bilge, revealing if any water was leaking in through hidden shotholes.

If you have given all the necessary orders, Ramage told himself, it is time you started thinking about what this damned French frigate's appearance means. Well, it means your original idea of sheltering in the lee of Giglio until the *scirocco* blows itself out, and then going over to Port' Ercole, has gone by the board.

So now you have to keep out of this wretched frigate's way for the next two or three days, so that the garrison commander on Giglio does not realize he was hoodwinked. Also it is vital that no alarm is raised by the French on the mainland so that extra guards will be watching the second group of hostages.

But just consider being chased for three days by this frigate, which is identical with the *Calypso*, and therefore of the same strength in terms of guns and, since there is no reason to suppose otherwise, as fast and weatherly . . .

179

So the *Calypso* has first to be a plover, protecting her chicks or the eggs she is hatching in the shallow depression on the ground that passes for her nest. On the approach of an enemy, be it stoat, fox or human, the plover runs away, one wing dragging as though she is hurt, trying to lure the threat away from the nest. Her shrill cries of distress and injured appearance usually work.

Could the *Calypso* be as effective as a plover? The more he thought about it, the more certain he was that she could not: by the time the *scirocco* blew itself out, the two frigates would have had to fight each other, and one would have been destroyed or captured.

Very well, he must make sure it was not the *Calypso*, and if the French were not to raise the alarm, then the fight had to take place out of sight of lookouts on the mainland. Or at least the French on shore must not be able to connect the sea fight with the Port' Ercole hostages.

Come to think of it, as long as the Giglio commandant did not connect the frigate with *his* former hostages, there was nothing to fear. More important, there was no reason why the commandant should, so long as that frigate to the south did not open fire on the *Calypso* while still in sight of Castello.

At that moment Ramage saw General Cargill coming up the quarterdeck ladder, buckling on a sword. "What's all the commotion about, eh?" he demanded.

Ramage shrugged and pointed at the small grey shadow now astern. "A French frigate."

"Ha, and how are you going to engage her, eh?"

"We're not," Ramage said calmly. "We're trying to avoid her – it will be dark in an hour."

"*Avoid her*? You mean you're running away?" Cargill shouted, banging the hilt of his sword. "Why, that's cowardice!"

Ramage walked to within a foot of the man, not wanting everyone to hear the conversation. "You will answer for that remark later," he said coldly. "In the meantime I must ask you to leave the quarterdeck."

"I'll be damned if I will!" Cargill exclaimed. "If there's going to be fighting, my post is here."

"You've already decided there's not going to be any fighting,

180

and I must remind you that I am in command of this ship. If you do not go below I shall place you under an arrest and two Marines will *take* you below."

Cargill, eyes shifty, suddenly realized that he had just called Ramage a coward on his own quarterdeck and that Ramage had challenged him to a duel. Perhaps he had been a little hasty, Cargill admitted to himself, but dammit the fellow *was* running away. And anyway, who was he to threaten to arrest a field officer? A pipsqueak of a captain threatening to arrest a general!

He felt a tap on the shoulder and whirled to find Sir Henry standing there; it was obvious the admiral had heard the entire conversation.

"General Cargill, I suggest you go down to your cabin."

"But this fellow Ramage is –"

"Go down to your cabin and wait for Captain Ramage's seconds to call on your seconds," Sir Henry said. "No gentleman can be called a coward without demanding satisfaction. And, if I might express a personal opinion, no gentleman would call the captain of one of the King's ships a coward on his own quarterdeck unless that person fully understood what was happening."

"But Sir Henry, I can see with my own eyes what's afoot!" Cargill protested.

"In that case," Sir Henry said quietly, "I should tell you that Captain Ramage has every right to arrest you if you refuse to obey his orders. Me, too, if I did the same."

Cargill swung round, staggering as the *Calypso* rolled, and then made his way to the ladder. Sir Henry, without a word to Ramage, returned to the taffrail.

Ramage sighed: if one had to fight only the French . . . He took the telescope from the binnacle drawer and balanced himself to inspect the French frigate. Yes, she was following precisely in the *Calypso*'s wake. Her guns were not run out – but because she was not suspicious or because she was rolling so violently? Topsails and courses set, the same as the *Calypso*. If there was an urgent need to overtake the *Calypso*, surely she would let fall her topgallants? Ramage looked aloft at the *Calypso*'s straining topsails and then decided only a gambler would set topgallants: a sudden extra gust in this uncertain weather could easily carry away a mast . . .

So what was that French captain doing and thinking? At first, no doubt, interested (and surprised) to see a ship of his own class off Giglio and obviously weighing anchor. A sensible captain would conclude that the ship was being prudent, shifting berth in the *scirocco* to the lee side of the island. So far so good.

Then the ship bears away and sets more sail without apparently answering the challenge. How important would the Frenchman judge that? His reaction would not be as rigid as a British post-captain, for at least four reasons. First, there were so few British ships in the Mediterranean that the Frenchman would not be expecting to see one – certainly not at anchor off Giglio.

Second, the French captain would notice at once that the ship was the same class as his own, and it was unlikely anyone would see in this wind that the sails had a British cut. Third, the captain of a French frigate in the Mediterranean was unlikely to have heard (or would have since forgotten) that a French frigate of this type had been captured by the British some years ago in the West Indies.

Fourth, the French were very casual about signalling, and this captain might not – since he would assume that any other ship would be French – be very concerned that his challenge was not answered.

However, Ramage decided, any French captain might be curious if the frigate he was following stayed on *this* course, which led to nowhere in particular. North-east could only mean somewhere on the Tuscan coast, fishing villages between Castiglione della Pescaia and Talamone . . . Turning to the northwest, though, would show clearly that the destination was Elba, which in turn meant Porto Ferraio. And of course Porto Ferraio, one of the safest harbours in the whole Mediterranean, was on the north side of Elba and well sheltered in a *scirocco*.

Ramage acknowledged Aitken's report that the *Calypso* was now at general quarters and nodded in agreement when the first lieutenant said he presumed Ramage did not want the guns run out yet. Ramage noted that Southwick had now joined Aitken. It was a deuced nuisance that Sir Henry had installed himself at the taffrail: Ramage wanted to pace the weather side between the quarterdeck rail and the taffrail, but if he did that now it would be obvious (and unnecessarily rude) to Sir Henry that he was avoiding conversation.

It was curious about plovers. In Kent they were called peewits, which was a fair approximation of their cry. But how did they learn that trick of shamming injury to a wing to lure intruders away from the nest? Or did it come to them naturally, like swimming to ducklings and baby moorhens? Hmm, night was falling fast: darkness was getting a helping hand from the haze, which was almost thick enough to log as a faint mist.

Time to reassure the French frigate. He called a new course of north-north-west to Aitken. This would be radical enough to be immediately noticed by the ship astern, and within moments Aitken was shouting orders which braced the yards and trimmed the sheets as the wind came round on to the larboard quarter.

Peewits. Curious how his mind kept returning to those black and white, crested birds! They were not even sea birds. If you walked across a field they wheeled overhead, with their irritating "peewit" cry, warning everything else, from partridges to hares. Some people liked plovers' eggs to eat but as far as Ramage was concerned they were small and fiddling; he suspected that to the gourmets the fact that they were seasonal and hard to find rather than their delicacy accounted for their popularity.

Southwick now came up to him. "Glad you came round six points to larboard, sir: I was about to remind you about those 'ants' – we were steering straight for them."

"Ah, yes: they'd be hard to spot in this visibility, especially if our course had taken us through the middle."

"Aye, we'd have lost the light by the time we got there," Southwick commented.

Peewits scratching at the top of anthills: again the black and white birds with the paddle-shaped wing tips came to mind. Yes, he could just imagine them pecking away at anthills, searching for a meal – providing, of course, that they liked ants. Perhaps they preferred mole burrows and molehills, new ones, a happy hunting ground yielding fresh worms.

He looked astern at the French frigate, now becoming a blur. Yes, she had altered course too. Perhaps she too was bound for

Porto Ferraio, or her captain had just decided to shelter there for a couple of days, and visit the sister ship. The island of Giglio was now out of sight – and Argentario, too. No, perhaps there was just a hint of a heavier greyness in the distance – Monte Argentario was big. From memory, though, in a *scirocco* the upper half of the mountain was usually hidden in cloud streaming to leeward, so it was probably his imagination.

He now looked over the starboard bow and let his eyes run slowly aft. No sign of the mainland of Tuscany. Punta Ala had mountains to the south, and Talamone some to the north, while in between (with the Bocca d'Ombrone in the middle) it was flat. The *Calypso* and the frigate astern could both be in the middle of the Atlantic as far as landmarks were concerned. The nearest land, if you wanted to flatter it with that description, was the Formiche di Grosseto, the ants. With peewits pecking at them.

Ramage suddenly saw it all clearly, and he turned to Southwick. "Do you think you can give me a fairly exact course to the Formiche di Grosseto?" he asked. "No, that's asking too much. No, first give me a course to meet the coast south of the Ombrone river: then we can check our position exactly once we spot those forts at the mouth of the river."

"But it'll be dark long before we get within miles!" Southwick protested.

"The moon, remember the moon," Ramage chided. "It'll be up very soon. It's nearly full and it'll penetrate the clouds just enough to be as useful as an ostler's lantern."

"We could just as easily run up on the coast!" Southwick grumbled crossly. "If you'll forgive me saying so, sir, it's just madness to try and dodge Johnny Frenchman astern by going inshore like that!"

Ramage grinned. "You know I always go slightly mad with a full moon!"

"Slightly!" Southwick sniffed, and made for the quarterdeck ladder and the rolls of charts in Ramage's cabin.

Chapter Sixteen

Ramage walked aft to speak to Sir Henry. The admiral was (as he accepted with perfect correctness) simply a passenger, but as a man he deserved some hint of what Ramage was planning.

"He doesn't seem to worry much about challenges," Sir Henry said, nodding astern towards the French ship. "Just follows us like a stray dog hoping for a pat on the head!"

"He probably thinks we are making for Elba, sir," Ramage suggested. "Porto Ferraio would be just the place to shelter from a *scirocco*. Or he may be based there."

"Anyway, you're leading him away from Port' Ercole," Sir Henry commented. "But no doubt you have plans for when you get nearer to Elba. For after dawn tomorrow. Tomorrow! I must admit I'm finding it hard to get adjusted: this morning we're prisoners in Castello at Giglio: this afternoon we're having dinner on board one of the King's ships; this evening we're being chased by a French frigate!"

Ramage noted that the admiral did not ask what Ramage's plans were. He was either being very tactful, or keeping his own yards clear. By not knowing about Ramage's intentions (and therefore neither approving nor disapproving), if Ramage subsequently faced a court-martial or court of inquiry, the admiral would be in the clear.

Ramage was sufficiently sure of himself not to give a damn, but he was curious because he was beginning to like Sir Henry and there was one class of people for whom Ramage had unconditional contempt and that was trimmers. What was it Swift had written? Ah, yes.

"To confound his hated coin,
All parties and religions join,
Whigs, tories, trimmers."

Trimmers: men who hovered, always ready to change sides or allegiances if there was any advantage to be had. Politicians were always trimmers by nature; no man not a natural trimmer would go into politics in the first place. But generals, admirals, prelates and the like could be trimmers by choice (turncoats by a less polite name). Was Sir Henry trimming or being tactful?

"Although we're now steering for Elba," Ramage said casually, "we'll soon be coming back to the north-east."

"North-east!" Sir Henry repeated, his brow wrinkling. "Oh, thanks for warning me: I'd have been alarmed, otherwise!" He thought a few moments, and then looked questioningly at Ramage, nodding astern towards the French frigate as he spoke. "Do you think he'll follow you? Especially if he's bound for Porto Ferraio? Might think you have some special orders."

So Sir Henry was being tactful, not a trimmer! "I've considered that, sir. If he doesn't follow, we'll just be grateful and go back to Giglio!"

"We need luck," Sir Henry said. "By the way, I hope I'm not in the way up here?"

Ramage, embarrassed at having such a senior admiral being so tactful, said quickly: "No, sir, of course not: you and Lord Smarden have the freedom of the ship."

Sir Henry smiled and nodded again, and Ramage sensed that he too shared his own distaste for Admiral Keeler, as well as for General Cargill.

Ramage saw Southwick coming up the quarterdeck ladder. "If you'll excuse me sir: the master is bringing me the new course."

Southwick handed Ramage a piece of paper.

"Nor'east by north a quarter north? Very precise, Mr Southwick. Are you sure you've allowed enough quarter points for a northgoing current?" Ramage asked teasingly.

"I wrote it down in the hope you'd bet me a guinea I'd be wrong, sir," Southwick said. "That course should bring us precisely between those two southern towers, the Torri dell' Uccellina. The northern one is tall and reddish, if you remember, and stands on a hill a thousand feet high, and the other is short and dark grey."

Ramage looked at Southwick, pretending doubt. "All right, a guinea. Mind you, it hasn't escaped my notice that we'll see Monte dell' Uccellina first, and from that we'll be able to spot the tall tower . . ."

Southwick grinned cheerfully. "Better a mountain well ahead than breakers under the bow! That sandy beach'll have just the right slope to put us high and dry if we hit it. And, sir, that course assumes you'll be altering course now . . ."

Ramage gave the piece of paper to Aitken. "We'll steer that and hope for the best," he said. "And watch our friend astern!"

Aitken gave the course to the quartermaster, who asked for it to be repeated. Southwick muttered: "There you are, sir, people think you've gone off your head!"

Aitken picked up the speaking trumpet and was already shouting orders to trim the yards and sheets as the four men at the great wheel turned it, two standing to windward and two to leeward, while the quartermaster kept an eye on the nearest of the two compasses and the weather luffs of the sails.

Slowly the *Calypso*'s bow swung round to starboard, putting the wind nine points on the starboard quarter. Such a change in course would hardly go unnoticed in the French frigate, even though the visibility was closing in rapidly as night fell.

There was no mistaking the tension in Ramage as he watched the frigate astern. She had not altered course: instead she ploughed on to the north, sails bellying, bow shouldering aside the waves in great smothers of spray. No phosphorescence, Ramage noted thankfully. But no hint of her altering course either: she is ignoring the *Calypso*. And that is ironic – but no! The outline of her hull is changing, her yards are being braced up, the distance between her three masts is narrowing . . . Finally the masts were in line. Once again the frigate was following in the *Calypso*'s wake.

"Wonder what they're thinking now," commented Southwick.

"Her captain has probably just remembered that we never answered his challenge," Ramage said. "I was hoping he'd carry on to the north and leave us alone so we could go back to wait in the lee of Giglio."

"It's an odd feeling, running away from a Johnny Crapaud," Southwick commented, "even if it's not really running away."

"You sound like that damned general," Ramage said coldly. "To him battle is 'a direct frontal attack in regular order' – no matter that the Austrians lost every battle where they tried it against the French." Ramage thought for a moment and added bitterly: "Why should I be responsible for killing even one Calypso if I can capture or destroy that damned frigate without losing a single life?"

"You know me well enough that I don't have to argue, sir. I'm not responsible for the present fashion at the Admiralty of judging a captain's skill in action by the size of the butcher's bill. I've seen that it's usually just the opposite: stupid captains have the heaviest casualties. Will you be challenging that general?" he asked in studied casualness.

"It won't be necessary. The man's a coward and a bully himself: he'll apologize." He nodded towards the quartermaster. "Tell him that if he steers a quarter point either side of the course I'll have him flogged."

"Aye, that'll scare him," Southwick muttered as he walked across the deck, trying to recall the last flogging that Ramage had ordered. Yes, Spithead, many years ago, a mutineer, and even then only a few lashes . . . Strange that some captains regularly ordered at least a couple of dozen lashes every week, yet Mr Ramage has never flogged a man since he was made post. Was it the ships' companies or the captains? That's a daft question; give a captain three months in command, and then it was rule of thumb: a bad ship's company pointed to a bad captain.

He warned the quartermaster, who warned the men at the wheel, but as he walked back, Southwick believed the quartermaster when he had exclaimed that they were holding the course so carefully it looked as if the compass needle had stuck.

"How far off is she?" Ramage asked Southwick, nodding at the frigate and wanting a second opinion.

"Half a mile. Hard to judge in this light, but I reckon no more. Another ten minutes and it'll be too dark to see her."

"It's more important she sees us. Get the lamptrimmer to inspect the poop lantern: I might decide to use that, and I don't want it smoking."

"But then the damned Frenchman will follow our every move!" Southwick exclaimed. "We'll never escape!"

"Exactly," Ramage said coolly. "Not only that: if by now he suspects we might be British, he'll be even more puzzled when we show a poop lantern for him to follow us. Might even convince him his suspicions are wrong . . ."

Southwick shrugged, borrowed the speaking trumpet from Aitken, and bellowed forward the order for the lamptrimmer to lay aft at once.

Ramage beckoned to Aitken. "Keep a lookout aloft when it gets dark, and we'll have the regular half dozen night lookouts on deck – one on each bow, at the mainchains, and on each quarter. Warn them particularly to watch for land – along the coast north from Talamone: they've seen it before."

Aitken nodded as Ramage said: "I'm going down to the great cabin for five minutes: call me if there's any change up here. Watch our friend, in case he claps on more sail."

With that Ramage went down to his cabin and, after pulling a chart from the rack, sat down at his desk. He unrolled the chart and weighted down the ends. It covered the area from Giglio to Argentario, then over to the mainland by Orbetello, northwards to Talamone, the mouth of the river Ombrone, and on far enough to show Castiglione della Pescaia, Rocchette and finally Punta Ala.

And there, almost in the centre of the chart, just about midway between the island of Giglio and the mouth of the Ombrone, were the three rocks and attached shoals that were neatly marked "Formiche di Grosseto". He took the parallel rulers, dividers and a pencil from the drawer and spent the next three minutes measuring off courses and distances, noting them on a small piece of paper which he tucked in his pocket before rolling up the chart and returning the navigational instruments to the drawer.

He did some calculations after checking depths of water, realized that the odds were against the great gamble he was about to take, and finally shrugged his shoulders. Often lack of an alternative made a man brave. This was a good example. He picked up the lanthorn to return it to the Marine sentry on duty at the great cabin door. The nuisance of being at general quarters was that lanthorns, giving a very dull light, replaced the glass-fronted lanterns.

Up on the quarterdeck he was surprised just how dark it had become while he was below. Looking astern, he could just make out the French frigate, a dark blur in the *Calypso*'s wake. But could the Frenchman still see the *Calypso*? The British frigate was sailing into the darker eastern sky and, even though the visibility was bad, it was still lighter to the west, where the sun, despite having long since ducked below the horizon, still gave some reflected light.

"We'll have the poop lantern, Mr Southwick."

The lamptrimmer, a hulking man, was carrying a lanthorn, and he opened the front so that he could use the flame of the candle to light the wick. The wind blowing hard over the quarter seemed to fence with the flame, although the lamptrimmer did his best to shield it with his body. Finally the big poop lantern was lit, and Ramage saw that Sir Henry was still standing at the taffrail. He turned to Aitken. "Send someone for my boatcloak: the admiral must be soaked with spray."

"It's all right, sir," Aitken said, "I had some oilskins brought up for him while you were below in your cabin. I have the impression," he added quietly, "that the old gentleman is enjoying himself: it's probably a quarter of a century since he rushed round in a frigate!"

The sight of the lamptrimmer making his way back down the quarterdeck ladder reminded Ramage, and he called over Southwick so that he he could give both the first lieutenant and the master their orders at the same time.

"Mr Southwick, first, when I give the word I want four or five strong men sent down to the cable tier, with a couple of boys holding lanthorns, so they don't fall over each other or get tied in knots."

Southwick nodded but was puzzled, although he knew better than to start asking questions at this stage.

"Second, I want three men on the fo'c'sle with axes. *Sharp* axes. And a couple of lads with lanthorns. And six men at the bitts." He saw that Southwick would have apoplexy if he was not allowed to ask a question, and eased his curiosity by adding: "We may be anchoring in a hurry, so I want the men down in the cable tier to make sure the cable is ready to run smoothly. I want the men with axes to cut away the anchor, which at the moment is catted; and I want men at the bitts to secure the cable after I've decided we've veered enough. Does that satisfy you?"

"Doesn't sound as though you've much faith in my navigation, sir," Southwick grumbled. "Good lookouts, a man in the chains singing out the depths as he finds them with the lead, and there shouldn't be much chance of running up on the beach."

"Well, we can't be too sure," Ramage said, amused that Southwick had drawn the wrong conclusion. "Now, Mr Aitken, I see you've set the lookouts. As soon as Mr Southwick reckons we've nearly run our distance to the coast, I want a man in the chains with a lead, and you make sure those lookouts are looking! We shall wear round soon after sighting the coast. Perhaps even instantly. And now you have five minutes to go below and tell our guests what is happening. Should General Cargill offer any remarks that reflect on anyone's honour, you have my permission to leave and come back here at once. Do not," he emphasized, "answer back."

Once Aitken had gone below Ramage walked aft to find Sir Henry. "If you would prefer to be with us at the rail, sir . . ."

"No, no, my dear fellow," the admiral said. "Your first lieutenant was kind enough to give me some oilskins, and I'm happy enough here. Isn't often I get the chance of a frigate action, you know!"

"Action!" Ramage repeated jokingly. "I thought we were running away!"

"Oh yes, we are, we are. What I believe our army friends would call a tactical withdrawal if they were doing it." He pointed at the poop lantern. "Would that by any chance be a red herring?"

"Why no, sir," Ramage protested innocently. "That's what we rough sailors call a poop lantern, so that any ship astern of us can follow in the darkness."

Sir Henry smiled as he said: "Ah yes, it's just like a big

coach lantern, isn't it. Well, I'll be your postilion, if you like."

"Much appreciate it, sir," Ramage said, giving a bow. "Now, if you'll forgive me, I'll rejoin the ladies."

As he turned away he was not sure if he could still see the frigate. The poop lantern was well screened so that it threw most of its light astern, but few stray beams reached the quarter-deck to interfere with anyone's night vision. Occasionally seas surged up so high that broken crests caught some of the light and threw reflections back on board as though the waves were momentarily swirling piles of sparkling diamonds.

Aitken rejoined him at the quarterdeck rail. "The marquis thanks you on behalf of the rest for letting 'em know what's happening, sir. The general – the junior of the two, I mean – said nothing." Aitken glanced up at Ramage, who sensed rather than saw the twinkle in the Scot's eye. "I had the impression that General Cargill was verra subdued. Aye, verra subdued. Like a man who has bet a lot more money than he has in his purse, and sees his horse starting to run lame."

Southwick sniffed contemptuously. "And that's about what he's done, with that cowardice nonsense. A pistol ball at twenty paces – yes, he can already feel it lodged in his gizzard! Probably he's already rehearsing his dying speech!"

Ramage laughed and turned to look astern. Yes, the frigate was still there, but he saw her bow wave rather than the hull. The French captain had not set more sail – surely an obvious move, once the *Calypso* altered course. Was the Frenchman fearful for his masts or unused to driving his ship in heavy weather? Or simply following the *Calypso* because he thought she was probably commanded by an officer senior to himself? Many questions and no answers, but as long as she followed the *Calypso*'s poop lantern all was well.

She was following all right, but Ramage realized that if his all-or-nothing gamble was going to succeed, she would have to be a good deal closer. A couple of ship's lengths, a cable at the most, although it was damnably difficult to judge a couple of hundred yards in this light.

How he hated the late twilight: distorting shapes and colours, it made him want to blink. Then, for a brief time after twilight one somehow could not accept that it was dark. Daylight is the natural time for human beings to hunt; only certain animals hunt in the dark, a time when the human is at a great disadvantage, lacking the animal's sharper hearing and sense of smell. And, Ramage speculated, an animal's sense of *position*. In the dark a human almost immediately loses his knowledge of where he is in relation to objects round him, but most animals remain sure-footed. Cats in a darkened room rarely (if ever) bump into chairs or knock over priceless china (although often blamed by careless maids).

There was no rush to shorten the gap, though. For the time being the Frenchman can follow astern at the present distance, Ramage decided. The longer he follows the more confident he will become. He knows that on this course we are heading for the Tuscan shore; but he also knows the frigate ahead would hit the beach first, giving him plenty of time to bear away into deep water.

The *Calypso* had been at general quarters a long time, but it was unavoidable. Hill, Kenton, Martin and Orsini were still standing by their divisions of guns – and they would be very puzzled. Steering for the Tuscan shore with a French frigate in pursuit? To them it must seem like running away up a blind alley.

Not only to them, Ramage thought: Aitken, Southwick and the old admiral standing bundled up in oilskins at the taffrail must be wondering. Yet that was one lesson Ramage had learned over the years – do not explain your entire plan to subordinates all at once: do it a section at a time, as it becomes necessary. Rarely can a plan be carried out from beginning to end in its entirety: there is usually a hitch somewhere in the middle, so the plan has to be amended to fit the new conditions. Subordinates, however, are often slow to change to a sudden new situation if their heads are full of the old plan. Somehow they seem to resist any modification, but if you tell them a section at a time – keeping them just ahead of events – they react quickly and decisively.

Ramage admitted that this system also allowed him to change plans radically at the last moment without all his officers knowing . . . In a way it was cheating, but few captains could have more loyal and eager officers than the *Calypso*'s, and because they were eager it was reasonable to conclude that the method worked.

Ramage's clothes felt damp, and now and again he shivered, but he did not want a boatcloak encumbering him. Curious how too many clothes seemed to make clear thinking more difficult, although that was not to say that pacing the quarterdeck naked would produce brilliant ideas.

"Deck there! Foremast here!"

Chapter Seventeen

The shout was faint as the following wind hurled the man's words ahead into the darkness but Aitken snatched up the speaking trumpet and, aiming it aloft, bellowed: "Foremast, quarterdeck here!" He then quickly reversed the trumpet, placing the mouthpiece against his ear and aiming the open end at the lookout.

Ramage could just hear the words without using a speaking trumpet as an ear trumpet. "Breakers ahead!"

"Down with the helm!" Ramage shouted at the quartermaster. "Come round to larboard and steer west."

Looking over the bow he could not see any telltale line of waves breaking on the beach, but the lookout had the advantage of height. Suddenly the lookout on the starboard bow reported breakers, but by then Aitken was bellowing orders which were wearing the frigate, getting the yards braced round and the sheets trimmed. From reaching along on the starboard tack, the *Calypso* was now turning seaward; by the time she was sailing on the course Ramage had ordered, she would be on the opposite tack with the wind on the larboard quarter.

Reaching in a strong wind is easy on the gear but hard on the men. Now the frigate was heeling as men braced the yards and made up the sheets as soon as the sails were trimmed. Was she overpressed? Many a ship running before a strong wind found she needed to reef when she put the wind on or forward of the beam. The reason was quite simple: running before the wind, the ship was making say ten knots, so ten knots was subtracted from the wind speed. But by putting the wind on or forward of the beam, ten knots had to be *added* to the wind speed – and that was usually the amount that entailed another reef and sometimes meant handing the topsails altogether. But the change from having the wind one point abaft the beam on the starboard tack to snug on the larboard quarter made no difference.

As the *Calypso* wore round, Ramage's eyes had swept in a circle. Starting at the bow he looked for the breakers, then inspected the topsails to see if the wind was too much as the frigate swung on to the new course, turned to see if the French frigate was following, and finally came round full circle to try to penetrate the darkness and haze to spot the beach.

"The Frenchman's coming round, sir," Southwick muttered, "though I'm damned if I know whether he's just following our poop lantern or has seen the breakers himself."

"Following us," Ramage said shortly. "I doubt if they have a masthead lookout aloft at night in this weather."

"That's true," Southwick said with a sniff. Anything describing French incompetence always found Southwick in agreement.

Ramage took the small piece of paper from his pocket and as he unfolded it he walked over to the dim light coming from the lanthorn in the binnacle box. He turned to the quartermaster, but made sure Southwick heard: "Now you'll steer exactly south-west by west a quarter west," he said.

"South-west by west a quarter west," the quartermaster repeated and then, taking a deep breath, said: "If you don't mind me sayin' so, sir, t'aint the sort o' weather fer steering quarter points."

Ramage laughed drily as he watched the men turning the wheel a few spokes. "You were quite happy with a quarter point on the other tack. A quarter point now might make all the difference between scattering your sovereigns at Portsmouth Point or drowning within the hour."

"I wuz only meanin' the weather's got worser, sir; I wuzn't sayin' it couldn't be done," the man said apologetically.

"No, of course not," Ramage said, and sighted the long white line of breakers now on the *Calypso*'s starboard quarter.

He turned to find Southwick standing beside him. "Sir, this course . . ."

"I know," he said. "You'd better get those men down to the

cable tier in a quarter of an hour and the boys with the lant-horns. And three men with sharp axes and half a dozen hefty men at the bitts."

"But . . . but . . . we're clear of the breakers . . ."

"Where exactly are we?" Ramage asked tartly. "Do you want me to tack inshore again so you can get a sight of a tower?"

"Well, I don't know what you intend, sir," Southwick said helplessly, unwilling to commit himself and puzzled that Ramage should be anxious to know the ship's position so precisely.

"Well, I just spotted the Torre Collelungo a moment ago, the old square one," Ramage said. Luckily he had been looking towards the beach as he spoke to the quartermaster; even luckier that the tower, its shape unmistakable, had appeared in the darkness beyond the line of breakers like the ghost of Hamlet's father peering over a wall. Had the tower been round and not standing on a small hill, he would have had to tack inshore again to pick up another, but square, and in that position . . .

Ramage tugged the watch from his fob pocket and while he bent down to let the binnacle lamp's feeble light show the face, he said to Aitken: "A cast of the log, if you please Mr Aitken." He did not need Aitken's reproachful look to remind him that he should have warned the first lieutenant so that the men would be standing by ready.

A hurried shout and three seamen ran up to the quarterdeck. One carried a reel on which the logline was wound; another had two log glasses – one called the long, the other the short. The long one, in which the sand ran out in twenty-eight seconds, was used when the ship was estimated to be making less than five knots; the short, fourteen seconds, was for above five knots.

The third man carried a triangular-shaped piece of wood, the logchip, which had three lines attached to it, one to each corner. One of them was secured only by a peg pushed into the hole, and all three were made up to the logline itself.

The man with the logchip went to the lee quarter, and as the second seaman with the reel held it above his head by its handles so that it could spin, the logchip man called: "Is the glass clear?"

"Clear glass," the third seaman answered.

The logchip was dropped in the water, and the reel started spinning as the logchip, now immersed in the sea, dragged it off. As soon as a piece of bunting passed the logchip man, he shouted, "Turn," and the short glass was inverted to start the sand running.

The line, unreeling fast, had a knot tied in it every forty-seven feet three inches, and the knots were in the same proportion to a nautical mile as the glasses were to an hour. If three knots ran out with the long glass, the ship was making three knots; with the short glass she would be making six.

The third seaman with the short glass called "Stop!" as the sand ran out, and the line was checked by the first seaman. This jerked the peg out of the logchip, which went flat, skating along the top of the water as the men counted up the knots. Four.

"Eight knots, sir," the man with the reel reported to Aitken, doubling the number because he was using the short glass.

While the seamen were streaming the log, Ramage walked over to the compass and stared down at the card. The black lubber's line was within a hair's breadth of the letters SW × W$\frac{1}{4}$W printed against a small black triangle, and he called to the men at the wheel: "Obviously your favourite course!"

The four helmsmen and the quartermaster were still laughing when Aitken reported: "Eight knots, sir. Will you be wanting another cast?"

"Yes, in ten minutes or so. Stand by."

And there astern the French frigate was now inching her way up to windward to get directly into the *Calypso*'s wake, having taken longer to wear round. Well, Ramage thought to himself, the odds are now almost in my favour. He took the slate from the binnacle box drawer and noted down the time the coast was sighted (a guess from the time he had ordered the course alteration and looked at his watch), the course they were now steering, and the *Calypso*'s speed. The lives of many people now depended on three factors, time, speed and distance – and yes, the breaking strain of hemp . . .

Now for the bloody mathematics. The *Calypso* had seven miles to run from the mouth of the Ombrone river, but they had turned away from the coast opposite the Torre Collelungo which was, he remembered, almost three miles south of the river mouth.

There was a northgoing current but running at no more than a knot at the moment. Seven miles to run at eight knots – that will take . . . yes, fifty-three minutes from the time we altered course. In fact we have to run slightly more than seven miles because we started off south of the Ombrone – but then, the guess of a knot for the speed of the northgoing current is on the low side. So the two, extra distance and current will, probably, cancel each other out. He went to the binnacle lamp and looked again at his watch. Forty-one minutes to go.

The quartermaster, misunderstanding why Ramage had gone to the binnacle, said defensively: "We're steering as close to a quarter point as makes no difference, sir. Coming off mebbe a quarter point either side as she yaws, and it evens out nice."

"It had better," Ramage said with a cheerfulness he did not feel, but not wanting to make the quartermaster think he was distrusted. "Otherwise all of us will be marked down 'DD' within the hour!"

The men at the wheel and the quartermaster laughed at Ramage's grim forecast: in wartime a man could leave a ship (and therefore the Navy) for one of only three reasons, which were written as initials beside his name in the muster book as "D" for Discharged (to another ship, or a hospital), or "DD" for Discharged Dead, meaning he had died or been killed, or "R", the Navy's curt way of saying that a man had Run or deserted, an offence which could end, if he was caught, with the man swinging by the neck from a yardarm. In fact in wartime the Navy was so short of men that a recaptured deserter was usually flogged and sent to sea again.

"Another cast of the log, if you please Mr Aitken, and I'll thank you to have a man ready in the chains with the lead."

The wooden triangle attached to the logline was thrown over the stern again and the seaman held up the reel by its handles so that it spun freely, while the third man turned the glass, timing how quickly the measured length of line took to run out. Aitken had shouted the order for the leadsman, and Ramage could picture the seaman tying on his leather apron and collecting the coiled up leadline, holding the actual lead (which looked like the weight of a grandfather clock) before going to the lee side to stand on the thick board fitted lengthwise along the ship's side abreast the foremast. This, known as the chainplate (there was one each side in way of a mast and the shrouds were secured to it), formed a good platform. The leadsman put lines round himself (the breast ropes) and made the ends secure to the shrouds, so that he would not fall into the sea if there was an unexpected lee lurch.

Holding the coil of rope (marked at various depths by pieces of cloth and leather, because he would be working by feel) in his left hand, he had the end of the line secured to the lead in his right.

When the call came for the cast of the lead he would let six or seven feet of line pass through his right hand and then swing the lead back and forth, like a pendulum, finally letting it go when he judged it was swinging far enough forward that the lead would plummet into the water and hit the bottom as the ship sailed above it.

As soon as he felt the weight coming off the line he would feel for the nearest piece of cloth or leather, and know how much line was in the water, and thus the depth. As he shouted it out, he would be hastily hoisting up the lead and coiling the line, ready for another cast. And the leather apron would prevent the water streaming off the line from soaking him.

Forty minutes. After telling Aitken he was going to the fo'c'sle, Ramage walked up to see Southwick, who by now was wearing oilskins as the *Calypso*'s bow butted into the seas, sending up showers of spray.

"She seems to like this length o' swell," Southwick commented. "The men are down in the cable tier, and I've the others up here." He was obviously hoping for some explanation and, knowing that the next orders would be bellowed at Southwick from the quarterdeck, the voice distorted by the speaking trumpet, Ramage described his plan in detail.

Southwick nodded from time to time as both men clung to the breech of the weathermost bowchaser, ducking occasionally from spray hurling itself into the air to be blown aft by the wind.

"Yes," Southwick agreed. "I think the cable will hold." He thought for a moment. "Anyway, it'll be all up with us if it doesn't!" he grunted.

"Ten fathoms," Ramage repeated.

"Aye aye, sir. I'll get plenty of cable up on deck, faked out and ready to run. I – er, well, if I may say so, sir, I wouldn't mention to Sir Henry what you intend doing . . ."

"Why on earth not?"

"Well, sir," Southwick said uncomfortably, "it's difficult to put it into words, but . . ."

"But what?" Ramage demanded. "Spit it out, man; since when have you come along blushing with a bunch of flowers in your hand?"

"Well, sir," Southwick started again, "I've sailed with you so long that I expect the unexpected; it's sort of – well, I've received some very strange orders from you, sir, but I've carried 'em out and later I see you were absolutely right, and you took Johnny Crapaud by surprise. What I mean, sir, is that Sir Henry hasn't – well, he hasn't sailed with you before and he – well, he might . . ."

"He'll probably think I've gone mad?" Ramage offered.

Southwick swallowed hard. "Yes, sir, he might. Aitken and the rest of the Calypsos know better; in fact few of 'em realize that half the time your orders'd sound odd to the usual run of frigate captains because you succeed, so as far as our fellows are concerned that's the way to do it."

Ramage patted Southwick's arm. "Don't worry, I understand what you mean and thanks for saying it. Anyway, Sir Henry seems happy enough wrapped up in his oilskins and sitting undisturbed on a carronade aft. Aitken says he's dreaming of the days when he was young and commanded a frigate, and not a fleet!"

Back on the quarterdeck, Aitken reported to Ramage that the *Calypso* was still making almost exactly eight knots, and the time and speed had been written on the slate. And the French frigate, Aitken added, was following in the *Calypso*'s wake, barely a cable distant.

Ramage went to the binnacle and looked again at his watch. Twenty-nine minutes. The damned timepiece seemed to be going backwards. Well, Southwick knew what he had to do. Now to give Aitken his instructions, then he would take a turn round the deck, telling Kenton, Hill, Martin and Orsini what was expected of them. And, even though the present quartermaster was a good man, Ramage had an almost superstitious preference for having Jackson as the quartermaster, watching the helmsmen and the weather luffs of the sails, when they went into action – not that they were going into action, but . . . He gave the order to Aitken, and while the word was passed for the American, Ramage told Aitken what he intended doing.

Ramage watched the first lieutenant's face closely in the darkness, having already absorbed Southwick's honest comments, but Aitken revealed no reaction: Ramage could have been telling the Scotsman something routine – such as that tomorrow morning they would be anchoring in a quiet bay and he wanted the ship's boats away wooding and watering because they were down to fifteen tons of water and the cook was complaining he was short of wood for heating the coppers.

Aitken repeated the course that Ramage had mentioned, asked for a confirmation of the distance to be run, and suggested that he should visit all the officers at their divisions of guns, nodding contentedly when Ramage said he would do that himself.

Then, unexpectedly, Aitken had nodded his head aft. "Are you telling the admiral what you intend doing, sir?"

The Highland accent was strong, and Ramage knew the Scotsman was more excited than he had revealed. Hearing Southwick's warning, Ramage shook his head. "He might think I'm trying to get his approval."

"Aye, he might that. And I'm thinking you wouldn't, sir; to anyone not used to our ways it does sound a bit of a gamble. Our necks in a rope, one might say!"

"Yers, s'obvious, innit," Stafford declared. He, Rossi, Jackson and the four Frenchmen were crouched down in the lee of the fourth 12-pounder on the larboard side. The black enamelled barrel of the gun glistened wetly with spray in the diffused light from a moon fighting through haze and fast-moving cloud. "Yers – we're tryin' to lead this Frog frigate a dance. The Capting's got some trick ready so's we lose the Frog in the dark. Justchew wait'n see."

"Gilbert," Jackson said, "just check that apron: some of these gusts are a bit fierce."

The Frenchman stood up and worked his way to the breech. He ran his hand over the small tent of canvas protecting the flintlock from spray and rain.

"Is all right," he said, crouching down again beside the other men. "Tell me, Staff, supposing these 'Frogs' have already guessed what Mr Ramage intends doing? What then?"

"Frogs is a daft lot," Stafford declared, completely oblivious that number four gun on the larboard side was served by four Frenchmen, one Italian, one American and one Briton. "Needn't worry yerself Gilbert. Here, Jacko, they're callin' fer you from the quarterdeck. Wotchew bin doing then?"

For a moment, as he listened again for the hail, making sure it was for him, Jackson tried to decide whether Stafford was anxious for his wellbeing or afraid he might have missed something.

Yes, the hail was for him. "You're gun captain now, Staff, and Rosey, you move up one. Right?"

With that he walked aft in a series of splay-footed zigzags, looking like a drunken duck while moving from one handhold to another as the ship alternately heeled to stronger blasts of wind and then came upright in the lulls, like an inverted pendulum.

Stafford is probably right, Jackson thought; that Cockney is shrewd, and he has sailed with Mr Ramage for several years. But if Mr Ramage intends throwing off this French frigate, he is going to have to do it soon: the moon will be up all night, and the Frenchman was quick enough to follow the *Calypso* round on that last tack and shows up again at a cable's distance. Tacking and wearing across the Tyrrhenian Sea is all very well, but those Frenchmen can obviously work their ship fast enough to match tack for tack.

Once he reached the quarterdeck ladder he saw the first lieutenant and the captain standing together by the binnacle. Mr Aitken was still holding the speaking trumpet and had obviously hailed him.

"Sir," Jackson said, "you passed the word for me?"

"Yes. You take over as quartermaster."

As Jackson relieved his predecessor he listened as the man first repeated the course and described the sails set and wind direction. The American saw that the four men at the wheel were reliable and a glance at the compass showed the ship yawing comfortably about a quarter of a point either side of the course. Very good: the men were letting the ship find her own way rather than sawing the rudder first one way and then the other – nervous steering which usually ended in frayed tempers.

Jackson knew very well that he was always Mr Ramage's choice as quartermaster when going into action. But action on a night like this? Was Mr Ramage suddenly going to turn and steer down towards the Frenchman? With the *Calypso* rolling enough to make gunnery as near as dammit impossible? The two ships would pass each other at a combined speed of at least sixteen knots, so there would be time enough for only one broadside, and that would do precious little damage. Anyway, by the time the *Calypso* came near, the Frenchmen would probably be tacking, to get out of danger. At the moment – he pictured it clearly – they were like a donkey going uphill with the peasant holding on to their tail. Everywhere the donkey went, the peasant (in the shape of the French frigate) was sure to follow. Some nursery rhyme came to mind.

Yet up here on the quarterdeck Jackson did not feel there was any tension: Mr Aitken had gone back to his usual place at the quarterdeck rail; Mr Ramage moved up to the weather side, out of the reach of the spray. And that man sitting on the after carronade, oilskins glistening, must be the old admiral. Hicks, the other quartermaster, had gone off without sulking, and the whole ship's company knew that Hicks sulked as easily as the shine wore off brass in the sea air: in fact within a month of joining the ship the fellow had been nicknamed "Brightwork Hicks". If he was not sulking now, then Mr Aitken or Mr Ramage must have explained why he was being replaced. So at the moment, the American thought wryly, "Brightwork Hicks" knows a great deal more about what is going to happen than I do.

At that moment he saw the captain going down the quarterdeck ladder on the weather side. Five minutes ago he had been up on the fo'c'sle, where Mr Southwick was still waiting with a handful of men. Jackson shrugged his shoulders, quite satisfied with

204

his present ignorance: with Mr Ramage anything could happen, and it usually turned out for the best.

Ramage found Hill at the first division of guns, eight 12-pounders forward on the starboard side. His men were cheerful and obviously the *Calypso*'s new third lieutenant was popular. More important, he had a knack of keeping the men on their toes, even after hours at general quarters, which with so much spray coming over the bow and sweeping along the lee side of the ship, meant they were in effect sitting in showers of salty rain.

It took only a couple of minutes to give Hill his orders and assure him that he should now explain things to his guns' crews. Kenton was equally cheerful but had obviously given up the task of trying to keep his hat on his head. His thatch of red hair, soaked with spray, looked black and was sticking out in all directions like sprouting grass in a high wind.

"Long time since we had a chance to fire these in anger, sir," Kenton commented, slapping the breech of one of the guns.

Ramage looked round at the seamen, who appeared more like pirates than ordinary seamen or men rated able in the King's service. Most had narrow strips of rag tied round their foreheads, intended originally to stop perspiration running down into their eyes in the heat of battle but, at the moment, serving the same purpose against spray. Although they had gone to general quarters wearing only trousers, all now wore shirts and some had jackets. Few had bothered with oilskins but had long since daubed jackets with tar, turning them into tarpaulin coats which kept out rain and spray – until the canvas began to crack with age and use.

"Yes," Ramage agreed, "it's a long time, but firing heats up the barrels and burns off the blacking, you know. And we have such a sloppy ship's company that when they have to paint the guns again they spill more blacking on the deck planking than they get on the metal."

"Aye, sir, that's true," Kenton said solemnly as the seamen laughed. "I've even heard it said that's why we never go into action."

"Of course," Ramage said equally seriously, to the delight of the men. "Why scrub the deck white if careless fellows are going to make it black again?"

205

After giving Kenton his orders, Ramage crossed to the larboard side, to find Martin sitting on the breech of a gun,
holding his flute and explaining its finer points to the seamen
gathered round him.

"Don't let me disturb you," Ramage told a startled Martin,
who had not seen him approaching in the darkness, "but tell
me, 'Blower', have you ever left aside the chanties and sampled
the delights of, say, Georg Telemann?"

"Why, sir," Martin said eagerly, sliding off the breech, "do
you know his work?"

"I do," Ramage said with mock irritation in his voice, "but no
thanks to you. I haven't heard you play a note of Telemann
while serving in this ship."

"No, sir, because the men prefer the popular tunes they know.
But I play Telemann in my imagination almost every day. I've
worked my way through the concerti with my imagination
providing the orchestra and any other necessary instruments –
oboes, violins, bassoon, harpsichord, whatever is called for.
Now I'm halfway through the overtures."

"But the music – you can't know it all by heart?"

"No, sir, but my trunk's half full of sheet music. I don't need
music for Telemann's fantasies, of course. And I've Handel's
sonatas for the flute – my mother gave me all fifteen for flute
and oboe just before we sailed."

Ramage cursed silently to himself. Music was the one thing
he missed at sea – he blotted out thoughts of Sarah, thinking only
of the time before he was married – and he had never thought of
Martin playing anything on his flute but tunes for the men. All
those evenings when he could have been listening to Telemann,
who was one of his favourites. Did Aitken like music, and
Kenton? Hill, come to think of it, probably did.

"Don't get that damaged," he told Martin, pointing to the
flute. "After tomorrow we'll try and improve this ship's appreci-
ation of serious music."

Martin grinned and said: "I have two flutes, sir. I always
think of this as my working one. My best is in its own baize-
lined case. I rarely do more than take it out and polish it."

"You can start sorting through your sheet music tomorrow,"
Ramage said. "Meanwhile time passes. What I want you to do

when you get the order is this." Quickly, with the seamen listening and most of them nodding approvingly without realizing it, Ramage gave his instructions and then made his way aft, to find Orsini.

The young Italian was standing at a gunport, peering out and trying to glimpse the frigate astern while the gun captains chatted and most of the crews sat on the deck, backs against the carriages. Some seemed to be asleep, despite the spray, the creaking of the ropes of the tackles and the grumbling of the trucks as the guns moved an inch or so with each roll of the ship.

Orsini listened attentively as Ramage gave him his orders, ending with: "Any questions?"

"Not about the orders, sir. But are we leaving Tuscany for good?"

Ramage shrugged. "It depends, but I doubt it."

He understood immediately that it was no idle question, knowing Orsini's deep love for Tuscany, since he shared it. Most British seamen seeing the Lizard fading in the distance as they started off on a voyage from England wondered whether they would ever see their home again. Paolo must be wondering if that fleeting glimpse of breakers in the darkness would be the last time he saw Tuscany. The last time, or anyway, the last time for many years.

"It depends on whether our trick works," Ramage said, "if 'trick' is the right word."

After joking with the guns' crews, Ramage went back to the quarterdeck to find that Aitken, in anticipation of his return, was waiting for the seamen with the logline to report the *Calypso*'s speed. While he waited Ramage looked yet again at his watch in the light from the binnacle. Fourteen minutes to go, and damnation, he had forgotten to have a word with the lookouts. Still, perhaps that was all to the good: in a few moments he would send round a couple of seamen to warn the lookouts that in ten minutes or so they should see . . . *should*, but with the darkness and haze *would* they . . ?

Chapter
Eighteen

Ramage slipped the watch back into his fob. "Send 'em off," he said, and Aitken snapped an order to two seamen, who hurried down the ladders to warn the lookouts amidships and forward. Aitken called over to the lookouts on each quarter, and Ramage saw the admiral stir as he heard the words above the howling wind.

There was no question now of being suspected of seeking Sir Henry's approval and, Ramage thought, not telling the old man at this stage might seem unnecessarily discourteous. He walked aft and Sir Henry slid off the breech of the carronade. "Expecting some action, eh?"

"I don't know what to expect, sir," Ramage said frankly. "I'm not sympathetic towards gamblers because usually a bit of thought lessens the odds considerably, but this time – well, I've got to stake everything on one throw of the dice."

"No second throw, then?"

Ramage shook his head, conscious of the minutes ticking away and listening: when the first shout came everything would happen with bewildering speed. "No, sir; we have to win the first time, or else we'll be done for. I'm sorry I've got you all into this situation."

"Not your fault," Sir Henry said gruffly. "Just bad luck that this damned frigate –" he gestured astern at the dim shape in the wake, "– should have arrived when she did."

"So I'm intending to do this," Ramage said, quickly explaining his plan. At the end of it Sir Henry turned slightly so that he could look straight into Ramage's face.

"You're quite mad, of course," he said quietly, "it's the craziest thing I've ever heard, and there's a good chance we'll all drown in the next few minutes."

Just as well I did not ask for his permission, Ramage thought to himself and, coming from Sir Henry, such a judgement was not very heartening – to say the least.

"No," Sir Henry said, drawing out the words as though he had carefully searched his memory for them, "I've never heard of anything quite so crazy." He slapped his thigh, and for a moment Ramage thought the admiral was going to give him direct orders, saying he was taking command of the *Calypso*. "It's so crazy that –" he paused, as though trying to construct some exquisitely insulting phrase, "– it'll probably succeed. From what I've seen and heard of you, young Ramage, you have three possible fates waiting for you: French roundshot lopping off your head; or you'll come a cropper and a court martial will make sure you end up in front of a firing squad like Admiral Byng; or you'll command your own fleet at an early age. I wouldn't wager a single guinea on which it'll be."

"Thank you, sir," said a relieved Ramage. "So keep your guinea waiting safe in your pocket, and please excuse me for a few minutes while I attend to the business on hand!"

He went back to the quarterdeck rail by way of the binnacle, where the flickering candle told him exactly five minutes remained. Aitken stood a yard to his left, holding the speaking trumpet but otherwise seeming no different from his usual stance during a normal night watch. Ramage sensed rather than saw that Jackson was watching the compass and the weather luffs of the sails with the same easy but acute attention of a hovering osprey. The third man, whose task was to turn the glass when the log was heaved, waited for his two mates to return from whatever they were doing running round the ship. The wooden reel on which the logline was wound suddenly began trundling across the deck, dislodged by a sudden and particularly violent roll, and the seaman hurriedly grabbed it.

Ramage finally counted to three hundred. The slow count, each number representing a second, meant that five minutes had passed. Now was the time – but nothing was happening. He began counting again, one-and-two-and-three-and-four . . . Six minutes and seven, eight and nine . . .

He walked over to the binnacle again. He stared at the watch, not wanting to believe what the hands confirmed. Yes, several seconds more than ten minutes had elapsed. He went back to the rail. It was absurd to be so precise; the log was not *that* accurate, nor the wind that constant. Any estimate of the speed of the northgoing current was no more than a guess, with the prize going to any number between one knot and three. Had that fellow Hicks been keeping to the course as precisely as he claimed? And had Ramage himself made mistakes in working out the course and taking it off the chart? It was easy enough when working with the dim light from a lanthorn to read a course off the compass rose on the chart and make a mistake of a point: Southwick's writing was small, and SW × W$\frac{1}{4}$W could easily be misread. And was the chart accurately drawn? After all, it was only a copy, with no indication who made the original survey. So the *Calypso*, followed by the Frenchman, could easily be sailing the wrong course at the wrong speed over the wrong estimated distance.

"Clew up the courses," he told Aitken. That would slow down the *Calypso* appreciably, and with luck the Frenchman would not notice: she would close with the *Calypso*, and probably put it down to a fluke of the wind.

Aitken's bellowed orders quickly resulted in the frigate's lowest and largest sails losing their bulging shape; quickly the clewlines hauled the corners of the rectangles of canvas up towards the middle; the buntlines hoisted the centres upwards, so that it looked as though a giant hand was squeezing the sails in the middle.

Almost at once the *Calypso* pitched and rolled less violently. Now the fore and maintopsails were doing all the work, but from astern, Ramage hoped, it would be difficult to see that the courses were not still drawing.

He took his telescope from the drawer and steadied himself. The Frenchman was ploughing on, showers of spray leaping away from her stem like a gull's wings. Even in the faint light she looked a fine sight: there was enough spray to outline her hull, as though the ship was a bird preening herself on a nest of

210

light. And yes, she was beginning to close the distance. At least, she seemed to be, but Ramage knew that was what he wanted her to be doing. "Aitken," he said, "get the nightglass and see what you make of our friend."

Aitken braced himself against the roll, after checking that the focusing tube of the telescope was out far enough to suit his eye. He seemed to examine the ship for an age before shutting the telescope with a snap and reporting casually to Ramage: "She's made up a lot o' distance; I have my doubts if she's half a cable astern of us now.

"And she's not reducing her canvas – at least, she hasn't started yet," he added. "And with this sea, I have my doubts if we were getting a proper reading of our speed."

"Faster or slower?" Ramage demanded.

"Oh, I think we might well have been going . . . well, quite a bit – perhaps half a knot –"

"Come on!" Ramage exclaimed impatiently.

"Half a knot slower," Aitken said, and Ramage realized that the Scotsman had deliberately taken his time, as a hint to Ramage that the tension was rising too high.

But damnation, Aitken did not have the responsibility for possibly drowning everyone. Still, Aitken would drown along with the rest, so it did not make a ha'porth of difference whose responsibility it was: death was always completely fair, carrying off the guilty and the innocent, the rascals and the good men.

The *Calypso* butted into three successive waves, her stem slicing off sheets of spray which flung aft like heavy rain-squalls. Suddenly Aitken pointed aloft and put the mouthpiece of the speaking trumpet to his ear, aiming the bell-mouthed open end at the foremasthead.

Ramage waited for Aitken to report whatever had been hailed. Instead the first lieutenant reversed the speaking trumpet and shouted: "Foremasthead: quarterdeck here. Repeat your hail."

Again the wind whipped the lookout's words away to leeward. Damnation, the lookout must have seen *something*, but in which direction?

Suddenly a man ran up the lee-side quarterdeck ladder. "Larboard forward lookout, sir – you can't hear us. Ship or

211

rock dead ahead, maybe three cables, and also breakers five points to larboard, mebbe four cables!"

"Very well, back to the fo'c'sle! Make sure Mr Southwick knows."

Which was which? Was the rock ahead the northern one, Formica Maggiore, thirty-two feet high and whitish, with a bank of rocks extending southwards? Or the middle, eight cables to the south-east of it, blackish and with a bank extending north-west? Certainly it was not the southernmost because there was nothing southwards of it to cause breakers.

A thudding up the starboard side ladder made Ramage turn. "Lookout, starboard bow, sir. Mr Southwick says the middle rock is dead ahead – it's not high enough to be the northern one; and the southern one's five points to larboard."

"Very well, my compliments to Mr Southwick and tell him to stand by."

Damn, damn, damn . . . they had found the ants, but which one to choose? He had hoped they would come up to the northern, the Formica Maggiore, but they were lucky to spot any of them.

So is it to be the middle one, now dead ahead, or the smaller one to larboard? Well, altering course five points to larboard will alert the frigate astern. More important, with the *Calypso* steering direct for the middle rock and the Frenchman precisely in her wake, the *Calypso*'s bulk will almost certainly be obscuring the rock, and anyway the French will hardly expect . . .

And there it was, dead ahead, a black smudge on what passed for the horizon. With the ship rolling and pitching it seemed to be bobbing up each side of the masts, the rigging frequently obscuring it as though a net was swinging in front. Distance? Two cables, perhaps less.

Aitken now had his nightglass. "Cable and a half distant, sir, judging from the seas breaking round it."

Ramage turned to look at the French frigate and was startled to see how much she had caught up. He snatched Aitken's nightglass and inspected her. "She's run her guns out!" he exclaimed. "She's decided we're British and is getting ready to run up alongside and give us a few broadsides!"

"Aye, that'd be likely," Aitken agreed. "She probably thinks that going to windward she has a knot or two's advantage over us."

"As long as everyone on her quarterdeck is concentrating on us! Hellfire, Aitken, quick, a cast of the lead!"

Ramage cursed his own inattention as Aitken shouted through the speaking trumpet, but almost instantly came back the cry: "By the deep nine, sir!"

Ramage told himself that if he lived he would promote that leadsman who had been sensible enough to take a cast the moment he heard the lookout's hail from the foretopmasthead – the hail which the quarterdeck had missed.

By the deep nine: fifty-four feet. Close. And the rock dead ahead, closing fast. And astern the Frenchman closing fast. Every damned thing closing fast.

"By the mark five!"

Again the leadsman's hail: five fathoms, which was thirty feet: the *Calypso* had a bare fifteen feet under her forefoot. He strained his eyes. The rock seemed to be racing towards them now like an approaching ship. Much less than a cable; perhaps only a hundred yards ahead, with the Frenchman a hundred yards astern and beginning to alter course a point, to run up on the starboard side? Damn her!

In an emergency, which way would that French captain turn – to larboard, which meant going about, with the danger in these seas of getting caught in stays, or would he bear away to starboard, bringing the wind round to three or four points on the quarter? That was the sure and safe thing to do, and Ramage guessed he would do it – when the time came!

And there was the rock. The *Calypso* was almost on top of it. No, make an allowance for darkness distorting distance.

"By the mark five!"

The leadsman was working fast; coiling up that much line between casts was hard work.

"Give me the speaking trumpet," he told Aitken, "but be ready: if we miss . . ."

Calling "Stand by" to Jackson, he jammed the mouthpiece against his mouth, took one more look at the rock, and shook his head: he had left it too late: the *Calypso* would hit the rock (or pile up on a shoal circling it) while making seven or eight knots!

"Mr Southwick – foredeck there! *Let go!*"

Almost simultaneously he felt rather than heard a series of thuds – the axes cutting the anchor adrift at the cathead; then, a few moments later he smelled burning. The anchor cable was now racing through the hawse and round the bitts, the hemp scorching with the friction against the wood.

"Larboard!" he yelled at Jackson and while the helmsmen spun the wheel with desperate urgency, Aitken snatched the proffered speaking trumpet and gave a stream of sail orders and then waited. Ramage could only imagine the anchor cable running out. Come on! he implored Southwick under his breath: snub the bloody cable and get that anchor biting home before we hit the rock! No, he decided, there is not room for the *Calypso* to swing round, like a running dog suddenly brought up all standing by its leash . . .

He pictured the men at the bitts struggling to loop over bights of heavy, stiff cable to slow it up and finally stop it running out. No, it was hopeless, the *Calypso* was sailing too fast: trying to stop six hundred tons of frigate like that – either the cable would break under the strain or the men would never hold it on the bitts.

But – yes! Yes, the rock was sliding to starboard – an illusion caused by the *Calypso* beginning to turn to larboard. And the blasted French frigate? There she was, topsails and courses in straining curves, and now on the *Calypso*'s starboard quarter. And not changing course.

Aitken was shouting, sails slatting, the yards were being braced round: then suddenly the *Calypso*'s stern seemed to slew to larboard, as though skidding on ice.

"The cable held, sir!" Aitken shouted jubilantly. He pointed down on the maindeck. "Sent the men at the sheets and braces sprawling. No ship ever tacked so fast! And look at the Frenchman!"

Within moments Ramage heard heavier thuds from forward and then, after a whiplash noise like a pistol shot in a valley, the *Calypso* leapt forward as Southwick's men chopped through the cable which had done its task of bringing round the *Calypso*'s bow in – a minute? Perhaps two.

"North-east by east," Ramage called to Jackson. That would

put the wind on the starboard beam – and mean she was sailing back almost along her own wake.

Suddenly Aitken was banging him on the shoulder and screaming: "Look! Look for the love of God look!"

Ramage stared into the darkness in the direction Aitken was pointing. There, almost astern, was the rock and, just north of it, a bulky black shape. Shape? No, it was almost shapeless! Ramage strained his eyes, then grabbed a proffered nightglass.

Yes, as he had guessed, the French frigate had turned to starboard after suddenly sighting the rock revealed by the *Calypso*'s unexpected turn to larboard. She had swung to starboard to miss ramming the rock but, as Ramage had intended, had run on to the hidden shoal stretching north-westward for a couple of hundred yards. Two hundred yards of innocent-looking sea – but only a few feet below the surface and like a monstrous lower jaw was the layer of jagged rocks of a shoal waiting to rip the bottom out of an unwary ship.

Then an excited Southwick was standing beside him, pumping his hand and bellowing: "It worked, by God! Snatched us round as though we were a bull with a ring in its nose. But," he added, his voice admonishing, "you ran it damned close, sir! By the time we had the cable snubbed and the ship began to swing, I could dam' near touch that rock with my hand. Did you hear the leadsman?"

"Don't tell me about it," Ramage said firmly. "We're still sailing and our pursuer isn't, and that's enough!"

The sudden impact, stopping the French ship as she was sailing at about nine knots, had sent all three masts by the board. And seldom, Ramage thought, had "by the board" been such an accurate description: the masts snapped at deck level ("by the board") as cleanly as trampled bluebell stalks and collapsed forward. The foremast went over the bow, tumbling down on the bowsprit and jibboom; the mainmast crashed down on to the stump of the foremast, and the mizen had followed. Spread over the wreckage, like a great fishing net tossed aside carelessly, the standing and running rigging softened the harsh line of broken masts and slewed yards. And beneath all that wreckage men must be trapped. Many would be dead. He turned away to face Sir Henry.

"You're a lucky gambler!" Sir Henry said, still almost shapeless in borrowed oilskins, and shook him by the hand. "How you judged when to let go the anchor so that it bit in time for us to swing and miss the rock, I don't know –"

"Better not ask, sir," Ramage said.

"Well, you did it, and in my letter to the Board I shall say it was fine judgement. And you, Mr Southwick. You must have been running about on the fo'c'sle, but you didn't even lose your hat!"

"It's well anchored down, sir," Southwick said, tugging locks of his flowing white hair.

"What now, Mr Ramage?" Sir Henry asked, and Ramage recognized the tone. That was the trouble with being lucky: everyone then started expecting miracles . . .

Chapter
Nineteen

Time and time again the *Calypso* pitched and snubbed sharply like an angry tethered bull as the cable groaned. Nevertheless, considering they had anchored the ship in the dark using only the lead to keep them from running up on to the shoal, and were determined to be within gunshot of the stranded Frenchmen at daylight, Ramage was quite content.

The *Calypso* was headed south-east, into the wind with the middle rock of the Formiche di Grosseto, for which they had been steering last night, now on the starboard bow, a jagged black tooth growing from a smother of spray. The French frigate was on the starboard beam, a cable distant.

"She's so much like us to look at . . . and all I can think is that's how we'd look if we'd run on to the bank!" Southwick said.

"I've been thinking that ever since I had a good look at dawn," Aitken said.

Ramage laughed drily. "I hope you've both learned a lesson: that's what happens if you have a poor navigator, or keep a poor lookout."

"That wasn't what put him up there," Southwick protested.

"No, and that's the third lesson: never assume the ship you're following knows where she is or is keeping a sharp lookout," Ramage said, "and if she's an enemy, assume she's going to play a trick."

"Don't keep on, sir," Aitken pleaded, "or you'll have me shedding tears of remorse over the way we led that poor Frenchman astray."

Ramage examined the "poor Frenchman" once again with his telescope. Yes, from the moment the Frenchman began his turn to starboard he was doomed. If he'd turned to larboard immediately, following the *Calypso*, he would still have hit the rock because he had no time to let go an anchor to stop and then turn him quickly. By turning to starboard he had just missed the rock, passing it close to larboard, only – as Ramage had intended – to drive up on the rocky shoal stretching north-west from the rock.

The frigate would bounce from rock to rock for a few yards with an impact that must have ripped her bottom as it sent her masts by the board, before heeling to starboard and coming to rest, still looking as though any moment she might topple off the edge of the shoal into deep water and sink.

Although the sea had eased down a little since last night, the waves still made a foaming white collar round the rock and swept on to hit the Frenchman's stern, frequently driving green seas unbroken over her quarterdeck. Already the sternlights of the captain's cabin had been stove in and seas swept through, to pour down into the gunroom. She must be holed badly: in fact, staring at her in the circle shown by the glass, it was clear that despite the largest of the swell waves swirling round her, she was not lifting to any of them: she was inert, resting (impaled rather) on the hidden rocks of the shoal.

The stricken ship was heeled so far that the men in the *Calypso* had the same view as a gull flying high over her starboard side.

As Ramage had seen fleetingly in the night before, her masts had gone at deck level, each falling forward. The foremast had crashed down on the fo'c'sle and launched the topmast on to the bowsprit, while the topgallant mast had gone like a giant javelin into the jibboom, carrying it away so that it was crumpled over the bow like a giant's broken fishing rod.

All the standing and running rigging – shrouds which should keep the masts braced athwartships, stays holding them fore and aft, the halyards for hoisting the yards, and the braces for trimming them – all this cordage looked like a carelessly thrown gladiator's net. The yards themselves were slewed across the deck; some, broken, hung over the side. Sails, what was left of them, fluttered like shredded bedsheets, dark patches showing

218

where the sea sluiced over the canvas and occasionally, like a dog shaking itself, throwing up fine spray.

Yet Ramage was less interested in all that than what was stowed on deck amidships and what was hanging from davits aft.

"There are two boats on the booms amidships which don't seem to be damaged," he told Aitken. "Why the devil they weren't crushed I don't know. Some wreckage – from the mizenmast, probably – has stove in the boat in the larboard quarter davit, but the one on the starboard quarter – the one you can see – looks undamaged."

"So some of the Frenchmen can row on shore and raise the alarm," Aitken commented.

"When the sea has eased down. They'd never launch a boat in this. In fact they've only one useful boat for the time being – the one in the quarter davits – because without masts, and thus stay tackles, they can't hoist out the boom boats."

"No, but with a calmer sea they can manhandle them and just shove 'em over the side, and then bail," Southwick commented.

"Oh yes," Ramage agreed. "We've got to smash them all before we leave. And, because she's so heeled over she can't aim a single gun at us, we can take our time."

"At the moment we can't aim a gun at them either," Southwick grumbled. "Not until we get a spring on our cable."

"Exactly," Ramage said, "and now you gentlemen have had a morning promenade and digested your breakfast, let's *get* a spring on our cable and start knocking some holes in those boats before our friends launch them and row on shore."

As Southwick bustled forward and Aitken started giving orders, using the speaking trumpet, Ramage looked towards the east. The coastline was little more than a bluish-grey line low on the horizon, rising slightly to the north to form Punta Ala, and again to the south where Monte dell' Uccellina slid down to Talamone. The *scirocco* haze was too thick to see Monte Argentario or the island of Giglio – and, more important, it was unlikely that a watcher on the nearest shore (the flat coastline each side of the river Ombrone) would be able to see a couple of frigates at the Formiche di Grosseto.

He saw Sir Henry coming up the quarterdeck ladder, and as

he could see the rest of the hostages examining the wreck from the maindeck, he was thankful that Sir Henry must have said something which kept them off the quarterdeck.

"Well, she's there for good, eh?" Sir Henry said cheerfully, gesturing at the wreck. "And I doubt if they'll be able to see a hulk like that from the mainland until this *scirocco* clears up. Her profile isn't much bigger than the dam' rock!"

"No, it's only the *Calypso* that sticks out like a sore thumb, and most likely we'd be mistaken for her, sir," Ramage said.

"Exactly. But her boats . . .?"

Sir Henry was being tactful.

"Two on the booms haven't been damaged, nor the one you see in the starboard quarter davits. Still, I'll soon be making sure they won't swim again: we're just putting a spring on the cable now, sir."

"Good, good," Sir Henry said, but left unspoken the "Then what?" Putting the French frigate on the shoal had – well, only wrecked the French frigate: it had not solved the problem of the wives. Were the former hostages wondering if he would now decide he had carried out his orders, declaring they made no mention of wives? The orders did not, of course, and Sir Henry knew that. And Sir Henry probably knew that many frigate captains (and captains of seventy-fours, too, for that matter) would stick to the precise wording and make for Gibraltar . . .

Ramage waved towards the big black rock of the Formica Maggiore in sight to the north of them, and forming the northern end of the Formiche di Grosseto, and then turned to gesture at the swirl of broken water in the distance ahead which showed the southernmost of the three rocks. "Favourite fishing area for the local people," Ramage said. "Boats come down from Punta Ala and Rocchette, and out from Castiglione della Pescaia. And up from Talamone and Santo Stefano."

"Yes, they would," Sir Henry agreed.

"Still, they stay in harbour when there's a *scirocco* blowing."

Sir Henry nodded, content to let Ramage make his point in his own fashion.

"Once it's blown out, they'll be out here fishing. And they'll see the wreck. They'll come straight over to see what pickings there are, expecting plenty of rope and timber. They'll find the

French crew still on board," Ramage continued, almost dreamily, and Sir Henry realized that he was thinking aloud. "Still on board because even if they'd made a raft, they'd never reach the shore with a northgoing current.

"But not for a couple of days . . . I can't see the fishermen venturing out before then. The French persuade or threaten, so that the fishermen take the captain and a few others on shore. To Talamone or Castiglione . . . No, most probably Rocchette, because that'd be a run or a broad reach.

"The nearest French headquarters to Rocchette?" Ramage shrugged his shoulders. "Grosseto, I should think. That must be a good thirty miles from Rocchette. The French frigate captain arrives in Grosseto and reports – yes, it would have to be to the Army – that he's stuck on the Formiche di Grosseto, and there's a British frigate on the loose somewhere."

Sir Henry laughed. "He wouldn't get a very sympathetic hearing, I imagine."

"No. And the commandant at Giglio still thinks he's handed over his hostages in proper form and doesn't realize they've been rescued. So neither the French frigate captain nor the French authorities at Grosseto have any cause to connect this wretched British frigate with hostages . . ."

"No," Sir Henry agreed, "they'd all think she was – or is – in the area by chance."

"So in Port' Ercole, no one would know anything about all this, and with average luck no one now in Grosseto is likely to be gossiping in Port' Ercole for a few days. It must be forty miles by land from Port' Ercole to Grosseto."

"So there's a chance, eh, Ramage?"

"They tell me the fishing off Port' Ercole is good, and most of us were round there a year so or ago with the *Calypso* and a pair of bomb ketches, so we know what the countryside looks like."

"It must be charming," Sir Henry said lightly. "The sort of view that watercolour artists like."

"Yes. I only managed some pencil sketches last time because we were in a hurry. Ah, I see they're at last getting a spring on the cable."

Sir Henry eyed the French frigate. "At this distance it's going to mean some good shooting."

"Yes," Ramage agreed. "Just smash the boats, that's all I want. No need to kill a lot of men who are in enough trouble already."

Sir Henry gave a dry chuckle. "Have you thought of what the French authorities will do to that captain when they finally work out what has happened?"

"Not in detail, sir; just enough to be thankful it's not me."

Sir Henry made no comment. It was now clear to him that Ramage still intended to try to rescue the rest of the hostages. The admiral thought soberly that he was damned if he could see how the youngster would achieve it, but then, who else would have had the thundering cheek to march up to Castello and coolly sign the commandant's receipt for the people he was rescuing?

"So there should be time," Ramage went on, and Sir Henry guessed that Ramage was both thinking aloud and letting him know his idea on the situation. "We wait near Port' Ercole for the weather to clear. By then the fishermen up here will be taking this sorry crowd of Frenchmen on shore. We land . . . we can't risk more than that night and the next day. And the following night, if necessary. Then away, round the coast south of Sardinia and hurrah for Blackstrap Bay and Gibraltar. All being well."

Sir Henry stayed at the quarterdeck rail with Ramage as the *Calypso*'s men started fitting a spring on the frigate's cable. Ramage always thought this method of training round an anchored ship so that the broadside guns could be aimed at the target was like a bull's head being held by one rope tied to a ring in its nose and the rest of the animal being turned bodily by tying a second rope to its tail and heaving.

Southwick had supervised the men securing a hawser to the anchor cable using a rolling hitch. The hawser was put over the larboard side and brought aft, outside all the rigging. It was then taken round the stern and led back on board, coming in through a sternchase port and then to the capstan.

As soon as Aitken was satisfied that the hawser led clear, directly from the cable, along the ship's side and back in through the sternchase port, he signalled to Southwick. The master's party veered some of the anchor cable so that as the *Calypso* dropped back several yards the hawser attached to it led forward and, as Aitken's men paid out more from aft, both it and the cable where it was secured dipped beneath the water.

Finally both first lieutenant and master were satisfied: the bull's tail, Ramage noted contentedly, was secured (by the hawser) to the rope attached to the ring in its nose (the anchor cable).

As soon as Aitken formally reported that everything was ready for them to begin hauling, Ramage said: "Beat to quarters, then, Mr Aitken; we may as well make an early start."

Sir Henry watched the drummer boy flourishing his drumsticks and commented: "Surely that lad's drum has French colours painted on it!"

"French colours and the name of a French frigate, sir," Ramage said, half apologetically. "We captured the frigate off Devil's Island last year. Up to then we'd used bosun's calls to send the men to quarters, but they liked the idea of a drum, and the Marine lieutenant had a boy ready, so . . ."

"Most appropriate," Sir Henry said. "After all, the *Calypso* is a French-built ship!"

Aitken was waiting for fresh orders. "We'll try with just one gun at first, Mr Aitken," Ramage said, "because if we start firing broadsides we can't spot the fall of individual shot. Which reminds me, we may as well start with grape. Now, tell Jackson to wake up at his gun and I want you to report as you start hauling in on that hawser and turning us round until his gun is aimed."

Aitken, speaking trumpet in his hand, began shouting orders. First a party of men removed the wedge-shaped drawers from the capstan and slid in the bars. The swifter was quickly passed round and the men ducked under it to stand upright, their chests against the bars.

On the maindeck the powder boys now sat along the centre-line, using their wooden cartridge boxes as stools and chattering happily. The deck had already been wetted with the washdeck pump as a precaution against spilled powder and sprinkled with sand to prevent men slipping; all the guns now had their locks bolted on, with the lanyards neatly coiled on the breeches. And beside each gun were several rounds of grapeshot, each of which looked like small black oranges embedded in a cylinder of pitch.

Aitken, reporting everything ready, looked questioningly at Ramage, who nodded. At a word from Aitken the men at the capstan slowly stepped out to start the capstan revolving while two other men hauled the end of the hawser clear as it led off the capstan barrel.

The first dozen revolutions of the capstan were easy because the men were taking in the slack: Ramage saw that the hawser leading from the *Calypso*'s larboard quarter vanished below the waves almost dead ahead.

The clunk, clunk, clunk, clunk of the capstan pawls slowed down as the strain came on the hawser. After a few more turns the men began to heave the *Calypso* round by her stern so that the stranded French frigate would soon be on her beam, within reach of her broadside guns.

The deck was now beginning to run with water as the straining capstan barrel squeezed the water from the hawser, and a seaman stood beside the men with a bucket, throwing handsful of sand on to the deck beneath their feet.

The sharp "clunk" slowed to a rhythmic "kerlunk" but the men at the capstan pushed with a will: this was nothing compared with weighing anchor in a high wind and nasty sea.

Ramage walked to the ship's side and sighted along the barrel of one of the carronades. He could not see the French frigate because she was still hidden by the side of the port, showing that the ship had not yet been trained round enough. Sir Henry joined him.

"I say, Ramage, I must admit I'm enjoying all this. Must be twenty-five years (think of it, a quarter of a century) since I trod the decks of a frigate. You lose a lot with promotion, you know. Manoeuvring a fleet isn't half the fun of handling a single frigate!"

"Then I'll stay in the lower half of the Post List, sir," Ramage said with a grin. "I'm more interested in handling a ship than a fleet!"

"What commands have you had up to now?"

"The *Kathleen* cutter was my first, sir. I lost –"

"Yes, I remember, you deliberately got yourself run down by that Spaniard, the *San Nicolas*, to help Commodore Nelson, as he then was."

"Yes, sir. After St Vincent Their Lordships gave me the *Triton* brig. I ran her on a reef in the West Indies . . ."

Sir Henry thought a moment. "Wasn't that after you lost your masts in a hurricane? You drifted up on a Spanish island – yes, Culebra, wasn't it? And found some treasure?"

"We were lucky," Ramage said. "Then another ship, and I was lucky enough to capture this frigate, which I was allowed to keep."

Ramage knelt and sighted along the carronade barrel again. He could just see the French frigate now, and the slow "kerlunk" of the pawls and Aitken's occasional shout showed that the *Calypso* was being hauled round only a degree at a time, to bring the guns to bear.

He stood up and saw that the hawser now running from the stern made a large angle with the anchor cable, which vanished away to larboard. He heard a hail from Jackson, followed by a shout from Aitken, and the capstan gave a single "kerlunk", followed by a relieved sigh from the men at the bars.

Kneeling once again, Ramage sighted along the carronade barrel and found himself looking directly at the French frigate's deck.

Aitken came up. "Jackson's ready to open fire, sir."

There was something about the first lieutenant's hesitation that made Ramage raise a questioning eyebrow. "Er," Aitken said, glancing at Sir Henry, "the gentlemen are down there among the guns, sir, and . . ."

"They can watch from the fo'c'sle," Ramage said. "Tell Jackson to begin firing as soon as the deck's clear."

He and Sir Henry waited three or four minutes, then Ramage excused himself and hurried to the quarterdeck rail, where Aitken was looking down at the maindeck. Hill was talking to General Cargill by Jackson's gun while the rest of the hostages were standing up on the fo'c'sle.

"It's that damned general, sir," Aitken muttered. "The rest went forward without any fuss."

Ramage, after looking down directly below the quarterdeck

225

rail and making sure that Rennick and his Marines were drawn up, said to Aitken: "I'll deal with this."

He clattered down the ladder, deliberately making noise; walking past the mainmast, he saw that all the guns' crews on the larboard side were deliberately facing outboard to avoid looking at Hill and the general, who were standing just inboard of number four gun.

"Good morning, general," Ramage said politely. "We shall be opening fire as soon as our guests are on the fo'c'sle."

"*Guests!*" Cargill exploded. "Damnation, man, I am a general in the King's service, and I want to watch these men. I want to make a report to the Board of Ordnance about their ability. Not often the Board get a report from an *unbiased* witness."

"How right you are, sir," Ramage agreed coolly, "but you'll see better from the fo'c'sle: no bulwarks and hammock nettings to force you to peer through a gunport."

"I'm staying here," Cargill said stubbornly.

"All guests – by that I mean everyone not forming part of the *Calypso*'s ship's company – have been requested to go to the fo'c'sle if they wish to watch the shooting."

"I'm staying here."

"General, you have the choice: the fo'c'sle or your cabin."

"What the devil do you mean by that?"

"The captain of this ship has given the guests the choice. He has given an order," Ramage said, speaking slowly and clearly. "The choice is contained in an order – that the guests will go *either* to the fo'c'sle or their cabins."

"And if I choose to ignore the order of some whippersnapper and stay here?"

Ramage turned and waved to Rennick, who promptly began marching forward, followed by Sergeant Ferris at the head of a party of three men.

As soon as Rennick stamped to attention in front of Ramage with a questioning "Sah?", Ramage turned to Cargill.

"General, I repeat; you go to the fo'c'sle or your cabin."

By now Ramage could sense the tension throughout the ship. From the fo'c'sle the rest of the former hostages watched, looking down and able to hear every word spoken since Ramage and Cargill were standing only a few feet from them. The seamen forming the guns' crews were now standing with resentment showing in their stance.

"You be damned, Ramage," Cargill sneered.

As Ramage turned towards Rennick, he saw Sir Henry watching from the quarterdeck. Rennick had a confident look on his face and Ramage had the impression that Sergeant Ferris would quite happily toss Cargill over the side.

"Lieutenant," Ramage said formally to Rennick, "escort the general down to his cabin."

Cargill had gone white. Did he realize he had gone too far? Had he realized that neither Sir Henry on the quarterdeck nor the other two admirals on the fo'c'sle had interfered on his behalf?

"Oh, very well," he said ungraciously, "I'll go to the fo'c'sle."

Ramage knew that now was the time to establish who commanded the ship: Gibraltar was many hundreds of miles and many lives away. "No," he said, "you'll go to your cabin." He nodded to Rennick, who said to Cargill: "If you'll come this way . . ."

"Ramage!" Cargill exclaimed, "you don't dare put me under an arrest! I've warned you, I am a general in the King's service."

"You have disobeyed the lawful command of the captain," Rennick said quietly, "with the third lieutenant and the lieutenant of Marines of this ship, and three admirals, one general, a marquis, two earls and a viscount as witnesses . . . sir," Rennick added as an afterthought.

Cargill looked round like a trapped animal and then walked to the ladder leading down to the gunroom.

As soon as the Marines had clumped away, Ramage walked the few paces to the breech of Jackson's gun. He looked at the frigate and then, after telling Jackson to carry on, went to the next gunport.

Jackson, with the long lanyard in his hand, stood behind the gun, far enough back to be out of reach of the recoil, and peered along the sight. Stafford stood close to the flintlock and Rossi and Gilbert were beside the breech, ready with handspikes.

Jackson gestured with his left hand. Both seamen slid the metal tips of their handspikes under the breech end of the carriage and levered it over a few inches. Jackson held his hand up, and they stood back. So much for traverse, Ramage thought to himself: always train "left" or "right" in gunnery orders. Now for elevation. Jackson signalled again, and the two men put their handspikes under the breech and raised it slightly as Stafford pushed in the wooden wedge, better known as the coin, which governed how high or low the breech was raised from the carriage, and thus controlled the range by the angle of the barrel.

Jackson gave another signal, and as Rossi and Gilbert stepped clear and Stafford cocked the lock, Ramage realized that Jackson must have been almost ready to fire before Cargill interfered.

The American went down on his right knee, with his left leg stretched out sideways to its full extent. Slowly he tightened the firing lanyard, his eye still along the sight. The anchor cable and the spring held the *Calypso* steady, with little more than a hint of a pitch and a roll. Jackson was obviously waiting a few moments for the combined pitch and roll to bring the target precisely into the sight.

Then in one flowing movement the lanyard went tight, the gun leapt back in recoil, spewing a flash and a stream of black smoke from its barrel and giving an enormous grunt which half deafened Ramage.

As men began coughing from the coiling smoke which the wind swirled across the deck, the rest of Jackson's crew moved with the speed that came from constant practice. In went the mop, the "woolly 'eaded bastard" as it was more familiarly known, sopping wet and both extinguishing and cleaning out any burning residue left in the barrel. A powder boy ran up with the new charge which Louis grabbed and slipped into the gaping muzzle, standing to one side as Albert thrust it home with the rammer. Gilbert stood by with a wad, which was rammed down, and Louis lifted up the cylindrical grapeshot, starting it off down the barrel. Albert's rammer thrust it down on to the wad and powder charge, and then rammed home the final wad.

Gilbert gave a bellow and the men grabbed the tackles on each side of the gun and hauled, running the gun outboard again. The ship was rolling so slightly that there had been no need to

228

hold the gun inboard with the train tackle while the men reloaded.

By now Stafford was ready: he thrust the thin, skewer-like pricker down the vent to make a small opening in the cartridge to expose the powder; then, seeing that the loaders were clear of the gun, he pushed a quill – a tube of fine gunpowder – down the vent, shook priming powder into the shallow pan, and then turned to Jackson.

The American had seen that the first round had missed by about ten feet: all the grapeshot had spattered round the frigate's quarterdeck just forward of the boat hanging in the quarter-davit.

Ramage, who had come down to the gun with his telescope under his arm, examined the frigate. Yes, one accurately aimed round of grapeshot would do it. The first round, hitting just forward of the boat, had sprayed the hull planking and every one of the shot showed up in the telescope as a rusty mark. There was no need to say anything to Jackson: the shower of dust which had been flung up (the splinters moved too fast to be seen) would have shown the American just the correction he needed.

Jackson looked across at Ramage, who realized that the American was worried in case Ramage let the other guns begin firing. Was it pride or concern over spotting the fall of shot? Ramage nodded reassuringly, and in that nod Jackson read all the message he needed. The captain understood the need for a sighting shot: now for the correction.

Jackson's gesture with his left hand set Rossi and Gilbert to work with the handspikes. Under the carriage went the shoes and both men heaved down on the opposite ends to lever the carriage sideways an inch or two. Both men watched the crouching Jackson as once again he peered along the sight. A small, impatient gesture to the left, as though the movement of his hand would be enough to train the gun the slight amount necessary. Gilbert and Rossi gave the carriage little more than a nudge and, as Jackson shouted, they leapt back and Stafford cocked the lock before he too jumped smartly back.

The firing lanyard twitched – Jackson had tautened it the moment he saw Stafford had cocked the lock and stepped clear –

and again the gun erupted flame and smoke, leaping back in recoil as it gave a loud, asthmatic grunt.

This time a random gust of wind swirled some of the oily smoke back through Ramage's port and, by the time he had finished coughing, number four gun had been loaded again and run out, with Rossi and Gilbert busy with their handspikes, pausing at the end of each thrust to look at Jackson. Stafford had his tin of quills open, ready to take a fresh one and then push it down the vent, and the powder horn from which he took the priming was slung round his neck.

But Rossi and Gilbert seemed to be taking a long time with the handspikes. By this time Ramage had at last cleared his throat and his eyes had stopped watering so that he could look across at the frigate. No wonder it was taking time to train the gun – the quarterboat hanging in its davits was now a shattered shell, a few thin frames sticking out from the keel like the ribs of a crushed skeleton, the remaining planking sprung and jagged, instead of swelling round in a smooth curve from bow to stern. It was as though, Ramage thought inconsequentially, a banana had exploded, opening up the segments of skin.

Two rounds at a range of a couple of hundred yards . . . one ranging shot and then a direct hit. Well, the *Calypso* was hardly rolling and pitching and, with a gun captain like Jackson, one could take bets that he would do it inside half a dozen rounds.

Ramage realized that smashing the two remaining boom boats might be more difficult. Their name came from the fact that they were stowed amidships on top of spare yards and booms, which were kept lashed down over a large hatchway and made a good platform for the boats. From there it was easy for the stay tackles to hoist them up and out over the side when needed.

Ironically, the wreckage of the main and mizenmasts was now giving them some protection: a couple of slewed yards, a bundle of thick cordage, a smashed mast two or three feet in diameter – all would be enough to make the grapeshot ricochet. But there were nine grapeshot in each round, and every one of them weighed a pound. Give Jackson enough time!

Ramage went back to the quarterdeck, where Aitken and Southwick stood talking to Sir Henry.

The admiral glanced aft and Ramage walked with him until they were out of earshot of both officers, the quartermaster and the men at the wheel.

"The general – what happened?"

"I told him to go up to the fo'c'sle or down to his cabin," Ramage said in a flat voice. "He refused: said he wanted to watch the shooting and report to the Board of Ordnance."

Sir Henry nodded. "And then?"

"My lieutenant of Marines warned him he was disobeying the lawful order of the captain of the ship. The general found this amusing. I told the Marines to take him below."

"Under arrest?"

Ramage shook his head. "No, sir; I didn't feel inclined to give him that satisfaction."

"Very wise, very wise," Sir Henry said. "I didn't interfere because – well, you seem to be able to take care of yourself. I'd be inclined to treat him like a naughty boy."

"Indeed sir, he behaves like one," Ramage agreed, pausing as Jackson fired again but fighting down his curiosity and not looking where the shot landed. He was thankful that Sir Henry was, very tactfully, giving advice, and even more thankful that the advice coincided with what he had already decided to do.

"Trouble with arresting people," Sir Henry said conversationally, "is that to set 'em free again, you've either to charge 'em or climb down, which is bad for discipline."

"That's what I had in mind, sir," Ramage said. "And I wasn't quite sure what the *King's Regulations and Admiralty Instructions* had to say about travelling generals."

"Ha!" Sir Henry said contemptuously, "the Articles of War are all you need, particularly with the ship in action against the enemy." He looked squarely at Ramage and smiled. "Why the devil d'you think I'm so well behaved, eh?"

Ramage laughed, and took the opportunity of turning so that he could spot the fall of shot. "I'd put it down to your natural kindness towards young captains at the bottom of the Post List, sir."

"I eat 'em for breakfast," Sir Henry said. "Majors-general I keep for dinner. Lieutenants-general I have served cold for supper."

231

Number four gun on the starboard side grunted again. "That gun captain is either very lucky or very good," Sir Henry commented.

"Very good, sir. He's served with me since I had my first command."

"While you were, er, attending to the general, your master (what's his name – Southwick?) was telling me he was on board the *Kathleen* when that Spanish three-decker rammed her and rolled her over. Must have been an alarming sight, her bearing down on you."

"We had a rather limited view, sir," Ramage said, "but other ships later gave us flattering descriptions. By the way, sir, our story is that *we* rammed the Spaniard, not the other way round!"

"Well, a mouse in the stable can panic a stallion, so you may be right. Oh – just look at *that*!"

Ramage glanced across at the frigate just in time to see the two boom boats disintegrate. The angle at which they had been lying on the booms (compared with the single boat which had hung horizontally in the quarter davits) meant that Jackson was firing down on to them, and obviously one round of grapeshot had spread just sufficiently, like an enormous flail, to hit the larboard side of one and the starboard side of the other, ripping them open like a pair of bananas in the hands of a hungry ape.

"I'll have the spring on the cable taken in, if you please Mr Aitken," Ramage said. "The men can stand down from general quarters. Then Mr Aitken, we'll see about getting under way."

232

Chapter Twenty

Ramage sat at his desk listening to the two men report. The lantern swinging from its hook in the deckhead threw dancing shadows which emphasized their features: Rossi with his round face, full and generous lips, straight black hair and large, expressive eyes could only be an Italian: his hands gestured as eloquently as he spoke and seemed part of the words. Orsini's face was narrower, the shadows exaggerating his high cheekbones. In this light, Ramage thought, he looked like a youth painted by one of the better Renaissance artists. For the moment, Orsini was content to let Rossi tell the story in his Genovese accent.

"We landed on the rocks below Forte della Stella without trouble, and then climbed the cliff. The goats, they must have a hard life. We frightened a mother and her youngsters – or, rather," he admitted with a grin, "they frightened us because they suddenly bolted from a ledge just above and showered us with stones."

"The hostages," Ramage said impatiently. "Tell me the details later."

"Oh, they are in there, in Forte della Stella. We were in position by sunset, and soon after we saw the French guards shut the doors, two big wooden doors studded with boltheads to blunt axe blades. There is also a small door, big enough for one man, fitted into one of the big doors."

"A wicket gate." Ramage said in English.

"Yes, a wicked gate. That was opened just before it was dark, and a sentry came and stood outside. Musket, no sword. He

233

stands to one side – the left as you face the gate – and leans against it. He's probably learned how to sleep standing up."

"Learned it from a sailor, I expect," Ramage said drily.

"Yes," Rossi grinned. "And we saw one sentry walking round the battlements."

Although he had already made up his own mind, Ramage asked Orsini: "Do you also think the hostages are there?"

Orsini nodded. "Yes, sir."

"Why?" Ramage asked bluntly.

"Well, there are no guns on the battlements, sir – we were careful to check all round the fortress. Why keep a garrison at Forte della Stella unless to handle cannon to cover the entrance to Port' Ercole? To prevent enemy ships approaching?"

No guns? Now Ramage was certain. He was already half convinced when Rossi told him of one sentry at the main gate and another up on the battlements: that was unusual enough at a French fortress in such an isolated place and would be justified only if they were artillerymen guarding against enemy ships trying to sneak past to attack Port' Ercole. But with no guns perched up on the battlements, then there had to be another reason for the garrison and for the sentries.

There must be something special to guard inside the fortress, and that would not be Bonaparte's favourite canteen of cutlery. What *could* it be, apart from hostages?

Ramage could think of nothing else that would not be kept more safely in a castle or fortress scores of miles inland, not on the edge of the sea. Except that the Orsini Palace was just that, a comfortable palace but hard to defend, while Forte della Stella was simply a fortress and (like Castello on Giglio) relatively impregnable.

He looked at his watch. Eleven o'clock. A garrison of how many men? What duty was each sentry doing – four hours on and eight off? Or two on and four off? Anyway, two sentries on duty represented six men, not allowing for sickness. And guards for the prisoners. Say at least a dozen men, with a corporal, a sergeant, a cook, a lieutenant and a captain. Probably a groom or two for the horses. Nineteen – so say a minimum of twenty officers and men. After all, they were guarding hostages, not defending the fortress.

234

How many hostages? And where were they kept? Did they have a guard with them all the time – guards who, at the first sign of a rescue attempt, would treat them immediately as hostages, threatening to kill them unless the would-be rescuers withdrew?

"There was this *contadino*," Orsini said casually. "He helped."

"What *contadino*, and helped what?" Ramage demanded impatiently.

"Well, sir, as we left we saw a man making his way along a track about two hundred yards inland from the fortress. He was not worrying about being seen from the fortress – although in fact he was hidden most of the time by sage and thyme and juniper bushes. We wouldn't have seen him except that we were keeping a sharp lookout."

"Come on!" Ramage said, still holding his watch.

Rossi said: "I walked along the track so that I met him face to face. He was surprised to see me, of course, but as I was obviously an Italian he was not particularly alarmed.

"He had just come from Port' Ercole and was on his way to Sbarcatella – that's the small cape at the southern end of this bay and south-west of Isolotto."

Clearly Rossi was going to tell the story at his own speed, and Ramage realized that anyway it was difficult for some men to grasp the most important point in an incident: to them they had to begin at the beginning and carry on to the end.

"Well," Rossi continued, "this man has a small boat down there and some lobster pots, and he was going to row out and lift the pots."

"To whom does he sell the lobsters?"

"I was just coming to that, sir," Rossi said. "He *used* to sell them to the garrison at the fort, but it seems that after the first month they halved the price they would pay, so now he sells them in the village. He was very angry with the French. This only happened three weeks ago."

"So he started selling lobsters to the garrison seven weeks ago?"

"I was just coming to that," Rossi said again, finally adding, "sir", but carefully timing the gap. "According to this man the fort was standing empty until eight weeks ago. He remembers

235

the date because it was a particular feast day and the French soldiers marching through the port interrupted a procession, which made the local people angry.

"Anyway, they went through the port and up the track leading from La Rocca, above the port, and on to the fort."

"Just soldiers?" Ramage interrupted.

"Just soldiers. About thirty of them, marching in four columns," Rossi said, hard put to keep the pride from his voice that the *contadino* could remember that. "Two officers, who were riding mules."

"No hostages, then?"

Rossi shook his head and then, in a typical Italian gesture, tapped the side of his nose knowingly with a forefinger. "Not then. They arrived a week later, with a special escort, and were taken to the fort. The special escort left again next day."

"So there's absolutely no doubt that the hostages are in the fort?"

"No sir," Rossi said blandly.

"*Accidente!*" Ramage exclaimed. "Why did you hold on to the information about this *contadino* for so long?"

Orsini took over the narrative, his manner defensive. "Well, sir, we didn't think you would believe us if we just said 'The hostages are there!' I thought you would need all the facts that led us to the conclusion."

Ramage sighed. These two mules were going to proceed at their own speed. "Go on, then. How many hostages?"

"The man didn't know because he did not see them: he was out fishing that day and his wife told him. Some women, some men. 'Many', the man said. But he could describe the inside of the fort."

"Wait a moment," Ramage said. "Why was this man so helpful? What stops him going to the garrison and reporting that there are two Italian strangers asking questions?"

Rossi gave a short and bitter laugh. "First, sir, he saw only me: Mr Orsini was hidden. Second, this man hates all Frenchmen. Apart from cheating him over the lobsters, two French soldiers tried to rape one of his daughters . . ."

"What happened about that?"

"Two of her brothers arrived, killed the Frenchmen and hid

236

the bodies. The French commandant made the port pay a heavy fine because two of their men were missing. The Italians told the French captain the men had probably deserted."

"So now everyone in the port is angry with the French?"

"Yes, sir!" Rossi exclaimed, "but this happened four years ago, with soldiers stationed at the fort on the other side of Port' Ercole."

"Go on," Ramage said, "what did you find out about the inside of Forte della Stella, then?"

Orsini leaned forward and gave Ramage a folded piece of paper. "When I came back on board I drew this plan, based on what the man said. It's only a rough sketch. The guardhouse is here on the right, just inside the main gate. Then officers, two of them, have their quarters here. The soldiers and NCOs are here."

"And the hostages?"

"Here, sir," Orsini said, pointing to the north-west corner. "There is a corridor and leading off it are two very large rooms – almost like cellars. The men are kept in one, the women in the other. No privacy. When he delivered lobsters, the man saw a sentry on each door – he came usually in the late evening."

"How long did it take you to get up to the fort from the moment you landed from the boat at the foot of the cliff?" Ramage asked Orsini.

"Less than half an hour, sir. That includes ten minutes of crawling like snakes through the sage bushes to get close to the main gate – it was still daylight then. We had trouble with the *macchia*: it's thick and waist-high up to about thirty yards from the main gate but it's so dry that branches crackle every time you move: it's impossible not to snap them."

"And attacking the fort?"

Orsini thought for several seconds, and then glanced at Rossi, who remained staring down at the desk, obviously not wanting to commit himself. "It would be hard, sir. The only way in is through the main gate – or the little wicket door. There's smooth, open ground in front of the sentry, thirty yards or more, with gravel spread all over it (the French must use it as a parade ground) and the gravel makes a crunching noise if you tread on it."

237

"Coming back down the cliff to the boat," Ramage said, "could women get down that way?"

While Rossi shrugged his shoulders, with the comment: "It's the only way, sir, and it depends how old they are!", Orsini nodded. "Yes, sir. There's only one really bad place, and that's a climb of about fourteen feet, almost vertical. But we could secure a rope ladder from a rock just above it, so they could use that. We could rig knotted ropes along the rest of the route, above and below the ladder, which would give them something to hold on to, and guide them as well. A seaman here and there to help them – yes, it could be done. If there is a *very* old lady," he added as an afterthought, "a strong seaman could bring her all the way on his back."

Ramage looked at his watch. *Macchia* that went snap in the night. A sentry on the battlements. A sentry at the door whose defence was thirty yards of crackling gravel. He thought of General Cargill's standard tactic, a direct frontal attack. "Thank you," he told the two Italians. "Pass the word for Mr Aitken as you go out."

The *Calypso*'s first lieutenant had obviously been waiting on deck, and once he was sitting in the armchair Ramage gave him the gist of the two Italians' report.

"Doesn't seem too hopeful, sir," Aitken said. "Do we try the Giglio trick tomorrow, march up and bluff 'em?"

Ramage shook his head. "I'd like to, but it's too great a risk. We'd have to go through Port' Ercole and anyway someone might have come over from Giglio in the meantime and casually mentioned something. I might have risked it," he admitted, "if all the hostages were men, but I can't (at least, I won't) risk women's lives. Not with these stakes."

"But nothing is at stake, sir!" Aitken protested.

"Exactly. If we sail off and leave them, they're kept prisoners until the end of the war and they're left alive and safe. My orders are to rescue hostages named in my orders from the Admiralty, and I've done that: they're all safely on board."

Aitken looked stubborn. He stood up and began pacing the cabin, his head bent to one side to avoid hitting the beams. The dim light of the lantern showed the muscles taut along his jaw-line. Ramage could never remember his first lieutenant pacing the cabin before. Obviously strong emotions were at work in the Scotsman.

Finally Ramage exclaimed, "For God's sake, sit down and spit it out! All the pacing back and forth makes me dizzy!"

Aitken sat down, took a deep breath and turned to look directly at Ramage. "These women, sir. I don't fully agree with you, if you'll permit me to say so."

"Since when have you had to ask permission to give an honest opinion?"

"It's not just that," Aitken said mournfully. "I'm not just expressing an opinion; I'm completely disagreeing with you, sir."

"Tell me about it, then. With what do you disagree?" Ramage was exasperated: he seemed to be spending the evening hauling information out of men like corks from bottles.

"You said the women are 'safe' while they are still prisoners. I canna agree. They're *hostages*. This fellow Bonaparte is holding them as bargaining counters. When the Admiralty gave you orders to rescue the other hostages (the ones named, and whom we found at Giglio), you can't be sure that when the Admiralty drew up those orders they knew anything about the second group – the ones now in the fort. In fact, I'm sure they didn't."

"What do you suggest, then?" Ramage asked coldly. "Shall we hurry back to London and ask Their Lordships if we should include these others? Or would you prefer that I go ahead and risk their lives?"

"There's no need to go to London, sir. You've several of the husbands on board, including Sir Henry. Why not ask *them* what they think?"

"Call a council of war, eh?" Ramage asked sarcastically.

"No, sir," Aitken answered calmly, knowing how his captain despised councils of war. "But husbands understand their wives," he continued. "Sir Henry knows what his wife would want us to do. Maybe just as important, Sir Henry knows what *he* would prefer. You can ask them individually: visit each one in his cabin. There's no question of a council of war and no question of evading responsibility. I'm a bachelor, I admit; but if I was a married man in this position, safe on board a frigate with my wife up in yon fortress, I know I'd like to have a say in what's to be done. After you know what the husbands have said, you can make your decision. The responsibility will be yours, and yours alone."

The more Ramage thought about it, the more reasonable Aitken's argument became. "Very well, I'll do that, and thanks for speaking up: I'm grateful – though I'm rather puzzled why you hesitated."

Both men sat alone with their thoughts for two or three minutes, until Ramage said quietly: "But even if all the husbands are in favour of us trying a rescue, how the devil can we tackle Forte della Stella? It's designed to hold off an army . . ."

"We're just reaching the place where we need the rope ladder," Orsini said. "You can see that sharp rock up there, sir: just made to secure it."

"Wait a moment," Ramage gasped, "let me get my breath back: I'm neither a topman nor a goat, and this climbing in the dark is hard work."

Below and slightly to the north of them, the rocky islet of Isolotto sat in the sea as though rolled down from the top of Monte Argentario and bounced out far enough from the coast to leave a wide channel. It was steep-sided with deep water round it, and the *Calypso*, anchored to leeward seemed – well, Ramage could only think she must look as though she belonged there.

Port' Ercole, over on her starboard quarter, was too small to provide a good anchorage for a frigate unless towed in with boats and it was too shallow alongside the jetty. So what was more obvious than a French national ship anchoring in the lee of Isolotto, only a brisk row or a short sail for one of her boats should the captain need to visit the port?

"Blast these mosquitoes," Ramage muttered, "they seem to be hiding in every bush I grab for a handhold."

"At least we frightened the goats off," Paolo said, recalling how he had sat in the captain's cabin while he and Rossi reported, and although his wrists, ankles, neck and face seemed one itching mass, he had managed not to scratch himself.

Orsini led the way upwards just as Stafford arrived on the small ledge with a party of cursing seamen, two of whom manhandled the rolled-up rope ladder while others with the coil of knotted rope were hitching it round rocks and bushes to provide handholds.

The moon was rising quickly now with the thinning cloud breaking up into patches to reveal many of the stars and planets. More important, Ramage realized, the moon was throwing enough shadow to show the seamen and Marines now coming up the cliff face where to put their feet. On a night like this, with a land breeze blowing from the edge of the cliffs across to the fort, a musket dropped a few feet on to a rock might well make a clatter loud enough to reach the ears of the French sentry on the battlements.

Those wooden buckets: he wished now he had risked using the leather ones because a wooden bucket if accidentally dropped (or grasped tightly by a man as he slipped and fell) would make almost as much noise as a dropped musket.

And the devil take climbing a cliff face with a brace of pistols jammed into the top of your breeches and a sword wrapped in canvas slung down your back, even if some marline prevented it swinging against the rocks. Nor did burnt cork smeared on the face and hands to blacken them add to the general feeling of comfort.

Ramage stopped feeling sorry for himself as he concentrated on the vertical climb that Orsini had earlier dismissed as "fairly easy" and then pictured Southwick at the end of the tail of seamen and Marines, jollying along the men and making sure they moved silently.

As he reached the top of the vertical cliff face and found Jackson only just behind him, Ramage sat down on a rock and watched the American unwind a light line coiled round his chest and shoulders, and drop one end over the edge. There was a call from below and then, two minutes later, another, and Jackson started hauling on the line. It was obviously heavier than he had expected and both Ramage and Orsini helped him. Finally the top step of the rope ladder appeared; then the second and third.

"Charge them a shilling a time," Ramage said as he left Jackson securing the heavier ropes of the ladder round the rock Orsini had pointed out. Ramage wiped the perspiration from his brow before it ran into his eyes. It was a damnably hot night, apart from all this climbing, and there was little enough breeze.

But was it dying? The thought suddenly alarmed him more than anything in the last forty-eight hours. He muttered to Orsini and both wetted a finger and held it up.

The breeze was steady, which was a good sign because a fitful breeze, coming in puffs, was usually a warning that it would die within half an hour. If only it was blowing at double the strength! Yet perhaps a gentle breeze would serve his purpose better: doubling the strength might halve the time available.

"Seems steady enough, sir," Orsini agreed, and led on when Ramage grunted. Orsini now knew how much depended on that breeze. Originally Captain Ramage had simply asked him whether he thought it possible to attack the fort, and he had answered that he thought it was. That was all, really: there was no mention of the size of the attacking force.

Orsini admitted to himself that the thought of attacking Forte della Stella (even using every man on board the *Calypso*) was frightening: only two hundred men to storm a fortress built to withstand an army. Then later he had discovered that Mr Ramage was going to use only two parties of men, ten in one, twenty in the other.

For a time (and Orsini freely admitted it) he was in such a panic that he debated whether or not to go to Mr Ramage and confess he had been stupidly over-optimistic in his report. Then, *Mamma mia*, he had heard Mr Ramage's plan and was thankful he had done nothing. Audacious! That was a splendid English word, so near the Latin and Italian, but just different enough to convey that extra something that Mr Ramage so often provided from out of nowhere, it seemed.

Every piece of audacity was so well tailored, whether attacking Port' Ercole with the bomb ketches a couple of years ago (more, actually), or dealing with the pirates at Trinidada (where Mr Ramage had met his future wife), or escaping from France when war broke out again and while he was on his honeymoon. Orsini stopped his memory working: Lady Sarah had vanished while Mr Ramage was crossing the Atlantic to Devil's Island. Yet Lady Sarah was, Orsini knew, just the sort of woman he would himself like to have as a wife. Now she was missing, probably drowned.

242

"So at last we reach the top, eh?" Ramage commented. "Thank goodness it will be downhill going back!"

"Do you think the ladies will be able to climb down?"

"You're looking a long way ahead," Ramage said banteringly, "but if we manage to get 'em this far, I think they'll get down all right."

Ramage looked across at the fort. As its name indicated, it was star-shaped and with the moon lighting some parts and casting deep shadow over the rest he was reminded of a starfish tossed up on a sandy beach: apparently it had no eyes, no mouth, and no way of moving yet, put back in the sea, it walked, ate, and seemed to know where it was going. Momentarily, Ramage had the uncomfortable thought that perhaps hidden eyes *were* watching from the fort; that there was more life there than he gave credit.

He sat down amid the coarse grass on the cliff top and waited for the men to get up the rockface. His watch showed it was just an hour past midnight. Plenty of time before dawn. In fact, a chilling thought, some of his own men and those of the French garrison might be living the rest of their lives between now and dawn. Not the hostages, though, he told himself. He remembered the arguments he had had with the husbands.

Sir Henry was hard put not to overrule Ramage and insist on coming, and so were the two other admirals, until Ramage had been forced to tell them brutally that they were out of condition, would be hopeless shooting with muskets and probably with pistols as well, were completely untrained for this kind of fighting (in which the Calypsos excelled) and – this had been the final argument – for every one of the admirals he took he would have to leave a trained Calypso behind.

The repulsive Cargill, not consulted since he was a bachelor, had started off by insisting that he should be in command, proclaiming that this was an attack for which soldiers were trained, and so on. Again Ramage had been brutal. No, he corrected himself, his contempt for Cargill had made him almost vicious, and when Cargill had tried to assert his authority in front of all the other hostages, Ramage had asked him where he had seen active service. When the general evaded the question, Ramage had dismissed the whole question with a curt: "It is no secret, sir, that you had neither seen a shot fired in anger nor heard one until the *Calypso* fired at that French frigate."

Yes, it was nasty, it was probably unfair, and it was many other things, but it was necessary and, Sir Henry had said to him privately afterwards, Cargill had asked for it. Had he kept his mouth shut, everything would have gone off smoothly, but once again Cargill had wanted to play soldiers, and this time the result could be not only disastrous for the Calypsos, but lethal for the hostages up in the fort.

Aitken scrambled over the edge of the cliff and joined his captain. Ramage was secretly pleased to note that the first lieutenant was also panting.

"That rope ladder was a good idea of Orsini's sir," he gasped. "It'd be a devil of a climb without it." He paused. "But you came up without it, sir."

"Yes," Ramage said, adding teasingly, "a question of seniority."

"Aye, there's many advantages in being a poor lieutenant if that cliff face is the price o' being on the Post List!"

Several seamen followed and squatted down in the grass behind the officers. Then Hill came up, leading several men who very carefully lifted wooden buckets over the edge and equally carefully set them down again. Rennick was next, followed by Sergeant Ferris and five Marines. Rennick had wanted to bring all the Marines, but Ramage had pointed out that Kenton, left in command of the ship, needed a force in case the French arrived from Port' Ercole.

Finally Southwick, puffing and blowing but very cheerful, arrived and announced: "There! If I can haul myself up this cliff, then a convoy of rheumaticky grandmothers can let themselves down! The boats have returned to the ship, sir," he reported to Ramage.

"Very well. Now, Mr Aitken, fall in the two parties and then we can move on and finish tonight's business."

Ramage again tested the breeze while Aitken sorted out the seamen, and then he inspected the buckets. They were doing their job and the men responsible for them knew what they were expected to do. Ramage walked with Hill until they were out of earshot of the men.

244

"Hill, I don't want to make you nervous, but I must make sure you realize the success of the whole attack depends on your positioning. Almost more important, you and your men mustn't be seen by the sentry – or the people roused out when he raises the alarm. Until you hear shots – *if* you hear shots – you keep out of sight. If there's shooting and if you've finished your job, then you can join in."

"Yes, sir, I understand. Seems a long way from the great cabin of the *Salvador del Mundo!*"

"If it all goes wrong, we may yet find ourselves back there!" Ramage said grimly and recalled the strange court-martial, where a captain's insanity had put his life in danger and Hill, a bored young lieutenant on the port admiral's staff, had asked Ramage to be allowed to sail with him.

Aitken joined them. "The two parties are ready, sir." Then he asked Hill: "You're sure you have enough men? Ten, and five buckets?"

"They'll be enough," Hill said confidently and excused himself.

"He doesn't seem nervous," Aitken commented. "Bit o' luck getting him when Wagstaffe was promoted. Now, sir, about our party. I've put the seamen in the lead, with Rennick's Marines following. Rennick's not very pleased but I pointed out that he would insist on his men wearing those clod-hopping boots!"

"You're quite right," Ramage said. "The most important part of this is going to be done crawling on our bellies, and seamen with just pistols and cutlasses are less likely to make a noise. Rennick will get his chance if any real fighting starts. Right, we're ready so –" he took out his watch and turned it so the moon lit the face, "– as it's almost half past one we can move off. We'll give Hill's party a couple of minutes' start along the edge of the cliff, then Orsini and Rossi can lead us to the fort."

The track (now used only by goats and sheep and the lone *contadino*) dipped and climbed and twisted as it led to Forte della Stella which, as the patchy cloud drifted across the moon, alternately disappeared in the darkness and then reappeared, almost ghostly and unreal, its grey stone walls fleetingly silvered, but stark, remote and menacing. As the track took a final turn which brought them in sight of the main gate – the only

245

gate, Ramage corrected himself – he decided that it was time for the final approach on hands and knees.

"This track curves round to the left on its way to Port' Ercole, and leaves the Fort on the right," Orsini explained quietly. "About two hundred yards farther ahead there's a fork to the right, a smaller track which goes off to the fort, but Rossi and I took a short-cut through the *macchia*, starting here. It's about one hundred and fifty yards to the gate."

Ramage again pulled out his watch, waited for a cloud to drift clear of the moon, and saw they had taken only ten minutes. Hill's men would not be in position yet, and the *Calypso*'s third lieutenant knew he was not to start until at least half an hour after leaving Ramage's party. Twenty minutes to go . . . More than enough time, Ramage decided.

Even after letting Rossi and Orsini get three or four yards ahead, so that the sage and juniper bushes they pushed aside did not spring back in his face, Ramage felt his cheeks and forehead smarting with many scratches from unexpected long twigs. The dam' pistols chafed the skin at his waist and seemed to have stove in his lower ribs. The cutlass lashed on his back thudded monotonously against his spine, despite the canvas covering and marline lashing, and every sage and thyme bush and juniper must be the home of a hundred hungry mosquitoes.

The smell of thyme and sage (and rosemary – "That's for remembrance") brought back memories of the desperate affair several years ago not far from here (in fact he could see the Torre di Buranaccio on the mainland from the cliff top) when he and Jackson had rescued Gianna. Another lifetime; now, crawling on his belly towards the fort, it was hard to believe he had ever been there, and that for years he had thought he loved Gianna, and cursed the differing nationalities and religions that prevented them marrying.

Then, some years later, he had met Sarah and married her. Now Sarah was probably drowned, and Gianna murdered by Bonaparte's men, and here was Captain Ramage back again, a few miles from where the first part of the story began. Only now he was alone. Alone, probably a widower though his thirtieth birthday was distant, and crawling on his belly, with Jackson once again close behind him.

One day this thrice-blasted war would end, and he would go on half-pay and return to St Kew to live on the family estate. Cornwall attracted him and there would be a job for Jackson, who did not want to return to America, and the widower and bachelor would gently slide into old age, nodding knowingly about a newly born foal, cursing a late frost which caught blossom on the apple trees, and making sure the men doing muckspreading had plenty to drink. Rheumatism would set in and he and Jackson would creak and reminisce over old times. About rescuing Gianna, capturing the *Calypso*, raiding Curaçao, sailing into Trinidada off the Brazilian coast (no, they'd both keep off that because it would remind them of Sarah), and they'd reminisce too about this affair.

Already his knees felt almost raw: there was as much rock here as hardened earth – indeed, it was the sort of ground on which sage and juniper thrived. Yes, in the quiet of St Kew they would sit and reminisce of an autumn evening – *as long as they survived the next hour*. And the nearer they crawled to the fort, which seemed to double in size every twenty yards, the remoter seemed the chance of this gamble succeeding.

It *was* a gamble, and Ramage recalled how pompously he had told Sir Henry a day or so ago that he was contemptuous of gamblers because the element of chance could usually be removed by careful planning. Sir Henry had nodded politely, although most likely he wanted to laugh aloud. Anyway, his stake was down; the dice were rolling. And now Orsini was whispering urgently that they were about thirty yards from the end of the *macchia* and the beginning of the gravel square in front of the fort. Ramage turned and passed the order back for the column to halt.

Giving enough time for the word to pass from man to man in a whisper, Ramage then told Aitken, who had been following him, that everyone should unwrap his cutlass (but keep it down low so that the moon did not glint on the blade) load pistols and put them on half-cock.

Ramage did not pass orders for the Marines: Rennick knew exactly what he was doing. Ramage pictured Southwick unwinding the long strip of canvas from his great two-handed sword, which could take off a man's head with a couple of blows. One blow, probably, if rage put extra strength in South-wick's arms.

"Report back when everyone's ready," he told Aitken, who started the order off on its whispered journey. By the time the answer came back Ramage had both his pistols at half-cock and tucked back into his waist belt, and the canvas off his cutlass, which was now waiting on the ground beside him.

"I can see your face very clearly," he told Aitken. "That cork blacking has worn off."

"Afraid you're the same, sir," Aitken muttered. "The perspiration has washed it away. And I didn't bring any spare burnt corks."

"Oh well, I don't expect we'll meet anyone we know," Ramage said lightly. He picked up his cutlass. "Very well, we'll go on until we reach the gravel, and then wait for Hill."

Five minutes later Ramage peered at the gates from the edge of the bushes as Orsini pointed and whispered. "There, you can make out the sentry standing just to the left of that black oblong, which is the small doorway. The door must be open. We called the others doors, but they're really gates, and what was the proper English word for the small door? I'm afraid I have forgotten already."

"A wicket gate. A Dutch word we've adopted, I think, although the Welsh refer to a 'wicked' gate."

"Like Rossi. The Welsh obviously mean a gate just like that," Paolo said. "It's a wicked long run to reach it!"

"If you're going to make such poor jokes," Ramage muttered, "we'll speak Italian!"

He rolled on his side and pulled out his watch. Five minutes to go. Or, rather, five minutes until the time from which Hill could start.

Paolo nudged him. "Look, sir. Up on the battlements to the right: there's the other sentry."

Ramage watched the soldier march – no, he was strolling – and saw that he was making a complete circuit of the fort. He was not keeping a lookout on the seaward side – in fact, from the way he progressed it seemed highly unlikely that he was keeping a lookout for anything in particular. Would Hill have seen him? And would he be planning to start the attack once the sentry was out of sight from him on the landward side of the battlements? From down here among the roots of the sage and juniper, it was hard to judge the breeze, but it was light enough for Ramage to hear the faint rustle of the leaves. Yes, the breeze was still there, and the clouds showed that at least high up it had not changed direction.

He turned to Aitken. "Crawl alongside me and have a good look round." He passed on Orsini's observations, and Aitken nodded. "Let's hope Hill has seen that sentry," he murmured, echoing Ramage's thoughts. "If he times it right, it could give us an extra couple of minutes . . ."

Chapter
Twenty-One

A nightjar in a clump of olive trees over to the west of the fort kept up its lonely and monotonous quark . . . quark, a call so regular that Ramage stopped timing the seconds and used the bird. Otherwise there was silence. Then the sentry at the wicket gate coughed and spat, the silence making him seem much closer than thirty yards. The moon shadows cast by the bolt-heads made the big wooden gates look speckled with a heavy black rash.

The sentry up on the battlements, now almost at the opposite side from Hill and his party, sneezed violently and apparently startled the nightjar, which missed a beat. Had something happened to Hill? Had he missed his way? No, that was impossible: he had only to follow the edge of the cliff and then strike through the *macchia* towards the fort.

Ramage stared at the sentry beside the gate. Not beside it but leaning back against it. He was too far away to see if his eyes were shut, but Rossi could be right: the man was probably dozing standing up.

Ramage sniffed, and sniffed again. He held his breath, trying to sort out the smells. Sage and thyme, yes, but . . . He sniffed again. Yes, there was the sharper smell of bonfire smoke. Both Orsini and Aitken then nudged him simultaneously from either side. Burning (smouldering, anyway) sage and grass – not a strong smell, just a whiff, really. And then another whiff, stronger this time, and a third.

He twisted his body to the right so that he could look over to the windward side of the fort, then he watched the sentry at the wicket gate. The man did not move: grass and *macchia* fires were common enough at this time of the year, and anyway once the *macchia* really started blazing there was nothing to be done. If the flames spread to olive groves, the effect was spectacular: an olive tree started flaming and then suddenly exploded like a great firework as all the oil in the fruit (if they were still on the tree), the leaves and the branches blazed fiercely with the heat of a furnace so that a small pile of fine grey powder would be all that remained of a large tree; the kind of ash left by a good cigar.

More whiffs and then the smell became constant – and yes, beyond and to windward of Forte della Stella there was now a faint pinkish-yellow glow, a glow which grew brighter as Ramage watched, and seemed to throb.

He heard Aitken sigh and mutter: "It's going to work, sir."

The sentry on the battlements suddenly started shouting and then the other sentry at the wicket gate seemed to wake with a start, pause a minute or two and then dash into the fort, yelling – presumably at the guardhouse because Ramage almost immediately heard more confused shouting coming through the wicket gate.

While the glow increased until the whole eastern side of the fort was awash in a reddish-yellow light, a bugle suddenly blared out urgently inside the fort, obviously sounding an alarm, and a moment later several men rushed out through the wicket gate and, pausing a moment to get their bearings, turned left and then ran round the fortress walls towards the glow which, even as they reached one of the points of the star, began flickering: an indication that what had begun as something small like a bonfire was becoming a rapidly spreading blaze.

"Eight . . . nine . . . thirteen . . . fourteen . . ." Ramage counted as Frenchmen came hurrying through the gate. "Most are carrying muskets. Here come more!" He continued counting. Twenty-one men had run round towards the burning *macchia* by the time he stopped, and Ramage was satisfied that even the sentry on the battlements had left his post to join the others, who presumably proposed trying to beat out the flames.

"The sentries guarding the hostages will be the only ones left behind," Ramage said. His stomach was knotted with tension; his knees seemed to have lost their strength even though he was lying down. He grasped his cutlass, muttered a warning to

251

Aitken and Orsini and, turning his head towards the men lying in the *macchia* behind him, snapped: "Get ready . . . on your feet . . . follow me!"

With that he rushed across the gravel towards the wicket gate, tugging a pistol from his waistband with his left hand. Aitken, Orsini and Rossi were racing each other to be the first through the little doorway while behind him it seemed a cart was unloading gravel as twenty men charged across the parade ground.

Although Orsini just beat him to the door, the moment he was through Ramage looked to his right: yes, there was the guardroom, and in front was an inner courtyard formed by the walls of the fort itself. The blazing *macchia* had become an enormous lantern which showed the guardroom door swinging open: every man in it must have bolted outside.

Half left – yes, that door must lead to the two big rooms where the hostages should be, and he swung round towards it, slowing from a run to a brisk walk. Suddenly, the door flung open and a man stood in the opening, saw Ramage and the men behind him, and grabbed a musket. As Ramage realized that he and his party were lit by the burning *macchia*, now behind them, the Frenchman took one look at the gleaming cutlass blades, shouted a challenge and raised his musket.

Hearing the click as the Frenchman cocked the lock of the musket and knowing he had no time to change to his right, Ramage fired his pistol left-handed. The man collapsed, his musket going off as he toppled over, and Ramage heard the whining "spang" as the ball ricocheted off one of the walls.

One down – but how many more left in there? Any one of us running through that door is a perfect target for other sentries inside. No time to think: drop the empty pistol, switch cutlass over to the left hand, tug out the second pistol with the right, cock the lock, and now he was hurling himself through the door, waiting for an agonizing pain as a musket ball slammed into his stomach.

A small hall – anteroom, rather. A man at the far side, crouching and shouting, a musket on the ground in front of him. Yes, another guard who did not understand what was going on but, seeing his comrade shot dead, had the wit to throw down his gun and surrender to whatever was the threat.

252

"Rossi!" Ramage shouted and saw the Italian dash past him heading for the cringing man, anticipating the order. By then Ramage had the next door open and found himself in a short corridor with a door at each end. Which first? He snatched a lantern from its hook and turned left. The damned door was locked but even as he tugged at the handle Rossi pushed him to one side without a word, trying one large key. No, it would not turn. He gave it to Ramage. "The other door," he said as he thrust a second key into the lock, wrenched the door open and flung it back.

Ramage saw that a lantern inside showed several people in the room and, turning to Aitken, snapped: "You look after this crowd. Rossi took the keys from that last sentry: I'll open the other door."

By now the corridor was full of men: Ramage found Jackson and Stafford beside him and the American grabbed the lantern, holding it up high as Ramage fitted the key in the lock of the other door. It turned easily and, flinging the door open, he jumped rather than leapt inside, covering as many of a group of men as he could with his pistol. None was armed but all seemed frozen as they stared at Ramage, who was lit from behind by the lantern which Jackson still held high.

"Who are you all?" Ramage shouted.

"English prisoners . . . British hostages . . . Are you British? . . . What's all the shooting? . . . Is the fortress on fire . . .?"

Ramage held up his hand. "Please, you're all shouting at once! I'm Ramage, from His Majesty's frigate *Calypso*. If you are hostages follow that man, Mr Orsini, and hurry: he'll lead you along a track to a cliff top and then down to our boats. But hurry: don't stop for clothes or personal treasures!"

"The women!" one of the men shouted, "they're in the other room!"

"By now they're on their way to the *Calypso*," Ramage snapped. "We found them first! Now, hurry along! Orsini? Ah, there you are. Get moving – you don't need any lantern thanks to Hill's men setting the *macchia* ablaze!"

He stood back as the hostages hurried out. He saw two men kneeling down on the ground. "What the devil are you doing?"

"Putting on shoes!"

253

"Get out!" Ramage said angrily. "Run barefoot – a few blisters on your feet won't matter: if you don't hurry you'll have twenty Frenchmen using you for target practice!"

The two men hurriedly followed the others, leaving Jackson and Stafford waiting for orders. Suddenly a cursing Southwick stumbled into the room. "So help me, all the damned birds have flown!"

"What happened to you?"

"That guardroom: you didn't wait to inspect it!"

"It was empty – the door was swinging."

"Ha!" Southwick sniffed. "Well, I found three French soldiers lying on cots, trying to sober up and understand what was going on! A fourth was already on his feet, roused by the shots and trying to load a pistol."

"Where are they now?" Ramage demanded.

"Waiting for a burial party," Southwick growled, and Ramage saw that at least a foot of the master's sword blade did not reflect the lantern light: instead it was a dull reddish-black.

"Right," Ramage said. "That's the two groups of hostages and the Marines on their way. I hope Orsini doesn't curse in Italian because it'll make the men suspicious."

"That's all right, sir," Southwick said. "I sent young 'Blower' along with him to whip up the dullards and no one'd ever mistake *him* for a foreigner."

"Just look round in here in case any of the prisoners did leave any treasures behind and start grumbling," Ramage told Jackson, who walked round with the lantern.

"Shall we blow this place up?" Southwick enquired eagerly. "I've a fifteen-minute length of slowmatch tied round my middle."

"Only fifteen minutes? A stomach like that will take an hour's length! No, we won't blow it up, it's more of an ornament than a threat if we ever want to attack Port' Ercole again. Nothing, Jackson, just clothing? Right, let's get back to the ship."

Outside the courtyard the light was by now even brighter: several acres of *macchia* must be burning, the fire steadily spreading across the sage, juniper and thyme, fanned by the breeze that had earlier worried Ramage.

Southwick paused for a moment, looking round at the fortress walls which were harshly outlined by the flames beyond. "Those buckets – must admit I didn't think they'd work, sir. I thought the banging about would put out the coils of slow match burning in the bottom."

Ramage shrugged his shoulders. "If the buckets didn't work, the alternatives were having men holding burning match as they made their way up the cliff and along the top, or having them scratching away in the *macchia* with flint and steel, and then lighting slowmatch. And you know that's the time when the flint won't spark – or it starts raining and the tinder gets soaking wet."

Ramage led the way out through the wicket gate and almost immediately a small red eye winked over on his left and a musket ball thudded into the heavy gates a foot away.

"Quickly – out, or we'll be trapped," Ramage snapped. "The blasted French are coming back!"

Several more musket shots sent balls thudding into the gate and Ramage could see that the French were returning the way they had run out, but keeping closer to the walls. He knew he had one advantage – the burning *macchia* outlined the French, while the four Britons were against the dark walls of the fort, lit only by the general glow of the flames.

But the French had muskets – which they were no doubt busily reloading now – while the four Britons had only pistols. The French could fire at two hundred yards' range; the Calypsos would be lucky to hit anything at twenty.

Did the hostages get away safely? They must have: there were no bodies lying between the door and the edge of the *macchia*. Very well, every minute he could hold this damned French garrison here at the fort gave the hostages an extra minute to reach the cliff and scramble down to the boats.

As he crouched against the fort's wall beside the gates Ramage could see the French troops forming up in two lines, the nearest kneeling and the second standing. He pointed them out to Southwick. "A regular firing squad!"

Southwick gave an uneasy sniff. "They must have twenty muskets. They'll just pick us off one by one as we bolt across this gravel . . ."

"That's five musket balls each," Ramage commented. "Still, gravel isn't suitable for a quadrille, so we must keep these fellows occupied for a while."

With that he raised his pistol, aimed carefully at the French (noticing an officer pacing up and down behind the two files of men, obviously giving orders) and fired. The ball might reach – with enough impact to break an egg.

Turning to Jackson and Stafford, he said: "Fire at them – not together, just enough for the flashes to make them nervous."

Hurriedly he reloaded his own pistol, cursing that he had thrown away the other one. Powder, wad, ball, ram, wad, ram: flip open the pan cover, priming powder into the pan, snap the cover closed, rammer slid back under the barrel, cock the lock . . .

He looked up to see the row of French muskets again winking red eyes but heard only an occasional ball ricochet from the wall.

"They can't see us: they're aiming at the flashes of our pistols. Reload, but don't fire again until I give the word."

Yes, the French would be puzzled, with a couple of acres of *macchia* to windward of the fortress blazing merrily and obviously set on fire by whoever was attacking the fort. Looking at the dancing flames, Ramage guessed that the garrison commander must reckon it was the work of more than twenty men. Then he had seen men – only four – coming out of the fort, but he would think that no enemy dare attack with fewer than – well, seventy-five men: fifty to attack the fort while twenty-five set fire to the *macchia*. The Frenchmen must be worrying where the other forty-six were . . .

No wonder the commander was not leading a charge back into the fort: he must suspect that by now the hostages were released, even though still inside the fort.

Ramage almost laughed aloud as he pictured the Gallic shrug: why walk into trouble when they could cover the gateway and pick off the attackers and hostages as they tried to escape . . .

The Frenchman would have counted four men and assumed that dozens more were to come. He must assume they were either Italian guerrillas or British, but it was unlikely that he realized that most had already left the fort before he came in sight of the wicket gate. He would think he was seeing the first four, never guessing they were the last.

"Southwick, work your way along there –" Ramage pointed inland, away from the flames and the waiting French, "– and after twenty yards fire at our friends over there."

"But it's hard enough to hit 'em at this range without adding another twenty yards!" Southwick protested.

"You're not *supposed* to hit them," Ramage said ironically. "The muzzle flash represents another twenty of us waiting to attack the wily French."

"Oh, I see," Southwick said. "A good idea."

As the master crept away, keeping close to the wall, Jackson said: "Supposing I do the same thing that way, towards the French, sir?"

Ramage looked along the foot of the wall. When the clouds let the moonlight flood down, the overhanging battlements threw shadows, and the flames from the *macchia* were increasing and making a confusing flicker. "Very well. Ten yards the other side of the gate, no more."

"That leaves me, sir," Stafford said. "Can I make a bolt for it –" he gestured across the gravel-covered open space, "– and shout loud enough to seem like a company of Marines gettin' ready in the *macchia*?"

One man crouching low and moving fast to make a surprise move? It would probably work. "Very well, but don't fire twice from the same place, otherwise you'll get musket balls falling on you like bird shot."

Stafford was off and halfway across the open space before Ramage had time to say anything more: the Cockney went off like a hare breaking cover – and, like a hare, he was jinking before disappearing into the *macchia*.

From behind, Ramage heard the thud of Southwick's pistol, followed a minute later by Jackson firing. Ramage glanced across the open square, looking where Stafford had vanished, but the pistol flash when it came was several yards to the left, nearer to the French. He guessed the Cockney was hoping to make the French think he had merely joined (taking orders to?) a group hidden in the *macchia* solely to cover the gateway.

That poor French commander, Ramage thought, must think he is almost surrounded. He was still chuckling when a row of red flashes beyond and to the right of the French sent the two files of soldiers rushing to the fort's wall so that it protected their rear while they grouped into a half-circle to defend themselves against more attacks.

257

Ramage fired his pistol at the group, not that he expected to hit anyone but the muzzle flash would show Hill (for obviously it was him with his bucket men) where some of his shipmates were.

Stafford fired again, from a different position, then Southwick's pistol barked, followed by Jackson's.

Where were the hostages now – at the cliff top? Embarking in the boats? Ramage cursed because he had seen only the men. They seemed spry enough, but what about the women? Was there a rheumaticky and querulous old dowager among them, arguing the toss all the way to the cliffs? Well, even if there had been half a dozen, Aitken and Rennick had enough sturdy men to piggyback them to the cliff top.

His watch showed that, surprisingly, time was now racing instead of slowing down: the hostages had been gone a good twenty minutes. Another crackle of pistol fire and red dots, like bloodshot fireflies, showed that Hill knew what he was about and was now closer to the French.

Nevertheless, Ramage decided that they had delayed possible pursuit by the French for long enough: now was the time for all the remaining British to disappear into the darkness, making sure only that the French had no idea of the direction they took. To the French the *Calypso* must remain a French frigate quite innocently anchored in the lee of Isolotto, unaware of a dastardly attack on the fort by – well, Italian guerrillas probably, since they had only pistols, not muskets . . .

Would Hill hear a hail at this distance? Did any of these Frenchmen understand English? While he thought of a phrase that Hill would understand, Ramage called to Jackson, Stafford and Southwick: "When I give the word, run inland until you pick up the track that went on to Port' Ercole. Turn left along it and run for the clifftop."

He took a deep breath, made a trumpet of his hands and bellowed: "Hill! Can you hear me?"

"Very well, sir!" Hill's voice answered from barely forty yards away. "I'm over here with Stafford. My men are looking after themselves!"

"You've all done a good job. Now back to the cliff top and down to the boats. Take your men back along the cliff, but put the flames between you and the French before you make the turn. We'll be coming along the Port' Ercole track. When you hear me barking four times like a dog, you'll know we're on our way. Now get back to your men."

Hill's voice acknowledged and a minute later Stafford fired just as Hill's men let off another fusillade. Southwick and Jackson, obviously not wanting to be left out, fired again.

Ramage, cursing at having told Rennick and his men to guard the hostages, looked at his watch and this time did not bother to tuck it back in his fob pocket: there were enough pistols firing to keep the French huddled where they were – and probably dreading the dawn that would reveal them to their unknown enemies waiting like a row of sitting ducks.

Three minutes . . . more pistol shots . . . two minutes, and as soon as they were back on board the *Calypso* Southwick would be complaining bitterly that there had been no real fighting . . . One minute . . . he eased the hammer of his pistol, and made sure it was on half-cock before tucking it into his waistband. He slid the watch into his pocket, picked up his cutlass, and called to the three men: "Right, now make for the track. Don't rush – we don't want to let the French know what we're doing."

Then he barked four times and Jackson's giggle started Southwick laughing, followed by Ramage. "A sea dog," Ramage explained, "with a sore throat."

The four men reached the top of the cliff above the rope ladder just as Hill was lining up his men and roundly cursing one of them for having lost his bucket. As Ramage peered over the edge of the cliff, he saw that there was no one climbing down: the *Calypso*'s cutter was waiting a few yards from the bottom, near the rocks that formed a natural jetty, and the men were resting on their oars. All the hostages must be safely on board.

As he looked back over his left shoulder at Forte della Stella he marvelled at the beauty of the sight: already one of the most handsome fortresses Ramage had ever seen, part of its star shape was burnished to a coppery red on the seaward side, and the flickering shadows from the burning *macchia* softened any harsh lines.

"Hill, get your party started down the cliff. The cutter will come in as soon as they see us climbing down."

Chapter
Twenty-Two

Ramage climbed on board the *Calypso* to find Sir Henry and the other two admirals waiting for him, with Aitken standing respectfully to one side. Sir Henry stepped forward, right hand outstretched. "Ramage, my dear fellow, all the hostages have asked me to give you their thanks. I . . . I . . ."

Ramage realized that the man's eyes were glistening with tears, and both the other admirals were standing sideways, so that the lantern did not show their faces.

"I . . . well, none of us ever expected to see our wives again, so . . ."

"It worked, sir, that's all that matters!" Ramage said briskly. "I hope the galley fire is alight so that they can all have a hot meal. I suggest we wait for the morning for formal introductions."

"Ah, quite so, quite so, and thank you, my boy . . ."

Sir Henry turned away, wiping his eyes, and the other two admirals followed him. As soon as they had disappeared down the companionway, Aitken said: "Kenton wants to see you, sir: he's waiting here –" he gestured to the *Calypso*'s second lieutenant.

Damnation, Ramage thought to himself: he felt tired, his wrists and face afire with mosquito bites, and sticky from cobwebs which seemed to be strung between every damned bush. From the smell of it, the knees of his breeches were caked with goat droppings. He pulled out a handkerchief and wiped his face. "Isn't it something you can deal with?" he asked Aitken wearily.

The Scotsman shook his head. "No, sir," he said gravely. "It's a matter for you."

Ramage turned to Kenton and said impatiently: "Come on, then, what's the matter?"

"It's one of the hostages, sir. Waiting in your cabin to see you."

"More blasted complaints, eh? Oh, all right. Here, take these." He handed Kenton the cutlass and pulled the pistol from his waistband. "That's loaded, so be careful."

Hell, his whole body seemed to be on fire from mosquito bites, nevertheless it was good to be back on board again. The ship was rolling slightly and the squeak of a particular block aloft reminded him of the "quark . . . quark" of the nightjar. Already the whole night's activities seemed unreal, as though he was recalling a tale told by someone who had taken part in it.

He clattered down the ladder, acknowledged the sentry's salute, and as he opened the door the dim lantern showed the hostage sitting at his desk. A woman – oh blast, she was going to complain that a seaman used bad language or pinched her bottom. She looked up, and oh God, how she looked like Sarah.

"Hello, darling," she said, and the cabin spun, and he just had time to grab the door jamb as he shut his eyes. Then he seemed to be climbing out of a deep black pit while vines or tendrils or something seemed to be touching his face, but after blinking a couple of times he found himself holding Sarah, and as she saw him recovering she said: "If you nearly faint away again at the sight of me, I shall think I'm not welcome!"

"It's the first time a wife of mine has come back from the dead," Ramage said weakly. "But kiss me, and I'm not moving until my lips are so bruised that you have a rest and tell me how you got here."

Some quarter of an hour later, when they were both sitting on the settee, Sarah told her story.

"Well, two days after the *Murex* left the fleet, taking me to Plymouth, she was captured by a French privateer from Toulon. They were terrible men – reminding me of those pirates at Isla Trinidada. I had time to throw away any papers that might identify me – I thought they might try to get a ransom.

"In a way we were lucky because as they sailed the *Murex*

261

back to Toulon, and we were somewhere off Cartagena, a French frigate arrived and took us off and put a prize crew on board the *Murex*.

"I guessed it was not a good idea to say I was your wife, so I called myself Miss Mary Smith. Anyway, I was taken to Toulon where there were many women *détenues*, as the French call civilians who were caught in France and regarded as prisoners.

"Unfortunately, one of these *détenues* recognized me, and told the French who I was. Who I was before I was married, I mean.

"Anyway, two weeks later the French told me that I was in a special category, an '*otage*', and at the Emperor's order I was to be taken to join others in this category. So I was taken along the coast to Italy . . . what a journey! But I continued calling myself 'Mary Smith', so none of the other women hostages at the new prison knew who I was. That was why, incidentally, Sir Henry had no idea that his wife was sharing a room with Captain Ramage's wife."

"But you've told them now?"

"No. Aitken recognized me but, bless him, he saw me shake my head, and said nothing. He made sure I was on board first, and your Mr Kenton caught on very quickly and got me down here before any of the other women came on board. Sir Henry and the other hostages were so anxious to see if their wives had been saved that – well, they did not notice me."

She turned and, holding Ramage's face in her hands, gave him another kiss. "That's for saving me from those wretched pirates at Isla Trinidada." She kissed him again. "That's for marrying me." She kissed him a third time. "And that's for rescuing me this time. Can we go home to England now – in the *Calypso*? I remember your cot is just big enough to be *uno letto matrimoniale*. You see, I've learned some Italian!"

"Yes," he said, "I'll teach you some more."